THE GO...   ...SSIPPI.
THE ...   DATE DUE ...ERA.

In the tur...   ...e Civil War, steamboats rule...   ...carrying the wealth of
a nation ...   ...eat river at its heart. These
mighty sh...   ...the lifeblood of America, and the
hopes an...   ...eams of the people who rode them
united the ...orth and South at a time when history
was trying ...o tear them apart.

The *Tem...t Queen* was among the biggest and
most luxu...us boats on the river, the pride of her
veteran ca...in. She was a floating palace, with a turn
of speed ...at rivaled even the legendary *Natchez*.
And on h...decks rode wealthy planters and reckless
gamblers, ...ioneers and slaves, glittering beauties
and dark ...speradoes.

*This is th...r story—the epic adventure of America in
the maki...g, of the proud men and women who
changed t...e course of history . . . and of the fabu-
lous rivel...oats that carried the dreams of a nation.*

Turn the page and meet the passengers and
crew of the *Tempest Queen* . . .

All Aboard the *Tempest Queen!*

THE CAPTAIN: William Hamilton was a veteran of thirty years on the river. Now he had his own boat—the finest and the fastest on the river, he believed. The *Tempest Queen* was his ticket to a better life—unless he threw it all away.

THE GAMBLER: Dexter McKay knew every trick in the book when it came to betting against the odds—and winning. But he'd never learned how to stay out of other people's fights.

THE LANDOWNER: Tall and handsome Clifton Stewart was the heir to eighteen hundred acres of prime cotton and sugar land near Baton Rouge. But sometimes, there was more to life than money and power.

THE RUNAWAY: Eli had escaped his master's plantation and made his break for freedom. He got as far as Arkansas before the slave hunters ran him down. Now he was on his way back—to more trouble than any man deserved.

THE CHAMBERMAID: Mystie Waters was a young woman with mystery in her past. Her charm and beauty caught the notice of every man aboard the boat—including one she couldn't afford to get involved with.

THE PILOT: A lightning pilot, Patton Sinclair knew the river as well as any man alive, and wasn't afraid to show it. When he took the wheel of a riverboat, not even the captain could tell him what to do.

THE FRONTIERSMAN: Shaggy-maned Klack was built like a grizzly bear, dressed in buckskins and red flannel. He looked like a man straight out of the back country—until you noticed his hands.

THE ENGINEER: Life in an engine room had stolen Barney Seegar's hearing, but that didn't keep him from knowing exactly how the engines were working every mile of the way.

THE SLAVE CATCHER: Tough and merciless, Randall Statler made his living bringing back the runaways. He was a black-bearded wild man, and it would cost your life to cross him.

THE CON MAN: Absalom Grimes was an out-of-work pilot, riding down the river to find work. He bragged that he could steal any boat on the river, if he had a mind to—or if somebody made it worth his while to try.

RIVERBOAT

Douglas Hirt

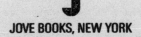

JOVE BOOKS, NEW YORK

RIVERBOAT

A Jove Book / published by arrangement with
the author

PRINTING HISTORY
Jove edition / March 1995

ISBN: 0-515-11566-5

A JOVE BOOK®
Jove Books are published by The Berkley Publishing Group,
200 Madison Avenue, New York, New York 10016.
JOVE and the "J" design are trademarks
belonging to Jove Publications, Inc.

PRINTED IN THE UNITED STATES OF AMERICA

10 9 8 7 6 5 4 3 2 1

PRELUDE

The cold rain drove down in raging black sheets, stinging his bare flesh like a million angry hornets—like the leather lash that Missus Canfield always kept by the back door, with the fire buckets. Yet Eli hardly felt the icy pelting at all. It was nothing compared to the fire that seared his lungs, the ache in his chest, and the pounding of his heart—at any moment it must burst, he feared. A vine reached out to snag his ankle. Briars clawed at his thighs, and the mud squished up between his toes with teeth of sharpened twigs.

Eli uttered a shrill cry, but the sound was lost in the driving rain. Lightning struck nearby, skittering him sideways. Its electric arc sizzled the air and picked out the naked tree limbs against the black and slanting rain. In the brief flash of light, Eli saw the swollen river ahead.

The Arkansas! Hope revived. The heavy muscles in his legs drove him on now, propelled by his renewed determination. The massive arms that could carry cane all day or heave bales onto the cotton floats pumped mightily at his sides.

Water streamed into his eyes and mouth, salty from his sweat. Eli crashed through the undergrowth, only vaguely aware of the oak and the yellow poplar that threw up a wall against him. His legs seemed to have a mind of their own as they carried him first this way and then that, dodging and weaving a trail around the trees that slowed his headlong plunge toward the river below.

Thunder rumbled over him. The sky flashed, crisscrossed by the slick, black tree limbs like the arm bones of dead men. In the flash, Eli was certain he saw Bouki clinging to the top branches, grinning down at him.

Lord! Even de spirits is a-comin' after me! Eli moaned and tried not to think of that mischievous Bouki, or of Zombi. A sharp branch jabbed his thigh. His hand came up red and warm.

Suddenly through the rain and the thunder, Eli heard another sound, and now his blood ran cold. The hounds were back on his trail. They were still far behind him, but their baying now was growing louder. He tried quickening his pace, but the forest was too dense. Once at the river, he knew he could hide in the water along its bank. That would be a dangerous thing to do with the river swollen so by the spring rains. The raging torrents would carry him clear out to the Mississippi if he got caught in them, and in this rising water no amount of cannon fire would ever bring his body up. Eli groaned pitifully to himself. But then that wouldn't be any worse than the beating he knew awaited him at Missus Canfield's whipping post! At least drowned he'd be forever out of Zombi and Bouki's reach.

Eli put that thought out of his mind. There was supposed

to be a safe house somewhere on the Arkansas River. A free nigger down in Louisiana had told him so. If only he knew where! He could find help there. Someone to hide him until a conductor could take him north to Canada.

Lightning slashed across his path, blinding him; its thunder knocked him aside. When the flash faded from his eyes, he saw that the river loomed nearer. Its high waters were roiling, bearing along a tree torn from the banks and the tilting shell of a cabin. Eli regained his footing and drove on, bursting through vines and branches, heedless of the pain of a dozen fresh wounds. His clothes were tattered shreds. The shoes he had worn when he had run off two weeks earlier had been lost days back in the clinging mud of some nameless bayou. Other than water to drink, which was about in plenty, he'd found a dead armadillo two days ago and had eaten it raw. That, and a crawfish he'd managed to claw up out of a mud bank, had been his only food in days. It was still too early for berries.

The horrible baying of the hounds was nearer now. Eli glanced over his shoulder and stumbled. He cracked his knee on a bole in the darkness and tumbled into a muddy depression. Moaning, Eli hefted himself up, tottered, and set off once again for the river. But all he could manage now was something less than a run and a bit more than a limp. Pain exploded with each step, and although the river was close, he knew he'd never be able to outpace the hounds.

Eli cast about, wide eyes big and white in the jagged flashes that rent the black sky. For a moment Eli thought he had a glimpse of heaven beyond the rip. Then the hole closed and he knew it was only Bouki up to his old tricks again. He wrapped arms and knees about the rain-slick trunk of a tree and shinnied up to a place where his fingers found a branch, and immediately he pulled himself up and clambered higher.

Perhaps the dogs would pass on by, confused by the rain. Eli clung to the tree and prayed, and his heart drummed as the baying grew louder.

Oh, why did I try at all? he lamented. All he had wanted to do was catch a glimpse of the slaves working on the levee. Why had Bouki and Zombi conspired to put those evil thoughts into his head? He had no doubt those spirits were somehow responsible. Eli had never seriously thought of running away before those two spirits had placed the temptation before him like Satan offering the apple to grandmother Eve. Somehow, it had happened. It had all come together as if ordained! Eli still had in his pocket the crumpled pass, soaked and now illegible, that had started this whole nightmare—not that Eli could have read what the words had said even when they had been freshly penned by Marster Canfield.

O Lord! Why was I so wicked to even have thought of running away? It was those spirits for certain! He moaned, and tears mingled with the rain that flowed off his face.

A gust of wind tried to shake him from the tree. He clutched tighter as if a helpless babe. Anything would be better than this!

The dogs were near now. Their baying changed suddenly, and Eli knew they had found him. In a moment a dog appeared below, and then another, and a third, leaping and howling, standing up against the tree, tails flapping, noses devouring his scent. It sounded like the very gates of hell had opened up beneath him. He squeezed his eyes, clutched the branch as if he expected God himself at any moment to come and shake old wicked Eli from the tree.

The dogs leaped about in crazy delight. Then he heard the men's voices, caught a glimpse of their lights dancing among the trees not far away.

"They got him treed!" a voice said.

"About time," another replied, short and impatient.

Thunder exploded. Through the sheets of rain the men appeared, lanterns in their hands, rifles wrapped in oilcloth hitched under their arms, the brims of their hats driven down in front of their eyes by the rain.

"Ho, Randall! Lookie here!" A man in a dark oilskin raincoat gave a laugh and held the lantern up high. "You were right. Got us a treed nigger for sure, and he do look a miserable animal."

The others gathered about the tree, dragged the dogs back, lifted their own lanterns. One of the men shouted. "Here now, boy. You come on down out of that—"

A crash of thunder drowned out his words.

"He ain't a-goin' to come down, Randall. Want I should shoot him down?" The fellow began removing his rifle from its oilskin.

Randall put out a hand. "Do that and I'll cut your balls! I don't bring back dead no niggers." He squinted up into the rain. "Now you listen to me, nigger. Get your black ass on down here or I'll rip you out of that tree like a bear cub."

Eli couldn't move. Fright had frozen him solid. He squeezed his eyes, certain the crush of his arms was about to snap that branch in two.

"He ain't goin' to come down, Randall. How 'bout I shoot off his toe?"

"Put that rifle away, Toby," another voice said. "He ain't going nowhere and we'll get him down directly."

"One more chance, nigger. Come on down or we are a-comin' up after you."

Eli knew he ought to give it up, but all he could do was cling to his perch.

"All right, we gave you your chance." Randall shook out a rope, handed the lantern and his rifle to a man at his side, and started up the tree. He got a loop fixed and in a minute had it tight around Eli's ankle.

Eli felt the tug, and the next instant his hip wrenched in its socket and he was certain they were going to yank his leg clean off. His grip failed. Down he slipped, catching himself on another branch. Below he heard their laughter. They pulled the rope harder. Something like a red-hot poker jabbed his hip. Eli cried out, grappled for another branch, fingers slowly unfolding from the soaking wood. Then he was crashing through the branches, coarse bark tearing at his skin. He hit the ground. Pain exploded in his knee. He squirmed in the mud, unable to see at first, lifted his face from the ground, and heard their laughter.

"We got us the nigger, we did, Randall."

Suddenly a knee crushed his chest, and Eli couldn't breathe. A rough hand grabbed up a fistful of hair and wrenched his head around. The white man unfurled a piece of paper and brought a lantern near. Through the rain, yellow light made a fearsome display upon the white man's fierce, bearded face. Unsmiling, he studied Eli's features and compared them to the picture in his hand.

"It's him all right," he said, standing finally. "Put the collar on him, Toby."

Eli was able to breathe again. One of the white men snapped a ring of iron around his neck and fastened it with a lock.

"Get up, nigger," the slave hunter called Randall said. "I'm taking you back." A boot slammed into his ribs. A streak of pain shot up his side. Another boot crashed into his spine. Laughter. Eli tried to protect his face, but now the punishment rained down like the torrents pouring from the black and angry skies.

He felt unconsciousness slipping away, and in those last moments, an arc of blue-white electricity turned the night to daylight, and he saw old Bouki up that tree laughing down at him.

A thunderclap exploded overhead, and then oblivion.

CHAPTER ONE

The thunder rumbled down the streets of Napoleon like cannon fire, rattling windows, startling mules, driving curious faces back from the black and streaked window-panes. Lightning ripped across the night sky while rain battered the buildings and turned the streets to gumbo. Through it all, Dexter McKay plunged on, a carpetbag and a walking stick wedged under his elbow, jacket clutched closed with one hand, top hat held firmly in place with the other.

Finding a haven from the storm, he halted on the boardwalk beneath a balcony and peered out at the down-pour that pounded the tin roof overhead like exploding grapeshot and cascaded in solid opaque sheets, turning streets into flowing rivers.

The sidewalk ended at the tips of his muddy, square-toed boots. He squinted through the unrelenting torrents at the vague outline of the sidewalk across the street where another balcony offered a bit of shelter that continued on in a haphazard fashion all the way to the river.

McKay frowned and shook the sleeve of his frock coat, which was already considerably heavier than when he had left the hotel. His fine beaver hat was drenched and limp. He extracted a gold watch from his vest pocket at the very moment a fork of electricity stabbed the earth, illuminating the white dial and gold hands. Thunder rolled through the streets again. He impatiently shoved the watch back into his pocket. He was already wet, so another drenching wouldn't make that much difference.

Top hat firmly clasped, McKay dashed down the two steps to the street, waded through ankle-deep mud, and leaped to the protection of the next boardwalk where he paused to take a breath and to shake himself like a wet dog. Then he was on his way once more, picking up his pace.

At the last building, McKay stopped again and patted dry his eyes, mustache, and small, pointed beard with a silk handkerchief, his eyes straining through the curtain of water. Thought no more than half a hundred rods off now, he was only barely able to discern the bulky outline of the wharf boat moored at the end of the pier. Beyond it sat the ghostly shape of two tall side-wheelers, one moment snatched from the darkness and driving rain, and the next thrust back again. The river itself had faded completely behind the slanting black shroud. Lights burned upon the two boats there, and on the wharf boat as well. Above the tall stacks of one of the steamboats cinders sprouted like Fourth of July fountains. Its furnaces were being stoked, and its boilers were building up a head of steam.

Is the pilot actually considering putting out in this weather after all? McKay wondered.

He glanced at the doorway of a saloon he had come to stop by. Past the windowpanes was a bar, mostly empty, and a scattering of tables around an inviting stove, but here and there men clustered about. His eyes moved unerringly toward the card game in progress. *Ah,* he thought, *if I only had the time.* His pocket was woefully light of recent because of certain financial setbacks—and a feisty gal by the name of Martha Jo. An hour spent here would certainly correct that deficiency, but, he reminded himself, bigger fish waited to be hooked. He had little to gain holing up here until the storm subsided, and much to be lost, McKay mused, grinning to himself.

Just then he heard the steamboat's whistle give two short shrills.

It was departing!

McKay dashed out into the deluge and dove headlong along the wooden pier and onto the wharf boat, which had been built upon the derelict hull of an old steamer and still wore a promenade running completely around the upper deck. He ducked under it, out of the rain, jogging around the other side to where the *Natchez* was docked; rather *had* been docked!

He arrived in time to see the foam churning beneath her paddle wheels, showing her stern light to the wharf.

"Damnation!" McKay shouted, dropping his carpetbag. His arms flagged furiously at the *Natchez*, but she ignored him and faded into the stormy night. For a moment only the red glow of her open fireboxes lingered, and then that, too, was gone. The pounding of her engines was lost in the roar of the rain, and McKay stood there, momentarily at a loss and becoming thoroughly drenched.

He picked up the bag and stepped into the wharf boat, shook himself off, found a bench in the empty waiting room, and flopped down upon it to think. An old Negro pushing a broom across the way eyed McKay curiously, keeping his head down.

"That was the steamboat *Natchez* that just departed, was it not?"

"Suh?" The Negro came half out of a stoop, seemingly unable to straighten up any further.

"The steamboat that just pulled out. Was it the *Natchez*?"

"Yes, suh. Him is de *Natchez*."

"Figured as much. And there goes my game as well. You know who was aboard?"

"No, suh."

"Devol, that's who!"

The Negro looked at him blankly.

"Well, never mind. It wouldn't make any difference to you, anyway, I suppose."

The black man went back to his sweeping.

McKay looked down at himself, made a face, and proceeded to squeeze water from his sleeve into a growing puddle at his feet. "You wouldn't happen to have a towel somewhere around here?"

"Yes, suh." The Negro set aside his broom and returned with a thin cotton cloth.

"Thank you." McKay shed his frock coat and wrung it out outside beneath the promenade, and dried himself as best he could. A stove in the corner drove the chill from the damp air. He wiped his shoes, then the puddle around his feet, and stood for a while in front of the stove as the lightning flashed upon the window and the thunder shook the wharf boat. Through the foggy glass McKay could see the other steamboat moored beyond. He cleared the glass with his sleeve, but the name on her paddle box was obscured by a pile of cargo waiting on the dock to be loaded.

The black man had finished his task and was making his was down the hallway when McKay asked, "What boat is that?"

He turned back, peered at the window where McKay was jabbing a thumb, and said, "Him be de *Tempest Queen*, suh."

"The *Tempest Queen*? Bound upriver or down?"

"I don't know dat, suh."

McKay frowned. "Well, it hardly makes any difference now." He was disgusted with himself for having lingered so long at the hotel—just the same he had to grin in spite of it all, remembering what had kept him. She had taken his last dollar, true, but then some things are well worth the price.

"Thank you, anyway," he said, and the Negro disappeared as McKay rotated himself in front of the stove like a pig roasting on a spit while the wharf boat pitched upon the back of the angry, swollen river. Shortly his clothes began to steam, and the warmth worked its way into his body.

Now that the steamboat *Natchez* had departed without him, he studied on his next move. He considered returning to the hotel and Martha Jo, but the bottom of his pockets held only lint, a crumpled handkerchief, and a worthless, soggy steamboat ticket. McKay knew well enough it wasn't his good looks that had attracted the pretty tart's attentions. Ah, well, there was always that card game back at the saloon. The briefest of grins came to his face, followed by another frown. McKay had no desire to dive back into this Arkansas storm.

He glanced out the streaming window at the white, three-tiered "wedding cake" moored there and wondered again where she was bound, then put that thought out of his mind. The *Natchez* was the fastest boat on the river, and this one would have no hope of catching her—even if she were ready to depart. The erratic streaks of lightning showed only the faintest wisps of black smoke above her stacks. She was not preparing to shove off anytime soon.

McKay's fist clenched as he thought of the opportunity missed. Devol was the most celebrated gambler on the Mississippi, and where he went, high-stakes rollers followed. Enough for an ambitious gent such as himself to siphon off a couple marks for a bit of fleecing of his own.

And it was his own fault—well, mostly. As he stood there drying himself out, he became aware of the voices drifting down the hallway, the muffled laughter, an occasional moan or shout of elation. McKay's mood was not such as he wanted company tonight. To be alone with his thoughts and to pull together a fresh plan were all McKay wanted. Perhaps he could find another steamer and catch up with the action farther down the river.

His glance went back to the riverboat outside, and a germ of a plan began to form.

Presently he grew aware of a new sound emanating from the hallway, and his full attention was at once riveted—as a prima donna's attention is galvanized at the opening bars of the orchestra or a factory worker at the whistle of a shift change. McKay listened again. Yes, he was certain now. It was the clink of coins being gathered up.

He thrust his hand into his pocket and came out with a soggy lint ball, but Dexter McKay was smiling anyway as he abandoned the comfortable warmth of the stove and grabbed up his valise and frock coat.

Along either side of the hallway down the middle of the wharf boat was an assortment of rooms: offices, storage rooms, waiting room, and finally the gentlemen's card room. The door was open, and beyond it six or seven men stood around watching the game in progress at the table. McKay stepped inside and nodded to the men standing about, but no one paid him much attention—except the gentleman in control of the cards at the table. He had looked over, quickly measured McKay at a glance, and returned his attention to the cards he was shuffling about on the tabletop, but not before McKay caught the fleeting look of concern—or was it irritation?—in the man's eyes.

Across the table was an older fellow clothed in a blue box-cut jacket decorated in gold braid, with a star on the cuff. He was wearing a dark blue billed cap, likewise emblazoned in gold, pushed back on top his head. He sported a gray beard, trimmed close to the face, and crow's-feet radiating out from his blue eyes, appearing deeper now by the intense scowl that had settled there.

McKay positioned himself next to the stove and draped

his coat over his ebony walking stick near to it as he watched the game.

The fellow in control of the cards gave a short, friendly laugh and said, "We will try it one more time. I think you finally got the hang of it, Captain Hamilton."

The other man, whom McKay had already figured out was a riverboat captain, and most probably the master of the very steamer presently moored to the wharf boat, gave a short grunt. He was not so convinced.

The gambler laid out the cards. McKay coughed into his sleeve to hide the grin that emerged. They were playing his game, three-card monte, and he recognized the pitch he had just heard as something he'd said perhaps no less than a thousand times before, to as many unwary souls who were about to give up the game in despair before they lost their last nickel as well as their watch and cuff links.

"One more try," the captain said, "then we play a real card game, not this fancy shuffle-and-guess gambit."

The gambler smiled as if his lips had been well oiled. "You're a shrewd opponent, Captain Hamilton. You sit there and place small bets until you have me figured out, and then you move in for the kill. I wonder if I shouldn't pull out while I am ahead?" He laughed.

'Twas a good line, McKay thought. He made a mental note to add it to his own repertoire.

The captain only barely managed to hide his own small smile. The man was hooked. McKay recognized the signs.

Another furtive glance at the doorway—then back at the cards now turned faceup on the table—and the dealer said, "Your choice, sir."

The captain leaned forward and squinted at the pictures on the three cards—a man, a lady, and a baby. "The lady," he said, pushing two gold coins across. The gambler matched his bet.

The man and baby cards were turned over, and finally the lady card. Back and forth they slid upon the tabletop.

McKay was only mildly impressed with the man's dexterity. He had seen better. Certainly he, himself, was more the master of the cards than this man. The gambler played it straight—as McKay would have done at this point to keep the captain interested.

Captain Hamilton studied the cards when they had come finally to rest in a line.

"That one," he said, turning over an end card. The lady!

The gambler fixed a most pained expression to his face and gave a long, heartfelt sigh of resignation. "You certainly have my mark, sir."

Captain Hamilton laughed and hauled over the pile of coins to his side of the table.

Very nice. Now raise the stakes some.

The gambler turned the cards faceup again and said, "You bested me that time, Captain. I wonder if my luck ain't all used up."

"One more time, Mr. Banning," Captain Hamilton said.

The gambler frowned and said dismally, "I don't know, Captain. I suspect I shall regret this in the morning," and as if to fortify his waning courage, he took a long sip from the glass of whiskey at his elbow and sleeved his lips dry. "Well, all right then, I shall go one more round."

The captain was delighted and worked his fingers across his palm as if he'd suddenly developed an itch. The gambler looked vaguely concerned, and McKay didn't think the expression was wholly for Captain Hamilton's benefit as Banning cast another surreptitious peek out the doorway.

Captain Hamilton selected the lady card again, commenting that she had turned lucky for him, and beyond that, McKay caught the gleam in Captain Hamilton's eye, for the captain, too, had discerned the smallest of a coffee stain or some such mark on the back of that particular card.

Money bet, cards turned over, the gambler shuffled them about and straightened them into a line with a slender forefinger.

McKay smirked.

The captain bent over, stroking his gray beard, considering. But he was poor at hiding the spark of victory that brightened his face. And now the gambler, as if unaware of the other man's advantage, cleared his throat and said innocently, "I may just raise this here bit, sir, if it pleases you, as I see you are in a quandary." That was a flat lie.

McKay coughed into his sleeve again.

The captain, who already had the winning card spied, leaped at this offer, although he tried—and not very successfully—to hide his delight behind a stern face.

"How much?"

The gambler considered a moment, chewing a corner of his lip, and said, "Fifty dollars?"

"Done!" Captain Hamilton thrust a fist into a pocket of his blue coat and tossed the appropriate coins onto the pile. The gambler added his money and said, "Turn over your pick, sir."

Hamilton turned over the marked card. He was stunned. It was the baby. "What's this!" he bellowed.

Some of the men standing about sniggered.

In an instant, Captain Hamilton flipped over the remaining cards. The man and the lady were there, as they should have been.

"But I—" he began to say, and then realized he'd been suckered, and he was too embarrassed to pursue the matter any further with so many men about.

McKay, of course, was not at all surprised, for he, and only he, had seen the original marked card slip into the gambler's sleeve at the very instant the replacement—identically marked—had slid out and taken its place.

Hamilton's neck glowed crimson, and to regain face he said, "Enough of this. No more fancy shifting of the cards. I'll have my money back, and I'll do it fair."

"Name your game, sir," Banning said easily.

"Old sledge," Hamilton replied.

The gambler agreed and played it smooth, but McKay wondered about the man's keen interest in the doorway, although no one else in the room seemed to have noticed. One of the men tossed another scoop of coal into the stove, and by this time McKay's coat had ceased steaming and he shrugged back into the still-damp apparel, although it was quite warm and toasty now. He leaned his weight on his walking stick and studied the careful manner in which the gambler returned his monte cards to an inside pocket of his saffron sack coat and retrieved a fresh pack of cards from somewhere else within it.

"I got my own cards," Captain Hamilton said, adding quickly to temper the accusation in the tone of his voice, "not that I don't trust yours, sir."

"Of course," Banning said, his slippery smile sliding across his face. "Your cards are acceptable."

At that moment, a woman appeared at the doorway. She paused a moment to shake out a dripping umbrella and then, smiling coyly as if surprised to discover the room filled with rough men who had suddenly discovered her standing there, said, "Excuse me, but I am looking for my uncle, Mr. Theodore de Winter." She glanced around at each of their faces and, discovering that her uncle was not among them said, "Oh, dear. I was supposed to meet him here, on the wharf boat, tonight."

A man in greasy overalls—an engineer or striker by appearance—said, "I don't know the name."

She said, somewhat dismayed. "He is Colonel Matthew de Winter's brother. The colonel is my father."

She spoke in a lovely, drawling Southern cadence that was music to McKay's ears. He'd been away from proper society too many years, he decided, drinking in the charm of her perfect face, her sparkling eyes. Her cheeks were somewhat flushed, her eyes very blue and wide; her complexion was what McKay was certain, in the South, would qualify as "peaches and cream."

The name de Winter didn't mean anything to the men in the room—and it certainly didn't mean anything to McKay, who had only recently arrived from the booming tent city along Cherry Creek, in the Kansas Territory, where the cry of *"Gold!"* had flooded the once peaceful land at the base of the Rocky Mountains with thousands of prospectors.

"Perhaps he has been delayed," she said hopefully.

"Maybe he left on the *Natchez*," said a stoutly-built man to McKay's left. He wore the rough clothes of a dock worker or stevedore and had muscles enough for such employment. The man continued, "She just pulled out, not half an hour ago."

"Oh, that's impossible. Uncle Theodore would not have left without me, and besides we had not booked passage on the *Natchez*."

She shivered then in a draft coming down the hallway, and McKay instantly doffed his hat and was immediately at her side. "Miss de Winter. I see you are chilled. Please take my place by the stove," he said, taking her by the arm despite her ever-so-slight protest.

"Well, all right, for a moment," she agreed.

Someone else in the room said, "You just stay as long as you like, missy. Your uncle will show up directly." There was at once universal agreement on this as the men stood and sat a bit straighter now, and their aim at the cuspidors improved some as well.

"My name is Dexter McKay," he said and bowed slightly at his waist. McKay pulled a card from his vest and pencil from his pocket and scrawled *At your service!* beneath his name and handed it to the lovely woman.

"Genevieve de Winter," she replied, smiling sweetly. She took the card, glanced at it, and put it into her handbag. "You speak like a Northerner, sir."

"Ohio."

"Oh." She only partly hid her disapproval. "I declare, I have never been farther north than St. Louis, although my father, the colonel, has traveled most all over the world."

"Really?"

"He is touring Spain and Portugal at this very moment."

"And your uncle is chaperoning while he is away?"

"Of course," she said most properly.

Banning took a cigar from an inside pocket, put a match to it, and offered one to Captain Hamilton. The captain declined.

The game began.

Banning had taken no notice of Genevieve de Winter. The captain had offered only a passing interest when she had entered the room. The cut gave Banning first deal. Hamilton's full attention was now on six cards he'd picked up off the table. The men looking on had their attentions divided, but after the game commenced, their eyes mostly remained on the two men facing each other across the table.

Genevieve craned her neck slightly to see the action, more than just a little curious.

McKay's interest was professional. He wondered what kind of gambler Banning really was. He had already figured out Captain Hamilton and decided that if the captain ran his boat the way he played cards, then passage aboard her would be a dangerous excursion indeed. The man had the *disease*, and he was an easy mark. He was an honest and open fellow, and his eyes either frowned or at once beamed when he gathered up his hand. He might just as well spread it out on the tabletop for all to see.

Banning, on the other hand, was a professional. Perhaps not as good as himself, McKay decided, but quite competent nonetheless. Just the same, he seemed to be doing exceptionally well.

An hour passed. Captain Hamilton was out a little over twelve hundred dollars by McKay's reckoning and more determined than ever to win it all back—even if it took all night and every dollar in his pocket to do so.

The men in the room forgot Genevieve de Winter, their

attention engrossed by Hamilton's spectacular losses as the cards went round the table again and again. McKay discovered that Banning seemed no longer concerned with the doorway and, just as odd, he seemed always to know exactly what cards Hamilton was holding, making no effort to soften the blows he had been dealing to the captain's purse.

With Genevieve de Winter forgotten—and how that could be was a deep mystery to McKay—their postures took the path of least resistance, and the cuspidors once again were safe from the continual streams of brown tobacco juice squirted in their direction.

McKay, however, the consummate student of human nature that he was, had not forgotten her, and now his curiosity went beyond the pale peach color of her crêpe de chine flounces, flowing in layers over the steel hoops of her crinoline, and the white, belled sleeves and ruffled cuffs of her shirtwaist, or the elaborately decorated straw bonnet upon her head. His eyes kept returning to the folded umbrella in her hands and the curious way it shifted slightly every so often. It took McKay but a few minutes of careful observation to discern the pattern.

Well, well, Banning was working with a capper—and a lovely accomplice she was. His admiration for the woman swelled. They were fleecing the captain admirably, and it really wasn't business after all. Now that he had the game figured out, it was easy to catch Banning slipping a card up a sleeve or dealing a second or slowly moving the edge of the top card over the shiny, flat-topped gold ring he wore on his little finger, turned around and facing up now.

McKay was suddenly thinking of the famous Devol aboard the *Natchez*, his own opportunities missed, and the woeful state of his finances at the moment. He had used most of his ready cash to buy the now worthless steamboat ticket, and the rest of it—well, he tried not to think of that, for he was endeavoring to concentrate on the moves Banning was using. He marveled at how blind everyone else in the room was to them.

If he could somehow find passage down the river, he might catch up with Devol and company. . . . Just then an idea took root and then bloomed, like a brilliant tulip in spring, and he could hardly restrain the grin that wanted out this time.

CHAPTER TWO

Now that McKay knew what he was going to do, timing would be paramount. He'd have to expose Banning for the cheat that he was in such a manner as to thrust himself into the good favors of Captain Hamilton and, in so doing, ensure himself passage downriver—McKay hoped the captain was heading downriver—but regardless, Napoleon was not the sort of town McKay cared to remain in, and if it turned out the good Captain Hamilton was heading upriver instead, well, so be it. Devol by this time was steaming away, and if the man was half as good as his reputation boasted, he would have fleeced all the easy marks by the time McKay caught up with the rascal.

His opportunity came not five minutes later when Miss de Winter twisted her umbrella in the palm of her hand and casually set the point of it upon the floor. Banning watched her past Captain Hamilton's shoulder as he dealt the cards. At her signal, he slipped the top card up a sleeve and continued counting the rest into his pile; as each card slid off the deck, Banning observed it in the polished surface of the ring he wore upon his little finger.

The game took its predetermined course, and at Banning's coup de grâce, Captain Hamilton angrily tossed his losing hand across the table and an oath caught on the tip of his tongue as he remembered the lady standing behind him.

"Ho, ho," Banning chuckled amiably, "you should have stuck with monte, my good Captain, sir," he said as he reached across the table for the pile of yellow coins that had grown quite impressive.

Crack! McKay's silver-crested walking stick hit the table, pinning Banning's arm beneath the scuffed ebony wood. The gambler looked up at McKay, and his eyes narrowed ever so slightly.

"Sir. You are intruding."

"You might say that, Mr. Banning."

The captain's view shifted between the two men. At first, he was confounded by McKay's actions and then slowly his expression hardened into anger as he began to understand.

McKay kept watch on Banning's free hand, for if he was like every other gambler McKay had known, he was certainly armed.

"I detect by your speech that you are a Southerner, Mr. Banning."

"New Orleans," Banning replied. "By birth," he added with a note of pride, carefully intoned to mark his indignation at McKay's flagrant interruption.

"I was under the impression that Southern men were gentlemen," McKay said. That, of course, was a flat-out lie, and McKay knew it, but it was spoken for Captain Hamilton's benefit, for the captain's accent was every bit as Southern as Banning's.

The men standing about had begun to mumble at the interruption, but McKay ignored them. He had the captain's undivided attention, and that was all he required. Miss de Winter was struck dumb where she stood, her pale blue eyes wide, the pretty mouth compressed into a single hard line, and the knuckles of her hands were turning white around the umbrella handle.

"Are you suggesting that I am not, sir?" The indignation in Banning's voice escalated to mild outrage.

McKay heard the murmurs around the room escalate, too, and now he caught a word being whispered that seemed to fan the flames of excitement among the men looking on.

Duel.

McKay said easily, "I would not call a *cheat* a gentleman, Mr. Banning."

The room seemed to heave in and hold its collective breath, and for a moment McKay imagined he could hear the ticking of the watch tucked away in his vest pocket.

McKay pressed his walking stick harder upon Banning's forearm and with his free hand shoved back the man's sleeve, revealing the tin holdout plate strapped to his wrist.

The room released its breath.

A flash of lightning and a crash of thunder punctuated the silence.

McKay casually withdrew the card that Banning had secreted there and held it up for all to see.

Instant outrage exploded.

"Tar and feather the cad!" someone yelled.

"Stretch his cheating neck!" another suggested.

Banning slipped from under McKay's stick and leaped out of his reach. The crowd shifted toward him and closed in. Banning riveted McKay with wild eyes and said, "You meddler!" and no sooner were the words spoken than a derringer appeared from beneath the folds of his coat and fired.

McKay felt the tug of the bullet at his sleeve.

Banning dropped the pistol, reached for another, and was already drawing out the second derringer when McKay's little .31-caliber Remington slipped out of its vest holster and cracked.

Banning staggered back, but before he could cock his own pistol, McKay fired again. The little revolver had not much in the way of firepower, and he continued to thumb the hammer and pull the trigger. Three . . . four . . . five. The hammer clicked on a spent cap.

Banning slumped to his knees, his derringer dangling a moment from his finger by the guard, then it, too, fell to the floor, and an instant later Banning himself atop it.

In the sudden stillness, thunder rumbled down the swollen river, more distant now.

McKay fanned away the thick cloud of black smoke that had filled the room and slid his little revolver back into its holster, out of sight beneath his vest.

The men crowded around. McKay turned the fallen gambler over. "He is still alive. Someone fetch a doctor."

"He won't be for very long," Captain Hamilton said, peering over his shoulder. "Just the same," he said to the fellow who might have been an engineer or a striker, "go find a doctor, and better hustle over the sheriff whilst you're at it."

"Yes, Captain," the man said, heading for the doorway where a black face had appeared, drawn by the gunfire.

McKay glanced back at the stove where Genevieve de Winter had been standing, and noted with a wry smile that in the confusion of the fight she had silently slipped out of the room and was gone.

A short distance away, in an upper room of the Fergerson and White warehouse, Stanley Fergerson paused a moment as he was about to pen his signature to the contract and glanced curiously at the younger man who had stepped suddenly to the window and was staring out at the wet night.

The lightning flashes were farther to the south now, and the rolling booms had moved downriver toward Chicot and Stop Landing.

"Curious," the younger man said, lifting the sash and sticking his head out the window. The breeze flickered the lamplight.

"That didn't sound much like thunder," Fergerson commented. He fiddled with the wick of the oil lamp on his desk and dipped his pen into an inkwell.

"No, it did not. More like gunshots." The young man's name was Clifton Stewart. Tall, well-dressed, forever nurturing a neatly trimmed beard that, although he tried valiantly to groom and coax it into something luxuriant, refused to be anything more than a fine, fleecy adornment to his cheeks and chin. An embarrassment at times, especially when pitted against old Jeremy Stewart's lavish gray beard, which still revealed traces of the fiery red it once had been.

Clifton looked toward his twenty-fourth birthday in two weeks, and with it the passage of his own plantation into his hands, the plantation that his father had purchased and readied for the occasion. In preparation for the time when he would be operating his own business, Clifton had been conducting the business of his father's cotton and sugar works since he was eighteen. Being the only male issue of old Jeremy Stewart, Clifton knew that one day all the properties his father owned would come into his hands, and he endeavored to please the old man in all that he did.

Clifton studied the black, wet streets below, and then the slick tin rooftops of the buildings nearby. The wharf boat was a short distance off, riding high up on the back of the swollen river, and beyond it he could see the chimneys of the *Tempest Queen,* puffing faint gray clouds of smoke into the stormy skies as the fire beneath her boilers was maintained to provide the small power required to keep the boat operating while at dock.

He caught a glimpse of a man hurrying down the pier from the wharf boat. The man mounted the levee and darted away along the muddy lane. Other than this single person, the streets of Napoleon were deserted. Clifton withdrew his head and shut the window. "It doesn't appear to be anything going on out there. At least the storm has moved off."

"How does the river look?"

"High," Clifton said, casually thrusting a hand into his pocket and returning to the desk. "But it is not near cresting, I should think."

Fergerson gave a snort that said he knew better and looked back at the contract beneath his pen. "She's as unpredictable as was my late wife Helen," he said. "Tomorrow morning you may be boarding your steamboat out of a yawl."

Clifton laughed. "I don't think she'll rise that quickly. Besides, I've a cabin aboard the *Tempest Queen* already. I shall be going there directly."

"Wise lad," Fergerson said, glancing about his long, narrow office. The office shared the space above the warehouse with discarded wooden crates, rope tackle hanging from the rafters, and other paraphernalia, lost from sight in the deep shadows at the distant ends of the place. But Fergerson seemed to be seeing beyond the clutter. "This town is not a healthy place, my boy. Napoleon is a den of pirates and thieves, and you'd do well to stay aboard your boat until she steams off in the morning."

He looked down at the paper then, freshened his pen, and signed his name in a tight hand with small letters precisely formed. *The carefulness of a bookkeeper,* Clifton mused, watching the meticulous strokes that marked the culmination of his yearly trip up to Napoleon. He'd return to his father with a signed contract for five thousand pounds of sugar and a bank draft for half the purchase price.

"There you go," Fergerson said, rolling a blotter over the signature. He folded the paper, slipped it into an envelope, and wrote out a draft and inserted it, too, into the envelope, sealing it. "Signed, sealed, and delivered. And you got an honest price, too. Not like you would have from those rascals up North."

"Thank you, Mr. Fergerson. It is well known that you treat the planters squarely." Clifton put the envelope into the inside pocket of his jacket.

Fergerson leaned back in his chair. "You know, as the years go by you begin to look more and more like your father. I look forward to our yearly visits, Clifton. Your family and mine have been doing business a lot of years together."

"Thirty-seven years come May."

"That long?"

"Father has mentioned it more than once."

"I miss the talks your father and I used to have, and we had us some good ones. Your father and me, we think alike." Fergerson huffed at a thought that came to him and continued, "I'll wager old Jeremy Stewart has some strong opinions about all this talk up North, and the ranting of those emancipators and abolitionists, and the railings of fanatical idealists like that John Brown. What right have they to dictate how we are to conduct our lives down here in the South?"

"I believe you and he . . . and I are in complete agreement there. He misses the old days, too. Perhaps you might come out to the house. You know that Father has some trouble getting around these days."

"Well, that happens to all of us. Don't ever grow old, boy," Fergerson said.

Clifton said, "Considering the alternative, I'd take a rocking chair and lap blanket over a cold grave any day."

"Well, you give your father my regards."

"I'll do that."

They clasped hands, and Stanley Fergerson walked the young man down the dark steps into an even darker warehouse and let him out the door. On the wet sidewalk outside, Clifton heard the heavy bolt being thrown on the other side of the door. He turned his collar up to the damp night air and buttoned up his jacket with the contract and bank draft safely tucked away in an inside pocket.

The storm had degraded into scattered drops flung about by the wind, cold and stinging to the cheek. Clifton turned his steps toward the levee and the wharf boat, thinking about the long ride ahead down to Baton Rouge. He hoped the weather would break so that he could enjoy the trip out on the promenade where he might watch the riverbanks scud by, decked out in their spring finery. The camellia were in bloom, their showy flowers like dollops of crimson paint spattered across the landscape. And the dogwoods, too, with their white bouquets looking ever so much as if someone had flung cotton balls onto the still-bare limbs. The redbuds, as well, were in bloom, adding their bit of glory to the season. He'd brought along a spyglass in the hopes of observing and cataloging the birds as well.

Spring along the Mississippi River brought not only the treachery of high water and the danger of crevasse, but the burgeoning of new life, and Clifton Stewart tried not to think about the former, even though a crevasse in their levees could destroy in a single day a season's worth of cotton or cane.

His thoughts were interrupted by voices. A group of men had suddenly emerged from a lane leading up into town, and they were making their way in a hurry toward the levee. Their boots pounded the wooden boards of the pier to the bobbing wharf boat, and Clifton found himself caught up in the rush and was soon being jostled down a hallway.

"Make room for the doc!" a voice shouted. Men stepped back and pressed along the walls of one of the rooms.

Curiosity piqued, Clifton found a place along the wall with the others to observe the happenings. A man was stretched out upon the floor, and it was evident from his torn-open shirt that he had been shot in no less than five places. Clifton recognized the captain of the *Tempest Queen* bent over the man, fingers pressed softly against the lifeless neck.

*   *   *

The doctor shoved through the crowd and dropped to his knees at the unconscious man.

"No pulse," Captain Hamilton said, giving the doctor room.

"Not surprising. He got himself shot up right dandy." The doctor fitted a stethoscope to his ears and put its cone to the man's naked chest. His eyes compressed slightly, then the corners of his lips dipped and he put the stethoscope back into his pocket. "Sheriff, he's your concern now."

A second fellow who had come into the room and was bent over the doctor, straightened up now. He frowned and surveyed the crowded room. "Someone tell me what happened here."

"I shot this man, Sheriff," McKay said, regaining his feet also.

The lawman considered him. "What is your name?"

"Dexter McKay."

"I hope you had a good reason, Mr. McKay."

"Self-defense."

The doctor looked up and said, "You have been hurt as well."

McKay glanced at the sleeve of his rain-dampened frock coat. A red stain was working its way into the material. "It is only a minor wound."

The doctor dragged the coat off and shoved up the sleeve. "Minor wounds can kill you just as dead as the major sort, sir, if not attended to. The only difference being that the former takes longer than the latter."

McKay allowed the doctor to proceed while the sheriff retrieved the two single-shot derringers from the floor. He considered them briefly and dropped them into his pocket. "Tell me what happened," the sheriff said, sounding weary. Being that this was the town of Napoleon, Arkansas, McKay suspected that this was not the first shooting the sheriff had attended to this evening.

"The man—his name was Banning—was cheating at

cards. Took a heavy toll on the captain's pocket." McKay glanced at Captain Hamilton, who frowned and nodded his head stiffly, as if the vertebrae there had suddenly fused. The truth was an obvious embarrassment for the captain to have to admit here in front of all these men.

McKay went on. "I called Mr. Banning on the matter, revealed him for a cad. He produced a pistol and fired. His bullet stung my arm as you can see. When he reached under his coat for a second pistol, I drew my own revolver and fired."

"Five times? Once was not enough?" the sheriff noted dryly.

McKay shrugged his shoulders and managed to find a grin somewhere within him, even though his heart was still pounding from the incident and there was a vague feeling of regret growing within him. "It was a very small revolver, Sheriff," he said.

"I see." The sheriff frowned, glanced around at the staring faces, and asked, "Anyone here know this man?"

They all allowed as that they had never seen him before. He had arrived at the wharf boat earlier that evening and claimed to have been waiting for a friend, was all they knew.

"Did his *friend* ever show up?"

Blank faces, shrugged shoulders, wagging heads, were the general reply. As far as anyone knew, he had not. McKay decided not mention the lovely Miss de Winter, and apparently no one else had considered her presence—or mysterious departure—worthy of note, either.

"Well, that's all right, I suppose," the sheriff said after giving it some thought. "I guess that wraps it up here. I'm going to need the help of a couple strong backs to haul this fellow up the mortuary. Then I'll see if I can't find someone in town who knows him and is willing to pay for his burial."

The doctor applied an ointment to the shallow wound that stung like sin and smelled like brimstone. McKay flinched.

The pain of it merged with the pain of the bullet hole and raced up and down his arm until it hurt to make a fist.

"Hold steady there," the doctor said. "I'm almost done here. Hurts?"

McKay shot him a caustic glance that spoke more eloquently than any words he could have said at the moment.

The doctor merely chuckled and wrapped a bandage around the arm, tying it off. "There. That should take care of it. You come by and see me on the morrow if you're still around."

The sheriff found himself two strong dockworkers for volunteers, and they gathered Banning up, hoisting him between them. The dead gambler sagged in the middle like a saffron-colored gunnysack filled with shucks as he was carried out of the room. The sheriff halted and turned back from the doorway and considered McKay a moment. "I got me a mighty handful of a job policing this here town of Napoleon, Mr. McKay," he said. "If you ain't got some pressing business here, I'd appreciate you moving on. I understand that the sheriff down Greenville has plenty of time on his hands. You might want to go visit his way."

"I'll tell him you sent me along."

The sheriff returned a tired grimace and left. The crowd slowly dissipated as well. McKay slipped his coat back on, winced, and noticed that Captain Hamilton was collecting his money off the table and shoveling it into those big, blue pockets.

"I feel the fool," he said, not looking at McKay.

"You had no way of knowing."

Hamilton turned. "That doesn't make any difference. I should have known better than to touch those cards in the first place. It . . . it happens most every time. You'd think a grown man of fifty-seven could control himself. Could set a limit and push himself away from the table once his losings reached it." He stopped then, glanced at his crew members still there, and said, "I thank you, sir, for your keen eye and your strength of character. It is always dangerous to call a man a cheat."

"I felt it my duty," McKay said.

"The sheriff wants you out of town. Have you a place to go?"

"Oh, of course," McKay said after only the briefest, carefully calculated hesitation, and as he had hoped, Captain Hamilton caught it.

"Come now, man. You needn't feel like you must lie to me."

McKay put on a distressed face and said, "I should have realized that you must see through my pride, Captain Hamilton. The fact is, I haven't a copper penny to my name, nor a roof to keep out the rain."

"You have a home, sir?"

"Ohio. But it has been a long time since I have been back. I have a sister in Baton Rouge. She is ill, perhaps on her deathbed. I was on my way to see her when I was suddenly trounced upon by a band of ruffians. They stole all that I had. Here, I managed to save this letter from Beth—that's my sister's name." McKay reached into a pocket, but his hand came out empty. He groped into another and with a growing urgency rummaged every pocket on his person, and when he didn't produce the aforesaid document, he looked most pained. He found his way into a chair and stared blankly at the black, rain-streaked panes of window glass. "I have lost it as well."

After a long, contemplative moment, he gathered himself up resolutely and said, "There is no need to burden you with my plight, Captain. I only came aboard the wharf boat to escape the rain. Now that it has ceased, I shall be on my way. I must make haste, for I have a long journey ahead of me. Perhaps I can find a passing cane wagon to catch a ride upon."

"Nonsense! I will hear none of this! You did me a service, sir, and I am not a man to allow a good deed to go unrewarded. Baton Rouge is the *Tempest Queen*'s home port. We leave in the morning. You will take passage upon her, and within a week you shall be at your poor sister's bedside."

"But I have no money," McKay reminded him.

"I will not hear another word about money either! You will ride as a guest of the Company."

"You can do that?"

"I am the *Company*," Captain Hamilton said.

"If you are certain it would not be a bother—"

"It is my pleasure," the captain said.

McKay and Hamilton, and the crew members there with them, left the wharf boat. As they mounted the gangplank to the *Tempest Queen*, McKay figured it hadn't been such a bad play for a spur-of-the-moment game.

He was feeling quite good about it all until he recalled the dead man he'd left behind. Afterward, it took a bit more effort to keep up the smile. Dexter McKay had had to kill only a few times in his career, and even though he reminded himself it had been in self-defense, there was a heaviness in his spirit.

CHAPTER
THREE

The clerk's office up in the main cabin was closed. With a hooked finger, Captain Hamilton indicated that Dexter McKay should follow him, and out the door he plunged. McKay found himself on the most forward end of the boiler deck, flanked on either side by the masts, overlooking the bow with its jack staff. Below was the main deck with its piles of cargo stacked in place; their dark bulk reflected a flicker of red light from an open furnace door. The right landing stage was lowered and secured to the wharf boat only a dozen feet off, and McKay could see it was still a considerably busy place—no doubt the owners had been informed of the shooting and had arrived to discuss the matter with the sheriff and check for any damage.

Captain Hamilton climbed a steep ladder to the deck above. McKay mounted the ladder next, pulling himself up with his right arm. His left he retained stiffly at his side, and he gritted his teeth against the sting of the wound and winced at an occasional bump that was inevitable ascending such a tight passageway.

The hurricane deck upon which he had mounted gave him a wider view of the river, although at present its dark waters were observable only out to about a hundred rods; the rest was obscured by the low clouds that wiped out any trace of moon or stars. The boat's lights fell weakly upon the swift current that rushed angrily past, bearing upon its swollen shoulders dark lumps of logs and boards, an occasional barrel, and a few half-submerged boxes of some obscure origin—jetsam scoured from the shores by the rising waters.

The wind up here had teeth; the few fleeting raindrops bit McKay's cheeks as he tramped along behind Captain Hamilton. To the south, infrequent flashes of the storm just past outlined the black, tumbling clouds that seemed in places so near to the water as to be piled up on the very back of the Mississippi River. If he strained to hear beyond the wind that buffeted his ears, McKay could faintly detect the distant thunder as it came rolling up.

Captain Hamilton made his way across the rain-slicked deck and up another short ladder and through a door into the texas. He shut the drizzle and chill wind out when McKay stepped in.

"Warm yourself at the stove," Hamilton said, and left McKay alone in a cozy little parlor. The floors were naked of any carpeting, painted gray originally, but mostly scuffed down to bare wood by the boots of the crew. Off to one side a potbelly stove sat upon a square sheet of tin tacked to the floor. Beside it was a nearly empty coal bucket. McKay moved a little closer to the stove and spread his palms before the radiating heat. He craned his neck to peer into the long, narrow hallway Captain Hamilton had disappeared down, but other than some lights at the far end, he saw nothing except closed cabin doors.

Three folding deck chairs had been placed near the stove, and two small windows were set into the wall, but McKay could not see out of them. Light from the swaying oil lamp overhead had turned the windowpanes black, except for the brief flicker of a far-off flash of lightning. He sat in one of the chairs to wait, and presently voices emerged from deep down the tunnel, and then the captain appeared with another man who was hitching an arm through a suspender strap and looking a bit bleary-eyed.

The clerk was a slender fellow of perhaps twenty-five years. He wore tan canvas britches and a stained, red union shirt, and stood about five feet eight inches tall, by McKay's reckoning, but appeared shorter, being at the moment round-shouldered and slightly stooped. His brown hair was an unruly patch that, no doubt, five minutes previous had been nestled comfortably into a warm pillow. His dark beard needed trimming, and the neglected cheeks above and the neck below required the attentions of a razor.

"This is Mr. McKay," Hamilton said. "He needs a cabin. His expenses will be borne by the Company."

The fellow yawned, eyed McKay neutrally, and gave a perfunctory nod of his head, but was in no mood to smile.

"Right, Captain," he answered, blinking in the lighted room and kneading his eyes. "Do it right away, sir."

Captain Hamilton said, "Mr. Belding will see you squared away. We will be under steam tomorrow morning at eight-thirty. Breakfast, of course, will be in the main cabin. We've a doctor aboard, and you might want him to check your arm afterwards."

"Thank you, Captain. You have been most gracious." His good fortune owing to his shrewd calculation at the card game had become most rewarding.

Hamilton discounted McKay's words with a wave of an

arm. "It's nothing. You have a restful night, and we will talk in the morning."

"If you'll follow me, sir," Belding said, yawning.

McKay nodded his farewell to Captain Hamilton and stepped out behind Belding into the chill wind.

The dark pilothouse was abandoned at this late hour, its stove cold. Captain Hamilton closed the door behind him, cutting off the wind, and stood for a moment in the silent gloom. To his left, the leather sofa was an undefined dark bulge against the rear wall, to his right the high benches only vague shadows. Although he could not see it, he felt the oilcloth beneath his feet as he stepped up to the big wheel. In the darkness its polished wood-and-brass fitting was not visible. The helm was merely a black-spoked silhouette, facing the black checkerboard of the forward windows, beyond which rose the black chimneys and the spider web of black hog chains and rods and cables. And beyond all that lay a veiled river churning beneath an inky night, enlivened here and there by the faint flashes of electricity so far to the south now as to be no more than the final punctuation marks at the end of a violent sentence.

He took his hands from his pockets and gripped the tall wheel, staring over the top of it into the night. Captain William Hamilton despised these storms. He despised spring as well, for it was then that the torrents came rushing down from the north, the west, the east, whipped into a frenzy by the violent thunderstorms, bastard children spawned by the mysterious union of warm Gulf air laden with moisture and the cooler northern winds. It was then, too, that the river surged like a sleeping monster shaken awake, writhing within its banks to free itself of unnatural barriers thrown up by feeble man in his attempt to tame the yellow beast.

Captain Hamilton's grip tightened about the helm, and he was not aware that his knuckles were blanching or that his teeth had clamped down and were grating.

The stormy world beyond the pilothouse windows faded, replaced by a scene that would hound Captain William Hamilton to his grave . . . and beyond, he knew.

The night in his vision is as violent as this very night had been. His yawl bucks upon the black, angry waters as his boatmen strain at the oars. He stands upon the prow, gripping a rope to keep from being tossed overboard—ever so much like George Washington—but without the exhilaration of victory. The urgent squall of the oarlocks are but a distant sound, for his ears are tuned only to the cries for help ahead. He peers ever forward, and his eyes reflect the flames that leap from the burning roof and dance like demons upon the black water that has overflowed its banks and now constrains the house in a death grip.

Upon the roiling water behind him, Captain Hamilton is vaguely aware of the steamboat that he had disembarked when she ran suddenly aground on the levee—a levee that restrains mere wood and iron but could never contain the angry Mississippi in flood stage.

Fighting the current, his oarsmen drag the yawl nearer and nearer until now he hears Cynthia's panic-driven screams clearly. He no longer needs the spyglass to see her upon the roof, above the torrents. She is up against the chimney, and all around her the fire crawls along the eaves and sizzles the soaking shingles, unquenchable even by the driving rains. She has the children there with her, both of them, clutched beneath her arms. Their voices cry out to him.

Now the yawl is near the portico. The oak trees along the private road that leads to the front of the house are half submerged, and the little boat struggles past their still-leafless branches thrust up like pleading fingers in the storm.

"Hard over, Mr. Finney! Put your backs to it men! . . . Let her fall off to larboard now. . . . More muscle, more muscle! . . . Pull hard! Swing her about smartly!"

The orders shouted those many years ago now ring anew

in his ears. The yawl is up nearly to the house that is a grotesque shadow of the grandeur it once presented to the world—and to the mighty river at which it snubbed its nose for so long from behind her protective levees.

How fleeting is mortal man, and the things of his hands!

Captain Hamilton yells above the shriek of the wind, "*Jump, Cynthia! John . . . Alicia . . . Jump!*"

Cynthia seems confused. She urges her children along the roof toward the river that laps below the gutters. Cynthia is uncertain, but she sees William's boat only rods from the house, and the strong oarsmen holding its position there.

Captain Hamilton encourages her.

She starts for the edge of the roof when lightning explodes in the branches of a tree nearby. Its crack drives her down to the slick shingles.

All at once the captain sees another figure moving across the roof. It emerges from behind one of the chimneys and rushes toward Cynthia and the children. A crash and a blinding flash explode simultaneously. In its fading, flickering light, he sees the panic in this fourth person's wide, white eyes and upon her black face where rain streams freely as she gathers up her skirts and once again scrambles over the sloping roof of the house.

It's Hester, the children's nanny.

The black woman helps Cynthia to her feet and draws the children close to herself. She is urging them to the edge of the roof.

"*Yes! That is right. Hurry! Jump!*"

The roof suddenly lurches beneath her feet. Hester falls back, the children with her. Cynthia goes to her knees. Hamilton sees the pain in her face.

"*William!*" she cries, stretching an arm toward him. He is still too far.

In another moment, hell itself opens up beneath them. The roof gives way, and in an instant his family is gone, swallowed up by the flames that leap into the stormy sky. For just the briefest of instants, Hester clings to one of the shingles, and then with a cry that shatters him to the bones and crumbles them to dust, Hester, too, is dragged down into the infernal . . .

"Captain? Captain Hamilton, are you all right?"

The vision retreated back into the den in which it dwelled. Captain William Hamilton shook his head once, as if dislodging the single remaining, clinging claw of it, and still half in a daze, he turned at the sound of the voice behind him.

"I saw you up here, sir. Came to check if everything was all right."

Captain Hamilton took a breath and felt his head clear. He grinned and said, "Of course, all is right, Mr. Sinclair. I was just watching the storm move off."

Patton Sinclair was one of the *Tempest Queen*'s two pilots. He'd been with Captain Hamilton three years and in that time had come to know this man. Now he frowned and said, "Another one of them dreams, sir?"

Hamilton knew he was mighty poor at hiding his feelings. It was why he fared so miserably at cards. It was why his pilot saw clean through his lie now.

Slowly, Hamilton nodded. "Yes, again," he said quietly.

"It's these storms what brings 'em on, you know," Sinclair said.

"I know that, dammit," Hamilton exploded. "What can I do about it? I can't change the weather on the Mississippi River! It's gonna rain, and it's gonna rain like hell, and if I can't stand it, then I ought to get off the river."

"It's gotten better."

Hamilton dropped his head to his chest and thrust his hands back into the pockets of his coat. "They don't come so frequent anymore, but it will never get better." He turned away from the dark wheel.

"Want I should have some coffee sent up, sir?" Sinclair asked.

"No. Thank you, Mr. Sinclair, but I think I will retire to my cabin. Good night."

"Night, sir." Sinclair stepped aside for him.

Hamilton lingered awhile out on the texas deck, staring south at the waning storm with the wind tugging at the hem of his coat, and then went down to his cabin.

The room was a neat, compact affair, with a bed along one wall, a wardrobe against another, and a writing desk with a well-stocked bookshelf above it against the third wall. Hamilton shrugged off the coat and hung it on a hook to dry. He put a match to an oil lamp and drew the curtains. Wearily, he lowered himself into the chair behind the desk, drummed his fingers upon the blotter, and then reached for the gilded brass frame, which always resided on the corner of the desk. It was battered and scraped from age, showing green verdigris in the seams where it had been long ago assembled. The daguerreotype in the frame had been taken on their honeymoon in Paris, France. Cynthia smiled out at him from it, her never-aging face lovely, innocent, forever twenty-two. The image had faded through the years, but in Captain Hamilton's thoughts it was still as fresh and enchanting as that brief summer in France almost two decades ago.

He frowned at the crack in the glass at the upper left corner, then put the frame back in its place, undressed, and went to bed.

Dexter McKay was restless in the neat cabin that the clerk, Belding, had assigned him. He glanced at his watch. Too early to even consider going to sleep, and besides, his arm pained him considerably. He pulled his coat gingerly over his shoulders and, leaving his hat, stepped out the cabin door immediately into the main cabin.

The main cabin was a long, stunning room, nearly the entire four-hundred-foot length of the boat, perhaps shy of that sum by no more than fifty feet. Beneath his feet, the floor was parquet, so shiny that he could see his shoes reflected back to him from the patterned wood surface. Above his head arced the ceiling, painted mostly white with green-and-gold trim, and with more scrollwork and carvings and wood turnings than McKay had ever seen in one place. The skylights that encircled the very top perimeter of the ceiling were of stained glass, and from the ceiling every fifteen feet or so there hung a crystal chandelier.

The inlaid wood of the parquet floor marched back to the rear of the cabin where it ended abruptly at a fine red-and-gold carpet that marked the beginning of the ladies' salon. Here the furniture was top-notch—not to say that the furniture anywhere in the main cabin was shabby, but in the ladies' salon it was heavily padded and brightly upholstered. A great gilded mirror, of such intricate design that even McKay's detail-oriented brain was at a loss to decipher it, covered two-thirds of the back wall, the other third being given over to a pair of dark wood doors that flanked the majestic-looking glass and opened out onto the deck and the very stern of the boat.

In the other direction, the meticulously polished floor headed forward, permitting the placement of tables and chairs upon its back as it made its stately way toward the bow of the boat. It ended at a bank of white doors, a considerable weight of leaded glass, and more scrollwork. Here was a reception area and the purser's and clerk's offices.

At this hour, only a few guests occupied the tables. Occasionally a waiter would respond to a lifted arm, take a request, and scurry, disappearing into one of the side doors.

McKay took a seat behind one of the vacant tables, removed a deck of cards from his inside coat pocket, and began a game of solitaire, moving his wounded arm as little as possible, for it ached mightily. When an inquiring waiter in a starched white coat came by, McKay ordered what he hoped might ease the annoying condition.

"Bourbon or Scotch?" the waiter inquired.

"Scotch, I reckon."

"Imported or domestic?" the waiter pressed further.

McKay raised an eyebrow. "You have imported Scotch aboard?"

"Certainly, sir." The waiter sounded vaguely offended by the dubious note in McKay's voice.

"Well, what kind of imported Scotch whiskey have you?"

He rattled off a litany of the varieties aboard, and when he had finished, McKay waved a hand in despair. He'd never ordered whiskey by the manufacturer's name before. The names meant little to him. "I don't care. Bring me whatever it is you drink."

"I do not drink Scotch whiskey, sir."

"Might I recommend the Glenlivet?" This was a new voice. The owner of it had materialized at the waiter's elbow. He was a young man, nicely attired in a light brown jacket, a pale vest, and burgundy tie. A fine, velvety brown top hat sat upon his head.

McKay studied this newcomer in a glance, and in that instant, he saw that he was well bred and presumably, McKay concluded, well fixed. He said, "I'll have the Glen-whatever-it-is this gentleman recommends."

"Very good, sir."

When the waiter had scurried off, McKay returned his view to the young man who still lingered at his table and appeared to have something on his mind beyond the helpful suggestion. McKay grinned and said, "Order something simple like a whiskey, and suddenly you realize how little of this world you know."

The young man said, "You are the man who shot that unfortunate fellow in the wharf boat this evening, are you not?"

McKay indicated the chair across the table. "Have a seat . . . and yes, I am he. You play cards?"

"Not very well." The young man lowered himself into the offered chair. "And never for money. My father says cards are a fool's game."

"He does, does he?" McKay gathered up the cards he'd been playing solitaire with; separated out a king, queen, and joker; and casually turned them over and began sliding them across the tabletop. "And what else does your father say?"

"He says never bet on anything but yourself."

"Interesting piece of advice." McKay finished shuffling the cards about. "Where do you suppose the queen is?"

"I have no idea. I was not watching."

"Take a guess."

"Well, if I was to guess, I'd say . . . the middle."

McKay turned over the middle card, and to the young man's delight, it was the queen.

"That was just a lucky guess," he said.

"Think so?" McKay turned up the other two cards, and then turned them over and once again shuffled them about on the tabletop. "What is your name."

"Stewart. Clifton Stewart of Baton Rouge."

"Pleasure to meet you, Mr. Stewart. My name is Dexter McKay. There, now I noted that you were watching closely this time. Think you can pick out the queen again?"

"Certainly, sir. It is on the end, right here."

McKay reached for the card, his hand momentarily obscuring the other two from the young man's view. When he turned it over, McKay let out a little cry of wonder, for amazingly, the card he turned over was the queen.

"That was too easy," Clifton said, sounding mildly suspicious. "This game is what they call . . . monte, I believe?"

"It is," McKay said, once again flipping over the remaining two cards to display that nothing was amiss. The waiter returned and set a glass upon a napkin imprinted with the *Tempest Queen* name and a line engraving of the riverboat.

"Sir, would you care for a drink?" the waiter inquired.

Clifton Stewart glanced up. "Yes, thank you. I will have the same as Mr. McKay." When the waiter left, Clifton said, "Let's see if I can do it again."

McKay chuckled. "I suspect the results will be the same. Some men have an eye for this game, you know. No way to put a move past them."

"Really? I did not know that."

"Really." McKay refrained from grinning and affixed a solemn expression to his face. "I have seen it only a time or two, but it is a fact."

He played the cards upon the table, and as before, Stewart made the correct decision. Both men were amused, but the younger man was warming to the game. McKay went another round, and this time Clifton made the wrong pick, but rather than discouraging him, it drove him on to try it just one more time.

"Where are you bound for, Mr. McKay?" he asked as the gambler set the cards up again.

"Baton Rouge," he replied, and just so his stories wouldn't cross each other, he played out the same line he had to the captain. "I have an ill sister living there."

Clifton's interest perked. "What is the matter with her?"

McKay put on a concerned face. "I don't know. The doctors say brain fever, but I don't think they really know, either."

Stewart nodded his head knowingly. "I had an aunt who suddenly took ill and perished. The doctors had called it brain fever, too. Horrible way to die." He fell into a thoughtful silence and then asked, "What is your sister's name?"

This caught McKay off guard. He had given Captain Hamilton a name, but for the life of him, he could not recall it now. Steward waited for the answer, watching him curiously. McKay feigned a cough and, when he had recovered, said smoothly, "Her name is Ruth."

"Ruth what?"

"Err—Provost. Yes, Ruth Provost."

Stewart pondered that and shook his head. "No, I reckon I do not know your sister."

McKay tapped the cards spread in a line upon the table with a slender forefinger. "Now, where is the queen this time?" he asked, drawing the conversation back to more familiar waters.

"Ah, let's see. This one here, on the end."

It was not the queen, of course, but when McKay turned the card over, the queen had instantly changed places with the joker and was exactly where Stewart had indicated.

"I think you have this game down pat, perhaps you would care to try another game?"

"No, I don't think so, Mr. McKay. I'm rather enjoying this one."

McKay said in his most nonchalant voice, "Then perhaps we can make it a bit more interesting?" He very nearly yawned, but figured that would be overdoing it a trifle.

Again Stewart shook his head. "If you want to play for money, well, I'm afraid I'm not up to that. Father says a fool and his money are easily parted, and that games of chance are the surest means to that divorce."

"Sound and true words. You have a wise father. But I wasn't thinking of money, although I am not opposed to placing a bet myself when I figure it's a sure thing. Are you?"

"You mean if I knew I couldn't lose?"

"Precisely."

Stewart gave this notion careful consideration, tugging thoughtfully on the scattering of thin, pale whiskers at his chin. "Well, I suppose if I knew that I could not lose my capital . . . ? Well, yes, I suppose I would take that sort of bet."

McKay merely grinned and gathered up the cards for another shuffle. The whiskey had taken some of the fire out of his arm, and he was rather enjoying the evening now. Young Clifton Stewart had relaxed, too, sipping his own drink and developing a fine red glow to his face.

Clifton said, "Well, what did you have in mind?"

"Matchsticks."

"Matchsticks?"

"Certainly. Have you never played for matchsticks?"

"No, I don't recall."

"It gives one the feel of placing a bet, but you see, nothing is at risk—save a few worthless matchsticks."

"Yes . . . yes, I see how that might add an edge of excitement—I think," he said, warming to the idea. Stewart thought a bit further, drained his glass. "But I do not have any matchsticks."

"Don't worry." McKay grinned and raised his good arm. Within a half dozen heartbeats a white-clad waiter was at his side.

"Matches?" the waiter repeated to ascertain he had heard the request straight. "I will have to inquire in the kitchen," he said finally and, with a vaguely puzzled look upon his face, departed.

CHAPTER
FOUR

"Are you the gentlemen who asked for the matches?"

Immediately both men forgot the cards that were spread out upon the table. Clifton Stewart instantly doffed his hat and stood, grinning. "Why, yes we are, miss."

She was a tall and slender woman, wearing a full, brown skirt, a somewhat wilted white shirtwaist, and a white but stained apron. Her hair was the color of a raven's wing, pinned up in a bun on top of her head, but after a long day's work, more than a couple stray tendrils fell limply down the perfect curve of her cheek. Her pale skin was slightly flushed: she had apparently been sent in a hurry from the kitchen upon this mission. Her large, dark eyes were openly curious as she handed Clifton the box of matches, and he saw the question that she was too polite to ask.

"They are to be used as counters—for this game of monte, you see."

"Oh. That makes perfect sense, now. It was an odd request." She stood there another moment, her hands folded in front of her, a pleasant smile for the two men.

McKay, although not as candid in his admiration as young Stewart, was no less struck by this woman's simple charm. He could not help recalling the lovely Genevieve de Winter. This woman was every bit her equal. How fortunate to have met two perfectly charming creatures in a single night. This, and the stately treatment Captain Hamilton was affording him, were almost more than a simple man could hope for. Leaving the swelling mining camps of the Rocky Mountain gold strikes with their burgeoning population of prospectors—men with heavy pockets and nowhere to spend all that newfound gold—had pained McKay greatly. Now, however, his fortunes were turning.

McKay gave her his most gentlemanly smile. Here was a diamond—perhaps still unpolished—but pure value through and through. "Perhaps you would care to watch?"

"Yes. That's a bully notion," Clifton blurted.

She merely smiled, and an angel could not have done so any more sweetly. "I'd really love to, gentlemen, but I must return to work."

"Where is it you work?" Clifton asked, as if groping for any ploy to keep her a moment longer by their table.

"The kitchen in the evening. I'm a chambermaid during the mornings."

"And the afternoons?" McKay inquired.

"Sir, I have the afternoons to myself. That when I catch up on my sleep. Now, I must be on my way. Enjoy your card game."

She turned and Clifton blurted out: "What is your name?"

She paused to look over her shoulder, holding them

captive a moment longer with her dark and haunting eyes. "Mystie."

"Mystie what?" he called after her.

"Waters," she said.

"Perhaps I will see you in the morning?" But she had already moved off, and if she had heard, she gave no sign of it. Clifton Stewart was grinning when he returned his attention to the cards. McKay was thinking about her, too, although he had more skill at keeping his feelings close to the vest.

"She is charming," Clifton said. "Do you believe that name?"

"She speaks with a Southern lilt. I was under the impression that Southern girls all had two first names. You know, Mary Jane, Betty Louise, . . . Martha Jo."

"That is commonly true," Stewart said. "The names are usually taken from the grandmother on each side. It is tradition, but it is by no means a law." He laughed.

"But that's precisely what I mean. Tradition is a heavy burden here in the South. I think it odd a woman would be given a name as . . . as different and poetic as Mystie Waters."

"I see your point, Mr. McKay. I will have to make a point of asking her tomorrow."

"You intend to see her tomorrow?"

"Of course." Clifton grinned suddenly and said, "Perhaps I will even drop by the kitchen tonight, for a something to keep the night hunger abated."

McKay's face remained impassive, but he, too, was thinking that if the card game continued late into the night, he might be induced to pay a visit to the boat's kitchen as well.

By midnight both men were weary of the game. The matchstick stakes had been most unrewarding as far as McKay was concerned, and Stewart had sidestepped his every attempt to shift the betting to more lucrative fare. But he could see that the young man was mentally tallying his winnings and losings in hard dollars, and McKay had made certain the winnings far exceeded what could have been, had the gambler been able to find the key to unlock the wealthy young man's closed fists. Well, he had made inroads this night, and perhaps tomorrow the tightfisted fellow would relinquish some cash.

These things took time, and the breaking of a particularly difficult mark was a challenge that McKay enjoyed. Nonetheless, McKay had noted in passing that the *Tempest Queen* was carrying a large number of passengers, and without a doubt, by the time they reached Baton Rouge a number of pockets would be considerably lighter, with his balancing the scales.

He grinned to himself at the thought as he collected his cards and put them away. His arm still ached, but not so much so now, thanks to the Glen-what's-it's-name that he'd been drinking.

McKay had learned through the course of the evening that this young man was the son of a wealthy planter, and a soon-to-be man of property himself. As the hours wore themselves out, Clifton Stewart, under the gentle hand of the scotch and McKay's own carefully placed questions, had loosened up. It didn't take McKay long to learn that besides eighteen hundred acres of river-bottom land, the lad's father owned sixty-seven slaves, a lucrative cotton business with firm business ties to an English textile conglomerate, and a thriving sugarcane business—not only growing the crop, but processing it as well.

For a while Mystie Waters had been the focus of their conversation. The Countess of the Kitchen, they had dubbed her almost immediately, but as soon as Clifton had discovered McKay's hidden interests in the woman, the talk turned back to cards, touching here and there on politics, but never lingering very long in that realm, for McKay merely listened to Stewart's complaints about the heavy-handedness of the

North, the unfair tariffs, and states' rights—and never once ventured an opinion of his own.

Not that McKay had any opinions on these issues that were smoldering across the land, on the verge of flaring into an ugly fire. He had learned early on that the wise man is the man who keeps his ears open and his mouth shut.

The two men said good-bye and drifted off toward their own cabins. McKay closed his door behind him but did not immediately light a lamp and instead reopened the door a crack and put an eye to it. When young Stewart had entered his own cabin, McKay shut the door and slipped out the opposite door onto the dark promenade and directed his steps toward the stern of the boat.

He hit an impassable barrier in the shape of the starboard paddle box and paused a moment to rethink his tactics. Eyeing a ladder, McKay climbed it to the hurricane deck, detoured around the obstacle, descended another ladder, slipped into the unoccupied ladies' salon by way of a back doorway, and then dove through another.

The kitchen seemed deserted, even though the place was still brightly lit. He stepped around a cupboard, past a long table, and then between a bank of ovens and a rack of iron utensils.

"Here now. What you doing sneaking around here?"

McKay drew up and smiled affably at a woman in a white apron who had appeared unexpectedly from a little room off to the side. She held a sack of beans in both arms and was glaring at him with a pinched face and an unlovely, belligerent mouth. "My sweet madam," McKay said. "Here, allow me to help you with your burden," and without a yea or nay from the surprised woman, he hefted the bean sack, despite the ache in his arm, and carried it to a counter where apparently the next day's soup was being prepared.

Brushing off his hands, McKay glanced around the kitchen. It was apparent the place was shut down for the night—except for the activities of this fearsome-looking creature whose glare told McKay she was still waiting to hear his reply.

He grinned and said, "I was looking for someone."

Her mouth had drawn up into a knot, and now the knot shifted to the left side of her face. Still she said nothing, allowing McKay to writhe a bit beneath her scowl.

"Err, a young lady . . . ?"

Sooty eyelids contracted.

"Err, a Miss Waters?"

"Ah-ha! I suspected as much," the woman gushed. "It ain't as if I've got four hands and can do all the work around this kitchen all by myself. You know how many mouths I'm going to have to fill come morning?"

McKay only just managed to wag his head before she drove on.

"Sixty-three, and that don't include what I'm expected to make available for deck passengers as well. And the crew! Why, they're expecting me and my girls to have breakfast sent up to them or over to where they are a-workin'. You tell me how long it takes me to do all that."

"I'm sure I have no idea, madam."

"Of course not. You try working your fingers to nubbins in this hot kitchen all day and half a night and then you'll have some idea!"

"But my sweet lady, what has all this to do with my inquiring—"

She had snatched a long-handled wooden spoon off the counter and was waving it like a deadly weapon in McKay's face. "I'll tell you what it has to do with it. I need all the help I can lay my hands on, and it don't help none when young men parade through my kitchen snatching away my girls to have romantic la-dee-das on the back deck, that's what it has to do with it."

This set McKay back a step. "Young men?" he asked.

"You think you are the first?" the woman said, and at once McKay detected a note of humor in her voice. "Ha! Guess you'll have to stand your turn, mister. Mystie is even now out on the kitchen deck with a young fellow who came sneaking in here just like you done not three minutes ago."

"Err—brown jacket, top hat?"

"The very one."

"I see." McKay peered across the kitchen through a door that opened onto the kitchen deck and saw the shadowy forms of two people standing there. It was clear from one silhouette that young Clifton Stewart had beat him to her.

"Why that young sneak," McKay said under his breath, but with no malice.

"Looks like you were bested, mister."

McKay glanced back and saw that the woman was actually smiling. "It looks that way, madam. I think I will be leaving now. So sorry to have interrupted your work."

"In another minute I'll be tossing that one out on his ears as well."

He merely grinned. McKay enjoyed a challenge and already young Stewart had elevated himself a few notches in the gambler's opinion. "Good night, madam," he said and returned to his cabin for the night.

The morning was gray with low clouds and the threat of more rain hanging over the *Tempest Queen* like a bad omen. Stewart was up early despite the late card game and the few moments in pleasant conversation with the lovely Mystie Waters before that old hag of a kitchen chief had chased him out.

Stewart leaned on the railing and watched the roustabouts on the wharf boat carrying the last of the cargo aboard and here and there an occasional passenger, with freshly purchased tickets in hand, climbing the stage, arms loaded down with baggage.

He had taken a turn around the promenade, ending up here, near the starboard paddle box. The boat was an immense, glittering palace, nearly three hundred feet long, he had been informed by a helpful crew member. Painted mostly white, the *Tempest Queen* fairly gleamed from bow to stern, even in the somber, overcast light. The handrailing was painted green, the decks gray—except down on the main deck where any paint that might have been applied was quickly worn off by the cargo stacked there. In late winter, she and other boats like her would be so heavily laden with cotton that her guards would dip the water. In fall, it would be sugar, and in between late winter and the next fall, every other imaginable item that could possibly be conceived in the fertile brains of Northern manufacturers and sold at great profit to Southerners.

Stewart frowned and recalled his father's words: *"Let the North have its factories. So long as the South has her cotton and her sugar, it is all we want—all we need."* For so many years that had held true, but the times were changing. Stewart felt it as surely as he felt the chill spring wind coming down from the North. The South was steadily losing its equality in the Senate as more free states were admitted to the Union. California had been wooed and admitted, and without even the due process that other states had been required to follow in the past! There was talk of the New Mexico Territory as well. Free states all, and on the flimsiest excuse that they were not suitable for slaves.

Stewart bristled at the thought. The time was coming, he knew, and it would only be a matter of a little while before the South would be free of its Northern tormenter.

His attention was drawn to a man coming out of the wharf boat. He had on a dark slouch hat that hid his face, but he carried a shotgun over his shoulder and wore a pistol in his belt. In his hand he had one end of a chain that he roughly tugged along. The other end of the chain was attached to a neck collar, which, in turn, was around the black neck of a frightened Negro. A runaway. Clifton Stewart had seen them brought back this way before, and the punishment was always the same. This one would be facing a whipping post in short order, Clifton mused, once back in the hands of his rightful owner. No wonder he looked so frightened.

"Good morning, Mr. Stewart."

He recognized the lilt of her voice immediately, and when he turned about, Mystie Waters's dark eyes were smiling up at him. She was wearing a white dress this morning, fresh and starched, and an apron of some slightly darker material. Her hair was put up in a bun, gleaming now in a rare streak of sunlight that had managed to find its way through the overcast sky. With both hands, she carried a wicker basket mounded up with clean linen: towels, sheets, pillowcases.

"Good morning," he said, smiling, and snatched his hat off his head.

"We are about to get under way," she said. "I apologize for the way Maggie threw you out last night. I was enjoying our little talk."

"So was I," he said, stammering a bit. He had never been a ladies' man, and he was unsure of himself. Not knowing how to proceed, he said, "I am looking forward to the trip. I only hope the clouds break up."

Mystie frowned slightly. "This is the time of the year when we get rain. There will not be many bright days on this trip."

"You sound like you know the river."

"I was born to it," she said. "My folks have a house overlooking the Mississippi."

"And where is that?"

"Cairo."

"You don't sound like a Northern girl," Stewart said, relieving her of the burden of the basket. "Let me carry this for you."

"I was not born in Illinois," she said, starting along the promenade with Clifton Stewart obediently at her side. "I was born in Carrollton, Louisiana. My grandfather lives there today. We moved North when I was twelve, but by then it was too late." She laughed, and to Stewart's ears it seemed to drive away all the gloom of the overcast morning sky.

"Too late for what?" he asked, amused.

"Too late to hide my roots, sir. Open my mouth, and at once the world knows I come from the South."

"And no reason to hide that either," Clifton said. "It is a thing to be proud of."

For an instant the clouds overhead seemed to settle in Mystie Waters's dark eyes, and then they brightened again, indomitably, and Clifton Stewart was aware of his heart racing.

"You do not know me well, sir," she said cryptically.

Stewart grinned. "A fault I hope to soon remedy," he said. He was shocked by the boldness of his words . . . and unaccustomed to the feelings suddenly flooding his being.

She halted by a door. "I must be getting back to work——" Her words stopped abruptly, and she looked past him to the landing stage below where the dockworkers were scurrying about like so many industrious ants.

"What is it, Miss Waters?" Clifton asked, his own view following hers. He could not detect anything out of the usual—but then, he did not know what was altogether unusual activity aboard a steamer, certainly not the frantic bustle of the dockworkers. He noted that the man with the runaway slave on a chain was boarding now, and he also recognized the sheriff from the evening before, climbing up the gangplank with them. There was another man boarding as well, wearing rude clothes of fringed buckskins and laced moccasins that reached nearly to his knees. A rough hat sat upon his head, and a huge knife hung at his side. Under an arm, he carried a heavy rifle in a leather scabbard. In the middle of the confusion, the clerk stood calmly among a small pile of wooden crates, marking notes on a sheet of paper in his hand. On the main deck, Captain Hamilton was speaking to the chief mate, pointing vaguely off in the direction of the bow. As far as Clifton could see, nothing was amiss—nothing that should have riveted her attention so.

When he looked back, Mystie seemed completely recovered. "It is nothing, really," she said, but was obviously distracted. "I must be getting back to work." She took the wicker basket from him, pushed through the door into a narrow gallery, and was gone.

Her thoughts were racing ahead as she went down the corridor toward the main cabin. She had received word of the *passenger* on the way, of course, but now she knew something must have gone wrong. Did they know? Should she risk making contact—

"Hello, Miss Waters."

His voice, so near, startled her. She wheeled about to discover him standing there, smiling easily, supporting himself upon his walking stick, a gleam of confidence in his dark gray eyes.

"Oh, I see that I have alarmed you. Please forgive me."

Mystie laughed a little uneasily and immediately assumed the image of perfect composure, even though her heart was pounding. "I declare, my mind was off somewhere when you spoke, sir. You . . . you are the gentleman who requested the matches last evening—Mr. Stewart's friend?"

"You are absolutely correct. Not only lovely, but you have a perfect memory as well. Here, please allow me," and accepting no word of protest, he relieved her of the basket—the second person to do so within five minutes. "Now, allow me to accompany you."

"I don't know if I should," she came back, but with growing confidence. "I do not even know your name."

"Dexter McKay," he replied at once, bowing at the waist to what little degree the basket in his hands would allow. "Forever at your service."

Mystie smiled. This Dexter McKay was quite dashing in his rich brown frock coat with the velvet collar, and his pale checked vest and striped trousers. He wore a ruffled shirt topped with a fresh collar and a brown tie fixed up in a neat bow at his throat. His boots had been recently polished, his hat likewise brushed. *Dashing, but too smooth.*

"I was taking it to the linen closet," she said.

"Lead the way."

Mystie nodded her head and said, "Very well, if you insist on helping me—"

"I do."

She refrained from smiling too broadly as she led the way through the main cabin where the tables were being shoved together and covered in white cloths and shiny silverware. Breakfast was scheduled to begin in less than an hour. The air was heavy with the aroma of brewing coffee, and spiffy white-clad waiters hurried purposefully about.

At the linen closet, Mystie finally persuaded McKay to relinquish the basket so that she could put the linen away, but not before he had made her promise to have dinner with him when she got off work that afternoon.

CHAPTER
FIVE

The chief mate, Mr. Lansing, looked past Captain Hamilton's shoulder and cleared his throat. Hamilton had been discussing the arrangement of the cargo on the deck, to keep his *Tempest Queen* in trim, and now his eyebrows drew together at his chief mate's soft warning, and he saw the mate's view dart toward the landing stage. When Hamilton turned, he recognized the sheriff coming across the deck. There was a second man with him, pulling a Negro at the end of a chain.

"Sheriff," Hamilton said briefly when the two men drew to a halt.

"Good morning, Captain," the lawman said.

Hamilton cast an eye to the gray sky. "I've seen better, but it's fair enough to be shoving off in. What can I do for you?" His view went back to the two men, and then shifted to the man in chains.

The Negro was a strong-backed man, a valuable field hand, it appeared to Captain Hamilton. But he was scared, and rightfully so. He had all the signs of a runaway, and the fellow who had him chained by the neck had the hard look of a professional slave hunter.

The sheriff said, "This here is Mr. Randall Statler, and he has a court warrant on this runaway slave." The sheriff presented Hamilton with a paper. "This is to show he has legal possession of this here slave until he turns him over to his owner, a Mrs. Susan Mae Canfield of Livingston Parish."

"Livingston Parish?" Captain Hamilton frowned and glanced at the document that appeared official enough. "What the devil is he doing clear over on this side of the river?"

The sheriff shrugged his heavy shoulders. "Hell if I know. He must have swum across. All I know is that Mr. Statler caught up with him just north of Napoleon, about to cross the Arkansas River."

Statler was not a big man, but he was built solid—like the proverbial brick privy, Hamilton mused. A black beard filled the lower half of his face, and a slouch hat covered the upper half, shading his sunburned cheeks, making them appear nearly as dark as the man he held bound in a chain.

Statler shifted the shotgun from his left shoulder to his right and spat a stream of brown tobacco juice onto the clean deck. "There is a branch of the Underground Railroad somewhere nearby. My guess is that this runaway was trying to make fer it."

"Is that so?" Hamilton considered the husky Negro a moment and then handed the paper back to the sheriff, who folded it, slipped it into a tattered envelope, and returned it to Statler. "I suspect you have already booked passage for the two of you?"

Statler shoved the envelope into the open neck of his sweaty, collarless shirt. "I booked me a cabin, Captain. Got the nigger here deck passage. What I need from you is a place to anchor him permanent. He sure ain't of the temperament to stay put 'less I fasten him down tight."

Hamilton glanced back at the prisoner, and the black man immediately averted his eyes, but not before Hamilton noted the swollenness about them, and the bruised and cut face. His clothes were in shreds, and he was shoeless.

Hamilton said, "Well, it's quite a run from down Livingston Parish a-way up here to Napoleon. I imagine the man's plain tuckered out. Looks like he caught himself in a bramble as well. He'll be wanting a place where he can get some sleep, and be out of the sun—that is if the blame thing ever decides to show itself."

"Don't fret about no comfortable 'commodations, Captain. Just any old place will do so long as I can lock this chain down tight."

Hamilton frowned. He had no particular affection for runaways, but he could tell that this terrified man had been treated mercilessly. Well, the Negro was fortunate to still be alive; he could just as likely have been dead. Perhaps when his missus got him back he would be. Hamilton had owned slaves once, and he well appreciated the need for discipline— it was just that some folks took too much pleasure in the task. He could see where this Randall Statler might fall into that category.

"Over here," Hamilton said. "You can chain him to the forward stanchion in front of the woodpile. He'll have protection from the sun and rain, at least, there beneath the boiler deck."

Statler made the chain fast, securing it with a heavy padlock, and then dropped the tethered key down the front of his shirt where the court warrant already resided. Giving the chain a final tug, he studied the wretched man huddled against the woodpile, and apparently deciding his prisoner wasn't going anywhere, he swung his shotgun back onto his shoulder and turned back to Captain Hamilton. "I'll be going up to my cabin now."

"Breakfast will be served in forty-five minutes," Hamilton said as a matter of duty.

Statler spat another stream of tobacco juice, nodded his head, and started off.

"You will find the *Tempest Queen* well supplied with cuspidors, sir."

Statler glanced back at the captain, and a scowl turned his swarthy face into something ugly, and dangerous. "I'll keep it in mind, Captain," Statler said. He then let loose a brown stream that splattered at the feet of the bound Negro.

"Not exactly the friendly sort," the sheriff noted when Statler had gone.

Captain Hamilton pulled at his short beard thoughtfully. "Well, I suppose you have to be a hard sort to do his kind of work."

"Reckon so," the sheriff agreed sleepily, and Hamilton figured the man had had a busy night. The sheriff started for the landing stage.

"Sheriff," Hamilton called after him.

He paused and looked over his shoulder.

"Any word on that man last night?"

"The gambler?"

"Indeed. Have you found out who he was?"

The lawman shook his head. "No. He was new in town, just like it was said. His name, as far as anyone could recollect, was Clarence Banning. Took some money off a couple unlucky strikers over at the Easy Way Saloon before finding his way down to the wharf boat. Nobody seemed to know any more."

"I was just wondering."

The sheriff nodded and started off the boat. He had a foot on the landing stage when he stopped again and turned back to Captain Hamilton. "I did learn one other thing, now that I think back on it. A couple fellows saw him having supper with a woman over at Mackie's Cafe. I asked around some.

Never could find out who the woman was or where she got to. I don't reckon it means anything." He let the pause lengthen, and when Hamilton did not add anything to the statement, the sheriff said, "Well, have a good trip, Captain."

"Thanks." Captain Hamilton watched the sheriff shuffle down the landing stage, hands thrust deep into his pockets, shoulders hunched wearily forward. When the man had disappeared around the corner of the wharf boat, Hamilton snagged the chief mate by the sleeve as he hurried past.

"Captain?" Lansing asked, distracted.

Hamilton inclined his head toward the Negro, huddled against the woodpile. "Get that man a blanket and something to eat, Mr. Lansing, and have a chamber pot brought down as well."

Lansing glanced at the bound black man. "A runaway?"

"Yes."

"I'll see to it once we're set up here, sir," Lansing said and hurried off about the business of loading and arranging the remaining cargo.

Captain Hamilton made his rounds. He checked in on his chief engineer and the strikers down in the engine room, then passed some encouraging words to the Negro firemen already heaving four-foot lengths of cordwood into the open furnace doors.

"Don't forget the pine knots," Hamilton told them. "We'll want some fine black smoke when we show our stern to the folks of Napoleon."

The heat in front of the furnaces was terrific, and it gave Captain Hamilton a tangible sense of the power at his command. The *Tempest Queen* was a grand boat, and in more than a few subtle ways she reflected the nuances of Hamilton's personality. He had watched her taking shape up on the ways in the Indiana shipyard, had fretted over her as a father might fuss over the birth of his first child. He had chosen her fittings; he had walked upon her unpainted decks and had stood in her pilothouse before her helm had been installed, peering out window openings before the glass had been fitted. She was a part of him. Even her name had been carefully selected after months of pondering upon it.

This was in fact his second *Tempest Queen*. The first, a smaller boat, had burned to the waterline below island some ten years back. Hamilton had taken the insurance money and with the addition of his own capital, and the investments of two silent partners, had built this boat. She was the finest on the river. The fastest as well, as Hamilton would be quick to boast to anyone who asked. And at one time he would have been equally quick to prove it. Racing, however, was a young man's sport. Hamilton had seen too many fine vessels blown apart because their captains had ordered on more steam in a side-by-side regatta, just to be able to display a set of antlers atop their bells.

Hamilton's *Tempest Queen* was too precious to risk in that fashion. He'd lost one boat already and had no intentions of sacrificing another to this demanding goddess known as the Mississippi River.

He made his way up to the boiler deck and looked in on the main cabin where the boat's guests were beginning to gather for breakfast. The tables had all been pushed together in a single row down the center of the cabin, and there were pleasant enclaves of conversation scattered about. Friendly greetings were cast toward him as he made his way through the cabin. He snatched a cup of coffee off a silver service tray and carried it with him up to the next deck—the hurricane—and presently stepped into the pilothouse.

This morning was Patton Sinclair's watch. The pilot was leaning against the wheel, puffing a green cigar and talking about the only thing Sinclair ever talked about—the river—when Hamilton entered. He glanced up and said, "Top of the morning to you, Captain."

Sitting on the pilots' bench with his long legs stretched out was a fellow Captain Hamilton knew. Absalom Grimes was a steamer pilot, catching a ride down to Natchez to "look at the river." Grimes was a frequent rider in the *Tempest Queen*'s pilothouse. He and Sinclair had been partners on the *G.W. Delany* back in '57, and it was common practice for out-of-work pilots to hop a steamer and ride up in the pilothouse to keep the river "fresh in their brains." The real reason they did so much "looking at the river," of course, was that it was cheaper being a guest on the boat than to rent a room ashore between berths. Hamilton had been a pilot years ago, before he was a captain, and he had ridden many a pilothouse himself when starting out on his riverboat career.

"Morning, Mr. Sinclair." Hamilton turned to the guest. "Mr. Grimes," he acknowledged briefly, finally glancing to the lanky lad there, Mr. Sinclair's apprentice, Jack Jacobs. In the seven months since Patton Sinclair had taken Jack Jacobs on as his cub, the young man had developed a cocky, self-assured stance, vaguely reminiscent of his chief, and had taken to smoking cigars as if he had been born with one in his mouth. "And young Mr. Jacobs," Hamilton asked, "how is our cub pilot doing this morning?"

Jacobs grinned. "I'm doing right fine, Captain," he said and glanced at Sinclair as if hoping the old master would verify that he really was doing fine.

Sinclair nodded briefly and withdrew the cigar from his lips. "He's coming along okay, Captain. A fair steersman already. Another year or two and he'll know this river almost half as well as I know her."

Ab Grimes chuckled, and Jack Jacob grinned indulgently at the good-natured fun at his expense.

"Well, so long as he keeps my boat off the shoals and out of blind chutes," Hamilton said, smiling.

"Oh, I'll see that he don't run you aground, Captain. It ain't likely anyway this trip—not with all this high water about. No, sir, we'll put out in the middle of the stream and go booming right on down to Baton Rouge. Of course, we may run over a flatboat or raft or two in the meantime."

There was a general round of laughter, and Hamilton

gazed out at the low, gray sky and at the impatient yellow-brown water rushing past the boat. The river was almost a mile wide here, nearly at flood stage, and he could only just make out the fuzzy shore over on the Mississippi side. He tasted his coffee again and fished a paper from his oversize pocket. "Here is our itinerary."

Sinclair studied the paper a moment and shoved it into his pocket with a bold arrogance orchestrated especially for the benefit of the men there. He had read it, had memorized it, and had absolutely no intention of referring back to it again for the duration of this trip.

Hamilton finished his coffee and set the cup where a passing waiter would be sure to see it. He extracted his watch from his vest, studied it, and said, "I plan on pulling out of here in about an hour. Is that all right by you, Mr. Sinclair?"

The pilot gave an indifferent shrug and cast an eye at the cloudy sky. "This day ain't gonna get no better, but then it ain't gonna get no worse neither," he said confidently. "I'm ready whenever you give the word, Captain."

Hamilton had never known Sinclair to say anything but in that annoyingly confident manner, and certainly never in a way that might let on that there was even an atom's worth of doubt in the man's mind. "Very well," Hamilton said, wheeling back to the door.

Atop the hurricane deck, the captain paused to survey his domain. A small bubble of pride developed as his eyes swept from stern to bow, lingering a moment on the impressive swell of the paddle boxes on starboard and larboard sides of the boat. His eyes shifted, and with his head canted back, Captain Hamilton studied the two tall chimneys—black against the gray morning sky, and filling the air with sooty smoke—rigged solidly in place with long, slender links of iron. The bubble of pride expanded and rose into his chest—and then it burst, and suddenly he was frowning.

Cynthia should be here as well. This vessel is as much hers as it is mine.

At once Hamilton's mood had become as gray as the overcast sky, and he climbed down to the main deck to see how Lansing was coming along with the loading.

With the *Tempest Queen*'s chimneys puffing thick black smoke from the burning pine knots being heaved into her furnaces, the brass bell upon the *Tempest Queen*'s hurricane deck gave out two heavy, melodious peals that drifted away over the town of Napoleon. Her landing stage was raised aboard. A visitor who had lingered too long leaped the short distance from her guards to the wharf boat as slowly the paddles began to turn, backing the bright, white-tiered boat away from the wharf and out into the river. Above her chimneys, as if being supported by two sable columns, was an expanding, black ceiling, held near to the sparking chimneys by the heavy air.

Hamilton stood atop the hurricane deck, the pilothouse to his back, the boat's bell at his left. The *Tempest Queen*'s bow came about, and faintly, above the pounding of the steam engines, he heard the ring of a bell way down deep in the engine room. Momentarily the chugging of the engines diminished, steam hissed through the gauge cocks, and then the pounding resumed with the puffing from her 'scape pipes becoming a smooth, rhythmic tune to Captain Hamilton's ears as the boat moved farther out into the stream. Behind him, in the pilothouse, Hamilton saw that young Jacobs was at the helm, with Sinclair nearby, an expert eye studying the swirling water ahead.

The boat picked up speed gracefully, chugging powerfully into the middle of the channel where Sinclair would take advantage of the swifter water to move them downriver. Now under steam, the boat was for all practical purposes under the pilot's command until they put in at Leota, below Greenville, where Hamilton would once again assume command.

Hamilton made his way down into the main cabin to catch the tail end of the breakfast still being served. He took his chair at the end of the table, and immediately a white-jacketed black waiter was at his side.

"Wheat cakes, bacon, and some coffee," Hamilton said out of habit, and he might as easily have said, "The usual," and the waiter would have known exactly what to tell the cook to put together. He had become a creature of habit, and comfortable in it. In two years, Captain William Hamilton would retire from the riverboating business, build himself a house on what was left of his land, and live out his remaining days on his porch, watching the river forever making its way down to the Gulf. He had vague plans to catch up on his reading and, perhaps, to someday write a book about the Mississippi. He might even travel again; see the Pacific Ocean, finally, or ride a steamboat on the Sacramento River.

There would be endless possibilities—in two years. Until then, Hamilton was content to handle the business of running his riverboat, striding her decks and chatting with the guests while under steam, arranging freight contracts and travel schedules when ashore—and ordering wheat cakes, bacon, and coffee for breakfast every morning.

He surveyed the cabin and watched busy waiters cleaning tables and passengers lingering to enjoy a second or third cup of coffee. He noted that Randall Statler had taken a table by himself. Statler had not bothered to change clothes, but at least he had left the shotgun and pistol behind in his cabin. In another corner of the room, a gathering of men was peering guardedly at the cards held close to their vests. Hamilton recognized Mr. McKay as one of them.

At the front of the cabin, a young man had entered through the leaded-glass doors and was glancing around as if searching for someone. Hamilton's breakfast arrived at about the same moment the young man spied his quarry, and Hamilton discerned within half a dozen steps that he himself was the fellow's destination. He set his coffee down as the young man pulled abreast. Hamilton did not know this man and figured he had taken passage in Napoleon.

"Captain Hamilton?"

"Yes," he replied warily, for he saw the impatience in the young man's stance, heard it in his voice. "I am Captain Hamilton."

"Sir, my name is Clifton Stewart, and I was told I might find you here."

"Well, you have done that. What is it I can do for you?"

"I must protest the *person* who has accommodations in the cabin next to mine."

"Oh, and who might that be?" Hamilton asked, not overly interested. Seeing to the petty complaints of his passengers was one aspect of his job that he would be happy to leave behind in two years.

"It is that fellow over there." Stewart pointed a finger conspicuously. "He is loud and rude and is not a gentleman."

Hamilton glanced across the room. "You mean Mr. Statler?"

"The very one."

"Well, I suspect you are correct on all three accounts, Mr. Stewart." Hamilton spread fresh, churned butter on his wheat cakes and flooded them with warm maple syrup that he had had sent by mail all the way down from Vermont. "What sort of problem are you having with him?"

Stewart said, "I was leaving my cabin when that man rudely pushed me aside. He cursed profanely when his key did not immediately open his door, and when it did, he slammed it open so violently the very walls of *my* cabin rattled. I do not know what transpired next, except that if the cacophony he made putting up his gear is any indication of the man's temperament, I shall not have a single moment's rest until we reach Baton Rouge."

"Humm," Hamilton mumbled around a mouthful of wheat cakes. He washed it down with coffee and said, "And what is it you would like me to do about it?"

"I would like you to assign me a different cabin," Stewart said, astonished that he would have to make it so plain.

Captain Hamilton leaned back in his chair and considered this angry guest. He could see by his clothes that Stewart was a man of means and heard in his tone that he was a man used to giving orders, and usually those passengers were the sort that caused him more grief if things did not go exactly their way. He said, "Perhaps, if you give it a night, you may discover that Mr. Statler will not be as boisterous as you suspect. He has only just boarded—"

"Yes, I know," Stewart interrupted. "I observed him coming aboard with that runaway slave."

"Well, then you know the man must have had a difficult last few days running him down. Once he has had a bit of rest, you may find him entirely different."

Stewart shot the slave hunter a superior glance and said, "I doubt very much that I have misjudged the man, but I will be patient, Captain. Be forewarned, if I hear so much as a peep out of him tonight, I shall insist on your giving me a new cabin." Clifton Stewart turned on his heels and left.

Hamilton watched Stewart stride briskly out of the cabin, and from the corner of his eye, he saw that McKay had noted the stormy passage as well. Captain Hamilton frowned. *Another annoying detail to see to*, he thought as he went back to his breakfast.

CHAPTER SIX

Chief Mate Edward Lansing eyed the cargo stacked about on the main deck. It was a mighty crowded place about now, what with the merchandise and half a hundred deck passengers milling about. He planted his hands upon his hips and frowned, not altogether pleased with the way the final piles had been laid out. He made his way to the guards and, bracing a foot on a cargo post, grabbed hold of a hog chain and leaned far overboard to eye the red strip painted around the hull, now half submerged in the yellow-brown water. The bow wake broke upon it forward, and the paddle wheel farther aft obscured it back in that direction with its frothy mix. Despite the haphazard arrangement of the cargo, the boat seemed to be running trim.

Still, Lansing was not altogether satisfied, and considering it a matter of pride, he whistled down a passing deckhand and said, "Get up a couple hands here, and let's do some rearranging."

The deckhand went off after some help, and while he was away, Lansing's critical, surveying view came across the runaway Negro shackled to the stanchion, and at once he recalled Captain Hamilton's orders. He wove his way through the milling crowds in their traveling attire—a colorful contrast to the gray morning and muddy river— and went up the wide, curving staircase to the boiler deck, feeling the boat bucking now as she knifed through the current. They were making a crossing, and he could hear the leadsmen shouting out the depth to Sinclair in the pilothouse most of forty feet overhead.

"*M-a-r-k three . . . M-a-r-k three . . . Quarter-less-three . . .*"

Lansing ducked into the main cabin where the noise of the passengers drowned out the leadsmen's cries. He saw Captain Hamilton still at his table, gave the boat master a brief nod as he hurried past, and a few paces before encountering the now-bursting ladies' parlor, he skipped through a door and cast a searching glance about the busy kitchen.

"Maggie!" he called, finally eyeing the kitchen chief.

She peered up from a bubbling black cauldron looking ever so much like a fairy-tale creature out of a child's picture book, created for no other purpose than to keep the progeny—and therefore the progeny's parents—awake throughout the night.

He dodged a cart of fresh-sliced fruit and sidestepped thirty pounds of roast headed for a yawning oven—this evening's supper—and finally made safe passage to Maggie's side.

"What is it, Mr. Lansing?" she asked impatiently, ducking

beneath a tray of eggs and sausage floating high on a
waiter's hand toward the door.

"Captain wants some food sent down to a runaway slave
who is bound to the forward stanchion." Lansing found he
was shouting to be heard above the clatter of pans, the rattle
of iron utensils, the gurgle of boiling water, and sizzle of
breakfast foods upon a spattering griddle. "Also wants some
blankets sent down to him, and a chamber pot, too."

"Chamber pot!" Maggie bellowed, and for a single tick of
the clock the kitchen seemed to fall into a dead silence.
Then the racket burst forth with renewed vigor, and twice
the volume.

"I will see to it, Maggie."

The kitchen chief turned and discovered Mystie Waters
suddenly at her side.

"I've got most my other work finished. It won't be no
bother," she added.

Maggie nodded her head. "Ladle up a bowl of grits, then,
and get whatever else it is Mr. Lansing says the nigger
needs. Now don't dawdle. I need you back here lickety-
split."

"Yes, ma'am." Mystie got the food together, adding a bit
of bread and a plate of bacon off the griddle. She put it on
a tray and, with Lansing closely following her out the door,
made her way down the corridor to a linen closet where
Mystie added a blanket to the load in her arms. After
another moment's delay to duck into a storage room for a
white china chamber pot, Mystie went out the main cabin
door with Lansing still at her heels. On the deck at the head
of the staircase, she stopped suddenly and smiled up at the
chief mate.

"You may go back to your work now, Mr. Lansing. I can
take these down to that runaway slave myself."

"I don't know as I should leave you, Miss Waters. I best
stick by your side. You never know what might happen with
a nigger like that alone with a white girl."

"Oh, don't be silly. You said yourself that he was bound."

"Yes, ma'am. A neck collar and chain, padlocked about the stanchion."

"Well, then, what could possibly happen?" she said with an easy laugh to show him how ridiculous the notion really was. "You must have much more important work to do, Chief Lansing. I'm sure Captain Hamilton would not want me to keep you from it."

Lansing glanced over the railing at the deckhands already gathered below, waiting on his return. A frown wrinkled his brow. "Well, I was about to rearrange a bit of the cargo, just to put the *Queen* on a level trim, you understand."

"There now, you just get back to your duty, Chief. It is far more important to see that the boat is in running level and trimmed than to follow me around, when, after all, I will be perfectly safe," she said.

Lansing thought this over. "If anything were to happen to you, the Captain like as not would hang my side on his wall—"

"Now you know nothing is going to happen. I'll be perfectly all right."

"He didn't seem so dangerous, really," Lansing admitted, backpedaling some now. "More scared than anything else."

"Well, no wonder!"

A smirk cracked upon Lansing's stern face. "I reckon I'd be scared, too, if I was in that nigger's shoes"—he laughed suddenly—"if'n he had any shoes on, that is."

Mystie smiled and said, "If I need assistance, Chief, I will be certain to call out."

Lansing considered that a workable compromise, and left Mystie standing there. His eyes suddenly fixed upon something below, and he went dashing down the stairs, hollering, "You lame-legged, half-blind son of a possum! I will tell you when you are to lounge about like a king atop that cargo pile!" Lansing stormed down onto the main deck and shagged the startled Negro deckhand to his feet, running him up one side and down the other with colorful and graphic metaphors, comparing him to every foul creature that came to mind. The Negroes all leaped to attention, quaking, and when Lansing had blown himself out like last night's storm, he said, "We are going to shift this pile over to that empty place by the jack staff and bring that small stack of fencing wire over here in its place. Now get moving. Hump—hump—HUMP!"

Mystie didn't linger to hear any more. She made her way down to the main deck and found the runaway slave with his knees drawn up and his head buried between them. He was down between two mounds of cargo, out of the way of the other deck passengers, and fairly hidden from view. His back was against the far end of the first of four woodpiles.

There were forty cords of firewood stacked there, and at the rate the firemen were heaving the fuel into the open furnaces, all forty cords wouldn't last but five or six hours before the *Tempest Queen* would have to pull into a woodyard or tie up alongside a raft to replenish the supply.

He didn't hear her come up, and when he became aware of her standing there, he spun about like a startled rabbit and wiped his eyes.

"It's all right," Mystie said soothingly. She came a little closer and bent down beside him.

He backed up tighter against the log stack as if he desperately wished to melt in between the chinks in the pile, and averted his eyes. "You got t' be goin' away, missus," he said. "I ain't 'pose t' be talkin' wit no white women alone."

"It is all right. I brought you some food . . . and some other things that you are going to need. The captain ordered it."

Trembling, the Negro still refused to look at Mystie.

She set the tray of food on the deck near him, and the blanket and chamber pot against the stanchion. She was aware of the heat from the furnaces not so very far behind them and the voices of the firemen feeding them and the rattle of their long iron rakes working the bed of coal back and forth. But they were only distant sensations, for Mystie's attention was full upon the frightened black man.

"What is your name?"

"Eli is my name, missus, and o' you need t' git goin' away from here 'fore someone sees you."

"I said it was all right. I am supposed to be here." Mystie paused and then asked, "Eli, were you crying just now?"

"Oh no, missus. Eli don't neber cry." But he refused to look at her.

"Where are you from, Eli?"

"I belong t' Missus Canfield."

"Why did you run away?"

"It was Bouki what make me do it. I ain't neber wanted t' run away 'fore. Lordy, I's a good nigger. Bouki, he make me do it. Now my missus gonna put me t' de stocks and whip me fer a month or more."

"Bouki is just old slave talk," Mystie said with a note of irritation. "Only darky superstition is all it is."

"No it ain't, missus. I's sees him!"

"Where?"

"In de top o' de tree. When I was runnin' from de dogs."

"Well, I don't believe that slave superstition for an instant, Eli." She paused to glance around before lowering her voice. "Listen to me, Eli. I know where you were bound. I got word—"

"What the hell are you doing here?"

Mystie nearly choked on her words, and her heart seemed to leap into her throat. She wheeled about, and in that instant, Randall Statler's angry scowl slipped slowly into a leering grin. "My, what a pretty thing you are." His eyes brazenly took inventory of her. His intent unmistakably clear upon his grisly and sweaty face, Statler advanced, and at the same time Mystie's fingers found the end of a stout length of white-pine cordwood protruding from the pile.

There are but three joys in life, Dexter McKay reminded himself again—for perhaps the fourth time that very morning—*a good game of cards, a lovely woman, and fine whiskey!*

He laughed aloud deeply, resonantly, graciously, as he laid his cards out upon the table, saw the expressions on faces head south in various degrees of sag or wrinkle, and heard their good-natured groans. The players threw in their hands, and McKay happily raked the little pile of coins to his side of the table.

"You have Lady Luck looking over your shoulder, Mr. McKay," the retired general said.

"He's got the devil in him," the wealthy planter amended, shaking his head and reaching into his pocket for more lucre.

"Beginner's luck. It is all the way the cards fall." McKay deferred graciously. *A good game of cards*. Well, he certainly was running no deficit on that account, not aboard the *Tempest Queen*.

The silent frontiersman, who went only by the name of Klack, was drumming the tabletop with his fingertips, seemingly trying to read something in the pile of cards the retired general was presently gathering up for the shuffle.

And indeed, it was a *good game of cards*! McKay had not once needed to bury a card or slip one from the bottom. These men loved euchre and had enough money to be able to play the game badly and afford to continue.

A waiter brought the coffeepot and refilled their cups. It was coffee this morning, but by this evening it would be some more of that delightful Glen-what's-its-name that Mr. Stewart had put him on to.

Fine whiskey, to be sure!

McKay had caught a glimpse of Clifton Stewart a few minutes earlier, speaking with the captain who was still seated across the cabin, himself sipping coffee and reading what appeared to be an illustrated newspaper. The young man had appeared unsettled and had left in a huff. McKay made a note to look the young planter up and again attempt to lighten his pockets some.

The retired general asked, "How about a different game?"

Klack peered at him from out of a forest of yellow hair

that fell like a shaggy mane from his head and sprang out in every direction from his chin. He had the look of a buckskinner. McKay had seen a few like Klack in his stay in the West, and this man had all the characteristics: the crude clothes, the quiet, thoughtful manner, the wary eyes. All the rough-and-tumble appearance of a man used to hard living—all but one, and McKay marveled how such a man could maintain such perfect fingernails, and fingertips as smooth and clean as a Sunday shirt.

Klack bit off the end of a cigar and spat it out, and the beard reached up and caught it, secreting it away with who knew what else in that golden mass. "What you got in mind?" His voice was oddly high-pitched coming from a man of such a burly visage. Klack was not a tall man, perhaps five feet six inches, McKay had judged when Klack had ambled to the table. But Klack was nothing if not hard as the Rocky Mountains he had said were home. He was built like a grizzly bear, and he smelled like one, too. His skin had been baked by the sun, desiccated by the dry winds, and run through a tannery for good measure. His arms strained the material of his red homespun shirt, and where they emerged from the turned-up cuffs, they were corded like bridge cables.

"Seven-up?" the retired general suggested.

The frontiersman's eyebrows dipped, and the wrinkles in his brow deepened further. "Don't reckon I know that game."

The wealthy planter to his right offered a brief explanation, and while that was going on, the retired general, who was casually shuffling the deck, said to McKay, "Where was it you said you were from, sir?"

McKay had started stacking his winnings in piles of similar sizes, larger coins in back, smaller up front. "The Kansas Territory," he said, not elaborating.

"Yes, of course. Out in the gold country, were you not?" He rolled the end of his magnificent gray mustache as he spoke.

"Yes. Along the Cherry Creek."

"I hear it was a big strike."

McKay frowned. "For some it was."

The retired general laughed. "I take it you were not among the fortunate?"

McKay grinned. "I learned early on that digging gold from solid rock was not my calling. And washing it from mountain streams fed by packs of melting snow high above can destroy the finger joints." McKay fluttered his fingers as if to prove they had retained their nimbleness. Indeed, that was one of the last things McKay would want to lose. Heavens! He'd have to resort to *working* for a living if he should lose his dexterity! The thought brought on a shiver, and he immediately put the dreadful notion out of mind.

McKay had followed the tide of gold seekers out to California in '49, but not to mine for gold—at least not in the generally accepted manner. No—heavens, no! It was infinitely easier to mine the yellow metal from no deeper than a prospector's pockets. They were forever eager to allow McKay to work that claim for all it was worth. And afterward, they would happily return to scrape at their claims in order to replenish his. A very equitable arrangement as far as Dexter McKay was concerned. When the California gold fields played out, he had made his way East, stopping briefly near the gold strikes in the Kansas Territory.

"And what brought you back to civilization?" the retired general inquired.

McKay drew on the stub of his cigar and just then spied Mystie Waters making her way through the main cabin with a man McKay knew was one of the crew, right behind. Her arms were laden with a food tray, a blanket, and a sparkling white porcelain pot under her elbow. He watched her bustle past and out the front doors. McKay thought wistfully of Genevieve de Winter. He felt the grin tug up the corners of his mouth, and he glanced at the retired general.

"Why, I returned for the lovely women of the South, General."

The retired general laughed. "Sir, I see you are a man of breeding and impeccable good taste."

The wealthy planter finished his explanation of the game of seven-up, and Klack allowed he would give it a try. McKay, however, had other thoughts, and he gathered up his winnings.

"Are you leaving us?" the wealthy planter asked.

McKay smiled smoothly. "I regret to have to depart so soon, but my presence is required elsewhere at the moment."

The wealthy planter was perturbed. "Sir, you must know that seven-up requires partners and we will be one short."

McKay shrugged his shoulders. "I do apologize, but something has come up. I am certain, however, that you will have no trouble finding someone to sit in." McKay grinned. "Perhaps later?" He gave each man there a smile and a nod, and tapping his tall hat firmly upon his head, he gathered up his walking stick and left.

On the deck out front of the main cabin, McKay made his way to the railing and peered back along the promenade. He moved to the other side of the boat and again observed the crowded railing all the way back to where it ended against the paddle box.

Looking forward, McKay heard a shout, and he saw the man who had accompanied Miss Waters through the main cabin. But the lovely lady was not with him now. The man was driving a group of deckhands to perform some task of moving cargo about. McKay dismissed the activity and began a careful search down among the deck passengers. He feared she had eluded him when, suddenly, he caught a glimpse of her beneath the overhang, and then she was out of sight.

McKay started after her, but then stopped. It was never good form to appear too anxious, he decided, She was, after all, about her job, and he could wait to see her later, when she had promised to have dinner with him.

Hitching his stick under his arm, McKay filled his lungs with fresh air, turned an eye up at the grizzled sky, frowned, and started for his cabin.

He tossed the butt of his cigar out into the rising river and cast another glance over his shoulder at the muddy water sliding beneath the bow. In that instant, he had a glimpse of young Mr. Stewart making his way around the stacks of cargo below.

CHAPTER SEVEN

Captain Hamilton peered across the room, the furrows deepened in his brow. Not because of what he saw, but because of that all too familiar force now rearing its fanged head within him. He suppressed an urge to get up immediately and instead directed his hand to bring the coffee cup slowly to his lips and then, just as deliberately, to set it back upon the saucer.

His hand had begun to tremble slightly. He swallowed hard and was vaguely aware of a dampness emerging upon his forehead. He allowed himself another glance. The seat vacated by Mr. McKay was still unoccupied.

Captain Hamilton commanded his thoughts back onto

boat business but found them abandoning their posts, like deserting soldiers running from the battle lines, and ending up back where he had shagged them away from in the first place.

Then, as if with a mind of their own, his feet pushed out from under the table, and before the captain realized it, they had carried him across the main cabin, and he found himself hovering near the card game.

He cleared his throat.

The wealthy planter glanced up, saw Hamilton standing there, and said, "Good morning, Captain."

The other players at the table, now aware that the captain of the boat had chosen their table to visit, momentarily set their cards aside.

"Good morning, gentlemen," Hamilton said, catching each eye, returning each smile. "I see you have a vacant chair."

"Mr. McKay had business elsewhere," the frontiersman said sullenly. "And just when we were going to have us a game of seven-up."

"Seven-up! Why that's my game, gentlemen."

"Really?" the retired general said, smiling cordially. "Perhaps you would care to join us then?"

Hamilton knew he should not take the seat. When it came to cards, however, the decision to join a game or leave it was never entirely his own. The first being a dictate of some inexorable force within him, the latter being a force of finances—or as the case usually ended up, the lack of finances. Just now he was flush, having recovered his losses of the night before, and no amount of urging to the contrary could have kept him from sitting in on the game.

"I think I have a little while, gentlemen," Hamilton said, hiding his enthusiasm and lowering himself into the chair with the dignity befitting the captain of a mighty Mississippi riverboat. Hamilton agreed to the frontiersman as his confederate, even though the bearded man from Jackson, Wyoming, had never played the game before. The first round would be with no bets, just to give the frontiersman a feel for seven-up before they got down to play in earnest.

In spite of his cheerfulness, Hamilton was unsettled. It was always like that when he found himself in a card game. Why could he not resist that beast that lurked within him, the animal that took control whenever a bet was waged, a card turned over? He had tried. Heaven knows, he had tried. But the results were always the same—and most dissatisfactory.

The wealthy planter drew high card for the deal, shuffled the deck, gave the captain the cut, and dispersed the cards around the table. Hamilton gathered up his cards, and slowly the guilt within him melted away, and then all that was important to him in the world were the cards in his hands.

Thwack!

Randall Statler staggered back, eyes wide with shock, stunned. When he withdrew his hand from his forehead, there was blood upon his palm. The shock and surprise on his face turned to rage, and the rage directed itself at the woman now on her feet, heaving the stick back over her shoulder again.

"You little vixen," he said, his rage now shaking his body.

"Stay away from me," Mystie warned, waving the stick threateningly over her head. The club had taken Statler by surprise, having emerged unexpectedly from the stack of cordwood at her side, and now he eyed it as he calculated his next move.

"I said get yourself away from me!" Mystie warned. Statler advanced a step. The Negro chained to the stanchion scrambled aside when the powerful slave hunter lunged.

Mystie swung again, but this time Statler was prepared for it. He reached out, grabbed the stick, and wrenched it away. Tossing it aside, he was suddenly aware that the black firemen feeding wood into the furnaces had suspended work and were now crowding near. Statler wheeled on them.

"Stay out of this if you know what's good for you."

Mystie's heart sank. The black workers halted and retreated, but she understood the price they would have to pay if they laid a hand on a white man—even one engaged in such folly.

Would that fear of reprisal have stopped me, she thought, *if the tables were turned? If I was a slave? Never,* she decided combatively, feeling her own anger flare now. *For, in fact, if they knew—*

Statler suddenly leaped at her.

Mystie sidestepped his reaching arms, but he managed to catch a handful of her skirts as she slipped from under his arms. Cloth ripped. Scrambling, Statler crashed through the tray of food near his feet, sending it scattering across the deck.

Mystie came around, fingernails bared like claws, and ripped three parallel furrows into his cheek.

The slave hunter recoiled, and once again his hand came away bloodied. The rage in his eyes almost blinded him. Mystie backed up and put one of the stanchions at her back. Her eye caught a glimpse of something white near her feet, and when Statler drove at her next, she grabbed up the chamber pot and shattered it upon his head.

Statler staggered back, stunned, and shook himself as if to reestablish the connections in his brain that had momentarily been broken, and in that instant Mystie darted past, making for an open avenue of escape between two tall piles of cargo. He caught her an instant before she could secure her freedom and pulled her roughly back, wrestling her to the deck.

She saw the violence etched in his swarthy face, the blind fury that filled his eyes . . . and then something else. Her breath caught, for all at once the fingers of this powerful man's right hand balled into a hard fist and his arm cocked back.

Mystie squeezed her eyes together and turned her face aside. It was all she could do with her arms pinned beneath his hard knees and the weight of his body crushing the breath from her lungs. She braced herself for the blow she knew would come in the next instant, and waited.

All at once Statler's weight was no longer restricting her breathing or pinching her arms.

There came a hollow thump and a sharp crack, and when her eyes opened, Statler was staggering backward with Clifton Stewart in pursuit. The young gentleman lowered his head and drove forward, hitting Statler in the gut and buckling the man over, sending him flying against the woodpile. Now voices rang out nearby as news of the fight spread through the boat. Statler winced as the cordwood jammed his spine, but when Statler advanced, there was still enough fight left in the slave hunter to stab out with a powerful fist that smacked the younger man's chin.

Stewart backpedaled, arms flailing. Statler, a wild animal, sprang away from the woodpile, his fingers latching onto the young intruder's throat. Stewart stumbled, and both men crashed to the deck.

Mystie scrambled out of the way of the two men. Clifton managed a knee to Statler's ribs, broke the man's death grip, and knocked Statler off of him. Gaining a moment's reprieve, Clifton struggled to his knees and swung out, clipping the slave hunter across the tangled mass of his black beard.

Statler reeled back. His foot came down onto the spilled grits and slipped out from under him. With a crash, the slave hunter went over backward and hit the deck, knocking the wind out of him. Young Stewart staggered as he regained his footing and sleeved the blood from his nose. He took a boxer's stance and made a pair of fists, windmilling them at the fallen man, himself puffing like one of the *Tempest Queen*'s steam engines.

"Get back up, sir—and face your just comings. I will— instruct you—on manners—where a lady is concerned," Stewart said while his lungs heaved.

Statler eyed the younger man wearily and slowly grinned. From beneath his shirt he pulled out a knife. Mystie gave out a muffled cry, and her eyes widened. The slave hunter got back to his feet, swaying a bit now, and came forward. Stewart's view had riveted upon the short, keen weapon, and now his bravado gave way to the better part of valor, and cautiously he retreated a step.

"Sir, a gentleman does not brandish a weapon in fisticuffs," Stewart stammered, backing up a second step.

Statler grimaced and shifted the weapon back and forth between his hands. "A gentleman don't put his nose where it don't belong," he came back, and without warning he lunged out at Stewart's chest.

Mystie gasped.

From nearby came a flashing streak of black that caught Statler at the wrist and sent the knife flying from his grip and skittering to a stop against the firewood pile. The stunned slave hunter wheeled to confront this new adversary and, giving hardly a pause, sprang for him.

With an effortless snap of his wrist, Dexter McKay flicked the ornate, silver horse-head grip of the walking stick, striking Statler in the temple. The slave hunter staggered, fell into the woodstack, and slumped to the floor in a daze.

McKay stepped over him, grinning down, and said, "Like Mr. Stewart says, a gentleman does not employ weapons in a contest of fisticuffs.

Statler shook his head, clearing it. He glanced about, and Mystie saw his view slant toward the knife, which had landed nearby. She was about to call out a warning to McKay when all at once Statler made a move for it.

McKay seemed to have been fully aware of the slave hunter's intentions, however, even expecting it, for with a twist of his wrist, the walking stick separated into two pieces just below the horse-head grip, and the next instant a seventeen-inch sliver of polished steel pressed itself against

Statler's throat. The slave hunter came instantly to a halt, his eyes wide and staring at the short sword. For a frozen moment neither man moved, and Statler barely breathed.

McKay's amiable grin broadened, and when he spoke, his words were so soft and easy that he might have been casually raising the stakes in a game of cards. "I have one hundred dollars gold in my pocket that says you cannot reach that knife before I sever your windpipe. What do you say?"

By this time, members of the crew had crowded in around the two men, and Edward Lansing took charge, bursting through the ring of gawking men. He came up short and first looked at Statler. Then his view moved up the short cane-sword and settled upon McKay's face.

"Put that thing away."

"Certainly," McKay replied, and in a moment the two halves of the black cane were back together, and it was casually hitched up under his arm.

Mystie noted the smug grin that came to his lips, and although Mr. McKay had come to her and Stewart's aid, she disapproved of such blatant confidence, and immediately she went to Clifton Stewart's side and examined his swollen lip and the eye beginning to blacken. With a handful of her apron, she wiped the trickle of blood at the corner of his mouth.

"Come and let me tend to this," she said.

"Hold up there," the chief mate snapped.

Mystie came about.

Lansing studied Mystie, and then the three men who most apparently had been involved in the fight. The Negro had come out from around the stanchion now, settling down among the shattered remains of the chamber pot and food. Lansing's attention shifted sharply back to Mystie. "And you said there would be no trouble, Miss Waters."

She squared her shoulders and narrowed an eye at

Lansing. "The trouble did not come from the slave." Her finger stabbed out accusingly. "That man is the culprit. He attacked me as I was bringing this Negro the food and supplies as you ordered—as the *captain* ordered."

"I thought she was trying to fetch the nigger free," Statler shot back, levering himself up on an elbow.

"That's a lie!"

"All right, Mystie. Settle down now," Lansing said, patting the air placatingly with a hand. He glanced at one of the members of the crew standing nearby and said, "Go get the captain. He's in the main cabin—"

"No, he isn't." Captain Hamilton's voice rang out, coming through the crowd. "He's right here." Hamilton drew up among them and studied Statler, who was wiping the blood from his nose with a sleeve. Then he spent a moment glaring at young Clifton Stewart, who was similarly mopping up his own face. Hamilton frowned and said, "I figured you'd two have a run-in before the trip was over, but never suspected it would be this soon."

Stewart looked stunned, Statler confused. Mystie was suddenly angry, and she said, "It was that man who started it, Captain."

Statler snatched up his knife from the deck and hid it away in the folds of his shirt and stood painfully, using the firewood at hand for support. "It ain't like it seems at all, Captain," he said. "I come down here to check on the nigger and find this woman bent over him. Looked to me like she was a-trying to free him. I says, 'Hey, what you doin?' and she turns about, all suspicious-like. Next thing I knows, she hefted a length of cordwood and gives me one across the head with it. See, look what she done." Statler stuck his forehead in Hamilton's face. "I was only tryin' to wrestle the cudgel away from her when that fellow comes out of nowhere, a-swingin' his fists at me."

Hamilton's gray eyebrows dipped suspiciously in Mystie's direction.

"I tell you, he's lying, Captain. I was only bringing the things down to him like you ordered."

Hamilton shifted his view between Statler and Mystie, and it was clear he didn't know what to believe. Suddenly he looked down at the bound slave. "Can you shed some light on this?" he asked.

Eli opened his mouth to speak, but Statler speared him with a look. Eli dropped his head to his chest and shook it. "I din't see nothin', suh."

Mystie stared incredulously at the black man, then hotly at Statler. "You know that he won't say anything that might earn him a beating later!" With fists suddenly clenched, she started for Statler.

Captain Hamilton snagged her by the wrist and gently held her back. "We'll have no more of this. You get back to work now, Miss Waters. Have someone else bring down a fresh tray for this man."

"He don't need no special treatment—"

Hamilton wheeled on Statler. "While the man is a passenger on my boat he will be fed and cared for, Mr. Statler. What you do with him onshore is not any of my concern. So long as you are in possession of that warrant, you have legal charge of him, but on the *Tempest Queen* I have the say-so. Is that clear?"

Statler's face blanched behind the black beard, and reluctantly he assented, saying, "Do what you must, Captain. Only, I don't want that woman anywhere near my nigger. Got that?"

"Miss Waters is an employee of this boat, and she will do the bidding of her chief; it is not up to you to dictate her job. I will, however, for the sake of avoiding another altercation, order her to stay away from the runaway."

He looked into Mystie's black eyes, and she thought she detected sadness there in the deep blueness of his own. "You heard, Miss Waters. For the duration of this trip, you are not to tend to the runaway's needs. I will have Mrs. Divitt assign someone else to see to it."

"Yes, Captain," she said, hiding an anger that wanted to explode in all directions—and one in particular. Her narrow stare settled upon Randall Statler.

Captain Hamilton surveyed the crowd standing about, mostly crew, and curious passengers farther behind, stretching to peer over shoulders. He noted, too, that the black firemen at the furnaces had slackened up and were watching curiously as well. Hamilton said to them, "You boys got something you want to say? Or have you devised machinations to persuade the furnaces to feed themselves?"

In the confusion of the fight, Chief Mate Lansing had forgotten them. Now he rounded on the firemen and made up for the oversight. "What's wrong with your arms, boys? Busted them up leaning on your elbows? I didn't hire no busted-arm firemen! You boys ain't fit for grinding into pig slop. No, sir! Why, I ain't never seen such a worthless bunch as you. My sixty-year-old mother can toss more wood than any four of you, and with one arm tied behind her and half-asleep in her rocking chair! You worthless excuse for alligator bait! Now get back to heaving that wood before we start to drifting down this old stream. Hump . . . hump . . . hump, you sorry gaggle of pop-eyed geese!"

As Lansing disappeared behind a volley of words, Captain Hamilton returned his attention to Statler and Stewart. "I will have no more fighting aboard my boat. Is that clear to you gentlemen? If not, I will put you both ashore at our next landing."

He received reluctant agreement on that point. Hamilton said to Mystie, "Be off with you now. Have Mrs. Divitt send someone down with a broom and mop to clean this mess."

"Yes, sir," she replied, and then to Stewart she said, "Let me take you up to the barber to clean that blood off your face." She paused then before leaving and smiled thinly at Dexter McKay. He *was* quite dashing, she had to admit again to herself, but oh so arrogant. "Thank you for your help," she said.

"You are most welcome, Miss Waters," McKay replied, his voice deep and smoothly resonant.

Mystie scorched Statler with a scathing glance, and then she took Clifton by the arm and led him away. The crowd broke up and went about their business, and as she climbed the wide staircase up to the boiler deck, she noted that below Captain Hamilton and Dexter McKay had left together.

By the stanchion, Eli had drawn his knees up to his chest and was pointedly avoiding contact with Statler's eyes. There would be a severe beating in store for the poor man once off the *Tempest Queen*, she knew, and she also knew that it was going to take all in her resources to prevent it.

"You did not witness the initial cause?"

"No, Captain Hamilton. I came on the scene as that ruffian was pulling the knife and about to run young Mr. Stewart through."

The captain grinned, putting a hand on the turned baluster at the foot of the staircase. "You seem to have a habit of showing up in the nick of time."

McKay laughed and nodded his head. "It would appear so, although I suggest both these episodes were mere coincidence. I just happened to be taking a stroll around the deck."

"A stroll? Humm." Hamilton started up the stairs with McKay. "Where is it you said you were from, sir? Ohio, I believe?"

"I was born in Ohio. I am most recently from the West."

"Far West?"

McKay shrugged his broad shoulders. "I suppose that depends on how far back you go. Ten years ago I was in California. Last month the Kansas Territory."

Hamilton looked over with a humorless glint in his eyes. "Working your way East? It is contrary to the flow. It seems to go against this popular notion of Manifest Destiny." Hamilton paused and then said, "Yes, I remember now you telling me about your poor, stricken sister, Beth." He pursed his lips, and a thought came to his head. "I know a few folks down around Baton Rouge. Perhaps your sister is one of them. What is her last name?"

This conversation was running uncomfortably close to another McKay recalled having had the night before, and as in that one, the name he had conjured up on an instance's notice eluded him. "Preston," he said finally, when the pause had stretched on as far as it was able before arousing suspicion."

"Preston?" Captain Hamilton shook his head. "I don't know any Baton Rouge Prestons."

McKay was not surprised.

They made the top of the stairs and Hamilton said, "Well, it is probably for the best that you are out of the Kansas Territory for the time being. It could still be a hotbed of more violence, although things seem quiet enough right now." He glanced below, but the runaway slave was not visible from his vantage point. "This whole issue of slavery certainly turned the territory into a powder keg."

McKay gave a brief laugh. "Believe me, where I came from, the issue of slavery is not nearly as important as the talk of wealth and gold and of new strikes."

Hamilton grunted, his voice suddenly weighed with concern. "I suspect that would be a most refreshing change. You will find that here in the South, however, the only thought given to gold is for the sort already minted, and the general feeling is that the wealth of the South is being threatened by the Northern abolitionists and emancipators."

Hamilton stopped at the leaded-glass doors to the main cabin. "I was in the middle of a game of cards when the shouts below drew me away. I filled your chair when you left. I shall see if the players have continued without me."

"You mean the retired general and his friends?"

"The very ones."

McKay grinned and winked. "Have a good game, Captain, and watch out for that rustic gentleman in the red shirt. There is more to him than meets the eye."

Hamilton was at once surprised and then grateful for the tip, and when he went into the main cabin, there was a lift to the corner of his mouth.

McKay, in the meanwhile, went off in search of the barber's shop.

CHAPTER EIGHT

Leota landing at six o'clock in the evening was still a busy place when the *Tempest Queen* nosed slowly out of the main channel. Captain Hamilton ordered the pine knots tossed into the furnaces, and under a ceiling of pitch smoke, the big white boat made the crossing, her engine crew moving sprightly, the leadsmen on the forward guards shouting out the depth across the channel, while Jethro Pierce, Patton Sinclair's partner and the pilot on watch, pulled a cord to signal the engine room to pour on the steam. He spun the helm over smartly with the aid of his cub, cramping it down and standing on it as the *Queen* slid past shoal water. The steam whistle atop the pilothouse sounded three times, signaling the landing.

They entered the slow water near shore, and Pierce signaled the engine room again. He lifted his foot, and the helm wheeled back, slipping under his palm until the pilot snatched the spokes at just the precise moment, and the *Tempest Queen* straightened out with such exactness that the casual observer might have wondered if she had not been connected to the wharf by an invisible wire that directed her unerringly to her landing.

With steam venting through the gauge cocks, and black smoke overhead adding to the gloom of the coming evening, Chief Mate Lansing spurred his men into motion, shouting with the rapidity of a steam calliope. In what might have been no more than a dozen heartbeats, he had the *Tempest Queen* secured to the wharf, and his seasoned crew was already manhandling the landing stage into position.

Dexter McKay found Captain Hamilton up in the pilothouse. "Captain," he said, stepping into the small, plush room. It was apparent who had the place of prominence on this boat. New oilcloth was tacked to the floor. A sofa stood off to one side, upholstered in green leather. The huge helm directly in front of the windows stood nearly as tall as the pilot himself, and the lower portion of it disappeared at his feet into an opening in the floor. The helm was of polished hardwood and heavily fitted with gleaming brass strips. Overhead hung the signaling cords, in easy reach of the man behind the helm, and off to the right a brass speaking tube rose from the floor and belled out at its end. The stove in the corner gleamed of nickel plating and radiated a comfortable warmth to drive away the cool, damp touch of the gray evening.

Hamilton looked up from a sheath of papers clipped to a board. "Mr. McKay. Can I help you?" His curt reply made it apparent that he was busy.

"I don't want to interrupt, Captain. I was only wondering

how long we are to be here in Leota and if I had time to go ashore."

Hamilton glanced at Pierce, who in turn cast a speculative eye at the low, gray sky and the spattering of raindrops beginning to tap upon the pilothouse windows.

"I reckon we will be spending the night here, Captain. Can't see how we will get off-loaded and on our way with this rain and fog moving back in."

"We shall be here the night," Hamilton said with authority.

"Thank you." McKay stopped off at his cabin for his coat and then made his way down to the main deck and through the flurry of activity as roustabouts tackled the cargo to be off-loaded, pushing to finish the job before another storm unleashed its fury on them. There were stacks of boxes on the wharf as well, waiting to be put aboard, and everywhere men were dashing about, heads turtled down into their collars, as the drizzle continued into the growing gloom of evening, hastened along by the gathering fog.

He glimpsed Mystie Waters standing on the guards, peering at something ashore, and startled her when he came up at her side and diverted her attention.

"I missed you at dinner," he said, smiling pleasantly.

She composed herself almost immediately and said, "I am sorry, Mr. McKay. But I had spent so much time seeing that Mr. Stewart was taken care of, that Maggie made me work through my break, and I have only just now been given leave of my duties." She seemed distracted.

"I understand," he said amicably, and peered at the wharf and the freight buildings beyond, where her attention had been focused a moment before he had come upon her. "Are you looking for someone?"

"Oh, no, I was just . . . looking." Mystie smiled, and those lovely dark eyes glinted brightly.

"Captain Hamilton says we will be laying over for the night. The weather seems to be closing in again. I am about to disembark and look the town over. Would you care to join me?"

"Thank you, but I think I will remain aboard. I have been to Leota, and once is enough."

McKay laughed and glanced at the paltry hamlet spread along the shore of the Mississippi River and up the wet, overgrown hillside. Drays and freight wagons pulled by mules were leaving furrows in the mud of the levee road beyond the wharf, and a crippled boardwalk staggered up into the town alongside the unpainted buildings, vaguely green with the mosses that covered everything in this section of the country.

"Then, I shall see you later, perhaps?" He tipped his tall beaver hat.

"Enjoy yourself."

He grinned. "We shall see." He found a break in the traffic and made his way briskly down the landing stage, his lively cane tapping the wood as he made his way through the gray drizzle and disappeared into the drifting fingers of fog that had begun to come off the river.

After McKay had gone, Mystie's smile faded and was replaced by lines of concern. Once again her attention returned to the busy waterfront, but the face she searched for was not there. Frowning, Mystie went up to her room for a shawl and an umbrella. Pulling on a pair of cotton mitts, she took up a handbag and left.

The town of Leota was as dreary when viewed from the local saloon as it had been from the deck of the *Tempest Queen*: mostly mud, clutter, and buildings set a trifle off the vertical—listing, not unexpectedly, toward the river. There was a card game in progress, but the attendees appeared old friends and not at all interested in having a stranger join in. McKay considered setting up a game of monte at a nearby table. With his winnings from that morning in a neat pile in plain view, he just might entice some riverboat man into a game.

The saloon, however, was not drawing many customers through its single, narrow door. After a few moments more, he sighed and stepped out into the drizzle to locate more productive grounds. Lingering a bit under the dripping eaves, McKay turned an eye along the gloomy street. It was an altogether depressing evening, and he had almost made up his mind to return to the boat, where at least he knew a game could be had, when he saw Mystie Waters come up the boardwalk from the river, a black shawl clutched about her shoulders, her head hidden beneath the canopy of a black umbrella.

Her march through the drizzle was determined, as if she knew precisely where she wished to be, and she had no desire to be distracted by the baubles displayed behind the store windows.

Odd, he thought, for a woman who had expressed no interest in this meager town. His curiosity piqued, McKay waited until Mystie had ascended the hill one block farther before he stepped out after her, turning his collar up against the gray drizzle. She did not turn aside once but proceeded to the edge of town and then followed a narrow lane, keeping to the high center where bits of grass kept her from the mud. Here was located a row of houses, really little more than shacks, appearing ever so much as if waiting for a good wind to relieve them of their struggle against gravity.

Mystie stopped suddenly and glanced about. McKay stepped behind the trunk of a gnarled oak. Satisfied that she was alone, she went to the porch of one of the shacks and rapped upon the door; three quick knocks, a pause, then four slow knocks.

McKay could not hear the voice from the other side, but he plainly heard Mystie's reply: "A friend."

In a moment the door opened inward and the face of an old woman appeared in the hazy evening light. McKay waited for Mystie to step inside, then hurried up alongside the house. Protected from the drizzle by the eaves above, and from view by a camellia bush in bloom, McKay sidled up to a dingy window and peered past a yellowed curtain.

Inside, Mystie dragged the shawl from her shoulders and rubbed her palms near a stove. The old woman who had opened the door poured Mystie a steaming drink from a copper pot atop the stove. She clutched it in both hands as if relishing its warmth, and they moved to a bare table and sat in sagging cane chairs. McKay could barely hear their voices through the closed window, and nothing at all of their words. Mystie spoke with animation, her face like shifting masks of concern and despair.

The old woman listened, not interrupting. When Mystie had finished speaking, the old woman stood, went to a dilapidated sideboard, removed a drawer, felt around in the darkness at arm's length, and pulled out a tattered black book tied with a green ribbon. She spread it open upon the table, and both women peered at it, turning the flimsy pages carefully.

McKay would have given his prized pair of weighted dice to see what was in that book. His imagination skipped ahead, considering all sorts of possibilities—each sporting a dollar sign. He strained to hear their words through the rippled glass, but it was no use.

After a few minutes turning pages, the two women appeared to agree upon something and, nodding her head, the old woman shut the book. She went into a back room, and a second later McKay heard a back door squall on rusty hinges. Beyond the corner of the shack, the old woman's gray dress flapped in the breeze as she hurried across a weedy yard and into a shed. When she appeared again, she held something dark in her hand. McKay could not tell what.

The door squealed again, slammed shut, and once more the two women were in view past the pale, torn curtains. He watched the old woman roll the object into a cloth and Mystie take that bundle and bury it in the bottom of her handbag. While he shivered in the evening chill, a lamp was lit inside and more coal added to the stove. Mystie, unhurried now, finished her drink. The two women talked over pie and more of the warm beverage. McKay imagined it might be coffee, and his thoughts skipped back to the warm, cheery main cabin of the *Tempest Queen*. He considered returning now that the conversation within had taken a decidedly leisurely turn, but his eye kept coming back to that black book with the green ribbon.

The minutes dragged out into half an hour, and then an hour, and despite the marginal protection here, he was becoming soaked to the skin and chilled through. The mist off the river was thick and deathly pale in the rising moon. When it seemed as if his torment would never end, Mystie stood up, wrapped the shawl about her shoulders, and gathered up her handbag.

The old woman walked her to the door and, after a few more words, sent Mystie on her way.

Finally! McKay felt a surge of warmth course through his body, and he rubbed his chilled palms together to get the blood moving. Now, if indeed it was coffee—or even tea they had been drinking—McKay calculated that it wouldn't be too long before the old woman succumbed to the necessities of life and made her way out back to the privy.

He had a glimpse of Mystie making her way along the lane, back into town, and then returned his attention to the warmly glowing windowpane. The old woman collected the dishes and put them on a counter against the back wall. She looked around the tiny room as if taking inventory of it, and it all must have tallied, for she nodded her head approvingly. Next, she peered into a looking glass on the wall and touched her gray hair back into place, brushed at the collar of her dress, smiled at herself, pinched her cheek, then turned abruptly and narrowed an eye at the window where McKay lurked.

He shrank away from it, then stopped, and told himself there was no way she could see him. By the time he had returned, the old woman had pulled heavier curtains across the window, permitting no more than an edge of light now.

For a while she bustled about noisily inside. McKay sank to his haunches to wait her out. He thought about what he intended to do, questioned his sanity. He could find himself waking up in jail, he reminded himself, casting an eye at the lights coming from the town below—that is, if Leota had a jail. Past the town, down at the river, all that could be seen through the fog were the faint sparks leaping from tops of steamboat chimneys.

The chill worked its way back into his skin again. He was about to give it up and return to the *Tempest Queen*, and dry clothes, when all at once he heard the squeak of the back door opening. In a leap, he was at the corner of the shack. From the back door a shaft of light stretched out, and in it was the old woman, bundled up in a shawl, an oil lamp in one hand, an old catalog under her arm.

In a moment another door closed softly. He gave her a few seconds to get settled down and then sprang from his cover and eased the back door open, wincing at the whine of the hinges, gritting his teeth, slipping through the narrowest of apertures. He eased it closed and turned to the table.

The book was gone!

In an instant he was at the sideboard. The drawer now upon the floor, McKay felt around in the back and his hand found it. His fingers fumbling, from both the cold and an urgent desire to be out of there before the old woman returned, McKay removed the green ribbon and flipped it open.

Names. Pages and pages of names. That was all. The first and last names of men and women, and alongside each, more names that McKay recognized as towns. There might have been ten pages worth of carefully penned names, and afterward only empty pages. Some of the names had been crossed out, and those that had been so struck had a date printed next to them. He scanned the pages and discovered the earliest such date was almost twenty years old and one was as current as the previous month.

This told him nothing. There could be no profit in a list of unidentified names . . . or could there? It certainly had not been worth shivering in the cold all this time. Frowning, McKay replaced the green ribbon and returned the book to its hiding place. His hand touched a second object. When he brought it to light, he discovered the object was another book, identical to the first except for a red ribbon.

His eyebrows dipped into a scowl. What was the old woman about? He removed the ribbon, and the book fell opened upon his palm as if it had been trained to do so from years of intensive use. Again, it was merely a list of names. Identical to the first—except that here there were only first names, not last, and each one had a date inscribed next to it.

McKay puzzled over this until the sound of the privy door slamming reminded him where he was. He fumbled the ribbon in place, tossed the book back into the shadowy recess, and struggled with the drawer, but the damned thing went in crooked!

Then the back door sang out. . . .

Clifton Stewart spied her at the head of the stairs, and instantly a smile was upon his face. His pace quickened. She had seen him, too, as she was shaking out the umbrella, and by time he reached her, she had it folded together and was looking lovely in a vaguely disheveled way.

"I have been looking for you, Miss Waters," he said.

"Oh, have you?" she replied with a cautious reserve, but was apparently pleased. He considered her smile at that moment the prettiest he had ever seen. Even in her simple clothes, and her hair wet now and threatening to burst from beneath the scarf, she was by far lovelier than any of the young ladies that came by his father's house, ostensibly to pay their regards to his parents, but Clifton knew better.

In particular, there was Charlotte Drysdale, a pale, talkative lass who would as soon surrender her very life than to be found out in the sunlight without the protection of a wide bonnet: *"Dear me, I shall shrivel up like a prune and look like a Negress if I remain in this sun one moment longer."* And straight away Charlotte would be seeking the nearest spot of shade, which was generally in the vicinity of his father's porch swing, and imploring him to keep her company—preferably on the swing beside her.

No doubt Charlotte Drysdale was a beauty in the classical way that a Southern man thinks of beauty. But suddenly here beneath the balcony of the promenade, with the soft glow from the chandeliers through the leaded-glass windows and the music of a string trio coming from the main cabin, Mystie Waters—even with her hair curling and her frock damp—had left poor Charlotte in the dust, had left her as far behind as his father's Thoroughbreds always left old Samuel Drysdale's horses at the Merryville races on summer Sunday afternoons.

"Where have you been? You are soaking!"

She laughed a little uneasily and said, "I just took a walk into Leota. Foolish me, I should have guessed I'd come back looking like a limp piece of lettuce. And I have to be back at work in half an hour. Look at me."

"You look beautiful." The words stunned him. Had they really come out of him? Mystie was surprised as well. Her eyes widened, and a faint smile touched her lips. Then a sterner look replaced it and her glance went to his face.

"That eye has about swollen shut."

"I can still see you."

Her head shook slowly as she frowned. "Does it hurt much?"

Clifton smiled bravely. "No. Not much." He permitted her to gently probe the puffy purple flesh with a soft forefinger, and hardly winced at all.

"You'll not see anything out of that eye come morning," she said.

"At least you are safe from that ill-mannered man, and that is all that is important. This small bruise does not matter—so long as I still can see you . . . in the morning."

"Why, Mr. Stewart. You are being impertinent." But her smile told him she didn't mind it at all. "I will be here, on the *Tempest Queen*, working quite diligently, so it is very likely that you will see me in the morning."

"That is not what I mean." He was suddenly very serious. "I mean, I should like to see you—socially. Perhaps when you are off work?"

"Perhaps," she said lightly, and then she continued with a heartfelt heaviness, "—although you do not know me very well."

"How else shall I?"

Mystie smiled faintly, ignoring that, and said, "Well, I ought to hurry up to my cabin and change out of these wet clothes. Maggie will be expecting me down in the kitchen in twenty minutes, and if I am late, she will have me against the whipping post for sure."

"Whipping post? An odd expression for a white girl. You make Maggie sound like a slave driver."

Her dark eyes became distant, as if for a moment her thoughts were elsewhere, and then she came back, but her voice was no longer gay. "It is just something I picked up from the Negro chambermaids. Maggie is really sweet, deep down inside. More bluster than anything else. Well, I really must hurry now."

"May I walk you to your cabin?"

"If you wish."

"I do."

A pleased lift came to the corners of her mouth, a glint to her eyes. She led the way up to the texas, where most of the crew lived, and said good-bye at her door. Then she was gone, leaving him standing outside in the drizzle with his head whirling. He was suddenly no longer aware of the stinging bruises on his face, and he was grinning despite them. A lamp was lit behind the curtained window of Mystie's cabin.

Clifton Stewart tipped his hat to it with the enthusiasm of a young boy and, feeling strangely light-footed, turned on his heels and went back down to the main cabin.

For a while after Stewart left, the hurricane deck seemed empty; nevertheless, the faint red glow of a cigar, brightened and then faded with a regularity in the shadows of the paddle box. After a few moments, Randall Statler stepped out, moonlight pale upon the fog that swirled about his legs. He narrowed an eye at Mystie's door and drew thoughtfully on the cigar.

A crew member suddenly appeared around the front of the texas, where Captain Hamilton had his quarters. As the man came near, swinging an empty coal bucket and whistling a ditty, Statler retreated once more into the shadows.

CHAPTER NINE

She inhaled sharply and stood there, stunned, her feet rooted to the floor.

McKay heard the catch of surprise in her breathing. He had only an instant to prepare for this, and now he quelled the fluttering that had taken flight in his stomach and forced himself to be absolutely at ease as he casually turned away from the looking glass on the wall where he had been smoothing his wet eyebrows in place. He feigned surprised then smiled at her.

"Well, I see that someone is home after all!" he said cheerily, and glanced at the front door. "I knocked several times but no one answered." The smile settled placidly upon his face, as if he had not the slightest guile to him, while his heart raced on.

"I apologize for coming in like this, unannounced and uninvited, my fair lady," McKay went on, his words honey-smooth, "but I was absolutely soaked from my long walk from Greenville, and chilled to the bone." Fortunately, McKay had spent a few minutes in the *Tempest Queen*'s pilothouse earlier that day, where there had been a chart of the river over which he had glanced while chatting with Mr. Sinclair. He was suddenly breathing a little easier, for a peek at the top of the sideboard had revealed two opened envelopes there, both addressed to a woman named Sadie Wilkes.

Now he paused and looked concern. "Oh, I see that I have startled you, Mrs. Wilkes. You are Mrs. Sadie Wilkes, are you not?" he asked, seeing her pale blue eyes widen.

"Who . . . who are you?"

McKay reached into an inside pocket, extracted a collection of cards, casually thumbed through them, and removing one from the bundle, placed it upon the sideboard where she could see it, pressing down a dog-eared corner with his thumb. He noted, too, that the drawer he had hastily put back in place had not fully closed, and now he stepped forward and casually brushed it with his hip, setting it aright.

"How remiss of me. I do apologize. Err, my name is Mr. Pettigrew. Philip Pettigrew of the Boston Pettigrews." A smile spread his lips.

She chanced a glance at the card, and her eyes shot immediately back at him. "I am Sadie Wilkes. Greenville is a long piece upriver."

He laughed. "You are telling me? Why, just look at my coat and my shoes!" Indeed, his wardrobe bore every appearance of a man who had spent considerable time out in the weather.

"What is it you want, Mr. Pettigrew?" she asked. The tension in her voice had lessened a smidgen, but the glint of suspicion still burned in her eyes. "And how do you know me?"

"I was given your name by a gentleman in Greenville. He said you would be able to help me." McKay was warming to the tale now, feeling his apprehension fade as he spun his fiction. Indeed, now that the initial encounter was past, he was actually enjoying the mental exercise of it.

"Me, help you?" The suspicion in her voice deepened. Her eyes narrowed as she set the tattered catalog aside. Her glance shifted to a wicked-looking iron prod near the stove.

McKay noted that and went on quickly. "You see, I am a collector. I have been searching for some very rare—er . . ." He stumbled and suddenly drew a blank, his brain refusing to supply him with a believable item. "Err—flowers." Now, what made him grasp at that straw? he wondered. Then he saw the bowl of bright red blooms on the ledge by the back door.

"Flowers?"

Another bit of frantic clawing, and his brain grasped the straw an instant before it slipped away. "Gold," he blurted out, ". . . yes, I collect gold flowers. Err . . . *The Blossoms of Troy*. They were made by a famous jeweler—a French jeweler. Err . . . yes . . . for the king of Spain . . . for his wedding to the queen, you see. Well, apparently the archduke—the queen's brother—was later given the gold flowers as a gift, and when he came to America in 1781 he brought them along. They were later sold when he died, and now I am looking for them." McKay felt like a complete idiot spinning such a foolish tale to this woman. If this had been St. Louis or Chicago, he would be planning to immediately leap through the door and make good his escape after doling out such a far-fetched lie, but here in this primitive hamlet he had no fear of being found out. There was no way for her to know of the existence of what he pretended to seek. ". . . And I was informed in Greenville that you have possession of one of these flowers and might be willing to part with it," he continued, ending with a wide smile.

She gave him a blank face, which was precisely what he had expected, indeed, anything else would have sent his heart palpitating again. "What's that you say?"

"*The Blossoms of Troy*. The gold flowers?" he encouraged.

Her stare hardened, and her mouth tightened into a knot.

McKay allowed his smile to falter. "You . . . you appear not to know what I am talking about?"

"Flowers made of gold? Sounds like a fairy-tale story, Mr. Pettigrew."

This was perfect. Now all he had to do was apologize profusely, make her feel his embarrassment, and perhaps in the process get a lead on what it was Mystie Waters was up to. Getting caught here had worked out better than if he had planned it that way.

"You mean that you do not possess *The Blossoms of Troy*, Mrs. Wilkes?"

"I do not!"

"But the gentleman in Greenville —?"

"I don't know anyone in Greenville."

"But he called you by name. He even gave me directions that lead directly to your home. I paid him *two* dollars for the information!"

"Hope you got the swindler's name." Sadie Wilkes was decidedly unsympathetic.

McKay staggered back a step and found his way onto one of the sagging chairs without being invited. "I do not remember his name," he said, clearly distressed. "But perhaps if you could give me a few, I might recognize it." McKay paused, debated how to continue next, and decided to plunge on ahead the direct course he had already set his feet to. "The gentleman told me that he was in one of your books — whatever in the world that means."

Her eyes widened, and McKay knew he had struck a nerve. So, there was something murky going on here, and that sweet and lovely Countess of the Kitchen was probably up to her pretty neck in it. Sadie Wilkes remained rooted to the floor a moment; then a strange twinkle flickered in her pale eyes and her white-crowned head nodded once and she said, "Perhaps I might have something here that will interest you, Mr. Pettigrew," and she moved toward the sideboard.

McKay refrained from grinning too broadly, but at once his grin faltered. Instead of the drawer where he knew the two books were hidden, Sadie Wilkes pulled open another, higher up. This was curious, and McKay's eyebrows hitched up and he straightened attentively in the chair. She had to feel around a bit, for the drawer she had opened was a trifle above her eye level. Then she found what it was she was seeking. For an instant her back was toward him, and when she again came about, her eyes had hardened and there was a fierce set to her mouth. In her hand was a Navy Colt, and she cocked back its hammer as if she knew precisely what to do with the revolver.

McKay nearly tipped over backward. He scrambled out of the chair, placed himself behind it, as if that would help, and reached for the ceiling. This was not at all what he had expected!

"All right, Mr. Pettigrew"—Sadie Wilkes came forward a step, the revolver thrust out in front of her, held with both hands—"what are you really up to? What do you think I am? Simple? I suspected you right off after hearing that outlandish story about golden flowers—but you made a mistake when you asked about the *book*. What are you really? A slave hunter? A federal agent? How did you get wind of me? Hurry up now, talk, before I pull this trigger and claim to the constable that you broke into my house and tried to do me harm."

"My dear lady!" McKay croaked. His voice had skipped up an octave or two. "I can assure—"

"Don't 'dear lady' me, Mr. Fancy Talker. Out with it. I feel my trigger finger begin to twitch, and you know how nervous old people can get."

"I'm . . . I'm merely a businessman . . . and your business is certainly none of mine!" McKay forced a grin, but his eyes remained riveted. "I really must be on my way—really." He took a single step backward. Sadie Wilkes didn't stop him. He grin became a foolish smile. "I am sorry to have bothered you." McKay reached carefully for the tattered business card, snatched it off the sideboard, and immediately lifted it toward the ceiling as he retreated a second step.

"You come snooping around here with your lying stories, you deserve to get shot."

"Now, we wouldn't want to do anything rash, would we?"

"*We* should have considered that before *we* came breaking into *my* house." Sadie advanced on McKay.

He continued his rearward shuffle until his heel smacked the door. With extreme care, he lowered one hand and reached for the knob.

"Why, if I weren't a Christian woman I'd have—"

McKay didn't hear the rest, for as soon as the door opened he dove outside and fled along the lane through the fog as fast as his high-pumping knees would carry him, left arm swinging like a weaving shuttle, right hand clasping the hat to his head. Behind him the revolver fired. McKay drew his head into his collar like a turtle and never looked back, never paused until his long legs swept him across the *Tempest Queen*'s landing stage and up the wide staircase.

On the promenade of the boiler deck, in the soft glow that shone through the main cabin windows, McKay finally came to a halt and fell upon the railing, heaving oxygen into his searing lungs. This drew the attention of those passengers strolling past, but right at the moment, McKay was in no mood to care. After a minute or two, his racing heart slowed, and he composed himself in a manner that befitted a man such as he. Straightening his tie back in place and pulling his jacket around upon his shoulders, McKay pretended not to notice their stares. He extracted a silver case from his breast pocket, fumbled out a cigar, and steadying a hand, put a match to it.

Inside the main cabin, he caught a waiter by the cuff. "Whiskey!"

"Scotch whiskey or bourb—?"

"I don't give a damn what kind it is! Just bring me whatever is nearest at hand!"

The startled waiter scuttled away, and a moment later McKay was pouring the drink down his throat.

"Another," he said before the amazed man had left, and when he had downed that one, too, McKay began to feel more himself. A pleasant warmth had begun to radiate from deep within him. It had been a most unpleasant encounter, and it brought to mind another close call that he only recently had had in the mining camps of the Rocky Mountains: an unpleasantness that had required him to leave such lucrative grounds in the dead of night, with nothing but the clothes upon his back, his valise, a couple of coins in his pocket, and a howling mob at his heels.

He shivered, and it had nothing to do with his soaking clothes or the chill night air, and went to his cabin to change into something dry and put his appearance back into proper order. His composure restored, McKay sat at a table in front of a mirror, methodically unloaded his Remington pocket revolver, dried it thoroughly, and reloaded it with fresh black powder and dry caps from a tin he kept in the bottom of his valise.

When he had finished, and the little revolver was once again in its hideaway holster, he lit a second cigar. As the tiny cabin filled with clouds of relaxing smoke, McKay opened a fresh deck of cards, removed the king, queen, and jack, and practiced shuffling them about on top of the table, observing himself in the mirror. His fingers limbered, McKay went through some more difficult cuts and shuffles and finally spent a few minutes dealing out the entire deck but never moving the top card. Satisfied, he repeated the exercise, only this time the entire deck was dealt from the bottom card, and even he could not detect the deed being done in the mirror.

McKay left his cabin forty-five minutes later, completely recovered from his encounter with Sadie Wilkes and feeling entirely himself again. In the bright and gleaming main cabin, he made his way through the crowd, heard pleasant talk, smelled the strong, pleasing cigar smoke. From the ladies' parlor came happy chatter. The waiters were busy hauling drinks and food. McKay took a table and in a moment had an attentive waiter at his elbow. He ate dinner, had another whiskey, and later, basking in a warm, contented afterglow, discovered that two of the three men he had played cards with that morning—the frontiersman and the retired general—were at a table across the way. Even as he became aware of them, McKay saw Captain Hamilton enter by the doors at the head of the cabin. The captain glanced around, spied the two men, and made his way to their table. They greeted him as if he had been expected.

McKay pushed back from his greasy dinner plate, downed the rest of his whiskey, and strolled across the room. "Have you room for one more?"

"Mr. McKay," the retired general said, pleasantly surprised. "Please, do join us. We missed you earlier this evening."

"I was out exploring the town of Leota."

Captain Hamilton chuckled. "Well, that might have taken all of five minutes."

The retired general laughed. The silent frontiersman merely grinned into his beard.

McKay grinned likewise and said, "I would have been back sooner but I . . . um . . . got caught out in the weather and was held up." His adventurous diversion had cured him momentarily of his curiosity, and he wished only to relax in the arm of his first and true love—a game of cards. He relieved his pockets of some of the coins he had won earlier and put them in a neat pile. "What is the game?"

They discussed this briefly and decided to have another

go at seven-up, with Hamilton once more placed in harness with the reticent frontiersman, and McKay with the retired general. That was quite all right as far as McKay was concerned. He had observed these three men before, and only the retired general had shown any finesse in the matter of cards.

McKay fished out another cigar from the silver case and offered them around. The retired general and the frontiersman both indulged themselves, but Hamilton declined. "Don't smoke?" McKay inquired.

"I haven't smoked in years." He smiled faintly, as if recalling something pleasant. "Cynthia would not allow it in the house. I resisted at first, of course, but frankly I found it too confounded inconvenient to go outside whenever I wanted to smoke. So, I gave it up. Never had any desire to return to it afterwards."

"And he doesn't drink, either," the retired general noted with a chuckle as he cut the deck for the deal. The deal went to the frontiersman Klack, and the rustic gentleman's fingers fumbled the shuffle so badly, McKay decided that the bumpkin could not have done much worse if he had been trying. McKay all at once glanced back at the man. It *was* almost as if Klack's intentions were to make himself appear inept.

"You don't smoke and you don't drink, Captain," McKay said, but his eye remained on Klack tossing out the cards and counting them wordlessly as they went around the table. "Have you no bad habits?"

"Only one, Mr. McKay, only one," the captain said with a sudden solemnity, and he did not elaborate, but there was all at once an peculiar glint in his eyes as he gathered in his cards.

Klack finished the deal and turned over the top card to determine the trump suit. The jack of hearts. The frontiersman smiled. Captain Hamilton said, "Bully!" and the retired general, who had volunteered to keep score, touched the point of a pencil to the tip of his tongue and marked a "1" on the scrap of paper at his elbow.

McKay arranged the cards in his hand. A waiter came by to see if they needed anything and went off bearing requests for brandy for the retired general, Bourbon for Klack, and two coffees. McKay never drank when playing cards.

As the game played out, the captain and Klack seemed to be doing very well. Klack was warming to seven-up and commented that up until that morning he had never played it.

"You learn quickly," McKay noted amiably.

"It ain't so difficult," Klack allowed, fanning out the cards in his hand and shifting two of them to a different position.

Captain Hamilton was thoroughly enjoying himself, and the pile of coins in front of him was growing handsomely. The retired general seemed frustrated at not being able to complete a trump, and it was only by McKay's intimate grasp of the game that they were able to take anything at all from their opponents.

All in all, the general, Klack, and Captain Hamilton had a fine time. McKay, however, had found himself continually distracted and unable to put a finger on the reason for his uneasiness. There was something important he was missing here, he was certain—

Klack laughed as he made a four-point trick, and once again he and Captain Hamilton won the hand. The retired general shook his head in mock despair, but was only mildly distressed. McKay discovered he was studying the frontiersman's ruddy, beard-infested face, and his perfectly manicured fingers, and he had no idea why.

McKay lost two hundred dollars that night—all the money he had won off them earlier and then some—but he left the table a little after midnight in grand spirits and with a smile wanting to burst out. His feet nearly danced across the floor as he made his way back to his cabin, and once inside, he dug out his valise and opened it up on the bed.

The money had been a trifle: an investment! It was only that faithful companion of his, Miss Lady Luck, that had kept him from plunging on at the start and sweeping the table clean. No, he had played the game just right—as a man familiar with cards, but nothing more than that. Perhaps he competed a little better than a fresh-faced tyro, but certainly no one there would have considered him a particularly skillful player.

He rummaged through his valise and removed a small, beautifully-made brass device with a keen cutting blade and an ivory handle. He opened his door and caught the attention of a waiter in the main cabin. When the man had come to his beckoning arm, McKay ordered three decks of cards. A few minutes later there was a rap on his door. McKay placed his hat over the card trimmer. The waiter deposited the cards in McKay's hand, and McKay rewarded him with a generous gold coin. Alone once more, McKay turned up the wick of the lamp. He dampened the corner of a towel in a glass of water and set about the task of patiently removing the stamps that sealed the cards in their paper wrappers.

Two hours later, his hat was filled with fine, curled shavings, and the three decks of cards were back in their wrappers, properly sealed and tucked safely away at the bottom of his valise. McKay put the tools away and took the hatful of shavings outside. The promenade was deserted. He looked at his watch. Almost three o'clock in the morning. No wonder. He grinned to himself as he made his way down the steps and onto the main deck. Most of the lights had been extinguished, and only a few lanterns on the wharf showed through the shroud of fog that had settled upon the *Tempest Queen* at her mooring. Stepping out onto the guards, McKay dumped the shavings into the river and watched as the evidence was swept downriver on the fast current.

From deep within the boat, beneath the boiler deck, McKay caught an occasional word spoken by one of the two firemen on duty. There was a momentarily cheery glow as a furnace door was opened and another length of wood tossed in, and then it was cut off. At this time of night the main deck was as tranquil as a mausoleum compared with the bustling activity of the place when the boat was under full steam and racing along with the current.

The bone-chilling fog seeped into his bones. The deck was still wet from the storm that had passed by earlier. McKay buttoned up his frock coat and settled the hat upon his head with a firm rap. Hands thrust deep into his pockets, he started toward his cabin.

His mind went back to the game and then to the plans that were germinating within his brain. He did not see the figure emerge from the shadows until it was too late, and by the time he did, something solid came whirling out of the blackness and struck him against the side of his head.

McKay staggered and tried to bring up an arm to protect himself from the knobby end of the club that had appeared out of the foggy darkness again. It loomed like a silver specter before his eyes an instant before his teeth crashed together. He was vaguely aware of the salty warmth that filled his mouth and then of something rock hard slamming into his gut, snatching the breath from him.

He buckled and momentarily lost consciousness, and when he came around a second or two later he was being dragged across the rough deck, too stunned to resist. McKay was only distantly aware of being lifted up to the guards— and then he was falling. Cold, swift water engulfed him and dragged him down to the muddy river bottom.

CHAPTER TEN

"Let me take a look at that eye."

Mystie Waters raised herself up on her toes and turned his face toward hers with both hands. She frowned disapprovingly, but secretly she was quite pleased with what she saw. Not only was the swelling going down and the dark purple no longer spreading, but beneath the scars of the battle he had fought defending her from the slave hunter, Clifton Stewart was a handsome fellow.

"Well, it doesn't seem to be getting any worse," she said sternly, pretending to be irritated that he had fought in her defense.

"No doubt due to your expert care, Miss Waters."

Mystie resisted the smile that threatened to destroy her demur. "You have become bold, Mr. Stewart."

Clifton smiled back at her. "I hope I have not become too much so."

"I will let you know when you do."

He started to speak, then hesitated as if to reconsider.

"Yes?" she urged, somehow sensing what was on his mind.

"Perhaps I am overstepping my place, Miss Waters, but it is odd—"

"What is odd?" They were strolling along the promenade, and for a change the morning was bright and lovely. An early fog had burned off with the rising of the warm spring sun, and the day promised to be delightfully clear and pleasant. The pilot had put out into the channel at precisely seven o'clock, under a full head of steam and a ceiling of black smoke, and now, at nearly eight o'clock, the *Tempest Queen* was booming downriver with the pulse of her mighty engines throbbing through the boat like a heartbeat: strong and steady.

The break in the weather had brought out a diverse company of river-going vessels—the symbols of commerce—from their safe moorings, and the traffic on the river was fairly teeming with crafts of all sorts. Some, like the *Tempest Queen*, under steam and running only a knot or two ahead of the current; some relying on square sails; and still others with nothing but the swift current beneath their flat bottoms for power and a side oar to steer by.

On the promenade where Clifton and Mystie strolled, black deckhands were busy sweeping, scrubbing the railings, straightening deck chairs, and emptying the black iron spittoons that were spaced about every twelve feet near the railing. Clifton drew up at the railing now, resting his forearms upon it and looking out at the wide, angry, yellow-brown water. The river was nearing flood stage, climbing the levees like a spider up a wall, bearing with it great quantities of mud from up North down to the Gulf.

"I worry when the river is like this," he said.

She peered out and her river-wise eyes saw beyond all the traffic. Raised on the Mississippi River, she was aware of the common dangers: the sawyers and planters and snags that high water always washed out from the shores. "Mr. Sinclair is an experienced pilot," she said, supposing that this was his concern. "The *Tempest Queen* is a good boat. I wouldn't worry."

"It's not the boat I fear for." His eyes fixed upon the distant shore. "It is high water like this that opens a crevasse. A break in the levee can destroy an entire plantation in a matter of days. Can wipe out entire towns if not checked, not to mention the lives lost."

She remained silent while he studied the river, waiting until he got around to speaking what was truly on his mind. A steamer passed them by, going North, hugging the nearer shore where the current was slower. The *Tempest Queen* was sticking to the middle of the channel, to take full advantage of the current carrying them South. Finally Mystie said, "The rising water is not what's really on your mind, is it?"

The corner of his mouth twitched, moving uncertainly into a grin. "No, Miss Waters. It is not."

"Then what?"

Once again he hesitated. "I do not know exactly how to say it." Clifton Stewart took his attention from the river and put it on her.

"Try straight out," Mystie suggested. "That's always the best when something is troubling you."

"I wouldn't exactly call it troubling."

"What would you call it?" Her dark eyes gazed up at him, impossibly wide and lovely.

Clifton Stewart straightened around to face her. He said, "Confusing."

"Confusing? What do you find confusing?"

"You. No, not you personally—but the way I feel about you." He stammered and cleared his throat. "I am suddenly no longer intimidated by your beauty, and I have become aware, in some small way that I do not understand, that you are unlike any other woman I have ever known. I . . . Perhaps I should not say this, Miss Waters, and I know it may sound preposterous, having known you only two days, but I feel irresistibly drawn to you."

All at once he seemed apprehensive, and suddenly Mystie knew why. He was expecting her to laugh at him. It *was*, after all, quite ridiculous for someone to feel so deeply in just two days . . . but if she were to be honest with herself, she would have to admit that in this brief time she, too, had felt the inexplicable pull, like the mysterious forces that dwell within a magnet.

"I don't think it is impossible," she said thoughtfully, "but you hardly know me—nor I you. You live in a different world than I. You have a large plantation and sl-slaves." She stumbled over the word. "I have nothing but this job on the *Tempest Queen*. I've lived my whole life on this river. I know no other." She wanted to tell him more, but stopped before admitting that secret known only to a few. That *dark* secret that even she, in her foolishness, tried to hide from herself.

"All that doesn't matter, really. Actually, I find the women in the world that I come from to be most frivolous." He grimaced. "I mean, most of them—and I fear I must include myself—have lived an overprotected life, and frankly, Miss Waters, I sometimes want to break free of that life. Burst my chains and be my own man."

She thought about that and said, "I imagine that must be much as that man chained below must feel."

Clifton was momentarily bewildered. "You mean the runaway? No. The Negro has no such desire." Clifton laughed gently. "They are, in fact, like little children. They look to their white people for guidance, for a purpose in life. Set them free and they wouldn't know what to do with themselves."

Mystie scowled and averted her eyes toward the angry

yellow serpent carrying them grudgingly south upon its back. "The firemen down below are freeborn, and so are the Negro chambermaids and cooks," she said, "and the dozen other people Captain Hamilton has working on the *Tempest Queen*." Mystie struggled now not to allow his words to poison the closeness they had only just become aware of.

"Yes, yes. That is true, but they have the captain and their chiefs to tell them what to do. They may be freeborn, Miss Waters, but they are still Negroes."

"That makes no difference," she shot back, her black eyes flashing, no longer able to contain her ire.

Clifton recoiled, surprised, and considered her a moment. He said, "I see that I have upset you. I apologize. I had no idea you felt that way. I was out of place to speak. I forgot that you lived up North, and I am certain that has influenced the way you see these things."

"I suppose it has."

"I shall not speak of it again, Miss Waters."

Mystie could not help but perceive the grave concern in his face over having offended her, and she truly believed it had been unintentional. After all, no two people ever agree on all things! As her mother used to say, if two people never fight, one of them has no backbone. It was just unfortunate that their disagreement lay so near to her heart.

Well, perhaps she was being overly defensive. There were, indeed, two sets of values here, and the South believed in theirs as fervently as she believed in hers. It was a nationwide point of contention. Some had likened it to a powder keg with a lighted fuse. She had even heard talk of the South's seceding from the Union if the North continued to chip away at their rights as individual states.

"We won't talk of it further," she agreed, suddenly aware of the power her words wielded. She could just as easily have said, *"Never speak to me again, sir,"* and with those simple words forever ended her acquaintance with this tall, handsome gentleman who had taken such a fancy to her — as she had to him.

Sudden relief swept across Clifton Stewart's face, and he was smiling once more. For a reason that she did not understand, that pleased her.

"I ought to be changing into my uniform. My shift is about to start," she said.

As they walked forward, toward the ladder that climbed to the texas, the *Tempest Queen* drew abreast of a large raft—large enough to have a little one-room shack built on the forward end of it, and a farm wagon, loaded and covered in canvas, tied down with ropes on the other end. There was a goat tied to the corner of the shack near a pile of hay, and a clothesline stretched from its roof to the uplifted wagon tongue that was tied back and served duty as a jack staff, where a scrap of green material flapped and a lantern hung, as the river law required for night travel. There was a man asleep on the deck near the shack. Two small children romped around a woman in a blue dress while she picked clothes off the line. An old, gray-bearded man, smoking a cob pipe, leaned casually on the long handle of the steering sweep at the stern. When the *Tempest Queen* drove powerfully past the raft, jostling it in her bow wake, the woman at the clothesline looked over and smiled.

"Oh, look, she is waving at us," Clifton said, and he and Mystie waved back.

"Travelers often do that," Mystie told him as the *Tempest Queen* left the raft leaping in her wake. "They are probably emigrants from up North, making their way southward. It's the only direction they can travel. Without steam, the river takes you in one direction. They will probably sell the raft for lumber in New Orleans, and by this time next year it will be the walls or the floors of some new house or store."

"Sounds like a most economical way to travel," he noted absentmindedly, and Mystie smiled, for she knew that his fascination was not with the raft they had left behind, but with the woman standing at his side.

*   *   *

"Mama?"

"Yes, Nathan?"

The boy had stopped chasing his sister, and now he drew up at Sara Gardner's side. Like his mother, Nathan was watching the splendid riverboat pulling out ahead of them, beating the powerful Mississippi River into a frothy submission beneath her mighty paddle wheels. Upon her gleaming white paddle box was a painted scene of dark clouds with the yellow rays of a rising sun bursting over and through them, and across the top of the box, following the upward curve of it, was painted: TEMPEST QUEEN.

"Mama, I want to ride a riverboat."

She smiled at the boy. "Put out your arms."

He complied, with the impatient look of youth being enlisted into adult chores. Sara put the clothes she had already picked off the line onto him. "If you really want it bad enough, Nathan, then someday you will do it."

"No, not *someday*, Mama. Why can't we ride a big boat like that down to Aunt Kathryn's house, instead of this old raft?"

The little girl, barefoot and in a worn but carefully mended dress, scampered up and thrust out her arms, too. Sara put clothes onto them while she decided on how best to answer her son's questions.

"Well, it costs lots of money to ride a big steamboat like that one yonder. Why, I would not be surprised if it would cost us twenty dollars apiece to ride it from Galena down to your aunt Kathryn's house."

The boy looked impressed, but Sara could see the disappointment come to his face. Even at his young age, he must have realized the impossibility of such a large sum of money. Sara was suddenly aware of a festering wound within her that her son's disappointment had once again brought to the surface. With a sudden scowl hardening her sunburned face, she shot a glance at the man asleep near the shack. *Asleep!*—well, at least that's what she told the children. That lie could not go on much longer. They were getting old enough now to begin to question why their father slept so much. Soon they would know the truth—if they did not already.

Her eyes narrowed as she gazed at the corked bottle cradled lovingly in the crook of one arm. She used to be jealous of all those whiskey bottles getting his attention like a mistress he no longer bothered to keep secret. But over the years even that emotion had died. Now, there was no jealousy. Now there was nothing, nothing but a growing, festering disdain. . . .

"I don't want to ride a big boat, Mama." The little girl's assertion thankfully distracted her thoughts.

"Oh? Why is that, Rachel Ann Gardner?"

"Because they blow up and make a big noise like at the mines back home."

At the stern of the raft the old man laughed. Jesse Green's voice was deep and easy; it was the voice of a man who, with more than seventy-five years of living, had come to terms with life. He and his wife, Claudia, had been against Sara and the grandchildren's moving away, but in a rare moment of sobriety, Gearson Gardner had persuaded Sara to move the family South. He had shown her the stack of letters from her sister, Kathryn, bragging about the economy and warm weather and saying that a man could get a job working along the coast—which had to be better than the cold lead mines up North.

Sara had doubted that anything could alter the course her husband had set himself on, but she had been willing to try, and indeed, the weather *had* gotten warmer as they moved farther south on this mighty stream, but nothing much else was any different.

Back at the tiller, Jesse said, "Rachel Ann, you are a smart little girl. Why, I remember a day in Dubuque back in 1837. I was down on the wharf watching the boats a-comin' and goin' when right there in front o' these very eyes, a big steamer—they weren't so big back in them days as that one what just passed us up, you understand—this big steamer he went an' blowed up a boiler. Why, it scattered that boat all up and down that river, sent timbers sailing clear over my head. Shook the river like a hundred thunderclaps all at once, it did. What folks didn't get killed right off, got boiled in the steam like crawfish and died in horrible agony days later. Some breathed in the steam, and it boiled their insides and they died, too."

"Father!" Sara said sternly. "Don't go filling the children's heads with such awful stories."

"But it's the truth, sure as I'm standing on this here raft and doin' the most foolish thing I ever done in my life, pulling up roots and moving South just because my daughter got a notion. Whatever got into my head?"

"Maybe it is the truth, but I don't want to hear it. Besides, you didn't have to come along."

The old man huffed. "Think I'd let *that* man take my daughter and grandchildren and move two thousand miles where your ma and I wouldn't never see them again?" He clamped back down on his cob pipe and leaned his weight on the sweep.

Sara frowned. Gearson never had been much of a husband, even in the beginning, before he'd fallen in love with the bottle.

"I still want to ride on a riverboat, Mamma," Nathan said.

"Someday you will," Sara said. "Someday."

Claudia Green came out of the shack, weathered face protected by a wide bonnet from the morning sun, her white hair rolled up inside it. She paused a moment to glare at the outstretched legs of Sara's husband and, with a disapproving tilt to her mouth, came briskly across the raft to give Sara a hand with the laundry.

"Victuals almost ready, Sara."

Sara could smell their breakfast cooking inside. Smoke came from the pipe in the roof of the little shack, and with only just a little imagination she made it out to be the chimney of a mighty steamer.

She sighed and put that foolishness out of mind. Dreams belonged to children. Her lot in life was already cast, and she would have to live with it. Maybe things would be different, but she didn't think so. If there was whiskey to be had in St. Charles—and Sara was certain that would pose no trouble—nothing would be different. At least she had her children and her mother and father with her. Everything else important, except what few belongings they were able to load onto the raft, had been left behind.

Sara, Claudia, and the children took the laundry inside and ate breakfast. Later, Jesse took his turn at the tiny table while Sara operated the sweep.

No one bothered to try to wake Gearson.

The sharp, bright sunlight through the window stabbed mercilessly into his eyes and sent pricks of fire into the joints of his jaw, as if his head had been placed into a smithy's vice and was being tightened down. He squeezed his eyes shut again and feared he might vomit. The sensation passed, and he lay there not wishing to move or open his eyes. There was a mild roar in his ears, like the sound of surf pounding the coast. Beyond the noise, he was distantly aware of voices.

Finally he could hold back no longer, and he gave a low, plaintive groan that so desperately wanted out. Somehow, that helped.

"Hello there," a voice he did not recognize said nearby. "You finally awake?"

McKay took a chance and parted his eyes again, cautiously. He blinked, turned his head from the window, and discovered a short, rotund fellow in a black suit, with a handlebar mustache, and small dark eyes behind a pair of spectacles. The man took McKay's wrist in his soft fingers and studied the face of a watch opened upon his other hand.

In a few seconds, he released McKay's wrist, and with a vague look of satisfaction on his small mouth, he put the watch back into his vest pocket. "For a while I thought we were going to lose you."

"Lose me?" McKay discovered that he could speak only barely above a whisper, his voice sounding like a frog's croak, and that his throat burned as if he had been ill. Only, he wasn't sick, at least, not so far as he could remember. But then, remembering was something he seemed to be having some difficulty doing right at the moment.

"Who are you?"

"My name is Dr. William Reuben, but folks just call me Billy."

"Where am I? . . . What happened? . . ."

"You are in your cabin, Mr. McKay. And as to *what happened*, well, I was kind of hoping you could shed some light on that."

McKay recognized Captain Hamilton's voice at once, and when he shifted his view, he found the captain standing on the other side of his bed. His eyes were narrowed with concern beneath the bill of his blue captain's cap; his mouth was a resolute line, framed within the closely cropped, neatly trimmed gray beard.

"Something happened to me?" McKay was confused. It pained him to talk, and he was suddenly dreadfully thirsty. He recalled doing something in his cabin—oh, yes, shaving playing cards—and he vaguely remembered going outside to dispose of the evidence . . . but beyond that, nothing. He shook his head upon his pillow and clamped his eyes shut at the explosion in his brain. "I can't remember. . . . Drink . . . of water . . . please."

Dr. Reuben helped him up, holding the glass and his head. Afterward, Reuben laid him gently back to the pillow, and McKay said, "I don't seem to be able to remember anything."

"Not surprising," Reuben said. "You took quite a blow to the head."

McKay felt the bandages tied there and grimaced. "No wonder I feel like someone dropped me down a mine shaft."

Captain Hamilton said, "You are fortunate to be feeling anything at all, Mr. McKay. If it weren't for one of the firemen on duty last night, you'd be at the bottom of the river at this very moment, waking up in eternity instead of here."

McKay looked bewildered, then his bloodshot eyes brightened a fraction. "I remember now—the water. It was so cold and swift . . ."—the glimmer faded—"but that is all, I'm afraid."

"That's too bad. I would very much like to know who did this to you."

"Yes," McKay said. "I would, too."

"No doubt." Captain Hamilton made a move toward the door, then turned back. "Well, if you remember anything, I'd like to know about it."

"Of course, Captain."

Hamilton appeared relieved at seeing him alert and lucid. He bid McKay farewell, and after he had gone, McKay lay there considering the sincere look of concern he had observed in the captain's face. Concern for *his* well-being. As far as McKay could remember, no one had ever been concerned over him. It confused him. He tried to sit up, but Dr. Reuben pushed him gently back to the pillow.

"You need to stay right where you are, young fellow. You have got a mild concussion, and I don't want you passing out and maybe falling into the river again. Next time, you might not be so lucky."

Lucky? McKay had considered himself lucky when he had first weaseled his way onto this boat with free passage. But since then, he had been in a fight with Statler and shot at by an old woman, and now he had nearly had his brains bashed in and almost been drowned. McKay was beginning to seriously question his luck.

He didn't resist Dr. Reuben's urgings to remain in bed. His brain had begun to feel a bit foggy again, and the room was whirling drunkenly. He closed his eyes to it and the next moment was asleep.

Outside McKay's cabin, on the promenade, Captain Hamilton lingered a moment at the railing, watching the river, but his thoughts were elsewhere.

"Captain?"

Hamilton glanced over as young Mr. Stewart approached. "Good morning, sir."

Stewart removed his tall hat and wiped his brow. The day was growing warm. "I understand that Mr. McKay was attacked last night. I was wondering how he was doing."

"Humm. You know Mr. McKay?"

"Not very well, really," Stewart said. "We spoke some the other evening. Played some cards—monte. Then, of course, he stepped in to aid Miss Waters and myself."

"Ah, yes, that scuffle about the runaway."

Clifton nodded his head. "So, when I heard from one of the members of your crew that he had been roughly thrashed, I was concerned."

"Well, 'roughly thrashed' is a not quite apt description. Mr. McKay was brutally cudgeled, apparently, and then thrown overboard to drown. He is fortunate to be alive."

Stewart frowned. "I hope you have the rascal in chains, Captain."

"Believe me, sir, I would if I knew who it was."

"Then there were no witnesses?"

"None that have yet come forward."

"Most unfortunate," Clifton said thoughtfully.

"I will locate the fellow, to be sure," Hamilton said. "I don't need this kind of trouble upon my boat."

"No, of course not. Ah, do you think I can step in to pay my regards?"

"The doctor is trying to keep him quiet. It might be best if you wait a few hours." Captain Hamilton started along the deck.

"Certainly." Stewart fell in step with the captain. "It is a shame to have this mishap befall him on top of his other woes. He seems a decent sort."

"Oh, then you know of his sister."

"Yes, he told me. Her name is Ruth Provost, and she is dying, he fears."

Hamilton stopped midstride and glanced over. "Ruth Provost? You sure that is her name?"

"Yes, Captain. Quite sure. I inquired after her since I know many folks around Baton Rouge. But I did not know of anybody named Ruth Provost."

"Humm." Captain Hamilton resumed his way until he reached a ladder to the hurricane deck. He put a foot to the step and a hand on the braided-rope railing. "If you should hear of anything further, let me know."

"I will, Captain, although I suspect I know the culprit even now."

"Whom do you suspect?"

"Isn't it obvious? It could be no other than that fellow Statler. I have already told you of his temper and ill manners, and then the way Mr. McKay bested him in the fight. Well, there could be no other. I am certain."

Hamilton frowned. "You have any evidence?"

"No. None but the surly nature of the man, which I have already observed, and the fact that he and Mr. McKay have already fought."

Hamilton didn't like the smug look on Clifton Stewart's face, and as he thought about it, he decided that he really did not care much for Stewart anyway. He was young, spoiled, still immature. Of course, all of that could be cured by a few years of honest, hard work. Still, Stewart's whining complaints, mixed with his superior attitude, grated on Hamilton.

Captain Hamilton kept these feelings from tainting his professionalism. He was, after all, in charge of seeing that the *Tempest Queen* ran smoothly, and that meant keeping the passengers happy as well as keeping the machinery working. He said evenly, "I'm going to need something more than that, sir. And in the meantime, I suggest you keep such opinions strictly to yourself. They can get you into a tar pit you might have difficulty climbing out of."

Stewart grinned knowingly. "I will not say a word, Captain. But you will see that I am correct. I only hope it doesn't take another near tragedy to prove it. Good day, Captain." Stewart strode briskly away.

Hamilton's frown deepened, and he climbed the ladder to the hurricane deck, feeling his age not only in the effort it took these days to ascend these steep ways, but in the increasing burden that command seemed to place upon his shoulders.

Atop the deck, with a wide, glorious view of the river before him, behind him, and all about him, Captain Hamilton paused and took heart. This is what he loved about his job, and why he remained on the river, he decided, as he made his way up to the pilothouse. And when he retired in another two years, this is the view he intended to live out his final years with, on what was left of his land overlooking the mighty Mississippi.

CHAPTER ELEVEN

Captain Hamilton stepped into the pilothouse — and into the middle of a challenge.

Patton Sinclair was lounging on the large green sofa while Ab Grimes had his legs stretched out along the high bench. Jack Jacobs was the steersman on duty, and to Captain Hamilton's way of thinking, Sinclair's cub-pilot was acting as if he was a full, daylight-licensed pilot. In spite of his huge monthly salary, Sinclair appeared to not be paying the slightest attention to the river ahead. Hamilton knew to assume such a thing would be a mistake. Sinclair was a superb pilot, one of the finest on the river, and Captain Hamilton also knew there could be little trouble that even a halfway competent steersman could get himself into with the Mississippi filling her banks as she was, and not an island or shoal in sight.

Besides, even though Hamilton was the ship's master, it would have been out of place to comment on the arrangement, and he no doubt would have gotten a sound rebuke from Sinclair if he had.

At the moment, Sinclair was studying the pieces on a chessboard set up on a three-legged stool between himself and Grimes. The smoke from three green cigars filled the room in a gagging cloud, even with the sashes up and the *Queen* booming along at a brisk pace.

Absalom Grimes was a slender little man with a graying beard, bright animated eyes, and thick dark hair. He was the sort of fellow who you always felt was telling you one thing, but meant something else entirely—and enjoying himself immensely at it. Grimes was waving an arm in the air at nothing in particular and saying, "I'll wager I can do it, Mr. Sinclair."

Sinclair studied the board a moment longer, then shifted a pawn up two squares and took the smoking cigar from his lips. "And I will wager that you cannot, Mr. Grimes."

"How much?"

Sinclair contemplated the cigar in his fingers. "One hundred dollars?"

Grimes smiled thinly and seemed unimpressed that the sum offered was more than some crew members made in three months. "Well, I would immediately take up your challenge, Mr. Sinclair, but I can see no opportunity to prove myself. Now, like I say, I could walk onto any boat on this here river and inside of ten minutes of her getting up a head of steam, steal it right out from under the captain's nose. I have no doubt on that point. What I ain't figured out yet is how to do it without landing myself in jail once I brought her back to shore."

Sinclair laughed. "See, I knew you couldn't do it."

"Oh, I can do it all right." Grimes displayed the same

insufferable confidence that marked most all riverboat pilots. He sucked on the cigar. "What I need is the proper motivation, sir, and your paltry one hundred dollars ain't it."

"What sort of motivation would entice you?" Sinclair asked curiously.

Grimes considered a moment, and blew an oval smoke ring at the ceiling where the bell cords dipped near the helm. "I reckon it would have to be something important. I'd do it if it meant saving a life, maybe. Or I'd do it if it meant helping my country—"

Sinclair exploded with laughter. "So, what you're telling me is that we got to go and get ourselves into a war before I can win a hundred dollars off you."

Grimes merely grinned back, like a satisfied cat, outwardly unmoved, but Hamilton could see the cogs and gears in the man's brain whirling at full steam. Hamilton cleared his throat. It was about time they acknowledged him standing there, even though they had been fully aware of his presence from the moment he had come through the door. Pilots were like that—an elite lot. Hamilton appreciated their lofty status, for once, a long time ago, he had been a pilot, too. Only it was always a bit difficult to deal with men who considered themselves but a single step below deity.

"Captain"—Sinclair looked over—"what brings you up this morning?"

"Just making my rounds, Mr. Sinclair." He glanced about the pilothouse. "Any problems?"

"Problems, Captain?" Sinclair sounded mildly put out that Hamilton would even consider such a outrageous notion on *his* watch.

"Hmmm. How's the cub doing?"

"He does passable well, so long as I keep a thumb on him."

Grimes chuckled, and Jack Jacob glanced over his shoulder, grinning.

Hamilton said, "We will be stopping at Princeton. It

wasn't on my list. Do you foresee any complications in that?"

"Princeton? Hardly a problem. Princeton's got good wharves. A might shoaly when the river is low, but not at this bank-full stage. We can take on fuel at the woodlot there."

By this time, Grimes had moved one of his bishops, and Sinclair was compelled to turn his attention back to the game. Captain Hamilton always felt a little like an extra left shoe whenever the pilothouse held more than one pilot.

His rounds brought him to the main cabin. Breakfast was being served. The tables had all been pushed together into a single, long column, and at least thirty passengers occupied it; elbows knocking elbows, waiters scurrying, forks and coffee cups rattling, coughs muffled in napkins, belches not so politely concealed, and a dozen different conversations going on at once. The main cabin reminded Hamilton a little of a barnyard whenever he came through at the height of feeding time.

He made his way through, shaking hands, nodding to the ladies, pausing a half dozen times to answer questions, to laugh at a joke, to grab a cup of coffee off a passing silver tray. He exited the main cabin by way of the ladies' salon and stood awhile at the larboard railing watching the frothy wake from the forty-foot red paddle wheel turning there.

Walking near the railing, Hamilton smiled and nodded his head at the passengers until he had worked his way around to the starboard paddle wheel where he lingered to view the wash from it, to smell the river, to listen to the steady rhythm of the steam engines thumping beneath his feet and the chuffing of the 'scape pipes overhead. The clean morning air upon his face was invigorating, and his view shifted to the smoke streaming from the twin chimneys— not so black now that they were away from a town and the firemen were no longer heaving in pine knots. Thick black smoke was a good show for the folks in the river towns who had come to expect such displays whenever a steamboat pulled in or out—and Captain Hamilton was always ready to give the people a good show.

He grinned a little, and his chest swelled as he made his way along the *Tempest Queen*'s deck, running a palm upon the green-painted hand railing. He descended a ladder and stepped into the engine room where his rounds usually took him next.

Barney Seegar, the chief engineer, and his strikers, were busy oiling the machinery, eyeing the gauges and manning the huge valves and levers that made the boat run.

It was a hot and noisy place, with steam hissing from escape valves and fat pipes, made even fatter in their asbestos wrappers, running across the ceiling and dipping downward to disappear into the floor or connect to one of the many steam valves, topped like whirligigs with bright red wheels, each a foot in diameter. Against one wall hung three signal bells, connected by lines up to the pilothouse, and dropping through the ceiling was the other end of the brass speaking tube, which, like the bell cords, had its origins in the pilothouse.

Barney saw the captain and wiped his hands on a red rag as Hamilton came through the maze of pipes and levers.

"Morning, Captain."

"All well, Mr. Seegar?"

"She's running like a clock, Captain!" the chief engineer shouted. To try to communicate above the thumping and slamming of the engines' pistons in a normal voice would have been all but impossible. And besides, Barney Seegar always shouted. Life in the engine room of a steamboat had stolen his hearing and he thought everyone heard as poorly as he did.

Captain Hamilton did not tarry long in the engine room. He visited with the barber next, then the clerk, spoke for a while with one of the carpenters, and by and by came upon Chief Mate Lansing, just as the man was bellowing double-time at his crew: "Move sharply now, you three-legged curs! What's the matter with you? Have you all been born of a turtle for a mother and a tired old snail for a father? I didn't hire on no laggards to work for me, no sir, sleep on your own time, yes sir. . . ."

Hamilton didn't have the heart to interrupt the chief mate when he was in such good form. He listened awhile, marveling at Lansing's ability to rail his crew and not once repeat himself. At the bow, Captain Hamilton watched the yellow-brown water breaking and rippling back. He took in a huge breath and let it out contentedly.

By the time Hamilton found himself once again in the main cabin, breakfast was finished and the tables had been separated and scattered about the floor. He spied the retired general and Klack at a table. They were forever playing cards, it seemed, morning to night. Hamilton's immediate desire was to turn back, but that indomitable force rose up within him and held him sway. As if an unseen hand were suddenly at his back, Hamilton found himself being shoved across the lengthy cabin.

The retired general spotted Hamilton immediately, almost as if he had his weather eye open for him, and next thing the captain knew, he was seated at the table, digging money out of his pocket.

Captain Hamilton won a considerable pot between Leota and their landing at Princeton to take on cargo. He went on to lose nearly all of it before Ducansby passed by on the Mississippi side of the river. When they took on fuel at Skipwith's Landing, Hamilton was again flush, and the wealthy planter had joined the game—about the same time that Klack had departed, walking out onto the promenade in the stiff-legged manner of a man trying to work the kinks out of his muscles.

Hamilton quit the game later that afternoon with considerably more money than he had entered it with, and feeling unusually confident in his gaming skills. The day had slipped past uneventfully, and now the heat of the afternoon was being dissipated against a wall of black clouds banking downriver. For the last hour, that wall had grown closer and closer, and the wind had picked up smartly. As Hamilton stood on the hurricane deck peering into the face of the impending storm, he could already see distant flashes in the angry, darkening skies and feel the sting of wind-driven rain upon his cheeks.

Mr. Pierce was now at the helm. Hamilton could see him through the windows. The pilot reached for a cord overhead and gave a yank, and far down below, Hamilton barely heard the bell clanging in the engine room. With the aid of his own cub, Pierce spun the helm to starboard, and the *Tempest Queen* began traversing the river beyond the foot of an island that loomed large to the north. The pilot reached for another cord. The big bronze bell on the hurricane deck resonated twice, and the wind carried the mellow sound far out across the waters. Pierce waited another moment, then yanked the cord again, and the watchman on duty yelled down to the leadsmen, who jumped to their jobs and began calling out the soundings from the far end of the boat. Their calls were picked up and relayed by other men stationed on the hurricane deck.

"Mark three! . . . Mark three! . . . Mark three! . . . Quarter less three! . . . Mark three! . . . Quarter less three! . . . Qua-a-arter twain! . . . MA-A-ARK twain!"

The *Tempest Queen* angled across the wide river, making for the levee at Providence, Louisiana.

Hamilton looked again at the storm they were nearing, and a tingle crawled up his spine. He hated storms. Hated them not only because of what they had done to him—but for what they still did to him. After all these years, you'd think the visions would eventually go away, yet back they came . . . always. In spite of his most valiant efforts to hold them at bay, the nightmares returned.

The first distant volleys of thunder rolled up the river and broke upon the *Tempest Queen*. Hamilton shivered again, thrust his hands into the big pockets of his blue captain's coat, and went up the steps to the pilothouse.

Jethro Pierce was a quiet man who, if like his partner Sinclair, he considered himself a notch below the Almighty, at least didn't go out of his way to let you know it. He was a tall, austere man, not given over to much smiling, but friendly enough in his own reserved way; and to his credit—at least as far as Hamilton was concerned—he did not smoke those foul-smelling green cigars. Pierce's cub was a lad named Theodore Miller. He was fifteen or sixteen years old, from a well-to-do family somewhere north of St. Louis, and that was all that Hamilton knew about the kid.

Pierce glanced over with large, gray owl-eyes when Hamilton entered the pilothouse. He nodded his long, balding head, greeted him with, "Captain," and put his attention back on the crossing he was making. The soundings were still coming up, being relayed from the leadsmen down on the guards.

Theodore grinned boyishly at the captain. "Evening, sir,"

"Good evening, Mr. Miller." He knew that Theodore Miller was thoroughly in love with his schooling and the career that awaited him on the other end of his two and a half years at the side of a seasoned riverboat pilot, and it was plain on his face he would slog his way to hell and back to get his license.

Absalom Grimes was asleep on the high bench, his head propped on his portmanteau, his feet hanging over the edge. The spittoon on the floor near his dangling arm was bulging with the butts of green cigars.

"Looks like we are coming into some weather ahead."

Pierce's scrutinizing gaze remained upon the river. He was reading the eddies and currents, watching for the snags that high water drags from the shores. "It's just a little old thunder-boomer, Captain. Shouldn't cause us no problems."

"Then you do not intend to lay over until it passes?" Hamilton kept his voice neutral.

"No, don't reckon I will. We will remain at Providence only long enough to take on fuel and passengers. What we got there ahead of us is nothing more than some noise and rain. Fuss and bluster is all. You won't find a stitch of fog in it, not with this temperature and those clouds taking on that shape."

"Humm." Hamilton would have preferred to have stayed tied up until it passed, but he knew there was no logical reason for that—not if there was to be no fog. "Very well, Mr. Pierce. I shall be down in the main cabin if you should need me."

"Right," Pierce said, but Hamilton knew he was only being polite. Most pilots would sooner run the boat aground than admit to anyone other than another pilot that they needed assistance.

A knock upon his door brought his head around. Dexter McKay pushed himself up out of the bed, placed his feet squarely upon the floor, and stood carefully, as if expecting the floor to lurch at any moment and toss him back into the bed where he had spent his day counting the minutes that dragged past by the seconds that made them up: sixty seconds to a minute, sixty minutes to an hour, one hour on top of another, and so on and so forth for an entire, insufferably boring day. By this time, McKay was willing to welcome anyone into his cabin to break the monotony.

Amazingly, when he stood, the floor remained firmly in place. That was a definite improvement over even two hours ago. McKay opened the door, and to his delight he discovered Mystie Waters standing on the other side, carrying a tray of food and wearing a pleasant smile—but one that did not fully hide her concern.

"I heard about your mishap, Mr. McKay," she said, coming inside. He left the door standing open to the long, white, bright main cabin while she set the tray upon the little table by the window. She turned and looked him over. "How are you feeling?"

"Much better"—which was the absolute truth. Her appearance outside his door and the aroma of the warm food lifted his spirits to heights they had not experienced all that day.

"I thought you would be starving by now. Captain Hamilton says Billy has confined you to quarters, so I brought you this from the galley."

McKay grinned. "Thank you, Miss Waters. Dr. Reuben fears I might fall overboard again if I leave."

"It is nothing to take lightly. The water is swift when the river is at this stage, and if you were to fall in the way of the paddles—" She didn't pursue that line of thought and finished the sentence with an unpleasant frown. "Well, let's just say that no amount of luck would do you much good."

"My intentions are to stay strictly away from the guards, Miss Waters, and I will keep the paddle wheel foremost in mind." He smiled. She seemed distracted. McKay had a feeling that there was more on her mind than his personal well-being.

Mystie lifted a napkin off the tray. "I fixed you a tray, but I was not sure what you would like, so it is sort of a little of this, a little of that. I brought you a piece of blackened catfish—really very good—some boiled soft-shell crab, dirty rice, a small bowl of gumbo, and here is some mirliton. There is a cup of coffee with a pinch of chicory, and I managed to find you a few pralines for afterwards. . . . Oh, and I almost forgot." Mystie took a paper bag from her apron pocket and set it on the table next to the tray. "Parched pinders, for later on."

"Pinders?"

She laughed. "I guess it's local slang. They are peanuts."

"Oh, peanuts!" He peeked into the bag, sampled one, and declared it very good. Mystie seemed pleased.

"Well . . ."—there was a catch in her voice—"I ought to leave you to your dinner before it gets cold. . . ." She started toward the door, but McKay had a hunch that she did not intend to depart—not just yet. She stopped then and turned back. He had seated himself already and was spreading the napkin upon his knees when she said, "May I ask you a question, Mr. McKay?"

"Of course." He looked over his shoulder at her.

She came back into the room and sat on the edge of his bed, her hands clasped upon her apron, leaning forward with a sudden earnestness in her lovely dark eyes. Her long black hair was tied up on top of her head, but just as the first time he had seen her, now two nights past, the day had taken its toll upon it and errant strands fell in long tight curls to her shoulders.

"What do you know about Mr. Stewart?"

The question was a crushing blow, and all at once McKay discerned the true cause of the bright glimmer in her eyes—and that cause was another man. He did not show his disappointment, of course. His expression altered not in the least. In his profession, it was economically disastrous to allow one's feelings to make an unexpected appearance on one's face. Instead, his smile remained perfectly placid, while his calculating brain raced ahead.

Here was the perfect opportunity. It was all a game, after all, and the stakes were high: the attentions of this breathtaking, black-eyed beauty. In an instant, McKay had his strategy laid out. All that was required was to let slip a few disparaging words about Clifton Stewart's character, properly doled out with the right amount of reticence, and he was certain he could turn her head in his direction.

Before he could speak, Mystie went on quickly, "I presume you two know each other. You spent the evening playing cards and using matchsticks for counters. Only men of honor who wish to be fair with each other would gamble in that manner. I take you for an honorable man, sir, and I believe Mr. Stewart is likewise."

An honorable man?

Her lofty words hit him unexpectedly and stung like a dirk that, to his surprise, had pierced his armor of disregard for anybody but himself. McKay felt his resolve waver, and he scrambled to repair the breached redoubt. Then a disconcerting thought burst upon him: *Perhaps it wasn't her words that had made inroads.* Perhaps a chink had been opened earlier and he had not realized it until this moment.

There occurred next a most unforgivable lapse. He frowned! Mending this intrusion upon his otherwise perfectly controlled face, McKay said, "Er . . . yes, I know Mr. Stewart . . . err, I know him well." The lie only twisted the dagger deeper.

Her concerned and absolutely guileless face brightened, and McKay struggled against a completely foreign enemy now—one he had seldom, if ever, faced. *Guilt? Yes, that must be it.* He was understandably unsure. McKay steeled himself against this intruder, knowing full well that if ignored, it would pass. He proceeded to fabricate a story that would include, if not directly, then at least by allusion, some of the more ignoble traits in Mr. Stewart's character. But when it came time to spin the yarn, what emerged shook McKay to his very roots.

"You are correct in your assessment, Miss Waters. Mr. Stewart is an honorable man. I . . . I stretched a point when I said I knew him well, for I do not. I have only just met the man, but from what little I know of him, I feel secure in saying that he is God-fearing. . . ."

This seemed to be very much along the lines of what Mystie wished to hear.

What was he saying?

He was dashing his own chances; crushing them beneath his honest words! And yet, when he resolved to undo this error, what he said next was, "Mr. Stewart has a high regard for family and loyalty, and . . . and . . ."

No, he could not possibly say what he knew he was going to!

"And, I believe he is smitten with you, Miss Waters."

McKay groaned inside. Oh, how it hurt! But he had said it just the same, and as he sat there watching her face run through a range of expressions that undoubtedly mirrored the thoughts racing through her brain, he was vaguely aware of the dagger being withdrawn, and now there was an odd sensation about him that he had never experienced before.

She seemed encouraged.

McKay was crestfallen. *What had come over him?* It must be a result of the bump on the head! Yes, that was it. He was slightly delirious, that was all. It would pass, and in the morning he would be himself again! No . . . that wasn't what he wanted, either.

It was all suddenly so confusing.

Mystie stood. "Thank you, Mr. McKay. I knew I could get a straight and honest answer from you."

"You're welcome," he managed to say, confused and slightly disconnected. She started again for the door, and this time it was he who prevented her. "Err . . . one moment."

"Yes?"

His brain was reeling, not yet able to grasp the change that had come over him. Didn't he read somewhere that near brushes with death did this? He hoped it would pass soon. "Err . . . I was wondering. The fireman who rescued me? I didn't get his name. Do you know it?"

"Yes. His name is Parker. Jim Parker."

"I shall have to thank him," he said, distracted and confused.

"Good night, Mr. McKay."

She closed the door after her, and he sat there staring at the food on his tray, not really seeing it. Something had happened to him this day, and for the life of him, McKay did not know what it was, or what to expect next.

CHAPTER TWELVE

He picked at his food but left most of it untouched, in spite of a hunger that had gnawed his stomach all day. He suddenly had no appetite. After a little while, McKay placed the tray on the floor by the door and spent time drumming his fingers on the table, thinking. His gaze lingered for a while on his watch. Someone had been thoughtful enough to place it on a napkin with its back open to dry out, and a whiskey glass turned over it to keep the dust from settling among the works. Absently, he thought he'd have to find a watchmaker who could clean and oil it to prevent any damage from its plunge into the river.

There were other items scattered about the table, too,

mostly papers removed from his pockets and now drying out. His revolver was among them. With a sigh, McKay got down his valise, removed the tools he carried in it, and set to work cleaning out the damp powder and caps, drying and oiling the piece, and reloading it. The holster was still damp. He set the little revolver aside and turned back to the valise. The three decks of cards were still there, untouched, as was the card shaver, a corner rounder, and a small punch designed to place dimples on playing cards, discernible only to the most sensitive of fingers. Strangely, the sight of these tools of his trade did not lift his spirits as he had hoped they would. They certainly had in the past—before last night's events had somehow shifted his life onto a different line. Well, it would pass. It *must* pass! In a day or two he'd be himself again.

He had no idea what the hour was, but it felt late, and a violent storm had swept across them, with sheets of rain slanting under the promenade's roof, though not making it as far as his window, which remained dry. He had opened it earlier, and now a warm, moist wind ruffled the curtains there, and lightning flickered upon them with its thunder obscuring the sounds of the riverboat's engines as she went racing downriver.

McKay stood and lifted his suspenders over his shoulders. His coat was still wet. At least he had a dry shirt and pair of pants tucked away in his valise. His shoes were still damp, but that couldn't be helped, for unfortunately he did not have a second pair of those in his valise. He put them on, laced them up, and after sliding the little revolver into his pocket, went outside.

Dr. Reuben had said he wanted him to spend the day and night in bed, but McKay needed to get out, needed to walk now that he was able. His head remained clear, and he was certain he would not be falling overboard this night. In fact, he half hoped that whoever had attempted to murder him the previous night would make another try at him. With a faint grin upon his lips, McKay slipped his hand into his pocket and his fingers wrapped around the Remington revolver there.

He stayed near to the cabin wall, away from the railing where the rain slanted onto the deck. The bolts of lightning picked out the river like a photographer's flash, freezing motion, burning into his eyes afterward the images of a raft, a steamboat fighting the current, the water looking like a writhing serpent stretching farther and wider than he remembered it last. He wondered if it was going to burst the levees, and if so, what human agency could possibly control the power of such a river. Well, these weren't his towns, his homes, his friends and family, so what difference should it make to him if it were all swept away?

McKay was frowning. Thinking about it, he did not have a town or a home, let alone friends, and whatever family he had was scattered about the country, and he had no idea where they were. They had never been very close. After his parents had died, his brother and two sisters went their own ways, and that had been—he had to stop and count— fifteen years ago? Yes, at least that long since he had had any word of them. Well, it didn't matter. He had himself, and that was good enough.

McKay went down the wide staircase to the main deck, his discontentment growing. He wondered why that should be, and could come up with no satisfactory answer. The torch baskets on the forecastle lit up the bow of the boat in a flickering red light. McKay frowned and stepped under the boiler deck, making his way around the woodpiles back to the boilers. The furnaces' yawning mouths glowed red from the fires inside while big, broad-shouldered black men heaved in firewood and pushed the coals about with long iron rakes.

Appearing like human machines, the firemen didn't speak much as they worked, picking up and tossing wood: their black backs shiny and red in the light of the fires. The heat was tremendous, and coupled with the humidity, McKay found the place most unbearable.

"Err, excuse me," he said to the Negro nearest him.

The man went right on raking ashes.

"Excuse me, sir," McKay said, louder. This caught the attention of one of the big Negroes, who glanced over. His broad forehead dripped with sweat, and he dragged an arm across it, slinging the sweat to the boiler where it sizzled.

"You a-talkin' t' me, mister?"

"Yes, I was."

The Negro straightened up. He must have been most of seven feet tall. He had the bulging muscles of a prizefighter and the wary look of a cornered bear. He leaned on the long rake handle, his powerful hands gripping it two feet above his head.

"What do you want, mister? Best make it quick. Mr. Lansing catch me loafing, he'll come down on me like a hogshead of bricks."

"I am looking for Jim Parker."

"Parker?" The fireman slung more sweat, then turned, and with his head facing over his shoulder, his voice rang out in a clear, deep baritone: "Ho, Parker! A white man here to see you."

"To see me?" came the response from clear at the other end of the boilers.

"Yes. Get yo'self over here!"

The man set a chunk of wood aside and made his way around the half dozen firemen heaving wood into the voracious furnaces—there were eight furnaces in all; McKay counted their fiery mouths as the fireman made his way past each of them.

"Are you Jim Parker?"

"That's me, mister," the fireman said with a hint of caution in his voice. Then his eyes widened. "Oh, you is de gentl'man I pulled out of de riber last night."

"Yes, I am, and I've come to thank you."

"Shucks, mister, yo' don't habe to thank me. I'd done it fer anybody."

"I am sure you would have. The fact is, you did it for me, and for that I am most grateful."

"Well, it ain't me yo' oughta be thankin'," Jim Parker said. "It's dat runaway nigger what's chained up at de stanchion. He de one what called out de alarm. Shucks, if it weren't fer him, I'd neber know'd yo' was in de drink."

McKay had hoped that Jim Parker had seen his assailant. "You mean you did not see the man who attacked me and threw me overboard?"

"No, suh. I only jumped in after yo' when dat nigger sang out."

"Well, I suppose, then, I ought to thank him, too."

"Yes, suh." Jim Parker seemed a little nervous, glancing around, and McKay suspected he had an eye out for the chief mate, hoping he didn't appear while Jim was away from his task.

"Well, I will let you get back to work, Mr. Parker. And again, my heartfelt thanks." McKay pressed a twenty-dollar gold piece into the man's hand.

"Yes, suh. Thank yo', suh! Yo' don't need to mention it no more, I is happy to do it." Jim Parker turned away and a moment later was back at his post, heaving wood into the hungry mouths of the furnaces.

Lightning showed McKay a way through the stacked cargo. He found the runaway slave with his back to the forward stanchion where he had been bound, his knees drawn up, his head between them. He appeared asleep, but when McKay stepped up, the Negro lifted his head, and he stared at McKay with large, frightened eyes.

"Good evening, sir," McKay said with a smile he hoped would put the startled man at ease. "My name is Mr. McKay, and I was told by one of the firemen that it was you who witnessed the fight here last night."

The Negro sat looking at McKay, not speaking.

McKay went on, "You see, it was I who was attacked and thrown overboard. You alerting the fireman saved my life, and I wish to thank you."

The slave still did not speak, watching McKay with a wary eye.

"Err . . . thank you."

It was the face of a very frightened man that McKay was looking into. He stooped nearer and said, "What is your name?"

The slave thought this over and then said in a low voice, "Eli. I's named Eli."

McKay grinned. "Eli. You can call me Dexter. Dex for short." He offered his hand. Eli only looked at it, and after a moment McKay withdrew it. "I was wondering if you happened to see who it was who attacked me?"

"I didn't see nothin'."

"But you did call out the warning?"

The Negro looked away. The lightning revealed the tortured features of his face, and in his eyes the fright of an enslaved man terrified about being whipped. Thunder rolled over the *Tempest Queen* like cannon fire.

"You don't have to be afraid. I know you saw my attacker. Tell me who it was. I'll see that nobody takes it out on you."

Still Eli refused to speak.

McKay grimaced. He glanced about the squalid deck where Eli was chained, at the tray where scraps of food remained, at the chamber pot nearby, stinking and needing to be emptied. "Well, can I bring you anything?"

"You won't. Not if you know what's good fer you."

"Why is that?"

Eli looked back. "It's dat Mr. Statler. Him don't like n'body a-messin' wit his nigger."

"You don't belong to him?" McKay was somewhat confused.

"I do 'til him turn me back ober t' Missus Canfield. It's de law."

"I reckon I don't understand Southern laws very well, then."

McKay stood and was about to leave when Eli said

something in a voice so low that McKay almost missed it entirely.

"What's that?"

Eli looked up. "I's didn't see his face."

"That's all right. Tell me, what did you see?" McKay's pulse suddenly stepped up, and he caught Eli's wariness as if it were infectious.

"Him was a gent'man. I sees dat much. Him had on a high hat."

"Yes. Tall hat. Good, go on."

"It were too dark to see by. Don't know'd what color it was. Him weren't no big man, though, and him carried a stick, wit a shiny knob on de end."

"And that is what he struck me with?"

"Yes, suh. Him hit you two, ma'be tree times. Den him dragged you ober and dumped you into de riber."

"Then what, Eli?"

The slave shrugged his shoulders. "Him run off and I's calls out. Next ting I's know'd someone jumps in after you and pulls you out and de boat is a-swarmin' with folks. Dat's all I's know'd."

McKay stroked the point of his beard thoughtfully. *At least it wasn't a little old lady with a cane,* he mused, recalling Sadie Wilkes.

"He left the boat then?"

"Yes, suh."

McKay stood. "Well, that at least gives me something to go on." He paused and looked down at the pitiful Negro. The iron neck collar rested heavily on his shoulders, and in the flashes of lightning, McKay could see a band of crimson where the collar had chafed the skin. "Can I bring you something, Eli? Something to make your trip a little more bearable?"

The bound slave dropped his head and shook it slowly. "Ain't nothin' you can bring Eli. This here is easy libin' compared t' what Missus Canfield will do t' me once't I's returned."

"Will she . . . will she whip you?"

"Like as not fer a whole month, and keep me in de stocks. Ma'be cut my feet so's I's can't neber run away agin'."

"She'd do that? Why, that's inhuman!" McKay was suddenly incensed. Here was a man who had saved his life, and the only reward waiting for him was a sound whipping. McKay had never before wanted to help any man if it didn't in some way fatten his own purse, but now he wasn't thinking about that. Wearing a scowl, he left the chained slave. If there was some way to help that man, McKay would find it, and to hell with Southern law. He paused and grinned suddenly to himself. When had he ever given a damn about the law—Southern or otherwise? He could see no good reason to start now.

He climbed the wide, polished staircase to the boiler deck, entered the main cabin, and discovered Captain Hamilton scowling at the cards in his hands. The retired general, Klack, and the wealthy planter were sitting around the table, looking a little, McKay imagined, like a school of hungry piranhas circling a floundering swimmer in some South American river.

She waited until McKay was gone, and then a few minutes longer to make sure no one else was going to barge in, and when she decided it was safe, Mystie Waters slipped from cover and was silently at his side. So swiftly did she move, that Eli was apparently unaware of her standing there until she spoke softly, and when she did, his head snapped up from his chest, his breath caught, and his large eyes bulged like beacons.

"It's all right," she said softly, kneeling on the floor beside him. "I am a friend."

Eli's voice quivered. "Oh, no. You got t' go, missus. If I's get caught wit a white woman, I's could get shot, or hanged!"

"No one will catch you. Keep your voice down. I want to help you." Mystie glanced around nervously. After a few moments, when she was sure no one had heard him, she looked back sharply and lowered her voice so that only he could hear.

"What was Mr. McKay doing here?"

"How can you help me, missus?"

"Never mind how. I can. Now, that man who just left. What was he here for?"

Eli put his large eyes on Mystie. "Him come to tell Eli thank-you for callin' out a warnin'.'."

"You did that?"

"Yes, ma'am."

She thought a moment. "All right. It makes sense. If that was all he wanted, he will be no problem."

"What *are* you talkin' 'bout, missus?"

"I'm going to help you get free, Eli. That's what I'm talking about."

"You can do dat?"

"Yes. I have friends who will help. Listen, a little above Natchez there will be someone to meet you. All we have to do is figure a way out of this chain before then." She pulled on it experimentally and sat back to think. "Eli, where does Statler keep the key for this shackle?"

The slave shook his head and said, "Him neber go nowhere wit'out it. Him keep it on a tong, and it hang about him's neck."

"That complicates things." She looked at the length of chain in her hand and gauged the links to be over a quarter-inch thick. It would take hours to cut through it with the old file Sadie had given her. Just the same, Eli had plenty of time on his hands. He could do it if Statler didn't show up unexpectedly and catch him.

"All right, Eli. I'll figure out something." She smiled thinly. A bolt of electricity lit her face, and thunder rumbled over the *Tempest Queen*. "Take heart."

"Yes, missus."

"Eli, why did you run away? And don't give me any of that nonsense about Bouki."

The slave shook his head and gave the question considerable thought before starting slowly. "I's can't say fer sure what made me do it. Marster Franklin, Missus Canfield's husband, him wanted a package taken to Marster Philip, de next place ober. Him give it to me, and him give me a pass, too, so's de pattyrollers don't ketch me and beat me. So's I's set out, de pass in my pocket, de bundle under my arm, but when I's gets der, de oberseer, him say dat Marster Philip is down to the levee wit some of his niggers lookin' fer crawfish holes on account dat de riber was gettin' squirrelly. De oberseer, him tell me to follow de riber road and take de package down to Marster Philip, so I's done it."

Eli paused in his narrative and looked suddenly sad, and Mystie's heart went out to him. His voice caught, "I's didn't mean to run away. I's was a-walkin' de riber road, and I's could sees de levee ahead and Marster Philip pointin' dis way and dat, and his niggers on der knees feelin' into de water, lookin' to find dem devilish crawfish holes before deys kin open up and crevasse de levee. Well, right along come another one of Marster's niggers, a-joggin' up de riber behind me, and him says him is goin' down to de levee and 'give me dat package fer Marster Philip,' so's I did. Him skip on ahead, and I's all alone wit de pass still in my pocket.

"I's was curious, so I's kep walkin' to see better if any of dem niggers finds a crawfish hole, and next ting I's know'd, I's on de levee maybe fifty rods away, and I's start to tink 'bout freedom. I's don't know'd what make me do it. I's a good nigger, I am. It was Bou—"

"Eli"—Mystie cut him off sternly—"I told you, none of that superstition."

He averted his eyes and dropped his head sorrowfully to his chest and said softly, "Yes, missus. It weren't Bouki."

"No, it was something that *you* wanted to do."

"My missus, she's a stern woman. I come wit her when she married Marster Franklin, but I's belong t' her, and she's hard wit de whip and believe in the stocks like it was religion. I saw my way t' leave and I's took it. I's slipped int' de riber, ketched a tree floatin' by, and ride it across. I's hide out in de cane brakes 'til night and den starts makin' my way north. Somewhere I's meets up wit a free nigger what tells me about de Underground Railroad, and a place called Canada where a nigger is free and de slave hunters can't get at 'em. Him says t' find Missus Fargo what libs on de Arkansas Riber, above Napoleon, and she will take me t' freedom. Him say him will pass de word. So, dat's where I's headed, and I's almost make it 'fore de dogs ketch up wit me."

Mystie smiled gently. "Don't give up hope, Eli, and don't tell anyone I was here."

"No, missus, I's won't tell nobody."

"I'll be back."

"Ole Eli ain't goin' nowhere."

"You will be soon," she said softly, and stood.

"Missus?"

"Yes?"

"What is your name?"

"Mystie."

Eli's eyes brightened, and unexpectedly he smiled. "My mama's name was Mystie."

"Was it?"

"Yes, missus. She was a fine woman."

"I am sure she was, Eli. My mother is a fine woman, too." Her smile faltered under the burden of what she knew had to be done next, and her voice fell back to a whisper. "I will be back later."

Mystie turned to leave and stopped suddenly, startled.

"Well, well, well." Statler stepped out of the shadows. "I had a feeling that if I kept an eye on you long enough, your trail would lead back to that there runaway nigger." The slave hunter came forward, putting himself between her and her only avenue of escape. "What is it about that nigger, anyway?"

It took a few seconds for Mystie to get her wits about her,

and she laughed, a little uncertainly. "I was just checking up on him. His chamber pot needs to be emptied. I was going to find the maid that Maggie put in charge of him and inform her of his needs."

Statler's smile thinned, and in a flash of lightning she saw his leering eyes taking stock of her. "Now, you don't expect me to believe a yarn like that, do you?"

Mystie's trepidation turned instantly to anger. "I don't care what you believe, Mr. Statler. Please stand aside before I call for help."

"Call for help? Go ahead," Statler said easily. "I'd like the captain to show up about now. Seems to me he warned you to stay away from that nigger. It looks like you ignored his orders. I wonder how he would take that? If it were me, I'd give you what pay you had coming and set you ashore at the next landing." Statler fished a cigar from his inside vest pocket, bit off the end, and put a match to it, puffing until it glowed. The flare of the match turned his face into that of a grinning goblin, and he seemed in no hurry now.

He shook out the match and ground it underfoot. "Now, the way I see it, the last thing you'd want is for someone to come by. That is, unless you want to risk losing your job . . . to risk being put ashore." His eyes brightened evilly and shifted toward Eli. "If that happened, you'll never see your precious nigger again." He grinned.

How much did he know?

He advanced a step, and Mystie was assaulted with the foul stench of his unwashed body. He extended a hand and lifted her chin and looked at her face, first from this direction, then that.

"You are a pretty little thing. You got fire in your eyes. I like that. It means you got passion in your soul, missy. I wonder just how much passion?" His eyes narrowed, as if he'd suddenly discovered something in her face.

She tried not to tremble as her eyes riveted on the leather thong about his neck that fell beneath his dirty red shirt. The key to Eli's neck shackle was there. There was a way to get it, but Mystie revolted at the thought of what she might have to do to steal it.

Mystie braced herself against his unholy advance. She would do what she had to, no matter how loathsome. Then quite unexpectedly Statler let her chin drop, and he backed away.

"I'm on to you, little lady. I don't know what your game is yet, but I will before this trip is over. And when I do, you will come crawling to me. Then we will see just how much passion there is in that soul of yours. Who knows, you may even discover you like me." Statler's grin dissolved into a mask of evil. "In the meantime, stay away from that nigger! I've got my eye on you." He strode away, and the shadows swallowed him up.

Mystie stood there awhile, trembling, and when her fear had subsided, anger poured in to fill its place. "I'll never come to you, never in a thousand years," she hissed hotly into the night. But even as she did so, something within her made her uncertain and fearful, and her distress would not leave.

She glanced down at Eli. Her mouth drew into a tight knot, and without another word, she left.

CHAPTER THIRTEEN

In late summer and fall, the Mississippi River is a willing mistress, a placid giant, wending her way south; a sleeping power contained within the wide, graceful swells of her banks. In some places, she even forgets she is a river at all, and leaves high, dry, once-inundated land to issue new growth. In the middle of this wide, lazy giant, shoals might sometimes reach out hundreds of yards just under the water, waiting for a careless pilot to bring his boat too close. Then they would suddenly rise up and trap the unfortunate trespasser. Great sport for a lazy river with nothing much else to do. In other places, sawyers and planters lurk like playful gremlins. Their mischief is of a more disastrous nature. They will happily rip open the hull of any passing boat if they can, and send her to an early grave, and put in place yet one more hazard for riverboat pilots to contend with.

Such is the Mississippi in summer and fall. In winter, she is mostly frozen over up North, allowing traffic only on her southern reaches. But in spring! In the spring, she comes alive, stirring from her extended sleep, stretching her long, tawny muscles, testing the bars of her confinement. She is well rested and hungry, and it is land that she craves most. Spring melt fills her from the north, west, and east as her tributaries swell, building muscles into her flanks. The torrential rains of the season serve to add peptone to help her digest her meat. She claws her way up her banks, fills them to brimming, and then nibbles at the levees. For a while, it is a contest between man's ingenuity and the river's massive power. In some seasons, man is victorious, in others the river wins handily and consumes thousands of square miles of rich cropland, chews it up and carries it away. Oh, the land finally works its way through her system, and she has to give it back, but what started out as an Illinois corn farm might very well end up as a Louisiana cotton plantation.

Captain Hamilton understood the workings of the river as intimately as he understood the workings of the *Tempest Queen*. What he did not understand so well were the workings inside his own head and why when the spring storms came they always brought with them the visions. . . .

As the boat surged powerfully along, her beating heart was silenced by the thunder that seemed to stretch out a hand and hold her back a moment. It was too much for Hamilton, and he was losing his concentration. He was ahead at this point; he always seemed to end up a little ahead of these three cardplayers, and he wondered vaguely why they persisted in the game hour after hour. Although in his more honest moments, he had to admit that gambling was compulsive to him, he never was quite able to fool himself into believing he was really very good at games of chance.

Yet he was able to best these men nearly two to one, and still they cheerfully played on. *Well, and why not!* Hamilton mused. But now he was losing even what little edge he had, and his thoughts were ranging farther afield, and with each clap of thunder that shook the boat, with each white bolt of frozen movement within the main cabin, Hamilton grew more and more uneasy, and he knew he ought to be leaving.

"Gentlemen," he said finally, gathering in his winnings. "This storm is becoming most severe, and I must be about ship's business."

"We understand," the retired general said. "You've got a large boat to run, and we certainly do not want to keep you from your duties."

Captain Hamilton grinned. He wasn't going to tell these men that once under steam a riverboat captain became a most superfluous entity. A mere figurehead. The real authority lay with the pilots. It wasn't Hamilton's intent to explain the law of the river to these men. "Yes, well, good evening."

"Will we see you tomorrow, Captain?" the wealthy planter inquired.

"Perhaps." Hamilton suspected that keeping him away from the game would be like keeping a pint of rum from a drunkard, but he at least liked to give the impression of a man still in control of himself.

Hamilton left them and made his way up to the hurricane deck, bending into the slashing rain. He angled for the texas deck, which was another three steps up. In the blinding flashes, he could see Sinclair up in the pilothouse, silhouetted against the helm, gripping it wide and powerfully, as if bracing himself. Hamilton turned his eyes back to the wet deck and in a moment leaped under the protection of the little balcony that stretched out from his cabin at the head of the texas.

He stood there shaking himself like a wet dog, shedding

his heavy coat. Rain slanted past the little porch where two cane-bottom chairs were stationed on either side of a small table. Water poured in sheets off the roof, and as he went to the railing, a shiver shook him, even though the air was warm and the rain, up from the Gulf, nearly the temperature of bathwater.

He never knew when they would come, only that stormy nights, nights like this, sometimes triggered them. Hamilton's knuckles blanched. He released his grip, staggered back, and fell into one of the deck chairs, shaking. His eyes focused on the flickering torch baskets ahead. There was little light out beyond the *Tempest Queen*'s bow, but the staccato of lightning more than amply illuminated the river in brief, blinding snatches. Sinclair knew the river well enough to run it "blindfolded and on smell alone," as he often bragged, but Hamilton had been out of the piloting business long enough to have lost the kind of intimacy Sinclair had with it. Besides, he could never again stand behind the helm of any boat and risk running smack up against one of those visions.

He squeezed his eyes and patted his face dry with the sleeve of his shirt.

"Captain Hamilton, sir."

Hamilton glanced over and discovered Dexter McKay standing in the rain just beyond his porch.

"May I come up, sir?"

Hamilton got out of his chair. "Hurry out of the rain, man. You are sick! I thought Dr. Reuben ordered you to cabin?"

McKay came around the larboard-side chimney and onto the porch. He was hatless, and he still moved a bit unsteadily.

"Sit down, sit down." Hamilton abandoned his chair to McKay and moved the other around. "Let me get you a towel." He ducked into his cabin and returned a moment later.

"Thank you." McKay dried his hair, his face, and his beard, and patted his sleeves to little avail.

Hamilton settled himself in the other chair. "What the devil are you doing out and about on a night like this?"

"I am really feeling quite better."

"You are white as a cotton patch. You'll catch your death in this rain," Hamilton said sternly.

McKay grinned. "I hope not. I had about as close a brush with death last night as I care to have for a good long time."

"Humm. Well, running about in a storm like this is tempting fate."

"Actually, I wanted to speak with you, but you quit your card game down in the salon before I had a chance."

"Oh? What is it you wished to see me about? If it is a complaint, you may present it to the clerk. I'm in no mood tonight."

McKay grinned. "No, I have no complaints, Captain. Indeed, you have been a perfect host."

Hamilton frowned suspiciously.

McKay continued, "I have managed a brief description of the man who attacked me. I thought you might be interested."

Hamilton's eyebrows hitched up. "Then your memory has returned?"

He shook his head. "I'm afraid not very much. But I have just spoken to the fireman who pulled me out—"

"Jim Parker?"

"The very one. He told me that, in actual fact, it was that unfortunate man bound in a chain who witnessed the attack and called out the alarm.

Hamilton leaned forward, his interest captured. "The runaway? Really? I was not aware."

"Apparently the Negroes are a close-mouthed group."

"Aye, they are that," Hamilton agreed.

"His name is Eli. He says the man who attacked me wore a high hat and carried a walking stick with a silver knob on the end. You know the passenger list. I was wondering if that meant anything to you?"

Hamilton gave a short laugh and settled back comfortably in his chair. "Well, that about describes three-quarters of the male passengers aboard."

McKay had to grin, too. It was true. It might even have described himself.

"Did he give you anything else?"

"Short stature."

"Humm. Now we've divided that three-quarters nearly in half."

"Still a long shot."

Hamilton nodded his head solemnly.

McKay said, "Eli said the man left the boat after hitting me."

"Now, that is something. Perhaps it wasn't a passenger at all. Have you any enemies, Mr. McKay?"

"None that I know of. I've only been away from the gold camps a little over a month, yet I can't imagine anyone there disgruntled enough to have trailed me here into the South."

"Then perhaps it was merely a case of attempted robbery with no forethought to the victim. You were, as they say, in the wrong place at the wrong time."

McKay pulled at his carefully trimmed goatee and then brushed his mustache in place with a finger as he considered this. "I suppose I shall have to go about with both eyes open, then."

"Always sound advice." Hamilton's words were punctuated by a blinding flash and a tremendous explosion overhead. It so startled McKay as to bring him up straight in the chair, and his face snapped around toward the forecastle. For an instant, he wondered if the lightning had struck the boat. When McKay looked back, Captain Hamilton seemed to be staring at something out beyond the bow. He had gone rigid in his chair, his face appeared etched in flint, his eyes wide and unblinking.

"Captain?"

Hamilton was suddenly out of his chair and at the railing.

McKay strained to see out past the water pouring off the roof. "What is it, Captain?"

"My God! It's on fire!" Hamilton's arms were stiff as jack staffs, his neck a mass of bulging corded muscles.

"The boat?" McKay leaped to his feet, catching the captain's alarm. "Is the boat on fire?" He scanned the deck below but saw no flames. Then he discovered that Hamilton's view was much higher, and McKay peered out into the driving rain where arcs of electricity showed only an angry, surging river. "Where? Where is the fire?"

"There, man! Right in front of us. The whole roof is an inferno!"

"Roof?" McKay looked again and saw only the river, but Hamilton's gaze was steadfast, his eyes frozen in a wide, crazed stare.

"There! Now I see them. They are moving across the roof, avoiding the flames."

Search as he might, McKay only saw the river and the rain.

Hamilton's voice rose, but his body remained fixed in place, as if a corpse. Only his eyes moved, in the chaotic manner of one tormented by a dream he cannot escape. McKay took Hamilton by the arm and felt rods of steel where he expected flesh and muscle.

"Hard over, Mr. Finney. Hard over! Put your backs to it, men!"

McKay watched in mild amazement, and with more than a little concern. Had Captain Hamilton suddenly gone mad? He considered alerting a member of the crew—the pilothouse was only a few feet overhead, and he was certain he could find help there—but he did not want to leave the captain in his current state.

"Let her fall off to larboard, now!" the captain roared, and whether or not there was a fire out beyond the boat, there certainly were flames of passion leaping in the man's burning eyes.

"Finney, have the men put their backs to it. More muscle, more muscle! Pull hard now, swing her about smartly!"

Hamilton's head tilted up and around as if he were watching something pass him by.

"All right men. Hold her steady."

Hamilton's look shot back into the storming night. His eyes rounded. "Hester?"

Then, with renewed strength: "Jump, Cynthia! John, Alicia! Jump! For God's sake, jump! I am here now!"

McKay could not imagine what this tortured man was seeing, for the rains still drove on, the lightning still lanced blue-white across the sky, and thunder still shook the boat. Nothing had changed in McKay's world. But in Captain Hamilton's world?

All at once Captain Hamilton's voice changed. No longer were his words driven by fear, but now there was a new, more powerful engine behind them: Fear had turned to terror.

"Hurry Cynthia! Hester has the children. Please hurry, to the edge now! Yes, that's right. Hurry. Now jump!"

Then an ax came down and chopped his words short, and Hamilton stood there more dead than alive, his eyes protruding, his lips thinned back.

McKay knew not what to expect next. Was the captain having an attack? A stroke? He held his breath and prepared to catch the man once he toppled, which he feared must happen at any moment now. Hamilton's hand was shaking. He put it upon the railing to steady it.

Hamilton all at once drew in a deep breath and shook his head as if coming out of a trance. He appeared surprised to discover McKay at his side. Slowly the surprise became reproach, and without offering a word of explanation, he went back to his chair and lowered himself wearily into it.

"Are you all right, Captain?" McKay remained standing over the man.

Hamilton did not answer him immediately. His eyes still remained fixed. After a moment, he said, "I must apologize, sir." Again his gaze shifted out at the rain and the night. He groped for a word and, when he had found it, he said, "I am a man who is haunted by ghosts."

McKay then sat down in the second chair.

Hamilton considered his next words carefully.

"It was a night very much like this one, sir. The rain had been heavy most of the preceding two weeks. The river bank-full, nearing flood stage. I was a pilot back in those days. I sometimes spent weeks away from home, away from Cynthia and the children." He grimaced and looked at McKay. "I don't need to bore you with my little tragedies, Mr. McKay."

"No, please. I want to hear it." A week earlier, McKay's thoughts would have been only about how he could turn a profit from this man's misfortune . . . from his *ghosts*. But just now he had no intent on gain, only concern for a man who had shown concern and kindness toward him.

Hamilton considered McKay's words. The corners of his lips twitched, and he said without any further urging, "I had a premonition, if you will. I had been most distressed for days before, and I was determined that on the next trip up the river I would put in at our levee and check in on Cynthia. She was living in the plantation house, which her parents had willed to her and which was mine by marriage." He paused and frowned.

"They had built it too near the river. They should have moved it a mile away where the land rose above the flood plain, but Cynthia's mother had wanted a view of the river, so they put it where they would have that, and they built a massive levee to protect it. But man cannot restrain the Mississippi, Mr. McKay. He is a fool to try. She is a willful woman who goes where she pleases! Takes what she wants! Destroys all who stand in her way!" Hamilton was suddenly shouting. His fist had clenched, and he had nearly come out of his chair. Discovering this, he unfolded his fingers and settled back, calming himself, falling into a brooding silence. When he next spoke, it was in somber tones.

"I will never know what happened that night—what caused the fire in the first place. I suspect that in their panic one of them must have upset a lamp, but it does not matter now how it happened. The unhappy fact is, it *did* happen.

"I was piloting a freighter at the time. The *Triumph* was her name. I'd come upriver on the west bank, having just left Pointe Coupee with three thousand sacks of cottonseed. I was making the crossing, heading for my home, which was only across the river and north a scarce dozen miles. From my place behind the helm, through the rain-streaked windows, I noticed as we drew nearer that there was a fire burning on that distant shore. And as I pushed the little *Triumph* up against the current, it became apparent that the fire was coming from my home. The river seemed to stretch on forever at that point, and then I realized the truth of it. Our levee had crevassed, and the river was spilling into the fields. It had already flooded the house to the third floor.

"Well, my first inclination was to take the *Triumph* right on through the crevasse and rescue whom I might, but the water was flooding in too swiftly, and there was not a single breech in the levee that was yet deep enough to clear her keel. I hit her keel and drew back. I then called down for my partner, and when he arrived, I put the *Triumph* into his hands. In the meanwhile, I had sent word to the chief mate, a man named Liam Finney, to prepare to lower the yawl and to round up the strongest men he had at his disposal.

"We put out then, in that violent storm, the lads rowing hard, me standing at the prow, looking ever so much, I suppose, as Mr. Washington must have when he crossed the Delaware." Hamilton's brief smile faded. "We made it through the breech finally, and it was a little like riding out a hurricane; then the men were pulling hard. At least beyond the levee we were out of the current, but the rain fell in mighty bucketfuls, and the lightning was like angry lances being hurdled by gods incensed that mere mortal man was attempting to fight the River.

"The house, where it used to stand, was a grand affair, built early in the century. A more stately home no man had, and when Cynthia's parents were killed, they left it all to their daughter, their only issue. There were a thousand acres of land and over one hundred slaves that came with the place. And now it was being consumed by the torch. When the men brought the bucking yawl closer, I could see by the light of the flames already eating their way through the roof that Cynthia and the children had made it to safety there. They were clinging to one of the chimneys. They saw me, I am certain. I even believe they heard me, for I shouted above the torrents for them to make their way to the eaves and jump into the water. We were near enough for us to pick them up. All she had to do was jump! Yet Cynthia was paralyzed with fear.

"I knew she must have seen us, for the lightning was so vicious that the night was almost continually being illuminated brighter than noon. It was at that point that Hester appeared. Hester was the children's nanny. She was at once at Cynthia's side, helping her and the children, moving in a zigzag to avoid the holes opening in the roof and the flames that were appearing most everywhere now."

A catch in his voice broke the narrative. McKay could see that Hamilton was struggling mightily with his emotions. His eyes glistened and blinked, and he sniffed and then steeled himself once more.

"They would have all made it to safety had they been but a few seconds faster. Nearly to the eaves they were when the roof suddenly opened up like the flaming gates to an infernal . . . to hell if you will! It gaped its angry, fiery mouth right below them and in an instant consumed them."

He remained silent a long, uneasy moment, then continued in a much softer voice. "We never did find their bodies. Afterwards, when the waters had receded, we went through the place, but there was nothing to salvage. The slaves rebuilt the levee, but the following year the Mississippi left her banks for good, cut a new channel, and what remained of the house disappeared forever."

"What did you do?"

"Do?" He made a wry smile. His voice took on strength. "I sold the place, what was left of it. It still had most of seven hundred acres of good cropland, you understand. Sold it all except forty acres on the hill where they should have built the house in the first place. I kept that for myself. It is a pretty site that now commands a superb view of the river—now that the river is so much closer." He smiled then. "I intend to retire there someday and build another house. Nothing as grand as the one that once stood. Can hardly afford to build homes like that anymore these days. I will sell the *Tempest Queen* and retire there someday soon. Spend my remaining years on my front porch watching this old river making her way down to the Gulf. I'll be sipping juleps, catching up on my reading, might even write a book about my life on the river. Who knows what I'll do. I've often thought I'd like to go West and visit rivers that I've only heard about: the Colorado, the American, the Sacramento, the Columbia."

"None can compare to the Mississippi. I have seen them."

"Have you?" Hamilton seemed genuinely impressed. "A well-traveled man, you are. I shall see them also."

"I am sure you will." McKay stood. "I wish you all the best, Captain Hamilton, and if there is some way that I can assist—"

"You mean my little lapses? There is nothing any man can do to help me there. It is something I will have to eventually confront alone and bury once and for all." He glanced up sharply. "Why am I telling you all this? It is not something I am comfortable talking about."

McKay shrugged his shoulders. "I don't know." He bowed slightly at the waist. "I wish you good luck on that. I ought to be leaving now. Good evening to you, Captain."

"Good evening to you, Mr. McKay—and get into something dry before you come down with pneumonia. Reuben will be impossible to live with if he should lose you now."

McKay left, and when he looked back from the hurricane deck before descending the ladder, he saw Captain Hamilton staring out into the rain, and for the second time in his life, he was aware of a disconcerting but genuine concern for someone other than himself. This wasn't working out at all as he had planned it. He'd never intended to care for anyone but himself—and now this old man had worked his way into the stony vault of his heart.

How long was it going to take for the effects of the knock to his head to wear off? he wondered. He wasn't sure how much more of this his nerves, or his pocketbook, could stand.

CHAPTER FOURTEEN

At four-thirty in the morning, Barney Seegar was awakened out of a deep sleep by an urgent knock at his cabin door. Coming groggily awake, he threw off the sheet and stumbled to his door.

"What is it?" the chief engineer asked, discovering one of his strikers, Walter Braun, standing there, sweat still on his forehead, a dirty, grease-stained kerchief about his neck. His dark overalls were smeared with oil and grease, and his cheeks had the swarthy appearance of an Arab—but the man was German clear down to his Black Forest stockings. His eyes were clear blue, bright and animated at the moment, and his accent still thick as fresh-churned butter.

"Ve have got a leak in the main feed on the starboard engine, sir!"

"A what?" Seegar canted a ear now in Braun's direction.

"A leak, sir," the excited German said again, louder.

"A leak? Steam?" Seegar suddenly cast off any remaining drowsiness.

"*Ja.*"

"Where, man, where?" Seegar was already reaching for his pants and stepping into them, hobbling in a circle and hefting a suspender up over his shoulder.

"In the starboard feed line," Braun repeated.

Seegar stomped his foot into a boot, then searched the cluttered floor for its mate, discovering it among a pile of dirty clothes in the corner.

"You shut it down?"

"*Ja*, Mr. Attebury is already doing so."

Seegar slipped on the second boot, not bothering to lace them up, immediately followed the striker down the ladder and then down another until he put his feet on the main deck, and hurried around to the engine room. When he entered, the shriek of steam being vented through the gauge cocks drowned out every other sound. The other engineer assigned to night watch, a dark little man with blond hair, was leaping from valve to valve, turning them down, shifting pressure away from the starboard engine.

Seegar crawled through a maze of pipes to the main feed line. The pressurized steam had breached the iron pipe all right. It had blown a section of asbestos wrapper clean off and was screaming like a banshee. He worked his way out of the plumbing and wheeled on the blond haired man, "How far down is she?" he yelled above the shriek.

"Two-twenty, and falling."

Seegar nodded his head. "Keep at it, Larry. We are going to have to bleed her dry. Anyone know where we are?"

"Just past the mouth of the Yazoo!" Braun shouted.

"Good. That will put us in Vicksburg in a few minutes, then—"

A bell on the board was suddenly ringing as if the arm at the other end of the cord wanted to rip it from its moorings. "What the hell is going on down there?" Jethro Pierce's voice echoed down the speaking tube. "I'm losing my rudder, and we are nosing to starboard!"

Barney shot a glance at Larry and Walter. "Cut the pressure to larboard engine. Try to keep them balanced."

The engineer and the striker leaped to the valves and levers, keeping the gauges under close scrutiny.

"Anybody down there this morning?" came an impatient inquiry, laced vaguely with a growing panic.

"Mr. Pierce," Barney called into the tube, "this is Seegar. We have a leak in one of the feed lines to the starboard engine. We will have to lay over for repairs. You should be hailing Vicksburg presently."

"Vicksburg is dead ahead."

"We will have to put over to make repairs!" he yelled into the speaking tube again.

"I heard you the first time, Seegar. Just keep those engines turning until I can bring her about and make the crossing."

"I'll give you what I can!" Seegar shouted back and leaped to aid his men. Overhead he could hear the big bell on the hurricane deck peeling out into the spreading dawn and a moment later the leadsmen's cries shouting out the depth. The steam whistle atop the pilothouse called across the river as Pierce signaled to the wharf that he was coming in. Even buried down in the engine room, Seegar could feel the *Tempest Queen* responding heavily to her rudder.

"We need to keep 'em turning another few minutes, men, then we can shut 'em down!" Seegar shouted.

The *Tempest Queen* sailed into Vicksburg with all the grace of a floating log, but Pierce brought her in safely, and by the time the lines were tossed out and the bow and stern made fast, Captain Hamilton was stepping into the pilot-house.

"What the devil is going on, Mr. Pierce?"

Pierce's gray eyes lacked expression, and his voice was laconic. "Some trouble with the starboard engine. Not sure what. Seegar said something about the main feed from the boilers."

"Humm." Hamilton glanced at the lights of Vicksburg that dotted the high ground. The ones farther up the hillside were already fading against the coming dawn. "Fortunate for us, we were near a town. Can Mr. Seegar effect repairs here?"

Pierce shrugged his bony shoulders and hooked a long finger under his suspender. "You will have to ask him that."

Hamilton intended to. He made his way through the still-sleeping boat, down to the engine room, and stepped in amid a cloud of steam, as the boilers were already being bled of their pressure.

"Mr. Seegar?" He shouted into the clouds, attempting to be heard above the hiss, "Mr. Seegar?"

Hamilton fanned at the steam and thought he heard something shuffling about back in the forest of pipes. Then Barney Seegar walked from the vapors like a specter from a foggy grave. He was wiping his hands on a filthy red rag and frowning.

Hamilton inclined his head at the doorway and stepped outside and onto the guards where the dark water rushed past, only a couple feet below. At least here the air was fresh and the noise of the steam somewhat abated. "What happened, Barney?"

"We were lucky, Captain. The main high-pressure line from the boilers to the starboard engine sprang a leak about halfway down its length."

"Can it be patched?"

Barney shook his head. "No. That's what I mean about lucky, sir. I've just been back there tearing off some of the wrapper, and it looks like the whole pipe was about to burst wide open. That little leak relieved the pressure, but the pipe is blistered all along its length. It could have all gone at once, sir, at any time, and if that had happened, there would have been lots of people hurt, maybe killed."

"Humm. Well, we should be thankful, then, that it wasn't worse."

"Thankful that it happened like it did. I had no clue there was anything wrong."

"How long to fix? I've got a schedule."

"Pardon, sir?" Seegar cupped a hand behind his ear.

Hamilton raised his voice. "How long to effect repairs, Mr. Seegar? I have got a schedule to maintain."

"You're going to be behind on your schedule, I'm afraid. First, we have to let the steam bleed and then let everything cool down. That will take several hours at least. In the meantime, I'll go into town and locate a piece of pipe that will work and then find a machine shop that can cut and thread it."

Hamilton said, "If the starboard pipe was damaged, you might want to check the larboard, too."

Seegar nodded his head. "I am going to replace them both. It won't take that much longer, and better safe than sorry."

"I agree. Any idea on how long, Mr. Seegar?"

"We will be tied up here most the day, sir. You might want to figure on staying over until morning. Since I have to tear some of the guts out of this gal anyway, there are a few things that ought to be checked."

"Humm. Very well. I'll inform the passengers of our delay. Get to it, Mr. Seegar."

"Right, Captain." Barney Seegar stuffed his red hand rag into his back pocket and disappeared amid the vapors pouring from the engine-room door.

For McKay, the layover was a much-needed break from the confinement of the riverboat: a chance to find a fresh game of cards in town and perhaps to revive the old fires that had once driven him on so faithfully. These last two days had been horribly depressing. He was discovering it was hard work trying to find something nice to do for someone else. *Oh, how so much easier when you had only yourself to look after.*

He filled his pockets with the necessities of life: his loaded dice, his marked monte cards, his silver cigar case with matching match safe, and a pocket roulette wheel. He slipped the Remington revolver into its holster and spent a moment polishing his gold signet ring against his trousers. He brushed his hat, slipped into his frock coat, and snatched up the ebony cane with its silver horse-head grip. Checking himself in the mirror, approving of what he saw, McKay noticed his gold watch and heavy chain still under the whiskey glass. A bit of condensation had formed around the bottom of the glass. Thinking he might happen upon a watchmaker, he dropped it, too, into his pocket and strode outside for his first glimpse of Vicksburg.

Coming down the wide, curving staircase, he marveled at the utter lack of activity about the boat. He decided that Vicksburg had not been a scheduled stop, and other than the baggage of a few passengers who might board, there was no freight to load or off-load. Amazingly, the deckhands were all lounging in the shade and chatting, and what was equally amazing, the chief mate was not ranting and raving over this arrangement.

McKay grinned as he tramped off the landing stage and put his feet to the road that climbed the steep hill up into Vicksburg proper. He felt good. The air was sweet with primrose, magnolia, honeysuckle, and a dozen fragrances that his Western-trained nose had not yet had the opportunity to make acquaintance with. The air was warm and humid, but not yet heavy. A pleasant change from the cold, dry Rocky Mountains he had only recently left.

The Rocky Mountains. He frowned, recalling the unfortunate circumstances of his most recent and rapid departure from the gold camps around Cherry Creek, and he wondered if Captain Hamilton had not hit the nail squarely on the head when he had suggested that someone out of his past had attempted to murder him the other night. McKay immediately dismissed the idea. It was too far-fetched.

He paused on the corner of Washington and Main, turned his face to the warm, pleasant sun, and closed his eyes. From out of the brightness upon his shut lids swirled a blob of silver. As it whirled closer, he could see the form of it. Eagle claws . . . or something very similar. That was it! That was the appearance of the cudgel that had hit him. Claws! The memory of it came at him so suddenly and clearly that McKay leaped back, startled, and his eyes sprang open.

A lady maneuvering a perambulator looked at him curiously. McKay tipped his hat and smiled affably, as if leaping about on a warm, spring morning was normal behavior, and he headed once more into town, elated that yet another piece of the puzzle had fallen into place.

A few blocks farther into Vicksburg, McKay turned south on Cherry Street and was almost immediately confronted with a gleaming edifice of quarried stone and towering columns. The Warren County Court House. On the top of the courthouse was a pretty little stone cupola. It seemed to command the highest viewpoint on the loftiest hill in Vicksburg, and it seemed also to have been only recently completed; indeed, not yet fully completed, for even now black workers were busy constructing retaining walls and cutting into the hillsides to lay out steps. Up nearer the courthouse, gardeners were digging in small twigs of trees, and on a corner of the lot, a small building was taking shape.

As McKay strolled around the building, he was drawn to a little crowd gathered on the steps near the south entrance. Beneath the portico, in the shadows of those exquisite thirty-foot Ionic columns, stood a tall man in a long brown frock and a beaver hat. He had his lapel gripped in his left hand and was gesturing with his right hand as he spoke loudly and with passion.

McKay's curiosity aroused, he climbed the temporary steps and moved among the crowd. After listening a few minutes to this man speak boldly about states' rights, and some notion that he called "squatter's sovereignty," which McKay gathered had something to do with the states' having the right to choose if they would permit slavery or not, McKay became bored.

He noted, however, that every ear there was tuned to this man's compelling tones, and when he asked a fellow nearby who it was that was speaking, he received a most surprised and acid expression in return. One would have thought the Savior himself had returned and McKay had failed to recognize him.

"Why, that there is Mr. Jefferson Davis." The man said it as if the name alone would clear away the cotton in this fool's head.

But it didn't—not immediately at least. McKay searched his brain. . . . Yes, the name was vaguely familiar, and then he had it. "Ah, the secretary of war!"

At this, the Vicksburgian gave him a most scathing glare. "*Ex*-secretary of war," he said, making clear his disgust at McKay's ignorance of what was most likely one of Mississippi's luminaries.

"Oh." McKay felt it time to continue on his way. He managed a thin smile for the gentleman, but the fellow chose to ignore it. McKay retraced his steps down to the street again and made his way into the business area of Vicksburg.

As he walked and thought about it, his anger stirred up the bile in his stomach. How was he supposed to know every ne'er-do-well who plied the backwaters of Mississippi? That man Davis would probably never amount to anything anyway! McKay's gut knotted, and he realized that his anger would only cause him indigestion, so he put the dolt out of mind and kept a sharp lookout for a place to set up business.

Vicksburg, however, did not appear to be overwhelmed with saloons or gambling parlors. He discovered a whiskey house, but when he stepped through the door into its cool darkness, there was not a single card game to be found.

Back out on the sidewalk, commerce was brisk; people coming and going, the lanes burgeoning with more than their share of busy gentlemen, and pretty ladies strolling with companions or pushing baby buggies.

Vicksburg seemed a most tamed and civilized town. On the one hand, McKay liked the civility of the place; but on the other hand, he knew intuitively that the pickings would be slim here. It was a pretty town, mostly of sturdy brick buildings that told him her citizens were serious about her future. The folks were friendly, and McKay figured that so long as he didn't ask stupid questions about local politicians they would remain that way.

He found an horologist who said he could clean and oil the watch and have it back to McKay by four o'clock. That was quite satisfactory, and he left the timepiece and went on his way, enjoying the warm, spring morning, observing the lovely ladies and polite gentlemen, and looking for a decent game of cards.

After three other failed attempts to find anything more adventurous than a friendly game of whist, McKay discovered what he thought might be the source of his trouble. It was in the form of an ancient yellowed, dog-eared notice that someone had mounted in a wooden picture frame behind a piece of glass, which hung on the wall of one of the saloons:

NOTICE

At a meeting of the citizens of Vicksburg on Saturday the 4th day of July, it was
Resolved, that a notice be given to all professional GAMBLERS, that the citizens of Vicksburg are resolved to exclude them from this place and its vicinity, and that twenty-four hours' notice be given them to leave the place.

Resolved, that all persons permitting Faro dealing in their house, be also notified, that they
will be prosecuted therefor.
Resolved, that one hundred copies of the fore-
going resolution be printed and stuck up at the
corners of the streets, and the publication be
deemed notice. Vicksburg, July 5, 1835.

July 5, 1835! That was nearly twenty-four years ago! This
was untenable to McKay's way of thinking. How can any
ordinance twenty-four years old still hold sway? That aged
document must have been framed for posterity's sake and
nothing more. Surely the modern folks of Vicksburg no
longer held to such Jurassic beliefs! McKay was determined
to test the resolve of these Vicksburgians, and at the very
next saloon, he turned in, took a table, ordered a whiskey,
and set up for business.

Clifton Stewart had been watching for her all morning,
and when Mystie Waters finally did appear, coming down
the staircase of the *Tempest Queen* dressed for a day in
town, her loveliness nearly took his breath away. Her eyes
were impossibly dark and mysterious; her hair glistened like
the flicker of a raven's wing where it hung loose about her
shoulders beneath the pretty blue-and-yellow sun bonnet
and was touched by the sun. She had rolled the ends of her
hair into ringlets. Under the morning sun her skin was the
color of almonds, and she looked to Stewart a perfect
princess in her blue tarlatan skirts, belled out above a
steel-hoop crinoline. Her sleeves were puffed, and she wore
a little silver watch pinned near her shoulder.

Regarding her with open delight as she came down the
stairs, Clifton Stewart became aware of something vaguely
disturbing, and he had no idea why that should be, so he
immediately put the problem out of mind and met her at the
bottom tread.

"Are you going into town, Miss Waters?"

"Since we will be staying overnight, Maggie gave me the day off"—she smiled—"and I wanted to do a little shopping. Also, Maggie has a list of items she wants me to pick up."

"Would you mind having company on your errands?"

Her dark eyes caught the sun like polished onyx—or at least Clifton Stewart imagined so. "I would be pleased to have you accompany me, Mr. Stewart. Your eye is looking much better," she said approvingly.

"I intend to avoid flying fists from here on, if I can." He grinned and offered his arm, and to his delight, her hand settled gently upon it, and it felt to him as if that was exactly where it ought to be—where it ought to remain forever.

They made their way through the busy wharf district and into Vicksburg. "Whatever made you leave the South, Miss Waters?" he asked when they had gone a little way.

"I had no choice, Mr. Stewart. It was my father's decision, and I was only twelve at the time. But I think my heart has remained in the South all these years. Illinois can be a cold and dreary place in the winter."

"I should imagine." He looked at her. "I would prefer you calling me Clifton, or just plain Cliff."

She glanced over with smiling eyes. "Only if you call me Mystie, sir."

"Then Mystie it is!" he pronounced at once, and his brain reeled with delight when her hand tightened ever so gently upon his arm. "I have never met anyone named Mystie. Does it mean anything special?"

"No, I don't think so. My mother insisted upon the name. She has a sense of humor that is unequaled, I am afraid, and is quite intuitive. I guess she just liked the sound of the two names together. 'They don't have to mean anything if they make music for the ears,' Mother has said more than once."

Mystie drew up suddenly and pointed. "Oh, look. Isn't that a—"

Before she could finish, Clifton blurted out, "A scarlet tanager."

She smirked and said, "*Piranga olivacea.*"

Clifton looked at her, impressed, and added, "Of the family *Thraupidae.*"

Now it was Mystie's turn to be impressed. "Are you an ornithologist?"

"Only an amateur. I find it a pleasant diversion from my work. I'm really quite fond of the study. I enjoy nothing more than to take a spyglass out into the field with my notebook, and scare up a species or two that I have not yet cataloged. I'd hoped to take some time for it this trip."

"I love observing and identifying birds!"

Clifton's heart was racing. This woman was really too perfect. An unpolished diamond, and to have found her in, of all places, a riverboat, working as a chambermaid and galley cook.

"All right, how about that one?" She had spied another bird in the branches of a magnolia tree.

He squinted a moment. "I cannot see it plainly, but it looks to be a warbler." Just then the bird in question fluttered from the branches. "Ah-hah! It is a warbler. A cerulean warbler."

"*Dendroica cerulea.*"

His jaw dropped. "I am dumbfounded. Wherever did you learn all that? Where did you go to school?"

"School?" Mystie laughed. "I have never gone to school. My father was my only schoolmaster. He taught both my mother and me to read. I taught myself about birds."

He noted the touch of pride in her words. "Your knowledge of ornithology is excellent!"

"One day when I was quite young, after my father and I had spent the day walking through the woodlots between the fields, having a glorious time spying birds and trying to identify them, he brought home several huge volumes with hundreds of colored pictures of birds. They were written by a man named John James Audubon, and some of the birds he had painted were the very ones near our home, for this

Mr. Audubon had been through Louisiana in the 1820s, catching them and painting them."

"It's true. It was before I was born, but my father met the man. I, too, own copies of the very books you describe!"

"I studied Mr. Audubon's book until I feared the pages would fall out, and I think I learned the scientific name of every bird in Louisiana by the time we moved to Cairo. And when we did, I started all over again, learning the Northern birds. It was really very challenging."

"You are quite an extraordinary woman"—and inwardly he added, *I think I am in love with you.* Of course, he would never dare voice such a sentiment on such a short acquaintance as theirs, but already he was making plans to introduce this marvelous woman to his parents immediately upon his arrival at Baton Rouge. Oh, they would probably disapprove at first. She was obviously of a lower station in life than they had hoped he would marry from, but that made no difference to Clifton. All the woman of his station were so—he had to grope for the proper word—*superficial.* Yes, that was it. But Mystie. Ah, here was an extraordinary woman. A woman of substance! One he could share his life with!

Clifton Stewart was determined not to let her slip through his fingers—not for all the cotton or sugarcane in the South!

CHAPTER
FIFTEEN

"Gentlemen, gentlemen, gather round. Keep an eye on the queen. That pretty little lady is your card to fortune, yes she is. First you see her here, now see her there"—McKay shuffled the queen about the tabletop, mixing her up with a pair of twos, but making certain his fingers fumbled just a bit, and the smooth flow of the cards faltered as if being manipulated by an amateur—"now over here. Keep your eye on that lucky lady. Can your eyes move faster than my fingers? This here is my regular trade, my good men of Vicksburg, yes sir, and if your sight is faster than my fingers"—which he made sure at the moment it was—"then you win; if not, I win. I will always have two chances to your one; this is my stock-in-trade, gentlemen. Who will wager twenty dollars?"

If he kept up the patter, he was bound to attract a crowd, and indeed, he was beginning to draw one or two curious faces. It was nothing at all like the boomtown of the West where entertainment-starved miners were beating down his door to give him their hard-won gold. The Vicksburgians were cautious folks, and they considered him with a jaundiced eye. Oh, their curiosity was being tickled, he could see that, but as yet not one had stepped forward to actually try his luck against McKay.

Persistence, he reminded himself. Ah, what he wouldn't give for a reliable capper just now. Someone to get the ball rolling here. He thought back to that night on the wharf boat almost a week past, and the lovely Genevieve de Winter. Now, there was a capper! And a most lovely one at that.

He finished a shuffle. "Anyone care to tell me where the queen is?" he asked to no one in particular. One or two men grunted and shook their heads. A young fellow gave a disinterested shrug and pointed at the end card. McKay turned it over, and sure enough, it was the queen.

"That gentleman has the eye of an eagle," McKay pronounced, flipping over the other two cards, then beginning again. "If he had bet twenty dollars, he'd have won twenty dollars and be buying all you gentlemen a round of drinks, and I'd be a poorer man. That's the way this game goes. Sometimes I win, sometimes you win. It all depends on how good your eyesight is. Can your eyes move faster than my hands? It only stands to reason they can. Now, who will go fifty with me? Someone out there wants to win an easy fifty dollars. I back my bets with gold." McKay went on for another couple minutes, playing the cards back and forth, attracting the curious, but not the daring.

No one tried to stop his game, so he figured that silly ordinance from 1835 was only a relic of history now. Just the same, the Vicksburgians seemed a sensible lot, not easy to part from their money, and McKay was frustrated at every turn.

Finally an older gentleman with a long beard and bald head peered over the shoulder of those men near McKay's table. He watched McKay move the cards ineptly, and after a few minutes said, "I'll go two dollars."

"Two dollars? Surely we can make it more interesting. How about twenty?"

"Two or nothing at all."

"Well, I see you are a man who knows his own mind. Very well, take a seat, and let's see the color of your money."

The men gave him room. The old man fished eight quarters from his pocket and set them on the table. McKay had no gold denominated that small, but the barkeep gave him change in the form of silver dollars on a ten-dollar note issued by the Bank of Boston.

Well, it was a start, McKay mused as he turned the cards over and began moving them across the table. "Now, the queen is the lady you must watch," he said, sliding the cards smoothly, but not too fast. This was his first nibble of the day, and it would not serve well to allow the old gentleman to lose his money. No sir, now was the time to prime the pump, and nothing primed better than a few dollars invested up front.

"Now you see her here, now you see her there, and now . . . now where?" McKay straightened up the three cards and asked the fellow to make his pick.

The old man considered a moment, winding a piece of his beard about his forefinger. Finally he decided. "She is in the middle." Behind him came a mix of groans and encouragement.

"Turn it over, sir," McKay offered.

He did and grinned broadly. "That was the easiest two dollars I ever made," he said, snatching up the money McKay had laid out.

"Well, you bested me that time, sir, yes, you surely did."

McKay turned the other two cards faceup. "You will give me a chance to win back my two dollars now? We might even make it more interesting. How about five dollars on the turn of the card?" McKay figured that was a reasonable step up from the man's initial wager.

The man stood. "Nope, I don't think so. I think I'll just take my winnings while I'm ahead."

"But you can't just walk away now." McKay could hardly believe his ears.

"I can and I will." McKay watched his two dollars march over to the bar, and a moment later the old man was sipping a beer. *Well, that was a failed attempt,* McKay scolded himself. He should have taken the man's two dollars when he had the chance!

But he kept a placid smile on his face and looked to the few remaining men standing about his table. "Well, gentlemen, you all saw how easy it is to win at this game," he said happily, trying to salvage something to build on. "Who will go another round with me? Who thinks their eyes are faster than my hands? Place a small bet—five dollars, ten, twenty?—and take a chance."

No one seemed too interested, and one by one they wandered off until McKay was alone, shuffling his cards, cursing the poison that had settled upon this otherwise delightful town. He considered going back to the *Tempest Queen* where he knew a decent game of cards could be had, but he resisted that. He had encountered something back there that he found disturbing, a thing some might call a conscience, and he wished to avoid facing that again as long as he could.

What he needed was a partner, a reliable capper who could step in at the right moment, place a big bet, win gaudily, and enthuse the others to take part in his—her?—good fortune.

Again his thoughts went back to that night, and he sighed, recalling the perfect way Genevieve de Winter had transmitted each card that Captain Hamilton held simply by the position in which she held her umbrella.

Now, she would be the capper!

The morning wore away and the afternoon marched on, and McKay had only a few nibbles, but no strikes, and at about three o'clock, he gathered up his paraphernalia and left the saloon, dejected, and made his way more or less in the direction of the wharves.

The afternoon was warm and pleasant, but McKay did not take much notice of it. Down on the wharves there were half a dozen riverboats docked and scores of men, black and white, moving freight and shouting orders. McKay didn't want to return to the *Tempest Queen* yet, and spying a dray parked in the shade of one of the wharf buildings with an old Negro sitting upon it, McKay wandered on over and sat next to the old man.

"Good day to you, sir," McKay said. "Mind if I join you?"

The Negro appeared indifferent about the matter and nodded his head and continued watching the activity on the wharves. McKay spent a few lazy minutes drawing circles in the dust with the end of his walking stick and after a while said, "It's a nice day."

The Negro just stared ahead.

"You live around these parts?"

The black man looked over slowly. His face was cut deeply with wrinkles, his cheeks gaunt, his eyebrows full and white. "No, suh. I live 'bout twelve miles south o' here."

"Well, then you're practically a resident of Vicksburg," McKay said, smiling. "What's your name?"

"Daniel."

"Got a last name, Daniel?"

"I belongs to Marster Briggs."

"I see. Well, nice town, Vicksburg, although not a very lively place," McKay said, trying to strike up a conversation. The day had been most depressing, and he needed some diversion.

The slave merely shrugged his shoulders. "If you say so, suh."

"It's very . . . civilized."

The black man seemed uncomfortable talking to him, and his eyes kept darting toward the darkened doorway of one of the nearby buildings. McKay fished around in his pocket and came up with a handful of the peanuts Mystie had brought to his room the night before. *What was it that she had called them? Ah, yes,* he remembered.

"Care for some pinders?" he asked.

The Negro glanced over, and his eyes brightened a bit. "Thank you, suh," he said, taking them gratefully and immediately cracking one between his teeth. McKay broke open a shell and chewed up the tasty legume.

"Pretty quiet town," McKay noted.

"Yes, suh."

"I've been all over the place and have yet to find a decent game of cards."

The Negro laughed and said, "Shoot. Hardly nobody goes into Vicksburg fer cards, suh."

"No?"

"No, suh. Why, thems what plays cards, deys goes over to dat wharf boat." He pointed down the wharf to a boat tied at the end of the line. It was a bustling place, but no one was carrying aboard cargo, and to McKay's untrained eye, there did not appear to be a trace of freight anywhere on her deck in spite of all the men wandering about. "Dat's where dey all goes to play cards."

"Ah-hah!" McKay suddenly understood, and he was hard-pressed to keep the elation from bursting forth with his words. "A floating gambling emporium!"

"Yes, I reckon, suh."

"Daniel!" a voice rang out.

The slave's head turned. A man was standing in front of

the door of a nearby building. He waved an arm and said, "Come along, Daniel. Time to get on home."

Daniel hopped off the dray. "Thanks fer the pinders, suh," he said and hurried off after his master, leaving a trail of shells behind. McKay likewise left the dray and started for the boat at the end of the line.

He noticed several things right off. The boat, indeed, carried no cargo. In fact, she had no wood for fuel anywhere upon her deck, and her boilers appeared partially dismantled, as if stripped sometime in the past for parts to be used on other boats. There was nothing aboard that resembled a crew, and she was not tied off with rope hawsers in the usual manner but was fastened in a more permanent arrangement by huge, black chains. In spite of her half-dismantled appearance, her railings were freshly painted, her decks scrubbed, her main cabin unusually busy.

McKay made his way up to the boiler deck. Near the stairs were two Negroes in black trousers and white shirts, strumming banjos. They had a hat turned up on the floor, and occasionally a passerby would toss a coin into it.

Noise and laughter came from her main cabin, and when he entered, the commotion of the gambling parlor was music to his ears, and he had to pause and catch his breath. A sea of green card tables spread out before him, with hazard boards and faro boards laid out, and roulette wheels spinning happily. A rising chorus of voices was urging a wheel of fortune on, while the click of the casekeeper, the rattle of the goose, and the call of the conductor swelled in the smoke-filled air; here was a riot of games with the clink of coins and chips sounding like the rustle of leaves in a fall wind.

Ah, this was paradise! "I love you, Vicksburg!" McKay sang out as he made his way into the crowd, feeling suddenly as if he had come home.

Mystie was feeling just a little bit guilty, but Clifton Stewart did not seem to mind. He was being the perfect gentleman, perfectly content to follow her around Vicksburg and wait patiently as she browsed the dress shops. Besides, she knew he would be insulted if she had insisted on carrying a single package of the more than half dozen she had already purchased. His arms were overflowing, his gait somewhat awkward, but what a perfect gentleman he was, and a true delight to be around.

Clever, witty, always proper. Clifton even laughed at her jokes, and somehow she had the feeling he was being sincere about it. And throughout the day they tested each other whenever one of them encountered a new species of bird. She held the superior knowledge, she soon realized, and on occasion missed naming a bird on purpose so that he could supply the correct nomenclature. More than her being always right, she enjoyed seeing his smile when he thought he was being helpful.

They had had dinner at a lovely restaurant, and he bought them ice cream afterward. He treated her special, as she had never been treated by any other young man. Much the way her father treated her whenever they were together. Although she had at first worried that their differences would be a wedge between them, she soon learned they had more in common than not. There was only that one stumbling block, and unfortunately, it was not a small one.

All and all, the day had been delightful. She had purchased everything on her list, including the kitchen items Maggie wanted. Mystie was thinking she ought to be returning to the boat, but she did not wish the day to end just yet. She was enjoying it too much, strolling along the sidewalk in the genial afternoon, at the side of Clifton Stewart—

Randall Statler stepped from a doorway and moved toward them to block their way. He was hatless, and his black hair was oily and unkempt. His ruddy and burned neck and cheeks above his black beard glistened in the sunlight. His shirt was opened at the neck, and a dirty bandanna was tied there, limp and wrinkled. His sudden presence startled her, while his leering eyes slowly surveyed her every curve, and an evil smile made its way onto his face.

Clifton Stewart appeared at first unaware of what had caused Mystie to come so quickly to a halt, but as she stood there watching Statler come nearer, he turned from her to the approaching man and recognized him as well. She heard him whisper beneath his breath, "Oh, no."

Statler ignored him and said to Mystie, "What a pleasant surprise running into you here." There was the odor of whiskey on his breath, and it made her recoil from him. "Why don't you and me go somewhere for a drink?"

Stewart stepped forward. "I must say, sir, you are most out of line."

Statler ignored him. "What do you say?"

"I say most definitely not!"

Statler only grinned more broadly, and with a dirty finger he raised her chin and looked at her, first from this way, and then that, in that same curious way he had the night he had followed her to Eli. He seemed to be looking for something, but what?

Mystie turned her face away, and he laughed. "You look pretty in the sunlight. Sunlight brings out the color in your skin."

Clifton Stewart shuffled the packages in his arms and stepped between them. "You are upsetting the lady. I must ask you to leave now or face the consequences!"

"Clifton," she interceded, sensing trouble coming, "let's be on our way."

"Not so fast, little lady. I figure you and me need to get to know each other better. Why don't you come to my cabin later on? I got a bottle, and we can have us a rip-roaring good time. Might even teach you a thing or two—"

"Enough!" Stewart roared. "You are foulmouthed and unscrupulous, and I insist that you leave us this very moment."

With no warning, Statler rounded on Stewart and brought

his knee up sharply into the younger man's groin. Stewart's eyes bulged, and with a renting peal of pain he buckled over. Not satisfied, Statler came up with a left hook that caught Clifton on the eye and jackknifed him backward. Mystie's packages went flying, and Clifton Stewart was sprawled out on the street, writhing in pain.

Grinning, Statler brushed off his hands and speared Mystie with a narrowed eye. "The kid never learns."

"You are a worthless bit of gutter scum," she shot back.

"Perhaps, but then, that still makes me better than you."

She raised an arm, and he reached out, snatching it in midair. He put his face close to hers and spoke softly, "I know your secret now, little lady. You might be able to hide it from most folks, 'specially moon-eyed fools like that one there. But I got you all figured out. I know why you find that nigger such a curious piece that you got to sneak down and talk to him in the dead of night."

"I don't know what you're talking about," she breathed. A bolt of fear had driven through her. *What did this awful man really know?*

"Liar. You know right enough what I mean, little lady, and if you don't want that fresh-faced dandy friend of yours to find out, too, you'll come up to my cabin and see me. Heh?"

Mystie licked her lips. She was aware of curious folks drawing near and of the groans of agony coming from the man curled up in a knot on the street. She desperately wanted to get away from Statler, but he held her in a viselike grip, and she had to learn how much he really did know about her.

In desperation, she nodded her head. "All right. I'll come up to see you," she said, loathing the words that he had forced her to utter.

"Tonight."

"No—" Her thoughts raced ahead. It could not be tonight. She had already made certain plans for Eli, and this evening may have been just the opportunity she was looking for, but timing was critical and she could not meet Statler tonight! "Tomorrow night," she said. "It's the earliest I can come."

He released her arm and slowly drank in her beauty. "I can wait. Tomorrow night will be just fine. Better not forget or get any clever ideas." Statler glanced down at Stewart. "Not unless you want the whole world to know your dark little secret." He laughed and pushed through the crowd and vanished into a nearby saloon.

CHAPTER SIXTEEN

Ah, the chatter of the chips, the ruffle of a deck of cards being expertly shuffled, the meteoric clicks of a wheel of fortune when first spun upon its axis—these were the things that gave him vitality! The "sawdust" in McKay's blood! Immediately the frustrations of the day melted away as he moved between the tables, peeking into a faro game here, pausing to see the results of a spin of the roulette wheel there. A bond of intimacy put McKay at once at ease. He had died and gone to heaven—or even better! He kept an eye open for a vacant table where he could set up his monte game as he strolled among the crowd with no immediate purpose of mind except to fill himself with the odors, the sounds, the colors of the gaming room.

Then he spied a table sitting all alone and waiting just for him, or at least so it seemed. With a grin of contentment, McKay angled across the room for that beckoning small island of green velvet. Yes, heaven could be no more heavenly, he mused, and he briefly entertained the notion of sending back to the *Tempest Queen* for his belongings and taking up permanent residence in this lovely, *civilized* town of Vicksburg. And if the owners of this gambling emporium decided to cast off and move its location farther upriver or down, McKay would have no trouble with that, either, so long as he could hitch a ride—

Just then a movement caught his eye that ripped asunder these pleasant thoughts and instantly riveted his attention. He drew up at once and peered hard across the busy room, not certain at first if he had seen what he thought he had seen, hardly believing it could be true. Then he saw her again, leaving a gaming table, floating across the floor like a angel. It was true, he had gone to heaven!

Genevieve de Winter!

He forgot the table and redirected his steps. Wouldn't she be surprised to see him. Had she already taken up with another gambler? He hoped not, but even so, he knew he could convince her to work at his side. Together they would be invincible. They might even make plans to take on the famous Devol himself! Oh, wasn't life sweet. Oh, its blessings! All one had to do was make a good and conscious effort to help one's neighbor—no, not *neighbor*, one's *brother* and *sister*—and all the good from above would come down to fill one's little world. Oh, what good fortune to have been clubbed over the head. That momentous occurrence had caused him to see the light and had changed his life!

Genevieve de Winter was making for a door now, and McKay picked up his pace, but he was slowed by the glut of sporting chaps laying their money down. He could not lose her now. He considered calling out, but that would be lowly, and McKay was anything but lowly. Instead, he waved an arm. This caught her attention, and she stopped to stare at him as he weaved a circuitous path across the room.

He grinned and waved again, and as he drew closer, he could see her eyes narrow down, and then the oddest expression came to her face, as if she had just discovered a fly in her pudding. The look of surprise turned to shock and remained only an instant, and the next instant Genevieve de Winter grabbed up her skirts and dove headlong for the door.

"Wait!" McKay called out. Lowly or not, he could not allow her to disappear—not now!

McKay leaped around the tables and in a few seconds found himself at the door where she had disappeared. Searching the crowded promenade outside, he caught a glimpse of flying blue taffeta one deck below, a flash of umber from her straw bonnet, a hint of gold in her flowing hair.

"Miss de Winter!" he shouted at the railing, and went charging through the crowd to a ladder that descended to the main deck. He had seen the crew of the *Tempest Queen* virtually slide down similar rope-and-wood ladders, their feet gliding along the outside of them, never wasting a moment to actually touch one of the treads. It was a speedy way to drop from deck to deck that he had admired from a distance, but now, as McKay attempted to duplicate the maneuver, his feet became entangled, his palms burned as the rope sped past. He struggled halfway down and was forced to stop and to reestablish himself on the ladder, and then resume his descent in the normal manner, having lost several valuable seconds.

He stumbled to the main deck in time to see Genevieve de Winter flying down the landing stage, dashing toward a street that led up into Vicksburg, her hat clasped to her head with one hand, her skirts held up a bit with the other. McKay scrambled around obstacles, and then he, too, was sprinting off the boat. He paused on the wharf, searched, caught of glimpse of her just turning the corner, and ran on. She could not get away. He had to catch up with her!

But his head was beginning to pound. Dr. Reuben had warned him that his concussion might cause dizziness and that he needed to stay calm. McKay felt the first waves of nausea hit him and wash over him. He drew up, breathless, fell against a building momentarily until it passed, and then plunged on. The corner was only a few dozen paces ahead, and he could see it was crowded with people. They seemed to be swimming in sunlight.

He was suddenly ill, and he had to stop again. His head seemed to whirl, and his legs wobbled like spindly sticks, not up to the task of supporting him.

"You cannot lose her!" he admonished himself aloud as he tried to ignore the dizziness and the pain beginning to throb in his temples. He pushed on out of the shadows of the tall buildings, into the bright sunlight of the street where the woman of his dreams had turned.

His gaze shot along the street, but his head felt as if it were spinning like a top. He pushed on, until his knees buckled and he slumped against a wall. Groping at a brick window ledge, McKay pulled himself up and leaned back with his eyes squeezed shut, wanting to vomit and struggling desperately against it. He heard voices all about him; worried tones, scrambling feet. He wanted to tell them that he was all right and that this would pass, but he remained there with his eyes shut, breathing hard, thinking of the lovely Genevieve de Winter and how she had once again slipped out of his life.

The spell passed. But still he heard the voices and a sound of commotion coming from his left. He was certain it was because of his strange behavior, but when he opened his eyes, to his amazement, no one was paying the least attention to him. Their attention was directed a little distance away, at a man moaning painfully and lying in the street with his knees drawn up, and at the pretty lady whom McKay recognized at once.

McKay put his own problem aside and went unsteadily to Mystie. She was bent over the man lying in the street, and the area was littered with packages which some of the bystanders were beginning to collect for her.

"What happened here?"

Mystie glanced up, and at once relief shone in her pretty eyes. "Oh, it is you Mr. McKay! Please help me with Clifton."

"Clifton?"

"Mr. Stewart has been injured."

"Ah!" He finally looked at the fellow close enough to recognize him. "What has happened to him?" McKay caught Stewart beneath his arms and helped him to his feet. The man came up heavily, reluctantly, still bent into a tight knot and unable to straighten up fully. Another man leaped in to help, and together they hauled the groaning young planter over to a chair beneath an awning and lowered him into it.

Mystie, with the help of the folks of Vicksburg, gathered up her packages and deposited them in a pile alongside the chair, and peered anxiously into Stewart's contorted face.

"Will he be all right?"

"I don't know," McKay said. "What happened to him?"

"It was that slave hunter, Randall Statler. He kicked Clifton. Kicked him in the—" She bit back her words, unable to find a suitably delicate way to describe the attack, but from the look of embarrassment on her face, and the distinctive way that Stewart was warped, McKay understood immediately.

He grinned. "Oh, yes. He will recover. And he will not soon forget this incident." McKay spoke from experience.

"The man is a rogue—and a lecher."

"Statler?"

"Of course!" She was miffed that he had to ask.

"What provoked this?"

"He accosted me, and in plain view. Clifton came to my aid."

"Again?" McKay figured he hadn't fared any better this time than the first.

Mystie scowled hotly, then her look shot back to Clifton's face and her expression turned instantly soft. "Oh, his poor eye. Will you just look at it? It was beginning to heal so well."

"It looks most painful." McKay grimaced.

By this time, Stewart had regained his senses and was gently probing his face and groaning.

"You said you were going to avoid fists from here on out," she scolded, and there was no reproach in her voice, only a deep sadness.

He managed a grin through his pain. "He overstepped the bounds of decency, Mystie. I . . . I guess I am not much of a fighter, though. I did not do a very good job defending you."

"It's all right." She gently brushed his hair from his eyes.

Stewart said angrily, "By all rights, I ought to challenge the cad to a duel."

"You'll do no such sort, Mr. Clifton Stewart!" Mystie retorted. "It will get you killed."

"A Southern man does not allow scoundrels like Randall Statler to speak insultingly to a lady."

"I'll not hear of this foolishness."

"But it's the proper thing to do. It is the Southern way of handling men like Statler."

"It's the dumb thing to do! The South has a lot of dumb notions that have become archaic in this day and age. It's 1859, for heaven's sake. People ought to act more civilized—ought to treat other people as they would have themselves treated."

Stewart hung his head, properly chastised.

"I'm sorry, Clifton. I didn't mean to get angry. It's just that I don't want to see you hurt."

"We ought to get him back to the boat," McKay said.

Stewart glanced up at the sound of his voice. Seeing McKay there, he gave a faint grin. "When did you show up?"

"Just a few minutes ago."

His grin faltered. "Afraid I didn't make a very good showing of myself."

"At least you made a stand." McKay's voice became suddenly serious. "You will never make a good showing so long as you try to fight men like Statler fairly. When you are feeling a little better, you and I need to have a long talk." He helped him out of the chair.

"I can walk on my own," Stewart said, rising painfully but steadily enough.

Mystie gathered up her packages. McKay bent to help her, momentarily felt the ground lurch beneath his feet, and discovered a second later that he was slumped against the building.

"Are you all right?" Mystie asked.

He smiled wanly. "A lingering effect of my concussion, I fear. I overdid myself today."

"I think we need to get you *both* back to the boat," Mystie said, taking over the reins of command.

"I think . . . I think that is a capital idea, Miss Waters." He didn't want to return now, not with Genevieve de Winter somewhere in town, but with his brain carrying on like a circus tumbling act, he had no choice.

If only she had not run off! What, he wondered, *could have caused her to react as she had?* He was puzzled, and he was determined to have an answer—but not now. Now he needed to rest, to get well. Then he would find his answer.

Slowly, the three of them started along the street.

"My watch!" McKay cried out. "I left it to be cleaned and oiled."

The troupe did an about-face and made their way to the watchmaker's shop where McKay collected his Jürgensen.

His head was clearing when he emerged from the small, dark shop. He was feeling better as they retraced their steps.

Suddenly it was Mystie's turn to remember something. The pharmacy sign on the shop across the street must have brought it to mind.

"Now, you two wait right here," she said at the doorway. "I won't be but a moment." She went inside.

"Quite a woman," Stewart said with bald admiration when she had gone. He was leaning against the building, touching his swelling eye.

"Yes, she is," McKay agreed absently. He was thinking instead of Genevieve de Winter.

"I think I'm in love."

This brought McKay's attention around. He hitched up an eyebrow. "Does she know?"

"I've not told her . . . not in so many words, but I am wearing my feelings on my shirtsleeves. I think it impossible that she should be blind to them."

This sounded serious. As he thought it over, McKay reached a hand into his pocket. "Care for a pinder?"

"A what?"

"Pinder. It's a local word for—"

"Yes, yes. I know what it means. It's not a local word, at least not for white folks. It's slave talk. Wherever did you pick it up?"

McKay was about to tell him, but reconsidered. He glanced through the window where Mystie was taking a small brown-paper package from the pharmacist across the counter. He shrugged his shoulders. "I suppose I must have heard someone on the *Tempest Queen* call them that. I don't seem to recall, exactly."

Stewart took the peanut and laughed. "Better be careful what you say in these parts. People might start to wonder whether you have Negro blood in your veins."

"That would be bad?" McKay asked innocently.

"Bad?" Stewart laughed again. "Sir, in the South, a drop

of colored blood makes you as much a Negro as that runaway bound to the deck of the *Tempest Queen*."

McKay grinned. "Well, then, I better watch what I say. I wouldn't want to be sold down the river for a slip of the tongue."

They laughed at his little joke.

Mystie appeared in the doorway then, tucking the paper package onto her handbag. "Now," she said, once again taking up the reins, "it's back to the boat for the two of you. To bed for you, Mr. McKay. And someplace out of Mr. Statler's way for you, Mr. Stewart."

"Aye, aye, Captain Waters." McKay gave her a mock salute and a grin. His eyes locked on to hers with a sudden curiosity.

She smiled faintly and shoved an extra package into his arms. "You are obviously well enough to carry one more of these." She took them each by the arm and directed them down toward the wharf. McKay went along without resistance, but he kept alert for a glimpse of blue and umber and gold and that perfect face of the woman he remembered so well from the wharf boat, standing near the stove, absently turning an umbrella in her hands.

But he also had become curiously engaged in watching Mystie Waters. McKay had always been a student of people, with an eagle eye for detail, and now she was to be his object of study.

"How is the work progressing, Mr. Seegar?" Captain Hamilton stepped into the busy engine room and out of the way of the scurrying crew members hauling out armfuls of discarded asbestos wrapping and lengths of rusty pipes.

"Hey, Captain?" Seegar shouted back, cupping a hand behind his ear.

"I say, how is the work progressing?"

Seegar was stretched out on his back on top of a pair of thick pipes, turning a huge monkey wrench attached to another pipe overhead. He released the wrench, letting it remain gripping the new pipe, and wormed his way out of the rat's nest of plumbing, mopping the sweat from his forehead with a dingy red rag.

"Work is coming along as can be expected. The new pipes fit perfectly, and that should cause no more delay. Got Mr. Attebury backwashing the boilers—figured since we was laid up here, now would be a good time, and it needed doing anyway. Far as I can see, it still is going to be late tonight before I get her all put back together. Another couple hours to build up a proper head of steam. You are looking at morning before we can get back on our way, Captain."

"Very well. It's better to take the time now and do the job right than to have an accident later on that will put us on the bottom of the river. Do it properly, Mr. Seegar. I'll be by to see how it's coming later on."

Captain Hamilton left the engine room and was making his way up to the texas when the retired general found him. It was late afternoon, but the sun still burned hot through the misty air overhead, and the humidity was climbing; a foretaste of the coming summer when most human activity draws to a slow crawl. Just yet, however, the heat and humidity were only a harbinger of things to come.

"Captain Hamilton, I have been looking for you. Are you engaged in ship's business?"

"At the moment I am not. What is it I can do for you?"

The retired general laughed slyly, lowered his voice conspiratorially, and told the captain that the wealthy planter was feeling lucky, and he was preparing to secure a large purse for an afternoon of *serious* card playing.

"Now you and I both know the gentleman is only a marginal card player," the retired general said, as if taking Hamilton into his confidence. "Since you have played cards with us more than a few times, I knew you'd want to get in on this game and perhaps pocket a handsome piece of change. It would add nicely to your retirement, which you have spoken of. We both know that concerning cards, you are a crackerjack player, Captain Hamilton, and you will profit easily if he is in a sporting mood." The retired general nudged Hamilton genially in the arm, grinning, and there was a glint of intrigue in his eyes.

Hamilton's palms had begun to itch. He slipped his hands into his pockets and said casually, "I am free for the afternoon. I was going to spend it in my quarters, but a game of cards might be an interesting diversion." He'd hoped he had sounded sufficiently indifferent about the matter, even though the retired general's words had stropped his interest to a razor-keen edge, and he could already feel a quickening in his pulse.

Damn it all! What is this hold that cards and games of chance have over me? At times Hamilton wished he could be free of them entirely. Yet whenever he tried to put them out of his life, the devil himself, it seemed, would mount up an attack against him, and the next instant he'd be scrambling for the nearest game—any game—and like as not lose every penny in his pocket while at it.

"Good!" the retired general exclaimed, clasping Hamilton on the shoulder. "Then let's hurry before some lucky fellows nab our chairs."

Hamilton allowed himself to be led along, disgusted with himself, yet elated at the same time. He never could understand these ambivalent feelings that came over him whenever he was around a gambling table. In the main cabin, Klack and the wealthy planter were at their usual table, chatting amiably when the retired general showed up.

"I found our fourth player," he announced, and they all seemed surprised and delighted when Captain Hamilton took the chair.

"Well," Klack drawled, "what will the game be this afternoon."

"How about something new?" the wealthy planter suggested, reaching under his coat for a fresh package of cards. "How about poker? Five-card draw."

Hamilton agreed to the game without thinking about it, for his attention had suddenly been drawn to the rows and rows of neatly stacked gold coins and the bundle of bank notes in front of the wealthy planter. A king's fortune in some circles. Certainly more money than Hamilton could ever hope to get his hands on without liquidating every possession he owned.

"Then poker it is," the retired general announced happily, unloading a pile from his pockets as well. Only Klack seemed to be short on the money side, but even a casual count told Hamilton that the small pile of gold coins in front of the frontiersman amounted to well over a thousand dollars.

This was going to prove to be quite some game, Hamilton thought grimly, and he had a sudden urge to make an excuse and leave it. Yet he could not, and as if under the control of someone else, he, too, put up his money.

CHAPTER SEVENTEEN

At the knock on his door, McKay threw himself into his bed and covered his eyes with an arm.

"Come in," he said weakly.

Dr. William Reuben stepped inside, closing the door behind him, and for a long while said nothing, but stood there with a pinched gaze and a displeased look upon his round face.

McKay peeked out from under his arm, looking contrite. "So, she told you." He returned his arm across his eyes. He figured Mystie would have informed the doctor of his near swoon earlier, and he had only been waiting for Reuben to show up.

"You don't seem to understand how serious a matter a concussion can be, young fellow," Reuben said finally.

"Believe me, doctor, my only intentions were to take a leisurely stroll on a lovely spring morning, and perhaps find a friendly game of cards. What could have been the harm in that?" McKay figured the bit about chasing Genevieve de Winter up and down the streets of Vicksburg might be a thing best left out.

"Apparently even that small endeavor has proved too much for you. Do I need to give you something that will make you stay in bed?"

"Such as?" McKay peeked curiously out at the doctor.

Reuben patted his black bag. "I'm sure I can find something in here that will do the trick."

McKay frowned and shook his head. "No, that will not be necessary."

Reuben put a hand to McKay's forehead. "Well, at least you don't have a fever. Now I must insist, sir, that you remain in your cabin tonight. Try to go to sleep early. If you think you might need something to help, I have a powder I can give you."

"I am completely done in, Doctor. I will be asleep almost immediately after you leave." He hoped the suggestion was not too subtly cloaked that Reuben would miss it.

Reuben chewed his lip in thought. "I'll take you at your word, Mr. McKay, but remember, it is only yourself you are hurting."

The doctor left, and McKay gave him a couple minutes before he swung his legs off the bed and stood, slipping on his coat and hat and taking up his walking stick. His head had cleared an hour earlier, and he could see no good reason to waste the rest of the afternoon and evening in bed. Besides, he had things he needed to do.

Opening the door a crack, he glanced up the promenade and then down. There was no Dr. Reuben to be seen, but there were plenty of folks around, and that would help him blend in. He slipped outside, locked his door behind him, and moving as swiftly as he dared without drawing undue attention to himself, McKay left the *Tempest Queen*. Once upon the wharf, he turned his feet downriver toward the gambling boat permanently moored there.

"Look, Mama, there is that big boat again. The one with the clouds and the sun painted on its paddle box. Remember, it passed us by two days ago?"

"What is that, Nathan?" Sara Gardner pushed a loose length of hair from her eyes and patted her brow dry with a sleeve. She was leaning hard on the tiller, forcing the lumbering raft to remain in the middle channel where the current had taken it safely around the spit of land that rose in high terraces to their right and poked out into the river like a long, pointing finger. Coming immediately around this spit of high ground, she spied the busy wharves of Vicksburg and the tall white wedding cake of a boat moored there, gleaming under a hazy late-afternoon sun.

Nathan pointed again. "See, there it is." He squinted and sounded out the name lettered across the upward curve of the boat's paddle box. "*Tempest Queen*," he read. "See, it is the very same boat."

"Why, sure enough, it is," Sara said distantly. Her concern at the moment, however, was not on fancy riverboats, but on keeping the raft's forward end pointed in the proper direction and in the middle of the channel where the swift high water could move them along away from the submerged dangers that lay closer in to shore.

"We are passing her up," Nathan exclaimed, and he jumped up and down clapping his hands as if this trip downriver was one grand race and their competition was the great steam-driven machines that belched smoke and beat river water into froth.

"So we are." Sara was distracted. She had been fighting the river for three hours and was exhausted. She considered calling her father to have him take over at the tiller, but the old man had wrestled it all morning and that was not fair to him. "Nathan," she said finally, her exasperation growing, "go try to wake your pa up."

The boy balked and glanced at the legs hanging out of the back of the wagon that was lashed to the deck. From under the canvas came erratic snores, punctuated occasionally by sputters and coughs. Nathan turned his large, fearful eyes up at his mother.

"I don't want to, Mama. Papa will get mad at me."

"Go on and do it. If he gets mad at anyone, it will be me. Don't worry, honey. I won't let him hit you again."

Nathan was still unsure. "Maybe Grandpa can wake him?" he suggested.

"No, you do it. Grandpa is resting, and it's about time your father began pulling his weight around here."

The boy started for the wagon, hesitated, then turned back. "Mama?"

"What, Nathan?"

"Why does Papa always fall asleep in the middle of the day. Is he sick?"

She turned her face up toward the hot sun that burned upon her skin, smelled the moisture of all the rain they had been having being sucked from the wooden planks beneath her feet, felt the climbing humidity. How did she answer a question like that? She answered it the only way Sara Gardner knew how to answer any question, and that was truthfully. "Your Pa is sick, Nathan," she said after a moment, "but not with the kind of sickness we usually think of. He's got a poison in him."

"Is that why he drinks whiskey? To get rid of the poison?"

She gave a short, bitter laugh. "The whiskey is the poison."

Nathan looked confused. "Then why does he keep drinking it?"

Sara shook her head. "I don't know, honey. It's all part of the sickness. I don't understand it." Her eyes narrowed, and her voice grew stern. "Only take heed what you see here,

Nathan. Don't you ever start drinking whiskey, for you will likely come down with the same disease."

"And I'd be like him?"

The disgust she heard in her son's voice toward his father sickened Sara. She nodded her head slowly. "Yes, you will be like him then."

She couldn't tell what the boy was thinking at that moment. His feelings remained hidden behind an unchanging expression, but his eyes had widened, and after a moment he made a tentative approach toward the wagon and the snoring man that lay inside.

"Papa?" his small voice said.

The man continued to snore.

"Papa?" Nathan repeated louder.

A snort, a sputter, an unpleasant snarl as he sucked phlegm from his lungs and spat it out. "What the hell you waking me for?" Gearson growled groggily. There was a sudden flutter of movement inside the wagon and then the sharp sudden crack of flesh against flesh, and the next instant Nathan was scrambling out of the wagon. He rushed to his mother's side, holding a hand to a red welt spreading across his face, tears welling up in his big, scared eyes, trying desperately not to cry.

"Damn you, Gearson!" Sara hissed as the man stumbled out of the wagon and stood for a moment swaying and staggering back a step to catch his balance. "You had no right to hit him."

Gearson shifted his reddened eyes at her, his voice was a dry croak. "I've told you before, no one is to bother me." Even after four hours of sleep, his words were a drunken slur.

"I told Nathan to wake you. You had no cause to strike the boy," Sara shot back hotly.

He advanced on her suddenly, swinging an arm. She ducked easily under his flying hand and released the tiller. The current drove it hard into his gut. "You're still drunk, you worthless husband. Try to hit me or my children again and we are leaving you."

"You ain't got nowhere to go," he answered, rubbing his stomach and working his dry lips. "Damn, I'm thirsty. Why the hell did you wake me, Sara?"

"It's your turn at the tiller."

He glanced down at the long rod in his hand, discovering it there for the first time. "Oh." He blinked, growled up more phlegm from his lungs and spat it out, but he missed the river that was only three feet away and left a yellow slimy smear on the deck.

"I got to take a leak." He pushed the tiller back at Sara, unbuttoned his fly, and peed a long yellow stream out into the river.

Sara looked away in disgust.

He finished, dribbling on the deck near their water barrel, buttoned up his fly, pulled a chair around, reached back into the wagon for his lover, and cradled her safely in his arms.

"Do you really need more of that?"

He ignored her and assumed the rudder, staring blankly ahead, tasting his lover's lips, smacking his own in delight.

She knew that she would get no rest, watching out that he did not run them up on a snag or bury them in the flooded shoreline, but at least Gearson was being made to do his part of the work, and there was, if nothing else, a modicum of satisfaction in that. Frowning, she took up a bucket of river water and tossed it onto the urine and phlegm. That done, Sara examined Nathan's face and told him to go inside the little shack for a while and play quietly with his sister.

By the time Nathan had gone into the shack, Vicksburg and the *Tempest Queen* were already far behind them. Sara forgot them both as she found a place to sit on an upturned barrel to keep an eye on the river ahead and the drunken fool at the tiller.

He found the place exactly as he had left it, still a bundle of joyous activity and luscious noises and smells, but this time Dexter McKay did not succumb to their magic. He had but a single purpose for being here.

He stopped inside the door and stood against the wall. Only his eyes moved, touching briefly each table, each gaming machine, each face. Genevieve de Winter was not to be found here. Well, she would most likely keep low until he had left, he decided, still not knowing why she should have fled from him in the first place. She could not have known he had discovered her part in Banning's ruse against Captain Hamilton, so what could she have possibly feared from him?

More than anything else, McKay needed to know the answer to that question.

He spent a full twenty minutes doing nothing but standing unobtrusively at the door, studying the people in the gaming parlor and those that entered and left. Satisfied that she was not aboard, he made his way back to the wharf and into town.

Strolling deep in thought along the sidewalk, he kept an eye alert for Genevieve, but now his goal was something else. It was almost six o'clock by his newly cleaned and oiled watch, and many of the businesses were closing their doors. He noted a general mercantile shop across the street and angled toward it. A moment before he arrived, the sign on the window flipped from Open to Closed. The proprietor was making his way across the floor toward a back door when McKay rapped on the glass with his walking stick and pressed his nose to it.

The shopkeeper, a young-faced man with a fringe of white hair about a bald head that looked most out of place against his pink, smooth cheeks, turned back. *"I am closed,"* he mouthed soundlessly, and pointed at the sign.

"I must make a purchase!" McKay shouted through the glass.

The young/old man shrugged his shoulders, turned up his palms in a helpless gesture, and shook his head.

McKay rapped again when he turned away.

A look of exasperation crossed the proprietor's face. *"Closed,"* he mouthed with exaggerated largeness.

McKay grabbed into his pocket and pressed a gold eagle against the windowpane. This brought the storekeeper's interests alive. With a show of reluctance, he shuffled back to the door, turned a key, and pulled it open a crack.

"I'm closed," he said, eyeing the gold coin. "What is it you want?"

"I must make a purchase, and it cannot wait until morning. It is an emergency." To the man's astonishment, McKay pushed past him and stopped in the middle of the store looking about.

"Err, what is it you are looking for?" the proprietor asked, attempting to regain control of the situation.

McKay turned on him, his eyes large and animated. "A file." Immediately he shifted his gaze back to the shelves of merchandise standing about.

"A file?"

"Yes, a file. You know, for cutting metal?"

"Yes, of course, I know what a file is used for. Only, what sort of emergency—"

"My dog you see. He is caught in a . . . um . . . a fence, yes, that is it. And I need to free him."

The proprietor viewed McKay narrowly. "Perhaps then, a pair of wire cutters would work better?"

"Wire cutters? I hadn't thought of that. Show me wire cutters."

"Just come this way." The man guided him down an aisle.

McKay examined the wire cutters there, considered their heft and size, and then shook his head. "No, these won't do. Too light."

"Too light? What sort of fence is it your dog is caught in?" the proprietor inquired, bewildered.

McKay turned on him suddenly, "Oh, it is a very big fence, indeed. Most heavy. You see, it was built to keep in the elephants."

"Elephants? In Vicksburg?" The storekeeper retreated half a step and gave McKay a pacifying smile.

"For the circus, man. It's for the circus!" McKay said with impatience and a wide grin.

The man glanced at McKay, and then at the doorway, as if measuring the distance to it and calculating his chances of escaping this madman.

"Um . . . what circus?"

McKay clasped the fellow on the shoulder. His head wagged condescendingly. "My dear man, the circus is not here yet." He fished into his pocket, fumbled through a sheath of business cards and extracted one, showing it to him:

Clarence Mus
Centerville and Gnottly Circus
Croakswood, New York

"The circus is coming in a couple of weeks, and then so will the elephants. You see now? I'm merely traveling ahead making arrangements."

The proprietor reached for the card, but McKay snatched it away and returned it with the others into his pocket. He would have to replace them all, he thought obliquely. They did not fair well from the dunking, and in spite of the care he had taken in drying them, the edges had curled and they were all water-spotted.

"Now, I need a file. The dog in question is a highly trained and valuable high-wire performing canine." McKay was warming to the tale and did not wish to relinquish it prematurely.

"Right this way, Mr. Mus."

McKay handled several different sharp files before deciding on a bright, heavy bastard. "This will do nicely."

"That will be twenty-seven cents."

To the proprietor's surprise, McKay dropped the gold coin into his open palm.

On the street, he slipped the weighty tool into his inside coat pocket and headed back to the wharf and the *Tempest Queen.*

He made it aboard without incurring the wrath of Dr. Reuben, went up to his cabin, put the file safely away at the bottom of his valise, and straightened up his coat, smoothing it back in place. He adjusted his tie, slicked down his eyebrows with a moist finger, and grinned at himself in the looking glass. He was finally going to do something good for someone else, and he wasn't quite certain how to handle the strange feeling coming over him. Approving of the image that looked back at him, McKay settled the tall hat onto his head and left by way of the main cabin door.

The main cabin was a busy place now that evening was approaching, and the passengers, back from a day's excursion into Vicksburg, were turning their attentions to other forms of entertainment. The little string band was playing unobtrusively off in a corner near the ladies' parlor, while most of the gentlemen aboard had gravitated toward the other end of the boat where cigar smoke, the clink of whiskey glasses, and the soft whisper of cards being dealt out lent a warm and friendly ambience.

McKay did not see Reuben about, and hoping the doctor had retired to his quarters for the night, he strode out in search of a card game, but almost immediately his view caught the back of Captain Hamilton. The captain was hunched forward with his head so tucked down that his blue cap seemingly rested on the tops of his collar. McKay diverted from his path and angled toward the captain's table. He was not surprised to find the same three men there . . . and once more he had an odd impression of vicious fish circling and about to attack.

McKay stood quietly for a moment, watching the cards go around. The captain appeared to be holding his own, but McKay understood that was only temporary. Unobserved as he was, blending in with the few other curious onlookers, McKay had an opportunity to see the three men in action, and it didn't take long for him to note the little signals that passed between them.

A touch of a mustache, a pair of crossed fingers placed casually by a coffee cup, a cigar tapped three times into an ashtray when no ashes were present. To McKay's trained eyes, the wealthy planter, the retired general, and Klack might as well have been shouting aloud the values of the cards in their hands across the table, but to every other eye there, nothing remarkable was happening, except that a large sum of money was making its way slowly around the table, with more than a few extra coins falling in front of Captain Hamilton to keep him interested.

But why?

Hamilton was well-to-do by the day's standards, but he was not a rich man, and McKay could see by the stakes on the table that these boys were fishing for bigger game than the old captain, only two years from retirement, could possibly hope to offer.

Then what did they want? What did Hamilton have that these men wanted to take away from him?

McKay's scowl deepened. Although he did not know what their ultimate goals were, he did, however, know for a fact that Captain William Hamilton was their designated pigeon. They had been carefully grooming him for something big since they had come aboard.

At another time, even two days earlier, McKay would have grinned into his hat and watched the outcome with a detached professionalism. But just now an anger welled up inside, and he was aware of an unreasonable concern for this old gentleman who had befriended him and had offered him aid when he had thought McKay had needed it.

He grimaced. Even now that lie, told easily enough back on the wharf boat of Napoleon, was a prick in his conscience. So much had changed for McKay that his entire being was wrenched, as if dragged out by the roots, shaken off, and set down in new soil. He did not particularly like it, he even resisted it, but there was no denying that this innocent trip down the river had changed him.

McKay cleared his throat and got their attention. The retired general grinned easily up at him while the wealthy planter seemed perturbed at the interruption, and Klack's stare darted up at him from the cards held close to his shirt.

Captain Hamilton looked over his shoulder. "Mr. McKay," he said happily, but with an underlying tenseness, as if he had been under enormous strain. "How are you feeling this evening?"

"Better, Captain. Err . . . could I possibly have a moment to speak with you . . . alone?"

"This is somewhat irregular. We are in the middle of a game, and the stakes are mounting," the wealthy planter said, irritated.

McKay smiled. "I see that, sirs, and I am certainly happy that I am only watching. That much money would give me the shakes."

The retired general's grin widened genially. "We are all pretty tense here. A break might do us all some good."

So, the retired general is the leader. These other two are his cappers.

Klack was nervous and unhappy about the interruption. He scratched at his beard, but not too hard, McKay noted, choking back his amusement.

The wealthy planter put his cards on the table, facedown, and pushed back his chair. "Oh, all right. I'll just stretch my legs."

Klack stood, too, but he remained within arm's reach of the cards and the gold, and McKay noticed for the first time that the buckskinner carried a big pistol tucked under his beaded waistband.

Hamilton said, "I won't be but a moment, gentlemen." He left his cards on the table and stepped off a few paces into the recess of a doorway. "Now, what is it that I can do for you, Mr. McKay?" He worked his arm in a circle and stretched the kinks from his back muscles.

"Err . . . how is the game going, Captain?" McKay tried to sound casual.

"It's going well enough. I've won more than I've lost, and that is all one can ask for, but that's not why you called me away." McKay detected a note of defensiveness.

"Actually, Captain Hamilton, that is why I called you away."

The captain's eyes became knife slits. "I don't need anyone watching over my shoulder, sir. I'm fully capable of orchestrating my own life."

There was too much force in the captain's words, McKay thought. Hamilton was under tremendous strain. Perhaps he had already wagered more than he could afford to lose. McKay wanted to help, but calling Hamilton's opponents out as cheats and frauds—a thing he had already done once with Banning, and once was quite enough—would only embarrass and embitter the captain. No, all he could do was offer a warning and hope the captain took it seriously enough to withdraw from the game.

"I don't mean to intrude, Captain, but having watched those three men play, I have a feeling that all may not be on an honest course."

The captain eased back from his hair-trigger setting. "I appreciate your concern, Mr. McKay, but I can assure you I have my game completely under control." He laughed then. Draining a bit of nervous energy, McKay suspected. "And besides, only our friend, the retired general, has any real skill. Those other two merely bumble along, losing their money. And I find the sport of it quite reward enough in itself."

McKay frowned. He could not force this man to do anything, but he knew the captain would not be smiling so easily later tonight, when the retired general decided it was time to draw in the net and haul his prize aboard. McKay had a fleeting vision of Hamilton's head upon a silver platter.

"Very well, Captain. I apologize for intruding. I . . . ." He stammered. The words he was about to speak were truthful, and for McKay, hard to bring out. "I . . . have come to regard you as a friend, Captain, and I do not wish to see you injured by men with quick hands and no scruples." There, it was said. McKay felt his head whirl, and he knew this time it had nothing to do with a silver-clawed walking stick that had crashed down upon it.

Captain Hamilton's scowl softened. "I appreciate the concern, Mr. McKay. But do not worry for my sake. I have this game under control." He laughed then. "Their money is as good as in my pocket even now."

McKay could not return his smile. About all he could manage was a fleeting grimace. "Very well, Captain. Then by all means, enjoy yourself tonight. Only—"

Hamilton had started away. Now he paused and looked back. "Yes?"

"Only one parting word of advice, and take it as you wish."

"Go on."

"Don't wager more than you can afford to lose."

Hamilton's eyes clouded. He nodded his head. "Always wise advice, sir."

"Good evening."

"Good evening, Mr. McKay."

Dexter McKay watched Hamilton return to the table. With a heavy heart, he made his way to the front doors and out onto the promenade.

CHAPTER EIGHTEEN

What were those three scoundrels after?

McKay tightened his grip on the railing, watching the river turn black ahead of the bow. A Negro deckhand was lighting the torch baskets. Their glow turned the main deck below, and the river that roiled past, a bloody red. The light from the main cabin behind him pushed his shadow far out over the cargo-glutted main deck where deck passengers huddled and talked and slept wherever they could find a place. As McKay watched, a second shadow moved across his own and stopped next to him.

"Mr. McKay?" the voice inquired behind him.

McKay kept his view on the torch baskets below and the

scattered points of lights ahead, where another boat was tied up at the wharf. "Mr. Stewart. Pleasant evening, is it not?" He looked to his left as the young planter joined him at the railing, resting his elbows on it, looking depressed. "Where is your lovely young lady companion?"

"Oh, Mystie had to go to work. She is on night shifts."

McKay returned his view to the dark water. "You look like a man with a problem, Mr. Stewart."

The young planter did not speak at once, but McKay was aware of his fidgeting from foot to foot. When his words finally did flow, they began as a slow trickle and gushed suddenly into a flood. "I made a fool of myself this afternoon. I should have known that I was no match for a man like Statler. I tried to defend Mystie, and it almost ended up the other way around, with my groveling in the street and her standing up to the rogue. What is it about me, Mr. McKay? Why do I bumble everything I try? I made a fool of myself that first time, did much worse the second. Mystie needs a strong man, one her equal. Not an inept milksop who ends up on the ground while men like Statler strut and push out their chests. He wants her, he has made that plain, and I see no reason why Mystie should choose a namby-pamby weakling like me over him."

Stewart blurted it out all in one breath, and now he heaved in a huge gulp of air and hung his head. His tone grew thoughtfully somber. "You seem always to be in control, Mr. McKay. I'd give anything to possess even a little of your confidence. Earlier you said something about a talk . . . ?" He ended on a slightly more hopeful note.

McKay fished out his silver case, offered Stewart a cigar, lit them both, and returned the match safe to his pocket. He drew in a long lungful of smoke and blew it out into the night where a warm wind snatched it up and dissipated it high above the main deck. He thought a moment. "How old are you, Mr. Stewart?"

"My age?" He seemed puzzled at the question. "I will be

twenty-four in less than two weeks at which time I shall come into my inheritance."

McKay raised an eyebrow. "I thought your parents were still alive."

"They are, but Father has seen to my future, and it is that I shall be taking possession of."

"I see. Well, I suppose yours is an enviable position to be in. Your future is all planned out and provided for, no worry, no need to fight for what you want. It has all been handed to you."

"You make it sound like a crime to take care of your own," he replied, now on the defensive.

"No, I don't think that at all. It is just that when people esteem you so highly as to lay fortunes in your hands, well, it's hard not to begin to think yourself actually worthy of it."

"You are saying I come across as superior?"

McKay looked at him. "You can at times come across that way."

He lowered his voice. "I don't intend to."

"I believe you."

"Then, it is my position in life that prevents me from having the sort of self-confidence you show, Mr. McKay?"

He chuckled. "No. I don't think so. But it is your kind of easy life, where all is supplied to you and you need not struggle for anything, that hinders you. I know personally several men of considerable means who are dynamos of action. Men you would dare not go crosswise with. And the only difference I can see between them and you, is that when they were twenty-four years old they were out there butting their heads up against the world. Fighting and clawing for what they wanted."

"Are you describing yourself?"

McKay grinned. "No, I am not rich, although I work hard at it. But in some ways, yes. I left home when I was young, have not heard from my family in years, have fought for everything I own. Perhaps I have not been scrupulously fair in my dealings with other men, and perhaps this is why you see something in me that you admire."

"I guess there is no hope for me, then." He dropped his head.

McKay frowned. "I agree."

Stewart's face shot up.

"With that attitude, there is no hope."

"Then what am I to do?"

McKay considered this a moment. "Well, first thing you need to understand is that although you may play fair, most men do not, and if you want to go up against them, you'd best do it on their level."

"I'm afraid I wouldn't know how to start."

"What was that fighting stance you assumed the first time you went up against Statler?"

"You mean this?" Stewart crouched forward, spread his legs, and began to wheel his fists in front of him.

"Precisely. Now wherever did you learn that?"

"In college."

"The boxing team?"

"Of course."

"Do you think Statler ever went to college?"

"No, I would think not."

"Then it is safe to assume he probably knows nothing of these brand-new Marquis of Queensberry rules."

"No, I suppose he probably does not, but then, most people would not know them."

"Of course. But the point is, instead of following some-one else's rules, he makes up his own as he goes along, so that, for example, when he sees a fellow fighting such as you do, rather than meet you squarely, he might just pick up a length of timber and—" Without warning, McKay stabbed out with his walking stick, striking Stewart softly in the stomach, and just as suddenly he brought the end of it up and clipped his chin, and before Clifton could react, McKay had swung around and smacked him soundly behind one of his knees, causing it to buckle. As the younger man went down, McKay drew the short sword from the cane and gently put it to his throat.

Startled, Stewart's bulging eyes stared up at the shiny sliver of steel.

"He might very well react thusly," McKay said.

Stewart gulped and said, "Yes, I suppose so. I see your point."

McKay withdrew and casually put the two ends of the cane together. "You have been raised to believe there are rules to govern every occasion, Mr. Stewart. You yourself said so earlier. A Southern gentleman would challenge Statler to a duel. The rules of the South?" McKay shrugged his shoulders. "And for another man raised as you, the rules might hold. But not for the likes of Statler. His only rule is survival, and he will shoot you in the back before giving you an even chance."

"I think I see," Stewart said, his gloomy face brightening a little. "In other words, I should do something completely unexpected, to throw him off. I should break the rules of manly combat, and when he is confused, lay into him with all I have."

McKay rolled his cigar between his lips, then blew gray smoke into the breeze. He had to grin at Stewart's sudden enthusiasm. "That is sort of the idea. The point is, Statler is not going to treat you fairly. Your only real defense is to understand that, and to never give him a chance to lay a fist"—McKay gave a short laugh—"or a knee on you. And never forget, if he can put his hands on a weapon, be assured, he will use it."

"I shall keep it in mind, Mr. McKay."

"One other thing."

"Yes?"

"His eyes."

"What about his eyes?" Stewart drew on his cigar, but the fire had gone out.

McKay struck another match for the young man. "Always be aware of his eyes. The eyes will always telegraph a man's intentions. It is a nearly universal truth. If he intends to throw a punch at you or if he is just attempting to bluff his way with a pair of deuces, his eyes will let you know. Learn to read them, and you will keep one step ahead all your life."

"How?"

"There is no way to teach it. You just have to start being observant. In a little while you will recognize the pattern."

"I shall begin immediately!"

Stewart went away in much-improved spirits. McKay, however, remained at the railing, suddenly pulling at his cigar. His thoughts rambled, but mainly they kept coming back to Captain Hamilton and the three sharks closing in on him.

After a time of fruitless contemplation, he returned to the main cabin, took a table, and began dealing monte to himself. The waiter came by and returned a few minutes later with a cup of coffee. McKay's dealing attracted the attentions of two or three men anxious to lose their money, which they promptly did. But McKay's thoughts drifted. He stole frequent glimpses at his watch and kept an eye on the progress over at the table where the retired general's gregarious laugh pierced the noise of the cabin at regular intervals.

Statler came in some time later, and he took a table by himself. The waiter carried over whiskey and kept up a pretty regular shuttle between the bar and Statler's table.

Mystie appeared a time or two on galley errands. She spied McKay and gave him a smile as she passed, but she was too busy to chat. She made a point of navigating a course as far away from Statler's table as she could. Once, however, her destination forced her to pass near, and he stopped her with a word, said something that made her back go rigid. After that, she did not return to the main cabin.

In spite of his distraction, McKay had a profitable evening. At around midnight, he watched Statler stagger away and disappear into his cabin. McKay wrapped up his little game, put his cards away, and wandered by to peek over Captain Hamilton's shoulders.

The tension was as heavy as a wet sponge. There was a huge pot in the middle of the table, and when McKay arrived, he was greeted with sharp, quick glances that stabbed out at him from handfuls of cards held close to their vests—well, in Klack's case, held close to his grimy red shirt and beard.

The game was attracting a crowd, and everyone seemed to be holding his or her breath. McKay observed the retired general cross his fingers, then he picked up his whiskey glass and brought it to his lips, but apparently only McKay noticed that he didn't drink. Almost at once Klack folded. He tossed his cards on the table and leaned back. "I'm out."

McKay watched the wealthy planter chew on his cheek awhile, then peel off a one hundred dollar bank note and put it on the pile. "I'll see you, Captain," he said coolly, but not before McKay had noted the meeting of eyes between the planter and the general. The retired general had given a nod of his head in return, imperceptible to everyone else standing there.

The retired general said, "Too rich for my blood," and like Klack, he folded.

The wealthy planter had developed a nervous condition and drummed his fingers on the tabletop. He was a very good actor.

Hamilton was as tight as a rusty bolt when he laid down his cards. Two aces, three sevens. He held his breath.

The wealthy planter stared at the cards, and then, with deep displeasure finding its way painfully to his face, he laid out a pair of kings and a pair of tens.

The crowd seemed to release its breath at once. Hamilton went limp in his chair, but he was grinning wider than the old Mississippi when he raked in his winnings. The retired general gave him a wink, for he had amassed a considerable pile as well.

With a mild curse, the wealthy planter chomped down on his cigar and said, "You were lucky that time. Next time it will not go your way, Captain."

Hamilton chuckled. He was in mighty good spirits, although the strain of the evening and the lateness of the hour were showing. When he glanced over his shoulder and discovered McKay standing there, he said triumphantly, "As good as in my pocket."

How could McKay tell him that they were allowing him to win? He couldn't. All he could do was wait for this charade to play itself out. He had a growing sense of doom. The retired general had permitted the captain to take a sizable purse off them; he would never have done that unless they were planning a truly grand finale at the captain's expense.

Captain Hamilton returned his attention to the pile of money in front of him and began to sort it and stack it.

McKay backed out of the crowd. The captain had been warned, and there was little else McKay could do except to hope that he would heed his advice . . . and with that hope sinking like a hundred weight of lead shot, McKay left knowing that Hamilton had not taken him seriously. Well, there was nothing to be gained by remaining to witness the final coup de grâce, and besides, McKay's attention was required elsewhere.

Raaasp!

"So, then he said to me, 'I found this here cuff link under my bed when I returned from Kansas City, and if I am not much mistaken, I shall find a match to it among your belongings!' Well, you can imagine my chagrin at being openly accused of such a deed, right there in that tent saloon with two dozen grinning eyes staring at me, and Big Brad Mcallister standing there, blocking the way of my only avenue of escape, heavy as an ox, a Colt's revolver in one fist and his wife's lovely wrist grasped in his other. Ah, the poor, beautiful . . . energetic woman. So starved for affection. If my embarrassment was great, hers must have been unbearable. The uncouth blockhead had dragged her into the saloon for all to see."

Raaasp!

"I know by now you must be wondering how I extricated myself from that one, aren't you?" He looked up at the black face and saw only mild confusion. "Aren't you? Well, I'll tell you just the same."

Raaasp!

"I already knew that this Brad Mcallister was all beef-steak and no gray matter. I'd taken a hundred dollars off of him in a simple wager that any schoolboy would have seen through, and I had been helping his poor wife with her . . . err . . . loneliness for over two months as well, without the dolt least suspecting. So, I figured it would be a simple task to talk my way out of this one."

Raaasp!

"'Sir,' I said to him as if deeply wounded, 'I fear you are mistaken and you will owe me and your poor wife an apology when the truth is finally known. I have not dishonored you, and that cuff link in your hand is certainly not mine!'"

Raaasp!

"Fortunately, I had the match to it in my pocket, and I slipped my hand inside and took it up. I stood and stepped out into the middle of the floor to plead my case before all the men there, and as I did so I brushed past the hulking, snarling Mcallister." McKay laughed. "I need not paint a picture for you. I'm sure you see already what I had in mind."

Raaasp!

Eli moved not a muscle, not a twitch, but watched him with huge eyes, and McKay half wondered if he were addressing a statue carved of ebony. What he saw was more fear than curiosity, and if those staring eyes were affixed to anything at all, it was the heavy chain across McKay's knees.

Raaasp!

McKay cleared his throat and said, "Well, I see you are not all that interested—"

"Don't stop now, Mr. McKay," a husky but restrained voice said from a little distance away. With the engines under repair, the firemen had the evening off and were craning their necks over the woodpile to listen to the story. These firemen, at least, appeared to be quite entertained by McKay's tale and his slow work at the heavy chain.

McKay shifted the file to his other hand.

Raaasp!

"Well, to make a long story short, I deposited the cuff link into Brad Mcallister's buttoned shirt pocket, *beneath* his vest. The slickest bit of handwork I had ever done since I . . . err, well that's another story. I proceeded to plead my case to all those who were there and said that I had never seen the cuff link before, although I used to own a set similar to them, but they had been stolen from me. Also, my own acquaintance with Mcallister's poor and much maligned wife was merely a chance meeting on the street one day about four weeks earlier."

Raaasp!

McKay grinned at Eli, and then over at his little audience by the boilers. "At that point I challenged everyone there in the saloon to disclose the contents of their pockets, and I would do the same. Naturally, among the odds and ends, and the pocket fuzz that emerged, not one cuff link appeared.

"Mcallister claimed that the exercise did not mean a thing. I countered that it did, and then I suggested that he empty his pockets. Well, you can imagine Mcallister's mortification when he drew out the matching cuff link—from a buttoned pocket! They laughed the man out of the saloon, and off he went, his poor wife buffeting along in his wake. Ha! It was glorious!"

Raaasp!

"Is that why you left the Kansas Territory?" one of the firemen asked quietly across the woodpile.

"Only partly, my good man," McKay replied equally softly, for not far beyond the crated cargo lounged other deck passengers, and somewhere out there was Chief Mate Lansing as well. "It seems that some few days later an itinerant preacher came through, pronouncing fire and brimstone on the sinners of Cherry Creek who didn't repent." McKay made a wry smile. "He was a very good preacher, and there was a lot of repenting going on. Unfortunately, more repenting than I could conveniently talk my way out of, especially since the sheriff's wife was one of those handsome young ladies who had gotten saved. Well, there was talk of tar and chicken feathers and open hints of retribution and a good stout rope perhaps. I considered the matter and decided the time had come to make a dignified but hasty retreat. And here I am."

"Lansing's comin'!" one of the firemen warned. McKay leaned into the shadows, silenced his file, and waited until the chief mate passed by the firemen and went on his way.

When it was all clear, McKay shifted subjects and said to the runaway slave, "Tell me about yourself, Eli."

Raaasp!

"Ain't much t' tell, suh."

"Does your master treat you poorly?"

"No, suh. No more den any other missus. But she don't take no laziness, no suh. She's hard when it come t' dat. And she will surely lay int' poor ole Eli for runnin' away once she gets her hands on he. She will hab the oberseer buck me a' whip me a lick o' times. Punishment is her religion, and de whip is de Word o' God in her hand, yes suh."

Raaasp!

"Well, Eli, I am going to see to it you don't have to go back to all that. You saved my life, and now I am doing the same for you."

"Are you really?"

McKay looked up, stunned. "I'm going to set you free, man!"

"A nigger ain't neber free. Dem slave hunters, dey can come an' steal a nigger away from anywhere in de whole country since dey passed dem new runaway slave laws. Least dat's what I's hear. Only'st place a nigger is really free nowadays is someplace I's hears 'bout called Canada, but dat place is a powerful piece up North, t' far t' runaway t' without help from the Railroad."

"The Underground Railroad? I have heard of it. Do you know how to contact the workers?"

Raaasp!

Eli shrugged his shoulders. "I's told der is a station house on de Arkansas Riber, an' a conductor der t' take me North, but I's neber make it. Dat slave hunter, Statler, him done catched me first."

"Then once I free you, you will not be able to find help?"

Raaasp!

"I's don' know. I's don' tink so, but I's will try. Freedom is worth de try. If not, I's rather die den go back."

"No, no, no, we need to do better than that." McKay paused in his assault on the chain to think. How did one go about contacting the Underground Railroad? He had read a little about the organization, how it was operated along the line of a real, working railroad, with station houses, stationmasters, conductors, workers, even presidents! They used the real railroads when they could, although mostly they shuffled the slaves up North at night. But all so secret. Only members knew one another. So how was someone like Eli supposed to make contact?

McKay pondered that, but before he could come up with a workable answer a figure stepped out of the shadows and said, "What the hell are you doing here?"

CHAPTER NINETEEN

"I ask you again. What are you doing here?" She stepped out into the open where the ruddy light of the torch baskets heightened the anger in her face. Her voice was forceful, demanding, but carefully restrained so as not to carry beyond the crates.

McKay was taken aback by her anger. "Err, I am freeing him."

Mystie came forward and went down on her haunches, her eyes level with his own now. "You can't do that."

"I know it is breaking some law or another, but I will not see this man sent back into slavery."

"No, that is not what I mean. I mean *you* can't do that."

Slowly McKay began to understand. "You mean that I can not free Eli, but someone else can?"

"Oh, you are going to ruin everything." In exasperation Mystie sat down beside him with her knees hiked up and her skirts tucked between them. "Listen. You are going about this all wrong. Look, do you even have a plan?"

In truth, McKay had to admit that he did not.

"There you go. You just get this notion in your head to help Eli escape, and you dive headlong into it with no plan. What is the poor man supposed to do? We are in the South, for heaven sakes. There is a warrant for his return. He has no papers. He has no map to follow but the stars above. In a matter of days he will be picked up again, and then what? Having run away twice, he will have no hope once he is back home." Mystie threw up her hands and glared at him, nettled.

"I hadn't thought about that. I just figured I'd cut his chain, and he could slip overboard and swim ashore."

"You weren't even thinking that through clearly," she shot back.

He narrowed an eye, confused. He had expected that if anyone would be sympathetic toward his endeavors, she certainly would have been considering—

"Now, look what you've done."

He glanced at the chain.

Mystie snatched it off his knees and held it in front of his eyes. "See?"

He studied the chain a moment. "No."

She said, "Look where you are cutting it. Look and think, Mr. McKay. You are severing it a good four feet from Eli's collar."

"Yes?" He still did not understand her point.

Mystie let her anger subside, and she said in a controlled voice, but one that might have been directed at a young boy puzzling over an arithmetic problem, "How much do you suppose four feet of thick chain weighs?"

At once he comprehended the dilemma. "Ah, yes. I see your point. He'd sink like a stone."

"More like an anchor—chain and all."

McKay grinned, embarrassed. "I guess I am not very good at this game. Never had any practice, you understand."

"There is no damage done, I suppose. Only, there could have been. And now what shall we do if Statler should come by and see the chain with a deep file cut in it?"

"I don't know. Maybe Eli can sit on it?"

Mystie sighed and then recalled the sack she carried in her hand. "Here, I brought this for you, Eli. I know you haven't had much to eat and you need to build your strength now."

"Thank you, missus," he said, taking it from her.

McKay studied her a moment and said, "Somehow I get the feeling you know precisely what you are doing."

Her gaze shot back to him. "There are proper ways of going about this and . . . and . . . Oh, hell. Yes, I've done it before. All right? Does that satisfy you?"

"In fact, I would guess that you make a regular habit of freeing slaves," he added.

Mystie's black eyes narrowed.

"In fact," McKay repeated, "I think I understand it all very well now."

"What do you understand?" Her voice sank to a suspicious whisper.

"Your concern for Eli. Your little trip back in Leota to visit that charming old lady—what was her name?—oh, yes, Sadie Wilkes."

Mystie's mouth fell open in a most unladylike manner. "How did you know—? You followed me!"

"You can hardly blame me. A little while before, you professed to not wanting to waste your time in a nowhere hamlet such as Leota, and then, through the most inhospitable weather you trek into town and up to this nondescript house. You give an odd knock, reply in equally suspicious fashion. What am I to think?" He gave her a quizzical look.

"But I must admit it was only this instant that I put it all together, and only now because Eli and I happened to be talking of the Underground Railroad."

He could see it in her eyes. He had struck a nerve, and before she had an opportunity to deny it, he said, "And you, Miss Waters, are a conductor."

Mystie sat there speechless, eyes hard as black flint. When she finally did marshal her thoughts, she said, "I'm only a worker. I am not a conductor."

"Then Sadie Wilkes is a conductor."

Mystie shook her head. "No, she is a station master."

"Mere semantics. The point is, you work for the Underground Railroad, and you intended all along to free Eli."

The slave was listening to all of this in what McKay figured was a most studious manner.

"We had word of a runaway coming north through Arkansas. There were people such as myself alert for him." She managed a halfhearted grin. "Working on a riverboat has many advantages. I have points of contact in most every town along the river. I knew there was a runaway slave coming north looking for a safe house and a conductor to take him into Canada. Imagine my disappointment when I saw Statler come aboard with Eli."

"So that's when you decided to make contact with someone higher up in the organization?"

"I don't know *all* the workers, only certain ones. Sadie helped me find the people farther south who could help. She then sent word ahead to them, and they are preparing to take Eli. But not until we get above Natchez. That's why you cannot free Eli yet. We planned it to happen at night. This delay worried me at first, but since it will be almost exactly twenty-four hours, we will still arrive at night. One of the things I did while in town was pass a note to another worker informing them of this delay."

"So, those were the names in Sadie's little black book?"

Mystie looked across sharply. "You really were spying," she said with understandable irritation.

He smiled smugly. "And the second book?"

"What second book?"

"The one with red ribbon."

"I know nothing of a second book. How did you—?"

"Never mind. It is a long and most unpleasant story."

She considered him a moment before continuing. "The plan is to free Eli below Natchez. There will be three lights arranged in a triangle on the Louisiana side of the river. He will have to swim toward those lights." She glanced at Eli. "Do you understand that?"

Eli nodded his head.

"The river is high, nearly at flood stage, but that can't be helped."

"I's a good swimmer."

She smiled. "I hope so."

McKay cleared his throat. "One problem. How are you going to free him?"

Her face went slack and color drained from it. "I have that all worked out," she said flatly.

McKay detected a shiver in her body, and something sinister in her tone. He did not like what he had heard in her voice. "I hope you know what you are doing."

"I'm doing what I have to." She came back like the strike of a rattlesnake.

He allowed her a moment with her thoughts. "There is another problem."

Her eyes flashed, but she did not speak.

"Mr. Stewart."

"What about Clifton?"

"He is in love with you."

Moisture gathered in her eyes, and she quickly brushed it away. "He doesn't have to know."

"But you will know. And, if I haven't missed my guess, you are feeling the same toward him."

She laughed bitterly. "You make very good guesses, Mr. McKay."

"He owns slaves."

"I know." Her soft voice cracked.

"A lie is not a very good way for the two of you to start out."

"When did you become so wise? Or have you always been this way."

McKay grinned and rubbed his head. "Oh, about two days ago," he said, settling his hat back in place.

"He will have to know how I feel about keeping humans as if they were animals. He will have to know what I do. If he cannot accept that, then it is best we know right from the start."

"But can you accept him?"

She fell silent and then shook her head. "I•can't think about that now."

He nodded and stood up. "I guess I won't be needing this anymore." He flung the file far out into the river. Mystie watched him straighten his coat and tie.

"Are you going to tell him?" she asked.

"Me? No, I figure that is your place."

"Yes, you are right. Only, I can't tell him now. Not until Eli is free. I can't risk ruining that."

"No, I suppose not."

"Promise me one thing. Promise you won't tell anyone that I am with the Railroad?"

"Of course." He was about to leave but turned back. "When it comes time, though, how honest will you be with Clifton?"

"I . . . I don't know what you mean."

"I mean, Miss Waters, when you tell him you are with the Underground Railroad, and that you deplore slavery, and he asks why, are you going to tell him the whole truth?"

She stared up at him, paralyzed.

"Are you going to tell him that you, besides being an abolitionist, have Negro blood in your veins as well?"

As McKay made his way out into the open and stopped by the wide stairs that climbed to the boiler deck and main

cabin, he recoiled at the still-vivid image in his brain:
Mystie's stunned look of surprise that had at once wrenched
her pretty face and the wide look of sudden sadness that had
come to her eyes—and he loathed himself for meddling—
for being the cause of her pain. It was none of his business!
Why did he not keep his mouth shut?

He was at once determined to kick this Good Samaritan
idiosyncrasy he had acquired and to go back to watching out
for himself and himself alone—*number one*! Let everyone else handle their own crisis. He was through worrying
about them: about the captain's folly with gambling, about
Stewart's identity problem, about the future that Mystie
faced . . . or about Eli.

It was none of his concern! He was through with it all!

McKay heaved in a deep breath and snorted it out, feeling
the weight suddenly rise from his shoulders.

There, that was better. He almost felt like his old self
again.

He put his foot to the stair tread when Mystie's voice
stopped him. He turned back. She came through the
scattering of deck passengers and peered at him, as if
weighing her next words.

"How did you know?"

"That you are part Negro?"

Mystie nodded her head.

"I didn't at first. You really show little of it, except for the
color and texture of your hair and the color of your eyes.
None of which is all that remarkable in itself. You might, for
instance, have a trace of Bohemian in you instead, or even
Italian. But then, there were the small things you said, and
today, with the sunlight upon your skin, I started to wonder.
And when I begin to wonder about something, Miss Waters,
I become absorbed. If one were to study your face, one
would have to notice small features—in your nose, in your
smile. Like I said, no one feature remarkable in itself, but
taken as a whole, quite telling."

"You are most perceptive, Mr. McKay." She forced a

laugh. "My mother is a mulatto. I have a quarter Negro blood in me, and in the South that's as good as being a full Negro. Very few people have found me out. It appears I have inherited almost all my father's traits, including his sense of justice, I am afraid." She paused. "Do you think Clifton knows?"

McKay grinned. "Mr. Stewart's head is swimming in bright and beautiful thoughts at the moment, and all he sees are lollipops and candy canes. No, Miss Waters, he sees nothing but a very attractive woman. He is blinded by love."

His words pleased her, but almost immediately the worried expression returned. "He will have nothing to do with me when I tell him."

McKay considered this. "I would not take that bet if it were offered to me. I think there is something substantial and tenacious beneath Clifton Stewart's pampered exterior. He will, however, need some time to digest that sort of news."

"You are much too much an optimist, Mr. McKay." She was about to add something else to that when a commotion up in the main cabin turned both their heads.

McKay's gut instantly knotted, and he plunged up the stairs two steps at a time with Mystie hurrying along at his heels. He burst through the doors and came to a stop. Captain Hamilton's table was bristling with men, some hooting and cheering, others scowling with either concern or anger. McKay could not see the captain through the crowd, but he did see the retired general standing there and beaming like a star.

"Drinks for everyone," the retired general bellowed, and as McKay made his way through the mass of gawkers, he knew that whatever those three's goal had been, they had reached it. Mystie was at his side, and when he glanced over, he saw the worry in her eyes that must have been reflected in his own.

McKay drew up at the table after elbowing aside one or two men and was immediately appalled by Captain Hamilton's frozen face. His skin had blanched to the color of his beard, the blue of his eyes faded against the wide, staring whites. He was immobilized. Struck dumb. Hardly breathing.

The retired general said, "Gather round, men, gather round. The bar is open, all drinks on the house." He clutched a sheet of paper with writing upon it and held it aloft. "I have hit the jackpot, and we will all celebrate."

At the table, Captain Hamilton emerged from his trance. Hands flat upon the table, looking like an old man, all vitality drained away, he pushed himself to his feet and stared at the retired general. "I will take my leave now, sir," he said, sounding like a man confined to the sickbed. "I will sign the proper papers once we reach Baton Rouge."

The retired general retorted happily, "I will, of course, want to retain you as captain."

Hamilton shook his head. "That will be quite impossible," he managed to say. Then he saw McKay standing there and immediately averted his eyes. The crowd parted for him, and the old man, bent and defeated, made his retreat.

"I don't understand," Mystie said at McKay's side.

He took her by the arm and removed her from the crowd. In the ladies' salon, he stopped and glanced down the length of the main cabin at the cheering, tumultuous celebration. Klack and the wealthy planter were equally pleased with the retired general's coup, and only McKay knew why. He discovered her rounded eyes upon him, staring. Although she did not understand it all, she seemed to realize that whatever had just occurred had somehow devastated her captain, and her eyes glistened.

McKay knew of no easy way to say it. "Captain Hamilton has just lost the *Tempest Queen* to those gamblers."

She staggered back, and the shimmer in her wide eyes gathered into pools, and a single tear traced a shiny streak over the curve of her cheek. "No" was all she could manage.

McKay had warned him, had tried to tell Captain Hamilton not to wager more than he could afford to lose. *Dammit, it wasn't his problem! No more Good Samaritan!* He turned away abruptly, drove his walking stick into the floor with a sharp smack that resounded through the carpeting, and without another word strode out the back door and up to the railing.

Black water rushed by, tossing about the moonlight and the lamplight from the *Tempest Queen* and those from the steamer moored behind her. Tumbling angrily past; powerful, and threatening to breach her banks and the levees built to hold her at bay. A perfect foil for his seething soul, McKay thought.

Silently, Mystie stepped beside him at the railing. Neither spoke, both allowing the river to do all the talking for them. Finally Mystie's quiet voice said, "What can you do to help?"

He looked over, amused. "Me? How can I help the captain?"

Mystie lifted her shoulders. "I don't know, Mr. McKay. But you are not the only person aboard this boat with perception," she said cryptically, and, without another word, turned away. Before disappearing around the corner of the promenade, she stopped, looked back at him, then she lifted her face to the sky, where in the distance dark clouds were building and roiling toward the moon. "Looks like another storm coming."

McKay stared at the place where she had disappeared until a jagged arc of electricity pulled his eyes away. Yes, it did appear another storm was on its way.

Captain William Hamilton fell into the chair as if a deadweight. He folded his arms wearily across the desktop, and his searching eyes stopped on the gilded picture frame that was growing green at the corners from age. Cynthia looked back at him, smiling, happy, never aging. Somehow he felt her there, placing a comforting hand upon his shoulder, running her fingers through his thinning hair. Whispering in his ear. If he turned his head, would she be standing there? And if so, how would she appear after so many years? Hamilton did not want to find out. He preferred to remember Cynthia as a young woman, as she appeared in the faded daguerreotype on his desk. Still, he sensed her presence, and a cold finger stroking his spine, and he chanced a glimpse over his shoulder.

You are acting like a frightened child, he chided himself. Just the same, he was relieved to discover no ghost from his past had come to visit. The little cabin was exactly as it was supposed to be. His bed made up and orderly. His coat hanging upon the tree that he had used for years. That very same tree that had survived the sinking of the first *Tempest Queen*. He looked about the familiar room. Nothing had changed. All precisely as it had been that afternoon when he had left it. Everything the same . . . except one small item. The *Tempest Queen* belonged to another man.

He had lost two mistresses in his life. The thought was unbearable, and he put his face into his arms, his body suddenly racked with shame—and disgust. If only he could turn back the hands of the clock, if only he had heeded McKay's warning!

Hamilton got a grip on himself. He had to face up to the truth. He had lost the most precious thing in his life. Had wagered it away in a most foolish manner. He had lost her because of his own folly. She had been snatched away from him because he could not control the beast within that reared its ugly head whenever the sound of ruffling cards reached his ears.

Hamilton sat up straight and stared at Cynthia. "I have loved but two women in my life. You first and foremost, my dear Cynthia, and the *Tempest Queen* after you. And I am not worthy of either of you."

His eyes shifted and stared at the desk drawer to his left. Hesitantly, his hand moved toward it, pulled it open. In the yellow lamplight, he lifted out the large revolver. Methodically, Hamilton checked the caps on their nipples, and assuring himself they were properly fitted, he turned the chair around to face the door, removed his cap, and flung it on the bed.

CHAPTER
TWENTY

The news of Hamilton's defeat ripped through the *Tempest Queen* like exploding grapeshot, and with nearly as much devastation.

McKay lingered at the stern railing, determined he was not going to involve himself in Captain Hamilton's problem, but that knock to the head was a tenacious thing, difficult to shake loose, and within a few minutes he was making his way up one of the ladders to the hurricane deck. By the time he had arrived, a growing assembly of officers and crew members had already gathered on the deck. McKay did not know all the faces, but he did recognize Chief Mate Lansing and a couple others he knew by sight but not name.

They milled about him like lost sheep, discussing the turn of events among themselves, as if they had personally lost the boat, looking over their shoulders at the light burning behind the drawn curtains of Hamilton's cabin, seemingly struck with the inability to act decisively. McKay wondered why, and then he understood. These men were all close to Captain Hamilton. Much closer than he was. Some of them had known him for years. They felt his pain more keenly than McKay could ever feel it, and were unsure as to how to approach and console their friend, for indeed they were still trying to console themselves as well.

McKay was not burdened by such close ties, and when he had lingered long enough, hearing all their suggestions bandied about, McKay said, "I am going over there and see how the captain is doing."

No one tried to overrule his decision. McKay crossed the hurricane deck, climbed to the texas and then onto Hamilton's porch. He rapped twice with the head of his walking stick.

The porch remained silent, as silent as the room beyond.

McKay knocked again. To the north the night sky flickered and lightning leaped from cloud to cloud, still too distant to hear its thunder. He was about to try again when a tired voice beyond the door said, "Come in. It is not locked."

McKay entered the somber room and closed the door behind him. Hamilton looked up from where he sat, a pale, gaunt reflection of the man McKay had come to know. McKay's view fell to the revolver in Hamilton's lap.

"Have you seen your future and decided it is too painful to bear?"

Hamilton's expression never wavered. "Desperate men sometimes think desperate thoughts, Mr. McKay. When Cynthia and the children died, I sat for twenty hours with a pistol on my lap."

"And is that what you intend to do tonight?"

Still void of expression, Hamilton said, "A man who

would wager all that he loves on three aces and a pair of queens doesn't deserve deck passage on God's green earth."

"You were swindled, if that helps any."

Hamilton managed a ghost of a smile. "It doesn't. But thanks anyway." He picked up the revolver and studied it in the pale light. McKay caught his breath. Then with a casualness born of a resignation to things that cannot be changed, Hamilton turned it over and handed it, butt first, to McKay. "Here, I suspect you would be more comfortable holding onto this."

McKay nodded at the picture. "Your wife, Cynthia?"

Hamilton followed his gaze. "Lovely, wasn't she?"

"Very beautiful."

Hamilton glanced back. "You knew, did you. You tried to warn me, but I'm an arrogant old fool! Now I have nothing left."

"You still have your property. Your dreams."

Hamilton shook his head. "No, no more. Oh, the property is still mine, but all my money was invested in this boat. I had intended to sell it and retire comfortably. Travel. See the Sacramento River!" he added with a wry smile. "But none of that will be possible now. What is it they say about a fool and his money?"

"They are easily parted?"

"Yes, that's it."

"You are sounding a little like Mr. Stewart."

Hamilton made a face. "Please, don't. I am feeling bad enough as it is."

McKay grinned. "Is there anything I can do for you?"

"No. Nothing."

"There are a number of your friends outside. They seem uncertain how to approach you, what to say."

Hamilton shook his head. "And I have let them down as well."

"I did not get the impression that they feel that way."

"Tell them I wish to be alone for a while."

"Will you be all right?"

"I'll get by." He turned to stare at the old daguerreotype. McKay left him there, lost in his memories.

The crowd had grown when he emerged from Captain Hamilton's cabin, and they watched him come across the hurricane deck.

"How is he?" someone asked him.

"He is in pain, but he will be all right." McKay was aware of a growing anger levering his jaw tight. How many men had he himself ruined at cards, he wondered. How many had the retired general? And how many more to come?

"What can we do?" another asked.

"Captain Hamilton wishes to be left alone. I suggest we honor that."

Sullenly they mumbled their agreement as the crowd slowly dispersed.

McKay handed Hamilton's revolver to Lansing. "This belongs to the captain. You might want to hold on to it until he feels better." That done, McKay returned to his cabin, exhausted. It was nearly three o'clock when he finally dropped onto his bed, the blow to his head catching up with him again. Yet, try as he may, sleep evaded him.

"Steam's up!" Seegar shouted into the funneled speaking tube. He studied the gauges, scrutinized the newly fitted joints and compression fittings, then went outside and around where he could see the black smoke belching from the chimneys. He put his hands on his hips and nodded his head in approval. When he returned, a bell was jangling, and he put his ear to the tube.

"I'm ready up here, Mr. Seegar." Sinclair's voice echoed down.

Seegar ordered the values opened, a huge lever pulled, and slowly the great pistons began sliding, the connecting rods moving, the huge paddle wheels turning. Stirred from her sleep, the *Tempest Queen* shook off her grogginess and pushed out into the river. Sinclair rang for the leadsmen, and their calls of the river depth began relaying up to him. Not that Sinclair had any fear of running aground. The river was at flood stage and threatening, but he knew the Mississippi well enough to never second-guess her. With a wary eye, he studied the river and the storm clouds that had overtaken them during the night.

"Here now, Ab, what do you say about this?"

Absalom Grimes shook out his match and, puffing a stream of gray smoke, peered out the glass wall of the pilothouse and scowled. "Lay you two to one she is crevassing the levees down aways." He squinted skyward. "No doubt with this rain we are going to have a rough ride."

"Just hold her to the center and ride it out," Sinclair noted.

Ab Grimes nodded his head. "That's what I would do." He went back to the high bench to rummage around in his portmanteau for a clean shirt.

Sinclair riveted his attention ahead and said to his cub, "Mind what you learn here today, Jacobs. There will be rough water ahead. You will see a crevasse or two if I'm not very much mistaken. Here is a lesson you best take note of."

"Yes, sir." Jacobs had become infected with Sinclair's sober manner.

Just a few feet below them, in the texas, Captain Hamilton stirred in his chair. He'd dozed during the night, and now he came awake at the shudder of the *Tempest Queen* moving away from her berth.

Hamilton stood, arched his back, and felt his spine pop. Momentarily confused, he looked down at himself, still fully dressed, and he remembered. The ache in his heart was a crushing weight upon his chest. He frowned at himself in the looking glass, pushed down his unruly gray hair, smoothed his beard and went outside.

If it wasn't already bad enough, now he was confronted with dark, rolling clouds hanging close to the river. The steady drizzle was only an omen of things to come, he knew, scowling. Overhead, a steak of blinding light turned the clouds momentarily translucent: an odd, pearly gray-brown.

An instant later, thunder rumbled across her bow and filled the little porch where Hamilton stood, looking out.

He ought to be making his rounds, he thought. He had duties to carry out. His job had not been terminated, even though his ownership in the *Tempest Queen* had been.

Reluctantly, he went back for his hat, his jacket, and his umbrella. He paused in the doorway to look back at Cynthia, and then, steeling himself against the barrage of questions and condolences he knew he had to face, Hamilton stepped out into the rain.

McKay stood at his window watching the gray sky and the surface of the river looking like a sheet of yellow sandpaper beneath the peppering of rain. He had not slept that night except in fitful snatches, always coming awake with a start, and then destined to lay awake while his brain scurried about trying to work out a puzzle, attempting to come to some sort of decision. Now that it was daylight, he did not have to worry about sleeping, and his thoughts had sharpened. The lack of sleep meant little to him, for he had trained himself to stay awake long hours, even days on end. It would be a poor showing if he should ever find himself in a card game that lasted two days and not be able to stay awake.

He grabbed up his stick and, putting on his hat, went out through the inside door that opened onto the main cabin. As was usual for breakfast aboard the *Tempest Queen*, the tables had all been shoved together and passengers sat elbow-to-elbow. McKay took a seat, and as he ate, he watched the retired general down the way. He was in a jolly mood, surrounded by his confederates, Klack and the wealthy planter.

McKay ate in silence, his brain whirling ahead almost faster than he could keep up, and by time he had finished, he knew what he was going to do.

Springing from his seat, his coffee untouched, McKay rushed back to his room and dragged out his valise. He dumped it upon his bed and separated out the three decks of cards he had already prepared. They were the Steamboat brand of playing cards, made by the A. Dougherty Company, and all three decks were number 220s and therefore identical—and precisely what McKay required. He slipped one of the packages with its seal still intact into his left pocket. The other two decks he carried to his desk and opened, discarding the carton. Taking his time, he built up two cold decks, one constructed to give his opponent a winning hand, the other put together to serve himself. The loser deck went into his left pocket, into a loop of material sewn in for just such a reason. The other deck he secured into his right pocket.

That finished, McKay turned back to his valise. Even empty, it had considerable heft to it. He removed the false bottom and lifted out two thousand dollars in gold. His emergency stash. This he never touched, except for business reasons, even if flat broke and destitute. There was a sheaf of bank notes there as well, and he put them into a pocket.

And finally—

McKay withdrew the envelope with respect that bordered on reverence. He had vowed never to touch it except for that one special game that every gambler dreams of. He had thought of it often when the stakes had skyrocketed and his purse had plummeted, but McKay had always resisted the urge to turn to it. Now he was not sure how he felt. If he should lose it— But no, he could not consider that possibility. With sudden resolve, McKay slipped the envelope into his inside coat pocket.

There, he was prepared, at least physically. Now came the hard part, the mental preparation. McKay swept clean the bed and fell back into it and blanked his mind except for one thought.

She was coming around the corner carrying a basket of clean laundry when he snagged her by the arm. So sudden was his appearance that a startled cry caught in her throat.

"You're a pretty thing in the morning," he said, his mouth moving into an easy grin, bristling the beard aside. He did not hide his open assessment of her, then the eager fire that burned in his eyes. "Just thought I'd remind you about tonight."

Mystie twisted her arm free. "I have not forgotten."

"What time?"

"Whenever Maggie lets me go. It won't be too late." Mystie could not afford to postpone it very long, for then she'd risk having the boat move beyond the meeting place Sadie Wilkes had worked so hard to put together.

He grinned evilly. Even at this early hour she thought she detected the odor of whiskey upon his breath. "I'll be waiting. I heard there was some excitement aboard last night."

Mystie's eyes hardened. "If you wish to call it that, yes. Captain Hamilton lost the *Tempest Queen* in a card game. I don't think that is very exciting, sir. I do think it is sad, and my heart goes out for the poor man."

He laughed. "Give him your heart, missy. So long as I get the rest of you." He laughed again and strolled away along the promenade.

Mystie was shaking when he left, and she was still shaking when Clifton Stewart emerged from the main cabin. She put on a happy face for him. So much had happened in the last twenty-four hours.

"Mystie!" He hurried to her side, concern showing in his face. "The news is all over the boat. Is it really true? Did Captain Hamilton lose the *Tempest Queen*?"

"It is all true, Clifton, and it has made me sick."

He studied her at arm's length. "You do look like it has taken you aback. Your face is drawn. I am sorry."

She could not tell him that Captain Hamilton's setback was only part of the problem she faced.

"Cards are such folly!" He noticed the basket in her arms then. "Here, let me take that, and I will walk a little ways with you."

"Clifton?"

"Yes?"

She was ready to blurt it out, to tell him and be done with it. There was so much to carry around as it was. To reveal her true heritage to him would help remove some of the weight of her problems, and the devil be damned. But at the last moment she could not. She knew that what McKay had said was true. She had fallen in love with Clifton Stewart in spite of the world of difference that separated them, and in spite of his awkwardness, which she was sure he'd outgrow. No, she could not confess just yet. She wanted to let the magic remain—even if it was only for one more day.

Mystie said instead, "Just how many slaves do you own?"

"This subject again? I thought we were not going to speak of it just yet?"

"I'm sorry. I won't—"

"Don't be sorry, Mystie, my dear. I don't mind, really. Actually, I think you will be quite pleased to know that I personally do not own any slaves."

Mystie's eyes brightened.

"Not yet at least," he went on. "But in less than two weeks I shall have a plantation of my own and a starting lot of slaves to operate it."

"Oh." She fell silent. No matter how entirely she tried to convince herself otherwise, she knew the rift between them was widening . . . would widen beyond the ability of either one of them to bridge once she told him the truth about herself. "Well, I believe we have arrived. Thank you." Mystie took up the basket and struggled to hold back her great sadness. She pushed through the door without a word of good-bye. Alone once more, she could not restrain her trepidation and unhappiness any longer, and she no longer tried. The tears burst in a flood and wracked her body as she buried her face in her arms upon the shelves of laundry.

The time had come. McKay sat up with a start and swung his feet to the floor in unison with a bolt of lightning and a volley of thunder from the storm raging about them. He looked at his watch, two-ten, slipped into his coat, and, looking in the mirror, straightened his tie and hat. Cane in hand, he paused by the door to tick off the list in his head: cards, money, envelope, revolver—? He checked the little Remington once more, even though he had carefully done so only a few hours earlier. Satisfied that all was in order, McKay locked his door and left in search of the retired general.

He found his quarry in the main cabin, but not at the gaming table where he had always been before, and not with his two cronies, but in the ladies' salon, chatting with two pretty women who were sipping strawberry frappés and smiling brightly, while the retired general had a whiskey in his hand, all puffed up and strutting like a rooster. McKay could not help notice the man's gaze continually moving about the glorious main cabin, as if unable to take in all the details in one pass—or perhaps he was still mildly stunned at having pulled off such a brilliant victory.

The retired general saw McKay enter the salon and flashed a wide smile. "Good afternoon, sir."

McKay tipped his hat to the ladies and returned the retired general's smile. "It is a bit dreary out there, but then I am learning one expects this sort of weather in the springtime. I heard of your victory, sir, and I have come to offer my congratulations."

"Why, thank you, Mr. McKay." His look made the rounds one more time. "A wonderful boat. I shall enjoy her for a while."

"A while?" McKay lifted an eyebrow.

The retired general chuckled. "What am I to do with this fine vessel? Can't tuck it into my back pocket and take it with me."

"No, I suppose not."

"I reckon I will spend a few months here, play a little poker, perhaps install a faro table or two. Then I will sell her and move on."

McKay nodded his head in open agreement. "I would probably do the same."

"I thought I'd go to the West. Maybe where you just came from, Mr. McKay. I've a feeling a man with a deck of cards might eke out a fair living in the gold camps."

Fair? McKay grinned. "I wouldn't know about that. I'm not much a hand at cards, you know."

"Oh, I wouldn't say that. I've seen you play. You do decent enough."

"Well, I really could use a few pointers."

The retired general's face lit up. "Have you anything to wager?"

McKay felt around in his pocket and came out with a fistful of gold coins.

The light turned into a beacon, and the retired general said, "Why don't we step over to a table then?" He'd already extracted a deck of cards from his pocket. "I'll teach you the finer points of poker, heh?"

"That would be wonderful!" McKay gushed and tailed the retired general like a lost puppy across the floor.

Seated, the retired general said, "Let's just play a few hands, low wagers, to get a feel for where you stand, Mr. McKay, heh?"

The sucker come-on. That was all right with McKay. It gave him an opportunity to study his opponent, as well, and he had no doubt the first few hands would be his, gratis. A carrot from the retired general.

McKay played only a mediocre first game, but not surprisingly, he won it just the same. The retired general chuckled and said that he was lucky. McKay took up the deck for the deal. His fingers stroked the edge and immediately located five cards that had been trimmed. He shuffled the deck as clumsily as he had played the first hand and identified all five trimmed cards—and discovered another five marked with minute dimples pressed into the upper right-hand corners. He grinned inwardly, half tempted to deal himself a royal flush from the retired general's own deck. But no, that would have to wait until later.

McKay had a long afternoon planned.

CHAPTER
TWENTY-ONE

The storm raged all day, bludgeoning the earth with its lightning, shaking the river with its thunder. But the clouds remained fixed overhead, not reaching down to the roiling, bucking waters. With only rain to contend with, and not fog, Patton Sinclair, after conferring with his partner Jethro Pierce, determined to ride it out and attempt to reach Natchez before midnight, which was the scheduled hour for their arrival, albeit was now twenty-four hours later.

Absalom Grimes had become Sinclair's third pair of eyes, and although Sinclair would not have admitted it, he was grateful to have someone of Grimes's experience and good reputation up in the pilothouse with him.

Sinclair and Pierce worked the day in their usual four-hour shifts, but each man lingered afterward to watch the angry river rising.

At four-thirty, Grimes spied the first crevasse and immediately the spyglass was employed. The river had breached a levee across the way, and a hundred workers, mostly black slaves, were handing up sandbags and timbers, but Sinclair could see as the *Tempest Queen* drove on past, that the river had won this time around, and the fields beyond were being stripped and washed away as swiftly as loose sand is washed down the stream.

"Mind you, Jacobs," the suddenly intense riverboat pilot said, passing the glass to his cub. "Get too close to something like that and unless you are very good, and you got a mighty head of steam behind you, you'll be sucked in as if caught in a whirlpool. When water is raging through a crevasse like that, it is moving twice as fast as that what's just flowing past it."

At dusk, Captain Hamilton made an appearance in the pilothouse. Grim, gaunt, silent for a long time, he studied the Mississippi River in her ragings—urged on by the violent storm.

"Evening, Captain," Sinclair said. Earlier he had expressed his condolences. There was nothing more left to say.

"We back on schedule?" the captain inquired.

"More or less—"

"Natchez-Under-the-Hill?"

"I'm figuring right around midnight?"

"Good." More silence, and then, "I think I'll go on back to my cabin"; and with shoulders stooped forward, Hamilton left.

Now, with darkness all around and her lights blazing, the *Tempest Queen* cut her way through the storm that shook her, heaved the river beneath her, and tossed lightning bolts like javelins. In a dozen places along the drowned banks, levees had crevassed and men fought the age-old battle against the river.

Hamilton sat in a deck chair upon his porch, protected from the rain, but not from the other things that storms like

these brought with them. Hypnotized by the fierceness of
this downpour, he felt himself being pulled into it, and he
had not the strength to resist.

Some miles ahead, Sara Gardner slipped out the door into
the deluge. Shielding her eyes with her arm, she clutched a
sheet of canvas about her shoulders and pushed into the
driving rain, grabbing for the tiller to keep from being
bucked off the raft.

"We got to put in to shore, Gearson!" she shouted.

A thunderbolt momentarily showed his face to her.
Emaciated. Lately he'd been drinking all day and shunning
food. His eyes stared recklessly ahead with rain streaming
off his face. He was even now drunk and grinning stupidly
into the wind-driven rain.

Water washed over the deck and tugged at the wheels of the
wagon lashed there; wind tore at its canvas cover. A barrel
went suddenly careening by and plunged into the river.

"Gearson!"

"Shut up, woman! You wanted me to pull my weight
here, well, now I'm doing that." He tipped up the bottle and
nearly lost his footing. Grabbing the tiller more tightly, he
laughed and then whooped like a wild Indian.

She braced herself as a wave washed across. The wind
snatched away her small sheet of canvas and flung it high
over the river. She noticed then that the lantern on the
uplifted wagon tongue had gone out.

"You have to light the lantern!" she shouted as the raft
leaped beneath her feet.

"Forget it!"

"No! Without a light we can be run down! It must be lit!"

"I said forget it! I ain't gonna try to light the damn thing
in this storm!"

Sara pulled aside the hair that had flattened across her
eyes. She knew it was impossible to try to reason with
Gearson when he was like this. "Let me take over the tiller,"
she said. At least then there would be someone sober at it.

"Get out of here!" He whooped again. "Hell of a ride, ain't it!" Gearson laughed wildly, eyes filled with a savage frenzy, water streaming off of him.

Blue-white electricity skipped across the arched back of the beast upon which they rode and made Sara's skin tingle. "All right!" she shouted, pulling more hair away from her eyes. "I'm going back to the children."

He waved her away and tilted the bottle up toward the crashing sky. Sara staggered along the pitching deck, and once safely back inside the little shack, she hustled her children under her arms and said to her parents, "He is mad."

Her mother and father did not reply. With arms locked, they braced against the tilted walls of the shack while the timbers creaked and groaned all around them. Sara knew they agreed with her, and she feared for all their lives.

Mystie braced herself and squared her shoulders. She had put the clock in motion with her visit to Sadie Wilkes in Leota, and now time was running out. She could delay it no longer. They would be closing in on Natchez in a few hours, and before then she had to have set Eli free. Right now, nothing else mattered—well, at least that was something she desperately needed to convince herself of.

Gripping her handbag tightly in one hand, she took two calming breaths and knocked on his door. She heard shuffling behind it, but before it opened, the door to the next cabin opened and Clifton Stewart's face peered out.

"Mystie!" he said. She could see he was at once surprised and then delighted. Her heart broke, and any resolve she might have mustered melted away. "You've got the wrong door," he started to say.

Statler's door yanked open just then. "You're earlier than I expected," he said.

Mystie did not speak for a moment, and in that short space of time Statler must have noticed that her gaze was directed one door down and that Stewart was there. He laughed and took her by the wrist. "She's mine for the night," he said. She felt the pull at her arm and went along without a struggle.

Statler closed the door and locked it. Once inside the little cabin, Mystie instantly came out of her daze. The slave hunter tossed the key upon the table and turned on her. "You got off work early," he said.

She resisted the urge to look away from his openly probing stare, and forced a laugh that she hoped would sound impulsive. "Actually, I told her I wasn't feeling well."

"Oh? Why?"

Mystie shrugged her shoulders and casually unbuttoned the throat of her shirtwaist. "I don't know. Whew, it is warm in here."

"I intend for it to get a lot hotter." Statler advanced a step.

"I've been thinking about this all day," Mystie went on, "and I just figured I didn't want to wait any longer. Besides, Maggie has plenty of girls to help her."

Statler took Mystie by the shoulders. His powerful fingers dug into her skin and hurt. She wanted to cry out as he crushed her to himself. His body smelled. His breath burned as his lips smothered hers. His hands moved, and she felt them suddenly upon her breasts. More than anything she wanted to turn and pull free. She had to remind herself why she had come.

Mystie managed a playful laugh and turned out of his grasp without appearing to stop his fondling too abruptly. "Now, Mr. Statler," she giggled, gently removing his grasping fingers. "A lady likes to start a little slower."

"Not too slow, I hope." He was breathless, and a fierce fire had been kindled in his eyes. Statler was a powerful man, and Mystie knew she could never stop him by force once he started. She laughed again, sat on the bed, and unfastened two more buttons, and then her eyes shifted to the whiskey bottle on the table. There were two glasses there, as there were in every cabin, but apparently Statler had not bothered to use either one.

"I want a drink!" she said suddenly and stood. "You, too?" she asked over her shoulder.

"Sure, only make it quick." He sat heavily into the chair, and it creaked beneath him.

Mystie reached out and touched his hand gently. "You *are* anxious, and, my, I can feel you trembling. Now, you just relax, let's have a drink together, and I promise you a night you won't soon forget."

"You really are a pretty little Negress."

Mystie stiffened as she turned back to the table. She uncorked the bottle, and as she carefully filled each glass, she asked, "How did you find me out?"

Statler's laugh rumbled behind her, a shadow of the storm raging just beyond the wall of the cabin. "Niggers are my job, missy. It didn't take too much to see it in you. When I go North, I got to be able to recognize the fair-skinned ones."

"I see." Her back was to him now, and from her handbag she extracted the little brown paper parcel she'd purchased from the pharmacist. He'd told her only a teaspoonful in a cup of warm tea. She had no idea what it would do to him mixed in whiskey. Nor had she the luxury of measuring out precisely as the pharmacist had instructed. She dumped half the package into the drink, and hoped he'd not taste it.

Statler went on. "I don't figure you got much nigger blood in you, but that don't matter down South."

"Actually, less than a quarter." She brought the whiskey over, put it in his hand, and with an easiness that belied her intense disgust for this man, she sat upon his lap.

"Even with that much nigger blood, you as much a nigger as that runaway I've got down below." He laughed. "I could take you to the block and sell you to anyone for a fair sum."

Mystie tasted the whiskey. It burned her tongue. "But *you* wouldn't do that to me?" she said playfully, and was again aware of his fingers working their way up her waist. Mystie steeled herself and said, "Come now and drink with me. I don't like drinking alone." She stiffened when his hand found her breast again.

"I might sell you," he said flatly, and emptied half the glass in a swallow. Statler made a face, then looked at the glass. "What the devil happened to that bottle?"

"What's wrong?" Mystie inquired innocently, but her heart leaped. Statler was frowning, then glared at her. He tossed his whiskey glass aside and grabbed hers, tasting it. The frown turned to a scowl, and without warning his hand lashed out and struck her along the face, knocking her to the floor. "What did you do to it?" he bellowed, standing.

Mystie scrambled to her knees and then to her feet. She eyed the locked door beyond him as he stood shaking in rage. Statler grabbed her handbag and found the package. Mystie's view darted to the second door that opened onto the main cabin. Had it also been locked?

He read the label and glanced up. "What the hell is this?"

Mystie leaped for the second door. Statler grabbed her and struck with a backhand that sent her reeling against the cabin wall where she crashed to a stop and fell stunned to the bed.

"Mess with me like this, will you?" He stepped forward, one fist balled at his side. "I'll teach you!" His other hand reached for her shirtwaist, and in a single yank all the buttons ripped away.

The game that afternoon had gone from friendly to competitive and finally to dead serious, and McKay felt *ruthless* coming on pretty soon. The retired general had begun by giving McKay a few simple pointers, but as soon as he discovered that winning off this man was not as easy as McKay had first let on it might be, the lessons stopped and the stakes climbed.

McKay still played as if a little unsure of himself, but he made certain the cards never fell so that either one of them would lose their entire stakes or so as to give the retired general a clean enough win to pull out on.

The retired general was frustrated, and although he tried not to show it, he was becoming angry. McKay decided the time had come to make his play. He smiled a little uncertainly at the retired general.

"I'm feeling a bit jittery," McKay said. "My, I have never played cards for such high stakes."

The retired general clamped down on his cigar, eyes narrowed, and merely grunted.

McKay flagged down a waiter. "Whiskey," he ordered.

"Sir, we have—"

"Don't run through it again!" McKay blurted, showing that his nerves were beginning to get the best of him. "Just bring me a glass of that Glen—Glen—?"

"Glenlivet?"

"Yes! Now, on your way."

"A bit anxious, aren't you?" the retired general inquired.

McKay's eyes glassed over as they darted between the two piles of coins and notes upon the table. "Huh? Oh, noooo," he drawled, making it sound easy, but failing miserably. "I'm just fine," he said, "and I think that I am about to abandon my conservative approach, sir, and have that stack of money in front of you for my own."

"Do you, now? Well, I shall have to see that you do not get it."

Both men laughed humorlessly. The game had become far too serious for levity. The retired general tossed out two piles of cards. McKay saw at once what he had done and folded on the raise, even though he held three kings.

His drink arrived. He took the smallest of sips, but in a manner that he hoped would convey a desperate man looking to build his nerves. The cards came to him. In his haste, his elbow knocked the glass, and both men leaped to their feet as the whiskey spilled across the table.

"You clumsy oaf!" the retired general roared. "Look what you've done!"

McKay grinned sheepishly as a nearby waiter rushed over with a towel. "I am sorry. Wasn't watching what I was doing."

"You've ruined the cards!" The retired general growled, and then quite suddenly he got a grip. "Well, no damage. I've another deck in my cabin."

"No. I will not hear of it. I ruined them and I shall replace them. Waiter, bring me some of the boat's playing cards."

"Yes, suh. Right away, suh."

They sat back down, and McKay could see the retired general was not happy. "Really, I do not mind returning to my cabin for the deck. After all, accidents do happen."

"I will replace the cards. It was my elbow that precipitated the damage."

Before he could protest further, the black waiter had returned.

"Here he is now. What do you have there?"

"Steamboat brand, suh."

McKay glanced over the selection. "Err . . . let me have the 220s. Thank you." He took the cards, switched hands, and reached into his pocket for a dollar. The waiter went away smiling broadly at the generous tip. McKay turned back to the table, grinning as well, while he broke the seal on the fresh deck.

The retired general bit down harder on the cigar. McKay ruffled the deck, set it up, passed it to be cut, and beneath the retired general's watchful eye, he reassembled it precisely the way it had been a second before.

"Now," McKay said tossing them out with a bit more proficiency, "we shall play some cards."

As he had predicted, dead seriousness became ruthlessness, and it was no longer possible for McKay to fully mask the smoothness of his hands, but that was no longer important. He had raised the retired general's hackles, and he could see that the man was going for blood, and so could others around them, for a little group had begun to gather, including the wealthy planter. Klack was nowhere to be seen.

McKay won a huge pot the next hand and prodded the retired general. "You may quit if you like, or shall we continue?"

"I'll see you wiped clean before I leave this table!"

McKay frowned for the retired general's sake, but inside he was beaming. He had the man where he wanted him. When came his turn to deal, McKay took out a cigar and removed the match safe from his left pocket, and when he had finished, he had the first cold deck safely in his hands.

This was the sucker hand. Well, McKay knew it was necessary, and he gritted his teeth as the retired general took ten thousand in gold and notes off of him. The crowd roared with delight, and more joined them. McKay had lost by the smallest of margins.

"Now, whose money were you intending to have in front of you, Mr. McKay?" he chuckled.

"Err . . . yours, sir," McKay answered.

The retired general laughed.

Another indecisive hand went by, and again it was McKay's turn to deal. The crowd pressed in about him. "Give me room!" McKay barked, feigning anxiety, and as they mumbled and backed up a step, he managed to switch to the second cold deck.

Cards dealt, McKay watched the retired general's eyes brighten almost imperceptibly, for he had dealt him a sterling hand in any man's opinion.

The wealthy planter had strolled casually around the table.

McKay turned his cards over upon the table, casually removed his revolver from its hideaway holster, and placed it upon the table. "I will not accuse anyone of cheating," he said easily, "but any man standing behind me may find himself shot through the heart."

A mass exodus put all the onlookers safely to one side of the table. The retired general's grim look remained unaltered. McKay smiled genially.

The betting began on a grand scale, and it was apparent the retired general was pleased with his hand and intended to end the game now and decisively—to show this brazen upstart and the whole boat what real card playing was all about. He did not draw, but stood pat.

McKay looked grim and saw the raise. He drew two cards. The retired general used his greater wealth to overbid. McKay looked worried. He set his cards on the table and studied the pot. He wiped his brow and said, "I have not the cash to see your bet, sir."

"Ha! then you fold!" The retired general reached for the pot.

"Wait. A moment to think, if you please?"

The retired general leaned back, smiling. "Take all the time you like." He drew long and easily at his cigar.

McKay drummed his fingertips upon the table, chewed his lower lip, then with hesitation, as if someone were restraining his hand, he reached into his inside pocket and withdrew the envelope.

"Here now. What is that?" The retired general sat straight in his chair.

McKay stammered, "It is all I have. I was to deliver it to my brother in New Orleans, to repay a debt, but now . . ." He let his words trail off.

"What is it?" The retired general's curiosity was aroused.

McKay shook his head. A heavy sadness swelled in his throat. "It was all I managed to save when the disaster struck."

"Disaster?"

"The cholera epidemic, of course."

"Oh. Yes, of course."

"And the wild Indians after that."

"Wild Indians?"

"They attacked without warning. I was fortunate. My dear brother—not the same one in New Orleans—was not so lucky."

"What is it, man?"

McKay drew in a breath and slit the envelope with a penknife. The papers half-withdrawn, he stopped and shoved them back in. "No, I cannot. It is better to lose all that I have than to risk this!"

"Here, let me see!" The retired general snatched the envelope from McKay and extracted the five neatly folded sheets of paper. The wealthy planter was at his shoulder, peering over.

McKay pretended to protest, but caught himself and sat back down as if a wounded man lost in wandering thoughts. The two men across the table read the papers, their lips moving but no sounds exiting them. When they had finished, the retired general looked over.

"This is a warranted claim to a gold mine in the Kansas Territory."

McKay nodded his head. "And if you examined the other four sheets accompanying it, you will see a detailed assay report."

"Yes." There was a note of awe in his voice. "It is quite impressive."

"You will note also the seal, and the signatures?"

Reluctantly, the retired general handed the papers back. "I see they are all in order." He glanced up and got a small nod from the wealthy planter.

"I can hardly put a value on this piece of property. If it wasn't that the debt I owe my brother was so great, I'd never consider parting with this. It has conservatively been estimated at two hundred thousand dollars."

No one spoke for a moment. The retired general said reluctantly, "I agree on the value."

After much soul-searching, McKay laid the papers in the center of the table. "If you will accept this?"

"I will," the retired general pronounced immediately.

"Err?"

"Yes?"

"Well, it is a little unbalanced at the moment, wouldn't you say?"

"Yes, I see your point." Now it was the retired general's turn to soul-search. McKay watched the silent communication that passed between him and the wealthy general. Finally, the retired general reached into his own pocket and extracted the only possible collateral that would equal McKay's gold mine. Without another word, he placed Captain Hamilton's signed transfer of the *Tempest Queen* onto the pile.

CHAPTER
TWENTY-TWO

Patton Sinclair's eyes rounded, and he grabbed for the iron ring overhead. The *Tempest Queen*'s steam whistle screeched out into the stormy night. Again it wailed out its warning, and then a third time.

"What the blazes is that!" he shouted.

Both Absalom Grimes and cub pilot Jack Jacobs were instantly straining to see through the rain-streaked windows.

Sinclair shouted into the speaking tube. "Reverse engines! Reverse engines! For the love of Pete, reverse them damn engines, Seegar!" Then to his cub, "Cramp her, now!"

Jacobs leaped to the wheel and helped Sinclair spin it hard to starboard. "What the hell is that?" he yelled again.

Grimes stared through the streaming windows then back at Sinclair. A wave of alarm had swept away his usually placid expression. "I think you're coming onto a raft, Pat!"

"Dear Lord in heaven!" He laid on the whistle again and then heaved at the signal bell below in the engine room.

"I'm reversing as fast as I can," came a voice Sinclair recognized not as Barney Seegar's, but that of the night engineer, Larry Attebury. "What the hell is going on up there?"

Sinclair had no time to chat. He had the wheel cramped down tight and was standing on it, but going downriver the boat responded sluggishly to her helm. Slowly she heeled over; too late—the front guards swung over the little raft. There was a grinding crunch as the *Tempest Queen* drove on and her larboard wheel walked over the raft.

The paddles finally turned to a halt and began working in reverse. The boat struggled against the current, straightened, and slowly stepped backward. Patton Sinclair held her steady in the current. He could hear her 'scape pipes chuffing, feel her paddles fighting to hold her in place.

"Do you see the raft?" Sinclair shouted.

"No," Grimes came back. Then suddenly, "Yes, there it is, just coming up about fifty yards ahead."

"Any people?"

Grimes shook his head. "No, none that I can see."

Sinclair's eyes swept the river. He glanced at a piece of a levee that had been partially dismembered, the raging river pouring through.

Captain Hamilton came through the doorway at that moment, letting blowing rain in as he leaned on the door to drive it shut again. "What happened, Mr. Sinclair?"

"It happened so fast I could not stop it."

"What happened?"

Sinclair looked over. It was the first time that Hamilton could recall seeing the man so affected. "We struck a raft. Walked over a corner of it with our paddle."

"Did what?"

"It wasn't burning a light like the law says!"

The door burst open again, and Jethro Pierce and Chief Mate Lansing came in with the rain. "We crawled over a raft," Hamilton said briefly, not waiting for the question he knew was on their lips.

Jack Jacobs pointed suddenly. "There, I see something."

In the lightning flash, they all saw it. Hamilton thought it looked like the roof of a building bobbing in the water. In the next flash, they were sure that it was the roof of a small shack. Hamilton went to the window, peered hard. "There are people clinging to it!"

"Won't be for long," Pierce said in his laconic manner. "Heading fer that crevasse."

Every eye shifted. The shattered remains of the shack were being pulled toward one of the breeches in the drowned levee. Hamilton blinked and shook his head as if to clear his eyes. Was that a flame starting to lick its way up through the shingles? No. He shook his head again. Blue-white electricity showed them clearly for the breath of a heartbeat. A woman, and a child . . . no, two children . . .

Hamilton wheeled on Sinclair. "Take the *Tempest Queen* there, Mr. Sinclair. We'll put men down on the guards to pick them up."

"No, sir."

Hamilton's gaze shot back, narrow. The pilot was in his right to refuse. Indeed, Hamilton would have been breaking the law if he had tried to insist on it. "We have to do something, for God's sake. We ran them over!"

"I agree," Sinclair came back, and Hamilton could see the panic in the pilot's eyes, and the concern. "But I can't take us in too close without running the risk of that crevasse pulling us through and wrecking us! We might lose the whole damn boat!"

Hamilton glanced back outside, and then suddenly he stepped close to the window and pressed his face to it. Yes, there were flames. He was sure of that now. The woman had climbed safely to the roof and was holding her two children beneath her arms. *Cynthia?* Hamilton shook that thought

from his head. Then he had to look back. Another woman
had appeared. The roof was blazing now. Hamilton was
certain! *Was that Hester darting from behind the chimney?*

"We've got to do something now!" he ordered. "That
place is an inferno!"

Sinclair looked again, then back to the captain. "Ain't no
fire out there, sir," he said.

"Why, are you blind, man?"

"Captain, are you all right?"

"Of course I am! Can you take her in a little closer, Mr.
Sinclair?"

"A little, but not too much."

Hamilton turned on his chief mate. "Ready a skiff, Mr.
Finney. Man it with the strongest backs you got, and let's
get it over the side."

Lansing looked at him. "Sir, there is no one named
Finney aboard."

"Oh, yes, of course. Well, hop to it, Mr. Lansing. And
attach a line from the skiff to the *Tempest Queen*."

"Yes, sir." Lansing dove back out into the storm, and
when he had shut it out once more, Hamilton turned on
Sinclair. "Hold her as close as you can. We'll play out the line
so we don't get sucked into that thing, and I'll be relying on
you to pull us out of there once we have those people safely
aboard the skiff."

"Aye, Captain."

Hamilton peered outside again. He could have sworn he
had seen flames a moment earlier.

"Captain, that shack is heading for a breech atop that
levee now," Grimes said, and the next instant it had entered
it and hung up on a tree washed into the crevasse. "Seems
to be momentarily stuck there—"

Hamilton did not wait for him to finish but was already
hurrying across the hurricane deck. Down to the boiler deck,
he sprinted around the promenade and nearly ran into
Dexter McKay coming from the main cabin.

"What has happened, Captain?" McKay asked, but Hamilton kept right on going.

On the guards, Lansing had the skiff already in the water, bucking in the current and forward wash of the huge paddle wheel not far behind. "Put a line to it and tie it off securely."

"Already done, sir."

They boarded, and Captain Hamilton took the prow as the skiff turned into the current and twelve strong oarsmen put their backs to it.

"Hard over to larboard, Mr. Finney—err, Lansing. Put your backs to it, men!" Hamilton peered ahead into the driving rain. A tongue of flame licked skyward. He blinked, and when he looked again, it had disappeared, replaced instead by a tiny, square patch of wooden roof and four people clinging to it. He turned to shout an order to Lansing and came to an abrupt halt. The frenzy left his eyes for a moment, and he said, "What the devil are you doing here, McKay?"

Dexter McKay glanced around, smiled sheepishly, and shrugged his shoulders. "I don't know."

"Well, never mind. Sit down so's you aren't thrown overboard. Mr. Lansing! More muscle!"

"Hump . . . hump . . . HUMP! We ain't got all year! Put your backs to it boys, sons of bankers, every one of you! Think you can clean your fingernails and sleep like city folk? Show me your mettle tonight, and I'll give you half a day in Baton Rouge!"

Hamilton turned back as the skiff fought the current and drew nearer. He swung his right arm in big circles and said, "Harder to larboard, now! We are almost there." Then across the water Hamilton yelled, "Hold tight a while longer!

"Finney, have the men put their backs to it. More muscle, more muscle!" Hamilton felt a hand upon his left arm. He shot a glance and saw McKay's concerned face. Hamilton scowled, wrenched the arm away, and shouted, "All right, Mr. Lansing, bring her straight in."

The skiff drew nearer and suddenly pulled up tight at the end of the line. Hamilton signaled the *Tempest Queen* to ease them in. McKay grabbed up a coil of rope, shaking open a loop in one end.

Hamilton cupped his hands and shouted, "Make ready to come aboard, Cyn—" He caught himself. McKay swung the rope, and it sailed out across the water. In a jagged lance of blinding light, the woman reached up and caught it.

"Keep it steady, Mr. Lansing," Hamilton ordered, but the pull of the current at the bow and the line on the stern was already holding the skiff steady as a compass needle.

Twenty feet separated them, and Hamilton could feel the deadly pull of the current where the river spilled through the breech. He shouted to the woman. "Secure the rope!"

She was confused. The shack suddenly slipped and moved deeper into the breech, and they grappled at the eaves to keep from being thrown off.

"We have to get closer, Mr. Lansing!" At that moment, McKay flung off his coat and, with the rope clutched in one hand, leaped into the torrents. The current pulled him under. He surfaced a second later, still clinging to the rope, pulling himself hand over hand and, in what seemed an eternity but was really only a little over a minute, McKay had reached the shack. Hamilton stood rigid, seized with fear as McKay scrambled up the tilted, rain-slick roof. He watched McKay put the rope around the woman and her children, snug it down tight. Taking the second woman under an arm and grasping the rope himself, they all five leaped out into the roiling water.

About the same instant that Patton Sinclair had spied the raft, two decks below, young Clifton Stewart came to a decision. He was aided in his struggle by the sudden and violent impact upon his wall from the cabin next door. Without another moment of hesitation, he plunged outside and, taking a running leap from the railing, hurled himself into Statler's door.

It crashed open and Stewart flew across the room, slamming into Statler and carrying him to the floor. Dazed, Stewart climbed to his feet, but not before Statler, and both men faced each other.

"It's you again!" Statler roared, circling in the little room.

Clifton Stewart shot a glance at Mystie, saw her wide, terrified eyes, her hand grasping the torn halves of her shirtwaist together. Clifton took a stance and showed his fists. "You have carried your foul behavior far enough, sir. Stand to and take your punishment." He windmilled his fists in front of him.

A small grin moved across Statler's face.

Stewart tried to remember everything McKay had told him, but all he could seem to recall clearly was something about *eyes*.

Statler straightened out of his crouch and said easily, "I don't want to fight you, kid. Take the woman and get out of here." His eyes shifted. "Go on, now get ou—OOOH!" Statler's heart shot up into his throat at the same instant that the point of Stewart's shoe shot up into his groin with enough force as to lift the slave hunter a full foot off the floor.

Statler's screech merged with the sudden shrill of the boat's steam whistle. As the slave hunter reached down for his vitals, Stewart came up with a jab that snapped his head straight up. Clifton heard a voice in the back of his head. *He will shoot you in the back before giving you an even break.*

Another volley of punches put Statler against the wall. The snap of an elbow broke his nose. Blood spilled across his shirt. Stewart grabbed the whiskey bottle, lifted it, but he stopped himself before bringing it crashing down upon Statler's head. *Perhaps I have to fight Statler on his own terms, but enough is enough.* Stewart released the limp body and let it fall to the floor.

He turned. "Are you hurt, Mystie?"

She flung her arms around his neck and let the tears spill, and then she was suddenly composed and wiping her eyes. "I am all right . . . now. Thank you, Clifton."

He didn't know what to say, and she didn't give him a chance. Springing from the bed, Mystie went to her knees over Statler's unconscious body and began poking her hand down his bloodied shirt.

"Whatever are you doing?" Stewart exclaimed.

She ripped the thong from Statler's neck and held it up as if it was a prize. Gripping the halves of her shirtwaist together, she headed out the shattered door, racing past startled passengers drawn to the cabin by the fight.

Stewart ran down the main stairs after her, caught her by the arm halfway across the main deck, and turned her around. Lightning showed him a wild, rain-streaked face.

"What are you doing, Mystie?"

Her eyes were big and staring. "Come on."

He followed her around the stacks of cargo, bewildered at this odd behavior, but allowing her to go on. Then they were by the runaway slave, and suddenly Stewart understood.

"You're going to free him?"

"I am," she said, fitting the key to the lock.

"But . . . but, you can't do that."

The neck collar came apart and fell to the deck. "I can do it, and I just did."

He watched, stunned while she helped the Negro to his feet.

"But . . . but," he stammered, trailing along behind them as they stole through the stormy night. All at once, the boat shuddered and threw them against the engine room wall.

"What happened?"

Mystie listened a moment. "The engines are being reversed." Without warning the *Tempest Queen* heeled hard to starboard and threw the three of them in a new direction. The boat was alive with men dashing about. "Come on, Eli." Mystie took him by the hand. She came to a crouch in the shadow by the paddle box where the big wheel had begun turning backward, throwing frothy water forward now.

"Mystie, think about what you are doing! This will get you thrown in jail."

"Who is going to turn me in? You?" Her black eyes were huge and intense.

Stewart was compelled to look away and shake his head. "No, I won't tell."

Suddenly she pointed. "There!"

A break in the low, tumbling clouds revealed the three faint points of light on the shore.

"That's where you go, Eli. Understand?"

"Yes, missus. I's sees 'em."

"You can make it, I know you can." She gave his hand a squeeze. Stewart was mystified; it all seemed so unreal. He watched the slave creep out onto the guards, then onto the narrow ledge in front of the paddle box where only a foot away churned certain death.

Eli looked back once, turned toward the angry yellow waters, and without another moment's hesitation leaped as far out into the water and away from the paddle as his powerful legs would carry him.

Clifton watched him bob underwater twice, saw his head appear once more before losing sight of him. When he looked back, Mystie was kneeling on the deck, gripping an iron cleat, staring ahead.

He looked at her, still confused. "Why did you do that, Mystie?"

"Because I had to."

"I don't understand. He belonged to someone—"

"He will belong only to himself from now on." She lifted her chin defiantly. "He will be free."

"You are an abolitionist!" All at once he understood.

Mystie nodded her head.

Clifton had no idea how to handle this. It went so against how he had been raised, the values of his parents, of himself. "This can't be true, Mystie. I love you."

"Do you really?" She considered him sharply.

"What does that mean?"

"Mr. McKay once asked me how honest I could be with you. He thought that if you knew the truth you would still love me. I didn't think so."

"Truth? Mystie, what are you talking about. If you mean freeing that Negro, well, of course I can forgive you."

She stood, uncaring about the ruined shirtwaist falling open. "That is not what I mean, Clifton. The truth is, I was born on a plantation, very much like your own, I would think. My father was in line to inherit it all, until he made two mistakes that my grandfather could never forgive him of. His first mistake was falling in love with a slave on his plantation, a mulatto. My mother."

Clifton took a startled step backward.

"His second mistake was that he loved me." She continued, not giving him a moment to speak. "I lived twelve years in the slave quarters. I was a slave as far as my grandfather was concerned. On my twelfth birthday, my grandfather gave me a present: I was told I was old enough to become a full fieldhand, and he put me out to do a full task of work. My father could stand it no longer. He had money of his own, not much, but enough to buy me and my mother from his father.

"He bought us, Clifton. His own family. Bought us just like he'd buy a horse. Got a receipt and everything. Then he took us North, to Illinois. He applied for and got our papers to prove that we were once and for all free."

She paused to collect her thoughts. "I have never been back there. I have no idea whatever happened to my grandfather, and if my father knows anything, he has never spoken of it." She stopped and drew in a ragged breath.

Stewart slowly came out of his shock. He backed another step and finally said, "You are a Negro?"

"About a quarter," she answered, suddenly drained. "But that doesn't make any difference in the South, does it?"

Clifton shook his head and retreated yet another step, too stunned at first to speak. "I . . . I cannot see you any further, Miss Waters," he finally managed, choking a bit on the tears that gathered. "Good-bye." He turned and rushed away.

"Clifton!"

He heard her call behind him, but his tears drowned out her words. He rushed blindly up the staircase, into his room, and bolted the door behind him.

The skiff docked alongside the bucking, diving *Tempest Queen*. Hands aboard reached down and hauled the woman up, then her two children, and finally the old lady.

"That all?" someone asked.

"That's all that made it," Captain Hamilton said, accepting a hand up.

Coat in hand, McKay leaped to the pitching guard. A strong hand caught his arm and pulled him safely in. He was still dripping from the plunge, and stepped out of the way of the scrambling hands. Hamilton said, "Take these people up to my cabin, Mr. Lansing."

"Mr. McKay!" Hamilton snapped.

"Err, yes, sir?"

"What the devil were you doing on that skiff?"

McKay smiled thinly at the scowling captain. "I guess I just got swept up in the rush."

"Humm. You could have gotten yourself killed."

"I didn't think about that."

"Well, fortunately it turned out all right. Only, let's not mention it to anyone? Insurance and all that, you know."

"Certainly." McKay turned to leave.

"Oh, Mr. McKay?"

He looked back.

Captain Hamilton stuck out a hand. "Thanks."

Sara Gardner sniffed and wiped her eyes. She put her arms around her two children where they sat on the edge of Captain Hamilton's bed, towels over their shoulders, and said, "We don't blame you, Captain Hamilton. I told Gearson to light the lantern, but he refused. Refused to put in to shore. He was drunk, and acting crazy."

"Humm." Hamilton glanced at the old woman beside her, crying painfully into a corner of her towel. "I am sorry this happened, and I understand your grief. We will be putting into Natchez-Under-the-Hill in about an hour, where you can disembark if you wish and make arrangements to return to Illinois. Or you may stay with the *Tempest Queen* until we reach her home port at Baton Rouge."

Sara patted her eyes dry again. "There is nothing I want

to go back to in Illinois, Captain." She glanced at her mother, who managed to nod her agreement. "And besides, we have no money to return."

"Mrs. Gardner. Money need not be a concern. I will stand behind any debt you may incur."

She smiled bravely through her grief. "Thank you for the kind offer, but I think we will continue on as planned."

"Humm. Well, we don't go as far as St. Charles, but I'll take you to Baton Rouge and then see you transferred to another steamer and assigned proper accommodations. And I will not accept no for an answer."

"Very well, Captain."

She was a handsome woman, Captain Hamilton thought, even in her grief. Her two children reminded him of his own—he put that thought out of his head. One family's grief was all he was able to handle at a time.

At the knock upon his door, Hamilton said, "Come in."

The clerk poked his head through and said, "You sent for me, Captain?"

"I did, Mr. Belding. Please see that these people are given a stateroom and are properly fed. See if you can find some dry clothes for them as well. They will be with us to Baton Rouge."

Sara gathered her children, helped her mother up, and said, "Thank you, Captain Hamilton." The shattered family followed the clerk out into the storm.

Hamilton was about to shut the door when an angry voice outside growled, "Out of my damn way!" and the next instant Randall Statler burst into Hamilton's cabin.

Hamilton scowled. "What's the meaning of this?" Then his eyes widened. "What the devil happened to your face?"

"It was that man, Stewart, and his nigger-lovin' friend, Mystie Waters. She put something in my drink, then they attacked me, knocked me unconscious, stole the key, and let my nigger free! They broke the law on your boat! What the hell are you going to do about it?"

"They set the runaway free?" Hamilton lifted an eyebrow and held back a grin. "I find that difficult to believe. Mr. Stewart is a slaveholder himself, if I'm not mistaken."

"I don't know what his part in it was, only that him and that woman were in it together."

Hamilton sat at his desk and said, "I will see to it immediately, Mr. Statler."

"You'd better!"

Hamilton turned and considered the man standing there in a quivering rage. "Sir, since the runaway slave is now gone, you have no further business on this boat. In a little while we will be docking at Natchez-Under-the-Hill. I insist that you disembark there. The clerk will refund you any fare you have coming. Good night."

Statler left, leaving the door wide open to the wind. A spattering of rain was making its way under the porch. Hamilton stepped out and caught the attention of the night watchman. "Have someone find Mystie Waters for me, Mr. Langley, and have her come to my cabin."

"Then what Statler says is true?"

Mystie Waters nodded her head. "It is." She sniffed and was unable to hide the sadness or the weariness in her voice.

Hamilton handed her a handkerchief. "And Mr. Stewart's part in this?"

Her eyes flashed up, suddenly wide. "He had no part in it! If anything, he tried to stop me. All Clif—I mean Mr. Stewart—did was come to my aid when Statler attacked me."

"Humm. I see." Hamilton paced his cabin floor, hands clasped at his back. After a few moments he said, "You have put me in a difficult place, you understand."

She nodded her head.

"You have broken the law, and I am bound as captain of this boat to turn you over to wharf authorities at my first opportunity."

"Yes, I know."

He turned suddenly on her. "Why did you do it, Mystie?"

Mystie shook her head. Her hair fell to her shoulders, unbound, black as midnight, curling from the rain. "I . . . I just had to. That's all I can say. And I would do it again," she added with resolve.

"Mystie, if it helps, I know."

"Know?" she asked, startled.

His head inclined once, solemnly. "I know about your— heritage."

She laughed bitterly. "It seem everyone knows now."

"It made no difference to me. You were a good worker. I am sorry to lose you."

"Then you will hand me over in Natchez?"

Hamilton looked away, and with his back to her he said, "We ran over a raft a while ago. Two people were killed. The larboard paddle wheel is probably damaged as well. I will have to file a report in the wharf boat and then decide with Mr. Seegar what's to be done about repairs." He turned back. "I will be quite busy, and probably shan't get around to your incident for some time. If you should be gone by then, well, nothing I can do about that, now is there?"

Mystie stood. "I understand, Captain. I shall pack immediately." She went to the door.

"Mystie."

"Captain?" She turned back to face him.

He reached into a can upon the desk and handed her a fifty dollar bank note. "This should cover any pay you have coming."

"Thank you, sir."

He gave her a smile then. "I'm glad you did it. I wanted to do it myself, Mystie, and I just might have, were I twenty-one again. Good luck."

Mystie managed a faltering smile. "Thank you, Captain."

When she had gone, Hamilton sat back down and looked at Cynthia's picture. "This has been a devil of a trip, my dear, and I am glad it's almost over." He stared at the picture a moment longer, then stood wearily, shrugged into a dry jacket, put on his hat, and went outside to confer with Seegar.

CHAPTER TWENTY-THREE

Natchez-Under-the-Hill.

Dexter McKay leaned upon the railing, drawing at his cigar, watching passengers disembark at the wharf boat while others carried their luggage aboard. The hour was late, and he'd had little sleep the night before, but McKay was not tired, and he was amazed at all the activity here. Perhaps like himself, Natchez-Under-the-Hill did not require much sleep. His view wandered up the high cliffs to the town of Natchez itself. A civilized place, he had heard, compared to this rowdy dockside community. Perhaps he could find a card game while the *Tempest Queen* was in dock.

Below, he spied Mystie Waters making her way to the landing stage, her arms filled with luggage. McKay hurried down the stairs and came up behind her. "Going somewhere, Miss Waters?"

When Mystie stopped and looked at him, he discovered a tear at the corner of her eye, which she blinked away. "Hello, Mr. McKay. I heard about your role in rescuing those poor people. You should be quite proud."

"And so should you."

"Me?"

"I see that Eli is gone. Safely away, I hope?"

"I pray so."

"Why are you leaving?"

"It is the best thing for now."

He took some of her luggage from her as they walked together. "Captain Hamilton has given me some time to make good *my* escape. I broke the law by freeing Eli."

"What does Clifton say about this?"

She turned on him sharply. "He does not know. That is the way I would like it to remain."

"I see. Then, you did tell him?"

"Yes. And he fled as if I carried cholera."

"I told you he would need some time."

She laughed. "Time is not something I have much of, Mr. McKay." She put a hand upon his arm. "Don't tell him about me—about my work with the Railroad. Please."

"I won't. Promise. But what are your plans?"

"I don't have any as yet. I will continue with the Railroad, of course. I'll get a job on another steamer as soon as I can. The river is my life. I will never leave it."

McKay walked her into town where he flagged down a carriage on Silver Street and paid the man to take her up to Natchez to a proper hotel. He helped her up, and when she was settled said, "My best. Perhaps we will meet again, Miss Waters."

"Perhaps. And thank you for being a friend."

"You watch out. I saw that Statler fellow disembark about half an hour ago."

"I will. Good-bye."

McKay watched the carriage climb up the road, and when it had turned a corner, he went back to the *Tempest Queen*. He came up short on the landing stage and stepped aside as the retired general, Klack, and the wealthy planter tromped off. The retired general stopped, peered hard at McKay, then allowed a tight smile to his face. "Someday, sir, you and I will find ourselves across the table from each other. Be warned, I will have my revenge."

"At your pleasure, sir." McKay bowed slightly and grinned at the three of them.

"What was that all about?" Hamilton asked when McKay once again was aboard.

"That? Oh, he was just wishing me good luck."

"Humm. Wonder why he is disembarking now?" Hamilton grunted. "Be a dirty shame if he misses our departure."

"I'm sure he can find his way to Baton Rouge without you, Captain," McKay said with a grin. He turned away, climbed the stairs, and went into the main cabin.

Neither McKay or Captain Hamilton noticed the short man with the walking stick and top hat who scurried aboard. The man hurried up to the boiler deck, swiftly checking cabin numbers. He halted at number 27. Put his ear to the door, then tried the handle. Locked. That didn't matter. In a moment he had a pick in hand, and the next he slipped into the dark cabin to wait.

The main cabin was still brightly lit, although only a scattering of passengers were milling about, talking of the accident, complaining that this second delay would hurt business, spoil a wedding, ruin an important connection. McKay sat alone at a table, sipping a glass of Glenlivet, which he had even ordered by name. Ah, life does progress! He considered the trip, and although not unprofitable, certainly it had not gone the way he had expected. And he never did catch up with the famous Devol.

Odd, he thought, *that does not seem as important now as it did only one short week earlier.* What was important to him now? He was struck with the question. Nothing but money and winning had ever been important to McKay. Why should he begin to question the foundation of his life now?

"A most confusing week," he muttered to himself. McKay set the glass down and stood. He was tired after all, he decided, and strolled across the main cabin to his room.

He stepped into his dark cabin and struck a match. In its flare, he froze as the man standing in the corner lifted a pistol.

McKay dropped the match and leaped aside as two feet of yellow flame spit out at him. Something tugged his sleeve, seared his arm. Blinded by the flash, McKay raised his walking stick almost by sheer instinct, an instant before the man's own cane skittered off of it.

His eyes cleared, and in the faint light coming through the window, McKay caught a glimpse of a silver streak. He ducked and jabbed out with his cane. He hit soft flesh, and the *whomph* of the man's breath going out of him was a satisfying sound. But then the attacker came back, and McKay staggered as a fist smacked into his jaw. Backpedaling across the table, McKay lifted a heel and rammed forward. The far cabin wall shook. Instantly he was up and swinging. A fist shot from the gloom and laid McKay out on the floor. He shook his head to clear it. Staring, glassy-eyed, McKay caught another glimpse of flashing silver and managed to turn out from under it even as the clawed cane resounded upon the floor. Grappling with his own cane, McKay narrowly avoided a second blow . . . he gave it a twist, separated it, and lunged forward as his unknown assailant took one last swing at him.

McKay felt the razor edge of the short cane sword meet with resistance, but the man's momentum carried him forward until he came to a halt at the grip. The man collapsed upon McKay. McKay pushed the body off himself about the same time as his cabin door burst open. Light streamed in, and McKay had his first glimpse of the man's face. Two men stepped inside and helped him to his feet.

"You all right, Mr. McKay?" a white-collared waiter asked him.

"Yes . . . I seem to be," he gasped, his lungs burning. He was aware of another burning as well and grabbed his arm and noticed the blood dripping from his fingertips. Someone lit the lamp and knelt down to turn the stranger over.

Hamilton stepped inside, glanced at the floor, then at McKay. "What happened?"

"He was waiting for me when I came in."

"Do you know who he is?"

"Never seen him in my life." McKay retrieved the man's cane from the floor and looked at the eagle-claw grip. "But we have met before. This is the man who attacked me the other day."

"Humm." Hamilton took the walking stick and felt the silver end. "You're sure?"

"Absolutely."

More folks were poking their heads through the door by now. Hamilton glanced at a waiter standing there. "See if he has any papers on him."

The man rummaged the pockets, came up with a wad of bills, a handful of coins, cards, dice, a watch, and other odds and ends, but no identification. He found something in the man's vest pocket. When he dug it out, he saw it was a card, and he handed it to the captain.

Hamilton's face dipped into a scowl. "You're sure you do not know the fellow?"

"Never seen him in my life."

"I wonder where he got this?" Hamilton handed the card to McKay.

Dexter McKay, it read in flowing script. And below, written in pencil in his own hand were the words *At your service!* McKay turned it over slowly, not fully believing what he was seeing. On the back, penned in a different hand was "*Tempest Queen*. Stateroom #27." He staggered back and sat in the chair.

"It means something to you?"

Suddenly dizzy, McKay looked up at the captain and shook his head. "No, I have no idea." He was too shaken to tell the captain he had given this very card to the lovely Genevieve de Winter that first night when he had killed the gambler Banning.

"You look pale."

McKay pulled his arm from the blood-soaked jacket. Hamilton saw the wound for the first time then and told someone to find Dr. Reuben, and the waiter to bring warm water and towels. "No wonder," he said, taking his pocket knife to the sleeve. "Look at the blood you've lost!"

The bullet had gone clean through the muscle, two inches beneath the furrow Banning's bullet had made a week earlier.

"Looks like you're starting all over again," Hamilton said, fixing a tourniquet above the wound.

"I hope not." McKay grimaced as the pain swelled. He looked away and gritted his teeth, but it wasn't so much the pain in his arm that had sent his head reeling. . . .

Does Genevieve de Winter want me dead?

Baton Rouge.

The storm had broken sometime that night, and McKay had slept soundly thanks to a bit of powder Dr. Reuben had used. The doctor's threats had finally been carried out. The damage to the paddle wheel had been slight, and the *Tempest Queen* had left Natchez-Under-the-Hill by two-thirty and traveled all night, stopping briefly at Ellis Cliff,

Tunica Landing, and Bayou Sara. Now, in the late afternoon, Baton Rouge lay ahead and across the river. Her levee had held, although many along the way had crevassed. Still, the danger had not passed, for it was "a bank-full river," as Captain Hamilton had told him.

They made the crossing, the leadsmen calling out the depth along the way. McKay sat in a deck chair watching the shore—rich green in the late-afternoon sun—move past. He was tired. Reuben said it would be so until his body built up the blood he'd lost.

"Mr. McKay," Clifton Stewart said, appearing suddenly at his side.

"Hello."

Stewart glanced at the arm in a sling. "Hurt?"

"Only when I move it." McKay could see the young man was gravely troubled. He nodded his head at a chair. "Sit down."

"Thank you." Stewart put himself half in the chair and leaned forward. "Mr. McKay, I have not seen Mystie all day. Have you?"

McKay pulled thoughtfully at the cigar. He said, "I understand you and she had a falling out?"

"I was an absolute ass! How could I have been so foolish, so uncaring! I have been locked in my cabin all day, going over and over it. Do you know what happened?"

McKay nodded his head.

"You do?"

"She told you that there is Negro blood in her veins."

Stewart became pale, and for a moment McKay thought he might swoon. "Yes. You have to understand, Mr. McKay, that here in the South she would be considered a Negro— well, a mulatto, and that is about the same thing."

"And that is a terrible thing?"

He looked away. "It is—for a Stewart."

"Then, perhaps it is for the best."

Clifton looked up sharply. "What is?"

"Mystie left the boat last night."

"No!" Stewart leaped to his feet. "I need to talk to her. To tell her that it doesn't matter. That I love her and wish to marry her, and the devil to those who will tell me I cannot!"

McKay shrugged his shoulders and winced at a stab of pain. "Perhaps you should have told her that last night."

"Where did she disembark?"

"I told her I'd not tell, but I'm sure your next stop would be Captain Hamilton and he'd tell you it was Natchez."

"I shall return there at once."

"You won't find her. She intends to sign on to another steamer. By time you get back to Natchez, Mystie might be anywhere on this river."

Stewart staggered back into the chair. "Then what shall I do?"

"I don't know," McKay said, "but if you really love her, you'll think of something."

"Marster Clifton. How was your trip up t' Napoleon?" Jenkin asked, taking Clifton Stewart's luggage and putting it in the carriage.

"It was fine, Jenkin," he replied briefly, climbing into the seat. Clifton Stewart stared ahead as the Negro driver took the reins and got the horses moving.

"Your father is anxious t' see you. Him's makin' big plans fer the sugar crop this year."

"I got the contract," he said as the carriage rattled down the streets of Baton Rouge and out into the country.

"You not sayin' much, Marster Clifton."

"Got a lot on my mind, Jenkin."

"Oh, I bets you got big plans t'. Jest like your pappy, you is." Jenkin laughed and urged the horses ahead.

Stewart Manor loomed through the trees in the late afternoon shadows. A tall, columned house built of white-washed bricks below the first floor, natural colored brick above. The shutters were green, and around the second-floor porch they went from ceiling to floor, slanted to keep the sun out and allow the breeze in. The house sat comfortably at the end of a long, sweeping drive. Jenkin brought the carriage up alongside the carriage stop, and another black servant rushed out to carry the luggage.

"Good t' have you back home," a black woman said at the door when he came through. The parlor was large and comfortable. Sparsely furnished. To the left was the ladies' sitting room; to the right, the gentlemen's parlor.

"Lila. Where is my father?"

"Clifton!" A woman's voice sang out. He looked ahead to where the long hallway led out to the back door and the kitchen beyond.

"Mother." Clifton met her in the hallway, gave her a hug, received one in return.

"We've missed you." She pushed him out at arm's length to gaze upon him as if it had been a year instead of only two weeks. Suddenly her eyes narrowed. "Is something the matter, Clifton?"

"No, of course not."

"Don't lie to me. I can always tell when something is bothering my little boy."

"Mother," he said impatiently, glancing, slightly embarrassed, at Lila. Jullene came in the back door carrying tall glasses of lemonade.

"Jenkin say young Marster Clifton is home and t' bring him somethin' cold."

Clifton took the glass, but his eyes remained fixed upon Jullene. She was a little over twenty years old. A pretty mulatto, fair-skinned. Perhaps this is what Mystie's mother looked like? He couldn't keep the woman from his thoughts.

"Somethin' wrong, Marster Clifton?"

He shook the thought from his head. "No . . . I'm . . . no, of course not!" He turned back to his mother. "Where is Father?"

"In his office, of course."

Clifton set the glass back onto the tray and strode purposefully toward the room in the east wing.

"Come in," the man's voice said from the other side.

When Clifton stepped in, his father pushed out from behind the desk and, despite the limp, came briskly across the room, smiling. "Good to have you home, son," he said, grasping his hand. "How did it go?"

Clifton removed the contract from his pocket and handed it to the older man, who immediately took it back to his desk. "Pour yourself a brandy, Clifton," he said, settling a pair of spectacles upon his nose.

Clifton filled a snifter of the liquor to the rim and immediately sipped it down a quarter of the glass.

"Well, well. These appear quite in order. You did a good job, Clifton." Jeremy Stewart removed the spectacles and looked over. "Have a good trip?"

"Father." He approached the old man, halted, and suddenly didn't know how to continue.

"Yes? Something on your mind, son?"

Clifton steeled himself and blurted it out. "I have met a woman, and I wish to marry her."

Jeremy lifted a bushy white eyebrow. A grin made its way slowly onto his face. "Well, well. I say it's about time. Someone you met on the boat?"

"Yes, sir."

"This has come about pretty quickly."

Clifton managed a faint grin. "I didn't plan it that way, I assure you."

Jeremy stood smiling and clasped his son upon the shoulder. "We never plan these things." He chuckled. "Well, at least we *men* never plan these things. Well, tell me about her, and then we'll go tell your mother. Is she from a good family? Does she live around here?"

"Oh, yes, I'm sure she comes from a very good family. I know her father loves her dearly. But, no, she is not from around here."

"Well that doesn't matter."

"She's a Northern girl," he said.

"Oh? Hope she doesn't have ice water in her veins." He

laughed. "I'm sure she will fit right in once she gets to know us. Where is she now? Did you bring her with you?"

"Father, there is a problem."

Jeremy looked at his son, for it was impossible not to hear the distress in Clifton's voice. "What sort of problem?" he said, suddenly wary.

"She disembarked in Natchez before I could tell her I love her. We . . . we had words, and I said some foolish things. Now I must return to find her before I lose her."

Stewart considered this. "You sure you want to go running after her like that?"

"I have to."

"I see. Well, you know you have my full support, and your mother's as well."

"Father—there is something else I must tell you."

For a moment Jeremy peered into Clifton's wide eyes. "I'm not certain I'm going to like what it is you are about to say."

Clifton nodded his head. "I am certain you are not going to like what I have to say. Mystie is a mulatto."

Captain Hamilton came slowly along the promenade like a man carrying a burden too great to endure. He ran his palm along the green handrail and paused to observe the crew below unloading the cargo in the growing shadows. McKay watched the captain awhile, then strolled alongside.

"Evening, Captain."

Hamilton looked over, surprised to see him there. "You are still here, Mr. McKay? I thought you'd be at your dear sister's bedside by now."

McKay grimaced. He had been afraid that would come up again. If he wanted to, he could have conjured up a believable enough story to explain the discrepancy, but he did not wish to lie to this man any further. "Captain, I am chagrined to admit this, but I have no sister in Baton Rouge. I lied to you in the hopes of attaining passage upon the *Tempest Queen*."

McKay saw the wince of pain come to Hamilton's face when he mentioned the boat. Hamilton looked back at the crew laboring below in the waning light. "Humm. It pleases me, Mr. McKay, to hear you say that."

"It does? Why?"

"Because, I have known for quite some time that you did not have a sister in Baton Rouge."

"But how could you?"

"Even the most inattentive brother does not forget his sister's name. She was Beth Preston to me, I believe, yet to Mr. Stewart, you called her Ruth Provost."

"I did? How careless of me. Please accept my apology, Captain."

"Apology accepted. Now, if you will excuse me, I have some unpleasant business to attend to in town. I've put it off this long, but it isn't going to go away." He started for the stairway.

"Err . . . Captain?"

Hamilton paused and turned back.

"Err . . . I was wondering if I could book passage with you on the return trip upriver. I have no reason to stay in Baton Rouge, and I found the *Tempest Queen*, for the most part, a most genial place."

Hamilton frowned. "Certainly you may book passage, but I am not the person to speak to. I shall not be going upriver again, at least not upon the *Tempest Queen*. You should make arrangements with the ticketing agent—or the new owner." Hamilton started on his way again.

"The new owner? I suppose that would be me, then."

Hamilton stopped abruptly and looked back. "Sir?"

"Err . . . the new owner. I presume the possessor of this paper makes one the owner, does it not?" McKay drew the document from his vest pocket.

Hamilton's eyes rounded. "Where did you get that from?"

"This?" He glanced at the paper. "I won it in a card game. From our friend the retired general."

"You?"

McKay shrugged and winced. "Well, I couldn't see any good reason to let the cad leave with it still in his possession."

Hamilton momentarily seemed to lose the capacity to speak. When he recovered he said, "Whatever could have made him wager the *Tempest Queen* after he had gone to so much trouble to win her from me?"

"Steal her from you, you mean." McKay withdrew his envelope. "This was his motivation."

When Hamilton finished reading it, he handed it back, his hand suddenly unsteady. "You risked a fortune to win back the *Tempest Queen*?"

"I assure you, Captain, I risked nothing."

"But that—"

"I went into the game knowing I would win. I do not play cards any other way. And as for my gold mine?" A smile came comfortably to McKay's face. "It is worth exactly one hundred dollars. That is the sum I paid to a friend in an assay office in Kansas City to have the papers properly drawn up and certified."

"You are a gambler yourself!"

McKay lifted his good arm, palm up. "I admit it."

Hamilton's eyes went back to the paper in McKay's hand. "What are your intentions now? As owner of the *Tempest Queen*, you will be quite wealthy."

"Me?" McKay laughed. "I know nothing about boats, or this wild river. No, riverboating is not my game." He handed the paper to the captain. "No, Captain Hamilton, riverboating is your game. Cards are mine. A man needs to stick to what he does best."

Hamilton stared at the paper, his hand trembling. He sniffed, then suddenly stood erect, as if a horrible weight had been lifted. "And you let me suffer like this all day?"

McKay took Hamilton by the elbow and started him along the promenade toward the main cabin. "Captain, some men are excellent riverboat captains, and then some are excellent cardplayers. Rarely is one man both. I just thought that if you had an extra day to think about it, well, then perhaps the next time some slick-fingered cardsharper decides to let you win a few hands—more than the odds would allow—you'd remember this and pull out with your shirt still intact."

"You scoundrel."

"Err . . . yes. We all have our callings."

"Captain Hamilton! Captain Hamilton!" A voice shouted from the wharf below.

They turned and bent over the railing. The owner of the voice was in shadows. "Yes, who is it?"

"Clifton Stewart, sir. May I come aboard?"

Hamilton looked at McKay. "Wonder what the devil he wants?" Then to the man below, "Yes, of course you can come aboard."

Stewart sprinted across the landing stage.

"Wonder what he forgot?" Hamilton said.

McKay grinned and leaned upon his cane with his good arm. "My guess is, he forgot his heart, and he wants you to help him find it."

"Whatever are you talking about, McKay?"

Dexter McKay gave him a quizzical smile and shook his head. "Just thinking aloud."

"Captain!" Stewart was breathless as he bounded up the stairs.

"Settle down, young man. What is it?"

"I must have passage upriver."

Hamilton looked at McKay, then back. "You, too?"

"Sir, I need to find Mystie. Sir, I love her and want to marry her. I must find her. Mr. McKay said she intends to find a job on another steamer."

"It's a big river, son."

"I know. That's why I want you to give me a job on the *Tempest Queen*. So I can stay on the river until I find her."

"Humm. I have no jobs open that I know of."

"Sir, I am a desperate man. I will do anything!"

Hamilton considered him. "A man in your position can easily book passage. You need not work your way."

Stewart glanced to the deck. "I have no money. My father, when he heard—well, he cut me off."

"Disinherited you?"

"I don't know if he will go that far, but for the moment I am a persona non grata. At least until I come to my senses, he says."

"Humm. Well, I suppose we can come up with something for you to do aboard the *Tempest Queen*. Go on down and tell Mr. Lansing I said he should put you to work."

"Thank you, Captain. Thank you very much!" Stewart grasped his hand and pumped it mightily, then dashed back down the stairs.

"Can you imagine that, Mr. McKay?" Hamilton said when Clifton Stewart had left.

"I find it quite encouraging."

"You do? Humm. Well, this next trip should prove interesting indeed."

"Indeed. Now, shall we talk business?"

"Business?"

"I certainly don't intend to ride the *Tempest Queen* free. And I don't want to have to keep booking passage each trip. I figure an arrangement can be made. Perhaps a percentage?"

"A percentage? You want to pay me a percentage of your winnings to ride my boat?"

"Exactly."

"Humm." Hamilton suddenly narrowed an eye at him. "I will have no cheating aboard."

"I wouldn't think of it, Captain! So, how about ten—? Hum? Or fifteen . . . ?"

"I think we can work something out," Hamilton replied, smothering a grin.